HANNAH
FOWLER

Janice Holt Giles

HANNAH

FOWLER

With a Foreword by
Dianne Watkins

THE UNIVERSITY PRESS OF KENTUCKY

This edition published in 1992 by The University Press of Kentucky

Foreword copyright © 1992 by The University Press of Kentucky

Scholarly publisher for the Commonwealth,
serving Bellarmine College, Berea College, Centre
College of Kentucky, Eastern Kentucky University,
The Filson Club, Georgetown College, Kentucky
Historical Society, Kentucky State University,
Morehead State University, Murray State University,
Northern Kentucky University, Transylvania University,
University of Kentucky, University of Louisville,
and Western Kentucky University.

Editorial and Sales Offices: Lexington, Kentucky 40508–4008

Library of Congress Cataloging-in-Publication Data

Giles, Janice Holt.
    Hannah Fowler / Janice Holt Giles ; with a foreword by Dianne
Watkins.
        p.   cm.
    Includes bibliographical references.
    ISBN 0–8131–1793–3 (alk. paper) : — ISBN 0–8131–0810–1
(pbk. : alk. paper) :
    1. Kentucky—History—To 1792—Fiction.   I. Title.
PS3513.I4628H3   1992
813'.54—dc20   92–14269
                                                          CIP

This book is printed on recycled acid-free paper meeting
the requirements of the American National Standard
for Permanence of Paper for Printed Library Materials.
∞

Foreword

In 1953, after four successful books, Janice Holt Giles turned from writing about the rural Kentucky region of her husband's homeland to historical fiction. "My personal love of history," she stated, "has had much influence on my writing. With regard to the historical novels I have perhaps a very ambitious project in mind. I want to develop, fictionally, the long movement westward, beginning with the outpouring through the Cumberland Gap in Kentucky, moving it on slowly and gradually as it moved in reality. . . . [The books] will develop as my particular research stirs my creative instinct."

Her commitment to historical accuracy in her novels is revealed through her own voluminous shorthand and typewritten notes resulting from the reading of numerous diaries, narratives, and journals in libraries and archives across the state. She also spent many hours examining microfilms of the Draper collection, which contained depositions and original stories of early Kentucky settlers, and she relied heavily on the bibliography and doctoral dissertation of Charles G. Talbert's "The Life and Times of Benjamin Logan."

Giles's first historical novel, *The Kentuckians* (1953), documents both real and fictional pioneers who entered Kentucky through the Cumberland Gap beginning in 1769 and peopled the original forted stations of Daniel Boone, James Harrod, and Benjamin Logan. Continuing through 1776, the book was the first in the *American Frontier* series that would eventually include nine titles. Giles planned to write several novels with Kentucky settings before following later generations of the families westward. Paul Brooks, her editor at Houghton Mifflin, suggested that the second book be about a woman.

Ready to move the settlers of Kentucky out of the forts and onto the farms, Giles liked the idea. It would be a challenge to create what she envisioned, "the new line, the new woman, a physically strong, enduring woman, who must furnish the seed for the generations of strong men and women to carry the balance of the series forward."

But the "woman" book would not come. Instead, Giles avoided the task temporarily by writing *The Plum Thicket* (1954), a story developed from her remembrances of childhood summers spent at her grandfather's home in Arkansas. Again, with her writing based on personal experiences, the novel proceeded rapidly. With its acceptance, Giles resumed her struggle to find a way to write "an entire book about the everyday life of a [pioneer] woman. Those pioneer women had to be physically and psychologically strong."

Giles's own ancestry boasted strong feminine characters. She knew well the stories of her tiny, five-foot-one maternal grandmother who journeyed across Arkansas with three small children in "a cindery, bucking, halting train" to the foothills of the Ozark mountains where her waiting husband had built a one-room log cabin. The cabin had a pounded dirt floor and a window and door covered with deerskin. While there, with only her husband's assistance, Catherine Babb McGraw delivered her fourth child. Giles's grandmother had borne twelve children by the age of forty-one and would live to be seventy-one.

At the turn of the century, Giles's mother, at age eighteen, left the large comfortable house her parents then owned to follow her new husband into the "rough, tough frontier country of the Indian Territory," where they were close neighbors to the last governor of the Choctaw Nation. John Albert Holt was the school principal and his wife, Lucy, a teacher in what would become Haileyville, Arkansas. As Lucy McGraw Holt almost lost her life during the stillbirth of her first child, she returned to her mother's home in Altus, Arkansas, for the birth of her second child, Janice Meredith Holt, in 1905.

Catherine McGraw and her daughter Lucy were proven examples of characteristic women of the frontier who stood by their men through fortune and adversity. In describing one prototype of the frontier woman depicted in novels from 1920 to 1950 in *The Pioneer in the American Novel, 1900–1950*, Nicholas J. Karolides wrote, "the basic equipment for the role of a pioneer heroine is an enduring strength, a strength which rarely falters before pain, grief, and hardship. She is maintained by a strong will, a confidence and courage, a determination to prevail" (p. 92).

There is little doubt that the strong feminine members of Giles's family provided idealistic imagery for such characters in her novels. But in *Around our House* (1971), she related the great difficulty she had in immersing herself into the "quiet, inarticulate" woman, Hannah Fowler, she had chosen as her heroine. Giles liked to "get inside" her characters. "My real problem," she continued, "is that this silent strong woman is not me," for she described herself as "high-strung and chattery."

Giles created Hannah as "tall, and big in every way. Her shoulders were square, her hips were broad, the reach of her legs was long. She was strongly built, not gaunt, but angular and spare fleshed." Her strength earned the respect of her father who said she "c'n do as good as e'er man." In contrast to her strength, the author designed Hannah with a spirit of quietude so unlike Giles's own expressive nature. As the death of her mother had occurred when she was a little girl, Hannah was reared entirely by her father. Missing the social interaction of brothers and sisters, Hannah knew only the placid companionship of her father and the men who were his friends.

Through innate determination, skill, and the persistent hard work of writing and rewriting, Janice Holt Giles did "get inside" the character Hannah Fowler. She chose to tell the story in author's narrative voice, with frequent use of the vernacular that she heard every day from Henry Giles's family and their neighbors in the western fringe of Appalachia where they lived. With the vehicle selected, she worked with such intensity that at the end of a good writing day, she felt she had to get back inside her *own* skin. "If I happen to pass a mirror, I am surprised to see the face reflected there. It should be dark-skinned, and thin, the strong face of Hannah."

Hannah Moore Fowler is best described in Giles's own words: "Hannah is like Mother Earth. She is timeless and durable and ample . . . ; in her children, she will endow her own physical seed with her strength and courage, and her own tenderness and love."

It is not surprising then that Giles gave the heroine the maiden name Hannah *Moore* to reflect Giles's personal identity in the adventurous spirit and enduring strength of the character. Married at eighteen to Otto Jackson Moore and giving birth to her only child one year later, Janice Moore struggled in a nonsupportive marriage for sixteen years before her divorce in 1939. Seeking a new life, she bravely ventured with her young daughter from the west to employment in Kentucky.

Defining herself as a "strong and durable woman most of the time," Giles noted, "I have had to be. I have had the strength and courage to rear my daughter, to be both father and mother to her as best I could, to earn a competent living and in a man's world to stand up to the toughest of them and fight for myself." Years later, she remarked of her life's experiences, "From prairie wind to Kentucky rain has been a long journey, but it has never failed to be interesting, challenging and adventurous."

Hannah Fowler has a long line of literary prototypes as well. Following the appearance of James Fenimore Cooper's *The Pioneers* in 1823, many writers have portrayed strong heroines in the dramatic conquest of the American frontier through historical fiction. Willa Cather's Alexandra Bergson and Antonía Shimerda in the prairie novels *O Pioneers* (1913) and *My Antonía* (1918) are seen not only as heroines of strength and endurance but also as the central characters of the novels, capable of doing a man's share of farming and toiling in the fields as they struggle for subsistence and livelihood in an unconquered land.

Edna Ferber's pioneer women in *Cimarron* (1929) are "women with iron in 'em. Women who wanted land and a home. You can't read the history of the United States, my friends, without learning the great story of those thousands of unnamed women in mud-caked boots and calico dresses and sunbonnets, crossing the prairie and the desert and the mountains enduring hardship and privation. Good women, with a terrible and rigid goodness that comes of work and self-denial. And if it's ever told straight you'll know it's the sunbonnet and not the sombrero that has settled this country."[1]

Bess Streeter Aldrich felt it was false to depict the prairie woman only as "gaunt, beaten, driven mad with despair," and wove the story of Abbie Deal into a tale that "faced up to the harsh truths of that early day" spirited with "faith, courage, and humor" in *A Lantern in Her Hand* (1928).[2] In *The Great Meadow* (1930), Kentucky's Elizabeth Madox Roberts positions the man's strength in the march toward a new world as "to the fore, in the thrust," while the woman's is "in the plane, enduring, inactive but constant."[3]

The manuscript of Hannah Fowler's story about the Kentucky frontier was completed on April 10, 1955. "I am glad to have the book finished," Giles commented, "yet I shall miss *Hannah* greatly." Once begun, the novel was written in three months. Unashamedly, she declared, "I have done a very beautiful book and I know it," but lamented, "At what a cost! My God, at what a cost! I have written my heart out in *Hannah*." In correspondence concerning a later manuscript, Giles wrote, "If I only enjoyed writing these books as much as I do the research all would be well, but alas, the writing is a heavy piece of work."

In February 1956, Janice Holt Giles received what she felt was "the most beautiful tribute to *Hannah Fowler*," a letter "lovingly written" by her daughter, Elizabeth Moore Hancock. "Dear Mom," it began, "This is a thank you note. To thank you for writing Hannah Fowler. It is a warm, lovely, strong book. Hannah is a dear person—once again a reader finds himself transported right into the center of that time, living right with the people. They are so alive—you are an artist at smooth dialogue. I believe the reason for the 'aliveness' of this book, even though it seemed another story to you—is that the description, history and action came alive through dialogue."

Janice Holt Giles dedicated years of research and writing to give Kentucky its place in this exciting epoch adventure. Her second book in the *American Frontier* series, about the woman Hannah, is as timeless as the story she tells. With this reprinting, *Hannah Fowler* returns to its honored place in historical fiction.

Dianne Watkins

Notes

1. (New York: Doubleday), 19.
2. Robert Streeter Aldrich, *A Bess Streeter Aldrich Treasury* (New York: Appleton-Century-Crofts, 1959), ix.
3. (New York: Grosset and Dunlap), 168.

1

THE WOMAN hunched by the ashes of the dead fire, her big shoulders squared forward. With a shingle of sycamore bark she raked back and forth, searching for a live coal.

Rain had fallen in the night, not heavily, nor stormily, for she had not awakened, but it had fallen soddenly and had put out the fire. The half-burned wood was sogged and the fire-blackened logs were glisteny with the wetness. The ashes were entirely cold and had begun to cake over.

She did not expect to find any fire. From the soaked look of the wood, and the packed look of the ashes, it had been put out in the early part of the night; but she raked the piece of bark back and forth carefully and methodically, from one end to the other, and from side to side. There was a chance a little coal had been left buried so deep that the dampness hadn't reached it, and it would save time and trouble if she could find one. To build a new fire was tedious. She scattered the ashes, piled them, sifted them through her fingers. There was no warmth at all left in them, so she gave it over, laid aside the piece of wood, and stood up.

With slow patience she set about her preparations to build a new fire. She looked around and chose a new place for it, in the clear, so that it was free of the drip from the trees. She dug down through the thick layers of dead leaves to the dryness of the ground underneath, piling the leaves to one side. The deepest buried ones would be dry enough to use for tinder. She carried the stones from the old fireplace over to the new and banked them around. She broke small dead limbs from the trees. They gave easily to her hand and as they broke, a silvery shower of raindrops sprayed over her. She stacked them near the fireplace, then she carried larger sticks from the pile of wood she had accumulated during the time they had been camped in this place.

When everything was ready she went over to an old log which had lain fallen and weathered so long it had rotted to a crumbly pulp and she dug into the heart of it with both hands, bringing them out full of dry punk. She laid this in the center of the fireplace, on a bed of leaves. Then she went to the lean-to, built under the shelter of a giant elm tree, and crawled under its low roof. A blanket-wrapped figure lay in one corner, but it did not stir. She moved quietly in order not to disturb the man. From among a pile of leather pouches and bags she brought forth one which held powder, and she took from it a scant handful, closing its neck carefully against the damp when she was through, putting it back among the provisions and covering it over. From another sack she took a flint. Then once again she squatted, hunching her shoulders. She poured the powder in a careful trail over the punk and set a rock exactly so that the first spark from the flint would catch the powder. The spark, which she struck expertly, ignited the powder which led a small line of fire into the punk, from which the leaves then caught. The woman nursed the little fire, patiently blowing on it, feeding it twigs and more leaves, one twig at a time, one small handful of leaves, scattering them carefully. After each feeding of the fire she blew strongly on it. "Ketch, drat you," she muttered once, "ketch, an' burn."

The smoke boiled up thickly and sullenly around her head and she squinted her eyes against it, but otherwise she paid no heed to it, not moving out of it or fanning it away. She squatted, her skirts draggled about her, spread fan-wise back of her, and alternately fed and blew upon the fire. A strand of heavy black hair loosed itself from the knot on the back of her head and fell across her forehead. With the back of her arm she brushed it up and out of her face, bending at the same time to blow once more upon the fire.

A sudden flame, like a hot tongue, sprang up. Quickly she laid more twigs on it, scattered another handful of leaves, turned and stirred the now crackling twigs. "Hit's about time you took a notion to burn," she said. When there was a good steady blaze she started laying the larger pieces of wood over, building them up into a pyramid so that there was draft room underneath. One at a time she laid them on, balancing them and turning them, propping them against each other. They spewed and sputtered, but the blaze beneath was hot enough now that she knew they would dry and catch. She added a final hand-ful of twigs and leaves and then stood, wiping her hands down strongly across her thighs. "Now, burn, drat you," she said, "jist keep on a burnin' whilst I git some water to make Pa's pone cakes."

From the place of the old fire she swung an iron pot up and hung it over her arm, looked once more at the now blazing flames, then walked over to the shelter under the trees. She had made it hurriedly, in sudden need of a shelter for her father, but makeshift though it was, it was stout, the poles sunk well into the ground, the roof branches thatched nicely together.

The trees still dripped from the night's rain, but up in their top branches the fog laced and swirled, and it lay like a band of white wool over the river. There was a clean line where the fog ended over the water, not ragged and edgy, but straight as if it had been drawn and the fog then told, This is as far as you can come. She had seen fog smoke up from water in wispy patches, like steam from a kettle, only whiter. But this fog this morning was solid and it lay boxed over the river, and there was this narrow space between it and the river so that she could see the dark water. Beyond the river there was nothing but the white wall of the fog. The hills beyond might never have been for all you could see of them, and when she looked behind, the hills that had stood there so solidly yesterday had disappeared, too. They, she and her father, were camped on a river in a suddenly vanished world. It did not trouble the woman. She turned her face upward and studied the drift in the upper branches of the trees. Already it was blowing away. "Hit'll brighten ere noon," she told herself. "When they's fog this heavy it allus means clearin' weather."

She peered under the roof of the lean-to. The blanket-wrapped figure stirred and she spoke. "Pa? You awake yit?"

"I'm awake." The man turned and groaned. "You git a fire goin', did ye?"

"I got it goin'."

"I didn't know whe'er you would or not. Some wet, warn't it?"

"Some." She stood and looked at the man. "Your leg hurtin' you purty good, is it?"

"Purty good. Kept me awake most the night." The man rolled over to face her, grunting. "I don't rightly know how we'll make out, Hannah," he said. "Lord knows how long it'll be till I c'n travel."

"We'll make out," the woman said, shifting her weight from one foot to the other and sliding the iron pot farther up her arm.

"I ain't wearied none," the man went on, "about us makin' out camped here. You c'n do as good as e'er man. That ain't what is wearyin' me. We ort to be travelin'."

"We'll travel," the woman said, "in time. Main thing is to git that leg of your'n cured up so's we kin. I'm goin' fer the water now, down to the river. Hit won't be long till I'll have you somethin' hot to eat."

"I'll relish it."

The woman swung off toward the river. She was tall, and big in every way. Her shoulders were square, her hips were broad, the reach of her legs was long. She was strongly built, not gaunt, but angular and spare-fleshed. Her face was long from the forehead to the chin, and her cheekbones were high and flat, making deep sockets for her eyes, over which the black brows grew thick and heavy. The eyes under the heavy brows were brown, a light brown mottled with green. The skin stretched over the prominent cheek and jawbones was brown, too, partly by nature, partly by weathering. The mouth was wide, with firm, full lips. She was a plain woman, but not an ugly one, and for all her twenty-five years there was something young and unfinished looking about her, an awkwardness that belongs to youth, as if, whatever time had done to her, it had not yet given her the whole of herself.

She made no more effort at handsomeness in her dress than she did in her person. There was no frippiness about the plain woolsey dress, no touch of soft collar at the neck, no apron on its front. It was a sensible dress, dyed with butternut, simple, serviceable and worn.

She was Hannah Moore, and here she stood on the bank of the Kentucky River, which some called the Chenoa and some called the Louisa, in May of the year seventeen hundred and seventy-eight, with her father, Samuel Moore, bound to settle in this new country and headed for the fort of Boonesburg, lamed now by an axe cut over his knee and laid up in a lean-to shelter there in the woods.

She stood on the rain-slippery bank of the river and watched its slow-moving waters glide past. Here it was wide, for they were less than fifty miles from where it ran into the Ohio. It was wide and deep, but not swift flowing, and it was forever curving in lazy, looping bends. It was a pretty river, she thought, deep-banded with trees, and colored blue-green like an agate stone, but differing greatly from the clear, swift streams of the border country they had left behind. It did not frighten her, though, as had the vast Ohio, which she had been happy to see the last of, slipping down it in the convoy of flatboats, families and soldiers making up the river train which Major Clark was bringing into the country. Soldiers or no she hadn't liked the Ohio. It was too broad and too deep, and she had felt too naked on its bosom. Besides not liking the water there had been the curtain of bushes and trees behind which had constantly lurked the threat of Indians. She had been glad when Samuel had decided to leave the flatboats at the mouth of this smaller, more friendly river . . . decided in spite of the opinion of the others that he was foolish and stubborn to strike inland and make his way up the Kentucky to Boone's fort.

It was only what they would have done anyhow, had the major stuck to his first plan to make a halt there at the mouth of the Kentucky and build a fort. But there would have been several, then, traveling with them. When the major had said he was going on, down to the Falls of the Ohio, and make his fort there, it had been a blow to many, for Samuel Moore wasn't the only one who had intended to follow the Kentucky to Boone's fort. But all had lacked the courage when the major had said he wouldn't build the fort there where the two rivers came together. The major had guns with him, and soldiers, and the families were protected so long as they traveled with him. They had counted on having him at their backs inside a strong fort when they struck up the Kentucky. Now, that was changed.

A whispering rumor had spread through the boats that this was an army the major had recruited to take against the British-held Illinois forts. No one knew how the rumor had got started. No one could say where it had come from, save that Reuben Harmon had told Isaac Holder, and Isaac had told his woman, and his woman had told those in the boat next to hers. Like a wind rippling through the trees it had spread all up and down the boats, that these soldiers with Major Clark hadn't been brought here to fortify Kentucky at all . . . had, instead, a long journey ahead of them, maybe to end up being taken by the British, or killed a long piece from home. It made the women eye them pityingly, think how young some of them were to be going into a fight against the British in the Illinois forts, think how some of them would never come back this way, ever again. It somehow made their own danger seem less, their own discomforts petty, their own unknown future more certain.

But one by one the men, gathered together, talking, talking, talking, had come to the same decision. "I'll go with the major."

"Makes no difference in the end. I'll look at the land close by the Falls."

"I've got my woman and young ones to think of. I'll stay with the boats."

"I've no wish to go off up the Kentucky without the soldiers betwixt me and the Ohio Indians."

They sat about the camp, chewed their tobacco, broke innumerable twigs into thousands of pieces, dug their heels into the rich Kentucky dirt, nodded their heads and made their decisions. All but Samuel Moore, that is. He listened, but it was as if he didn't hear. "I am headin' fer Boone's fort," he had said stubbornly.

"You're a fool, Sam Moore," they had told him, uncomfortable before his determination. "You'll never git there alive."

"Mebbe," he'd said, "but I'll chance it."

"It's too big a chance, this time of year."

"Man don't risk nothin', don't git nowhere," he'd replied.

"You'll be took," they'd warned him.

"I'll risk it," he'd kept on repeating.

"The Indians'll find you out on that river."

"No likelier than on this'n."

"We got the soldiers on this'n."

"Don't take but one bullet to snuff out a man's life, with or without a soldier standin' by his side."

Even the major had counseled them against leaving the boats. "If you are determined," he had said, "to head for Boonesborough, there will be parties traveling from the Falls later. Some of my men will be going to the interior forts later on. You would be better advised to continue with us and travel under their protection."

Major George Rogers Clark was a tall, sandy-haired man, tight-lipped and stern looking, and young to be the head of the Kentucky soldiers. Now that he had decided not to build his fort at the mouth of the Kentucky he was in a great hurry to move on to the Falls, and while he took the trouble to have talk with Samuel Moore, it was plain to see he was not an overly patient man.

"I thank you," Samuel had said, carefully courteous, "but the season is late. I have a wish to git on with what I come to do."

"There are just you and your daughter, I understand," the major had said.

"Jist me an' Hannah."

"Why not let your daughter go on with the boats, then, and join you later?"

"That c'n be as she'd ruther."

But she had not hesitated for so much as a single second. When approached she had replied as stubbornly as Samuel. "I thank you, but I'd best go with Pa."

All her life Hannah Moore had done for her father. Since she was a little girl and her mother had died she had taken over the care of herself and him. By his side she had worked in the fields, hunted with him in the woods, dressed out and cooked the game, made, stitched, mended and washed their clothing, been in all ways the keeper of their house and their lives. It was inconceivable to her that she should now seek the protection of the boats and let him go alone up the Kentucky. At her reply her father had looked once at her, approvingly, and then he'd said, "Hannah ain't never been from my side."

The major had shrugged his shoulders. "It is your own responsibility then."

"Hit is my own responsibility," Samuel had agreed gravely.

They had then moved their belongings from the boat—the axe, the two

[5]

rifles, the small store of provisions, corn and meat and salt, the bar of lead and bag of powder, the bullet mold, Hannah's spinning wheel, the iron pot and two pewter spoons, and the bundle of clothing and odds and ends. They had removed these things from the boat which they had shared with the Williams family, told their goodbyes, and stood, watching, as the flatboats shoved off into the stream.

Before the boats were out of sight they had turned, with one accord, to the task of building a raft. "I'm glad to be shut of 'em," Hannah had said.

"You done real good, though, Hannah," her father had told her, "makin' out with the Williamses."

"Nothin' else to do, way I seen it," she'd replied. "Jist the same, I'm glad to be on our own again."

"An' me."

They had built the raft, felling a tree, trimming off its branches, chopping its great trunk into equal lengths and binding them together with the wild grapevines they pulled down, green and twisty, from the trees. Then foot by slow foot they had poled their way up the river.

The woman made her way down the bank to a tongue of beach onto which they had pulled their raft two days ago, not thinking but that they would be leaving by first light the next morning—not thinking at all that Samuel's hand would slip on the handle of his axe while he was chopping wood for the night fire . . . would slip and the blade of the axe would sink deep into his flesh and bone, and the blood would gush out and he would have to hold the leg with both hands while she tore a petticoat into strips and tied it up to keep the blood from spouting such a stream as to bleed him to death. The raft was there, now, high up on the tongue of beach where they'd left it, ready and waiting their wish to go on up the river. Not their wish, for they had no wish to stay on in this place . . . that was what kept fretting Samuel . . . but their ableness to go on. The leg had swollen and he was fevered, and they could in no way venture on.

At the water's edge Hannah pulled a long shingle of bark under her knees and knelt to wash her face and hands. The water was warm, for May. It came over her how different water was in different places. At home now, there had been the branch back of the house, swift and clear-running and cold every day of the year. Spring-fed it had been, never ceasing in its flow no matter how droughty the summer. It had been a pleasure to her, always. She had dipped up the wooden pails full for the house, and had taken their clothing down to the branch to wash in its clear-flowing stream. All her life she had drunk it, bathed in it, used it. She remembered one still pool which, when she bent over it, had given her back her reflection, unbroken until she herself stirred the water. It had given her back her plainness, the long, bold, unsoftened lines of her face. However gently she bent over the pool, wishing to see loveliness, it had always shown her the truth. "I am plain," she had been compelled to admit, "I am a plain girl and never in time will I be different. Hit's no use to wish for e'er thing else." And then she had reached out her hand to stir the water. Here, now, in Kentucky, she could not see her face. The water ran too swiftly across the low tongue of beach.

She washed her face and hands and then unbound her hair and let it fall about her shoulders. Like nearly all very coarse, heavy hair it was too curly. Only its great length and heaviness kept it in bounds. She had no comb, so she shook it and ran her hands through it to remove the snarls. Then she wound it into a knot again and slipped the horn pins in place. She remembered once when she had had the fever and her mother had cut all her heavy hair off. It had grown back slowly, for months being a tousled mop all over her head. Like a little nigra's, her mother had said, laughing.

She thought, then, on the home they had left, not sadly, but with an affectionate remembering. It had been a pleasant place, the cabin under the shadow of the mountains. In all her life she had never lived any other place. She had been born within its walls, had seen her mother die there, had swept its floors, hung her mother's kettles over the fire, tended it and kept it, not knowing any other nor wanting any other. But it had been in the border country, claimed by both Virginia and Pennsylvania, and in the end Samuel had wearied of not knowing whether he could ever claim clear title to his land. He had his title under Virginia law, but as time went on it looked more and more as if Pennsylvania was going to claim the country, and if it did, what happened to a man's land? What happened to the land he had laid out himself and surveyed and staked, and worked and grown his crops on year after year; that he had built his cabin on and lived in, and buried his woman from and raised up his girl child in. After thirty years of it he wearied, and the time came when he said to Hannah, "We'll be goin' out to the Kentucky country. There a man can claim a clear Virginia title."

So they had sorted through their belongings . . . this to take, that to leave. To take, the iron pot and the pewter spoons; to leave, the wooden pails and noggins, the long-handled spider; to take, the two heavy blankets; to leave, the feather pillows, the hand-woven coverlids; to take, the axe, the hunting knife, the two guns; to leave, the big loom that since Hannah could remember had sat in the corner; to take, the spinning wheel . . . "They ain't room, Hannah," Samuel had protested. "The old horse is loaded beyond carryin' now."

"Then I'll pack it myself. I ain't leavin' Ma's wheel."

She would have carried it, too, he knew . . . every step of the way she would have carried it. So against her stubbornness he gave way, took a small anvil he had thought he might need off the load and, sighing, tied on the spinning wheel. There was then to take, a small bundle of seeds carefully tied in squares of linen cloth—pumpkin, turnip, squash, beans, corn; to leave, the apple trees, the lilac bush and the Rose of Sharon lily by the chimney corner; to take, the little horde of silver; to leave, the hearthstone under which it had been hidden; to take, heart, nerve, muscles, strong for the journey and hardened; to leave, stout walls of home, memories, and a lonely gravestone on the hillside.

They had loaded the old horse with all she could carry and then, footing it themselves, had turned their backs on the border country. They had made their way to Fort Pitt, where the Monongahela and the Allegheny rivers joined to become the great Ohio, and there they had learned that Major George Rogers Clark was taking an army of soldiers down the river by flatboat to the mouth of the Kentucky, and that he would convoy any families wishing to travel with him.

It had taken the last of their silver to buy lead and powder and to pay for a place on one of the boats. To two accustomed to seeing none but their own faces for weeks on end the journey downriver had been tedious beyond all description. The necessity of being with other people all day long, the need to talk with them and sit and eat with them and listen to them, had punished them both and Hannah had spoken truly when she had said she was glad to be shut of them. Even now, with Samuel laid up and the time unknown when they could venture on, she was glad to be shut of the boats and the people.

She dipped the pot full of water and climbed the bank again, made her way back to the fire. There she dug into the leather sack which held their meal, mounded it on a clean slab of bark, wetted it with the river water, added a pinch of salt and rapidly and deftly molded it into cakes. She set them on a flat stone and moved it into the heat of the fire. Out of another leather pouch she took a handful of dried meat. She took a long piece of curled bark and laid the meat in it, pouring water over the strips to soften them. Then she lifted out half a dozen strips and stretched them across the prongs of a forked stick. Two pieces she left soaking in the water.

She hunched by the fire and held the stick of meat over the coals. The fire was very hot now, and the heat dried and burned her face. She shielded it with her arm, but held the stick in place patiently until the meat had sizzled out its fat and curled, crisp and brown around the edges. Then she pulled it off the stick onto another piece of bark, and taking the tail of her dress she slid the stone on which the corn pones were baking out of the fire. One by one she took up the cakes, shifting them rapidly to keep from burning her fingers, onto the bark with the meat, then lifting it and swinging the iron pot over her other arm, she took the food to the man. "Here's your vittles," she said.

With the help of his hands braced against the ground Samuel raised himself and inched back until he was sitting almost erect, and leaned against the back of the lean-to. Hannah handed him the slab of bark and he took it on his lap. He ate rapidly, gulping the food down, the woman watching him. When he had finished he wiped his hands on his buckskin shirt front and reached for the iron pot of water. He drank deeply, then sighed. "I c'n still relish my vittles."

"I was hopin' you could," Hannah said, taking now for herself the remainder of the meat and bread. "Long as you c'n eat good, you'll keep up yer stren'th."

He eased himself back down into his blanket and Hannah went on eating, silently. When she had finished she threw the piece of bark away, and turning up her skirt front wiped her hands on the underside. "I got two pieces of that meat a soakin' in some water," she said. "I thought to put 'em on the slash, if you'd agree."

Samuel nodded indifferently. When she returned with the meat Hannah knelt by Samuel's side and uncovered his wound. She frowned when she saw it and when Samuel saw her frown he raised up to look for himself. It was a wide, deep gash just above the knee, going well into the flesh to the bone. The edges of the wound were beginning to knit together, but they had a pallid look and above the cut the leg was swollen and red. Hannah suddenly put her face down and smelled. There was a sickish, sweet smell, faint but unmistakable. She took a deep breath. "Hit's mortifyin', ain't it?" Samuel said.

"Not so's you could notice yit," the woman said, "but they's a poison in it needs drawin'. This meat ain't fat enough, but it'll have to do till I git somethin' better. If I could meet up with a bear, now . . . they's nothin' as good as bear fat fer drawin' out the poison. But even slippery elm bark is better'n this lean meat."

Swiftly she laid the soaked meat over the wound and bound it again with the same strips of petticoat.

"I d'know," the man said, "I jist don't know how I could of been so keerless as to slip that axe. Jist standin' there choppin' . . . jist a measly little bit of firewood, an' of a sudden the axe was buried in my leg, stid of the wood."

Hannah nodded. "Hit'll happen thataway. No need frettin' over it now, Pa. Hit's done. Man's axe is bound to slip, times. Yore'n ain't never, that I know of, before."

"Not ever," Samuel affirmed. "In all my time, not ever before. Oh, I have cut myself on the sharp blade of a axe, but not ever did I slip it into my leg or foot before."

"Hit was jist bad luck."

"Yes," Samuel agreed, brooding, "an' they's no way a man c'n turn his luck. Not that I know of, they ain't."

"No. I've not never heared of any either. You spit over yer shoulder, I reckon."

"Jist had done so. Hit warn't that."

"No." The woman looked reflectively out beyond the trees. "I heared a whippoorwill last night."

"I heared him, too."

"I d'know as I ever heared one this early in the year."

"I d'know as I ever did, either. But we been comin' south down the river a right smart piece. Reckon they commence callin' sooner down here."

"Hit could be they do. Time the corn was planted."

The man groaned. "Don't name it. The Lord knows if we'll git e'er bit planted this season."

"We'll git some planted." She stood and pulled her skirts free around her. "I'll be goin' into the woods now."

She picked up the rifles which lay at the farther end of the lean-to, laid one beside her father and slung the other one easily into the bend of her arm. Then she bent her head and passed out into the open.

Samuel watched her stride swiftly across the clearing, pick up the hunting knife and belt it securely to her dress. He did not call out to her to take care, no more than she would have called out to him. He himself had taught her the ways of the woods. She knew her way about in them as well as any man. If she ran across game today she could kill it and dress it out. Dressed, she could then pack as much of it as they needed into camp. He watched her run her hand into the pouch of meat and dig out a few strips. She tied them into a square of cloth and stuck it in the bosom of her dress. Then she tied the pouch securely, tied the pouch of meal and brought both of them to the lean-to. "If you git a notion to eat," she told him, "the meat an' meal will both be handy."

He nodded. "You aimin' to stay this side the river?"

She brushed her hair back. "I thought to," she said, "unless I git on the trail of somethin' like a bear an' it crosses over."

With no further word she left.

The man watched her out of sight. He had not asked her when she would be back. It was a useless thing to try to tell. She would be back when she had either found and killed game or had decided it was useless to try longer. Maybe she wouldn't be gone more than a couple of hours. Maybe she would be gone all day. He doubted if she would lay out the night, though. At home she might have, if the need arose, but not in this new country and not with his leg stove up. She would be back by dark, he guessed. He set himself to get through the day as best he could.

2

QUICKLY Hannah left the camp behind her and out of sight. She kept to the trees and downstream, walking with an easy stride and almost noiselessly. At this time of year she had already discarded her moccasins, but the soles of her feet, she noticed when she stepped on a stone and winced, were not yet well hardened. It took a time, she thought, after being softened over the winter, but it was none too soon to be toughening them.

Back to a depth of a hundred feet the trees grew thickly along the riverbank, letting no sunlight through. They were great, tall trees and she noticed the different kinds as she walked through them, hardly aware that she was noticing, so used was she to immediate identification of all woods things. She noticed only with the surface of her mind as her eyes shifted rapidly here, there, and beyond. Samuel had taught her that a good woodsman never fixes his eyes on an object. He shifts them constantly, from side to side and as far ahead as possible. "Git to starin' at somethin'," he'd told her, "an' you c'n be trapped. Kind of freezes you, like."

So her mind clocked the trees and their uses. There was ash, now, stout for paddles and oars and for leaching lye, and good wood for a puncheon floor. It whitened under use. There was hickory, best of all wood for an axe or hatchet handle, true-grained . . . and lasty for burning in the fireplace on a cold winter's night. There was oak, for sill logs and for framing, as enduring as all time. There was beech, which gave down the least little nuts in the whole world she guessed, and made nearly as good a floor as ash. There was honey locust, gnarly, but not to be beaten for posts or for fence railings. There was sycamore, the wood pithy and not good for much, but the bark was wondrously manageable, thin and curled and white. It always grew on the banks of streams and wouldn't live where it couldn't root close to the water.

She marked a young elm bordering on a hazel-nut thicket. If she didn't run onto game, when she came back she'd cut enough bark from it to make Pa's poultice.

It went odd, she thought, the ways of trees. It was as if they could think for themselves their own needs and wants. You never found them out of pocket the way you did folks. It would be good, she thought, if folks could know their own needs and wants like the trees and have a care for them as well. She, now, she knew *her* wants and needs. They were Pa, a cabin, a clearing, a garden patch, some woods close by and running water handy. Give her those things and *she* wouldn't be out of pocket anywhere—the border country or Kentucky, it made no difference. But put her down in a town, with folks near at hand talking and clattering the livelong day as they had done at Fort Pitt and on the flatboats, just put her down in a town, now, and she had to admit that would be different. Oh, put her down in a town and she'd be out of pocket for certain. She couldn't in any manner of way put down her roots in a town, with a house this side of her and a house that side of her, shutting and closing her in, folks coming and going all hours of the day and worse than the birds chattering in the treetops for picking at some kind of talk. I misdoubt, she told herself, I'd draw e'er other free breath should I ever be. Well, it wasn't likely she ever would be. Pa couldn't abide towns, either.

Some note of uncertainty slid into her thoughts here. Pa's leg was bad. Anxiety crept like a worm into her thinking. That leg was going to be a trouble and there was no use hiding it from herself. He'd had cuts before, plenty of them, and so had she . . . knife slashes, nicks with the saw, and once she'd cut her hand bad with the hatchet. Fat meat bound to it a few days had always healed the cut; never had she seen one turn angry and red this way, or smell that sickly, sweet smell. She wished she knew a good charm. Back in the border country, now, she could have traipsed over the mountain to Granny Poe's, and Granny, who knew all the charms that had ever been devised, would certainly know a good charm for Pa's leg. Maybe a cobweb tied on under the slippery elm bark, but then she wasn't going to put her dependence in the slippery elm if she could run up on something that had a sliver of fat on him. Fat meat was the best, everyone knew. There was pus and poison in that leg, for sure. And if that sweet smell got any worse, bad as she'd hate to do it she'd have to open up the cut and let it out. It was things like that that made a man lose a leg, and Pa, one-legged, wasn't to be thought of.

She doubted if she was going to run across anything on the river now. The mist had entirely lifted and the sun was well up in the sky. She ought to have left the camp sooner, she thought, for early morning was the best time, when the animals came down to water. She decided she'd better cut across the cane thicket to the hills. She might come on a bear, there.

She angled through the woods to the edge of the stand of cane, and there she took a bearing on the sun. The cane was fully ten feet high and so thick she'd have to fend her way through. It would be easy to get lost in such a tangle. The sun, two hours high, was on her left shoulder. She sighted to the foot of the hill. She wanted to come out at the foot of a little white cliff. She plunged into the cane.

An hour later, having shoved, pushed and hacked her way through the thicket, she came out exactly where she had intended. She stopped to rest a moment, pushed her hair back and wiped her face with her dress-tail, looked back on the cane. "Hit may be," she said to herself, "it's good feedin' fer animals, but in no way is that there cane a thing to pleasure a body gittin' through."

She did not search a way to the top of the hill up the cliff. Instead she wound along its base till it ran out into a heavily undergrown, bushy slope.

This she took and, almost crawling because of its steepness, made her way upward. At the top she found a plateau, flattened as if some great hand had smoothed the wrinkles of stone and gullies and roughness to a level. It was a fine tableland of forest, carpeted with the fall of last year's leaves still soft underfoot. High overhead the green of new leaves not yet fully opened were already making a roof to shut out the sky. Slanted beams of sunlight made bright shafts, and there was a busyness of birds all about—a kind of panicky busyness which told that her coming had disturbed them. She stood quietly, waiting for them to be reassured. Then, quietly she moved into the forest.

She had no luck, although she came upon the track of a bear soon after entering the forest. It was an old track, though, fully twenty-four hours old. The rain the night before had blurred and softened the edges of the prints, and the hollows were still filled with water. She followed it for a time, but she had little hope of coming up on the animal. Sometimes she stopped and hid herself stilly beside a down log, immobilizing herself, making no noise or gesture, waiting like something turned to stone for any wild creature that might pass. She saw only the squirrels and birds, never any real game. She thought it must be true, as she had heard, that in parts of Kentucky game was getting scarce. But then, she remembered, even with a plenty of game there would be times when your luck was out and you wouldn't run across any—plenty of times you did. The way your luck ran had a lot to do with it, and a body just never knew.

She kept doggedly on, however. It was midafternoon when she came to a small rill of water running flatly along the top of the ground. She traced it to its source, a small spring seeping from between some rocks. She was thirsty, and thinking of water she realized she was also hungry. She'd rest a spell here, she decided, and eat, and then she might as well start back. She'd just have to make do with a slippery elm poultice for Pa's leg, for it was plain she wasn't going to run up on any game now.

She dug the leaves out of the little pool under the rocks and waited for the water to clear, then she dipped it up with her hands and drank. "Most," a voice said suddenly at her back, "would of laid down and drunk from the pool. You been raised to the ways of the woods I'd say, ma'am."

She was scared so badly she froze momentarily, with her hands lifted to her face, and the fear went tingling down her arms into the skin on the backs of her hands, heating the skin and prickling it. She dropped one hand to her gun as she turned. "Not good enough," she said, "or you'd not a crept up on me from the back thataway."

The man laughed. "You'll not be needin' yer gun, ma'am, an' no need to be afeared of Tice Fowler. I didn't aim to skeer you."

"Oh, you never," she said, instantly denying her fear. "A Indian wouldn't of spoke. Hit startled me an' astonished me, but it never to say skeered me."

"Hit's mutual, then," the man said, drily. "I never looked to see a woman here. I was aimin' to git me a drink an' bait at this here spring afore goin' on, but I wouldn't of allowed to see e'er other human person, much less a woman. You give me a right smart of a start."

"I would think it," Hannah agreed, smiling a little.

The man stood there, leaning easily on the barrel of his gun, a little bent over it. He was a tall man . . . around six foot she guessed, and broad and hefty with it. He'd have to stoop, she thought, to go through most doorways, and swing a little sideways. She tried to place his age, though it was difficult because of the stubble of beard on his face. He was weathered about the eyes, and the hands folded over the gun barrel were rough looking and had lost the smooth fullness of first youth. His neck, though, was firm and solid looking, not gaunted or slack-muscled like Samuel's. She thought, maybe, he would lack ten years, or even fifteen, of being as old as Samuel. Samuel had lost the exact count of his age, but he figured it to be fifty, or thereabouts. This man would be about forty, she thought, though he *could* be a mite younger.

She watched him as he squatted by the spring, then. He took off his old battered buffalo-skin hat and creased it, making a drinking vessel of it. Dipping it in the water, he drank long and deep. His hair, Hannah saw, was a sandy, nondescript brown, clubbed carelessly with a thong of leather, and none too thick on top, and now that he was nearer she could see that his eyes were the same sort of light blue as Samuel's . . . the kind of blue eyes that were so light they looked faded, but remained keen and sharp in a man's head to the end of his life. She judged that commonly he did not wear a beard, for it was no more than a stubble and would easily have grown out in a few days in the woods. Seeing her looking at his face he rubbed it ruefully with his hand. "I hadn't thought to stumble up on a lady, as I told you, ma'am . . . but I don't commonly pack a razor with me noway."

Hannah dropped her eyes and made no answer, not knowing what answer could be made to such a statement. Pa shaved when the notion took him. Sometimes he'd take a spell of shaving every few days. Then again he'd go all winter without. Just depended on his notion. She did not know what the man meant, so she stood, eyes lowered, and made no reply. "You got anything to eat with you?" he said, then, shaking the water from his hat and putting it on.

She withdrew the bundle from her dress. "Meat."

"Not, I reckon," the man said, grinning, and she noticed that when he grinned there was a small pucker at the corner of his mouth . . . it whitened with the movement of his lips and sank inward, not much, but enough, she thought, that if a body laid a finger there, it would fit, "not enough to divide?"

Hastily she untied the cloth and laid the meat before his eyes. "I'd of brung more," she said, "had I knowed."

"I got nothin' left but corn," he said, and from the front of his shirt he pulled a pouch.

"From the looks of that there bag," Hannah said, laughing, "you ain't got much of *it* left."

The man's laughter joined hers. "I been travelin' light an' fast. Is it fur to yore camp?"

"Not more'n a few miles."

"Hit wouldn't disfurnish you, then, to divide up the meat?"

[14]

"Not e'er bit." She handed him the cloth which held the meat.

He took it and laid it on the ground. Then he spread the mouth of the pouch and poured the parched corn on the cloth beside the meat. "Well," he said, "hit ain't no feast, but it'll stay the roilin' of yer stummick fer a time. Let's eat."

Hannah shook her head, feeling shy. "You eat. They's a plenty at camp, an' I c'n do without till I git back."

Tice Fowler laughed. "Well, I baited good yesterday myself, so I ain't exactly starvin'. Come on an' set."

Indecision sat hard upon her, and she pondered, not knowing what to do. But she *was* hungry, and if the man had baited good yesterday and was heading for some place not too far away, she might as well eat too. Deciding quickly she sat down with her back to the rocks and began eating. The man squatted nearby, his hand reaching out for the food and his eyes kept constantly glancing about. Neither of them talked as they ate, but when they had finished all of the meat and corn, and both had drunk again, the man said, "I ain't to say as full as I've been in my time, but that'll keep me from hurtin'." Ruefully he added, "I warn't fixed to travel so fur afoot. I been over acrost the river, an' I had a little brush with the Indians an' lost my horse."

"I reckon you hated to lose yer horse," Hannah said.

"Well, sure . . . a man does, but," he grinned, "hit's better sometimes to lose yer horse an' keep yer hair."

Hannah nodded. "I'd think it." She picked up the square of cloth, shook it, folded it and slid it inside the front of her dress.

The man watched her. "You never said what yore name is," he said, finally.

She slid her look over him. He confused her. He shifted from one thing to another too fast for her. Pa, now . . . Pa never left off one thing till he had it worked over properly. He worried a thing till he had it summed up one way or another. That was what she was used to, Pa's worrying a thing till he had all the juice out of it.

Now, if *he'd* been telling about having his horse taken from him by the Indians he would have told precisely what he was doing when it happened, every thought he had, every move he made, and he would have weighed both his actions and his thoughts against each remote possibility. It gave a body time to think, listening to a long-winded man as she'd done all her life. With Pa she always had time to know what to expect, and time to think what to say. But this Tice Fowler, now, he moved around amongst his words too fast for her . . . telling about a brush with the Indians one minute and then shifting to ask her name without hardly taking a good breath in between. She brushed her hair back. "Hit's Hannah Moore," she told him.

"Pleased to make yer acquaintance, ma'am. Matthias Fowler, yer servant." He was standing, making a small, stiff bow, which still further confused her. It made her feel foolish and awkward . . . made her feel stiff-handed and clumsy, and a deep embarrassment spread within her, making it impossible for her to look any longer at the man. Her eyes dropped to her feet, bare and scarred with briar scratches. A feeling of heat crept up her throat and into her face. She could barely make herself mumble, "Pleased to know you." Then she whirled and picked up her gun. "I'd best be gittin' on back."

The man picked up his own gun. "Hit wouldn't displeasure you none, would it, fer me to go with you?"

"You kin if you're a mind to," she said. Without waiting to see whether he followed or not she strode off through the woods. Her ears, however, told her he was on her heels.

She was still ashamed that her carelessness had let him come up on her unbeknowing to her. It filled her with discomfort. She didn't see *how* she could have been so careless. She wished she could find a way to tell him it had never happened to her before. She wondered if she might not say, off-handed, that she'd just looked about and had seen nothing, which would be the truth. She hadn't given over watching . . . and she had just looked. But it was also true that she had seen nothing, when he was there, somewhere, to be seen. Naming it, she decided, trying to make out she hadn't been careless, would be worse than just leaving it lay, for any way you looked at it, she had been. If, watchful as she was used to being, she hadn't peered out a grown man, then she'd been careless in some fashion and there was no getting around it. She wished she could know where he'd been to escape her eyes, and she pondered on a way to ask him, but finally gave it over. Since he hadn't told her, she didn't think she ought to come plain out and ask.

In the broad stretch of the forest, free of undergrowth so that there was no need to walk single file, the man came up beside her. She glanced at him sidewise. "You said yore name was Tice, before."

He laughed. "Commonly that's what I'm called . . . Tice, short for Matthias."

"Oh."

"Hit puzzles me," he said, after a moment, "what a lone woman would be doin' in the woods."

She slid another quick look at him to see if he was poking fun at her, for his remark went foolish to her. What would *anybody* be doing in the woods? It ought to be plain as day what she'd been doing. But his face was serious, so she gave him an answer. "Huntin'," she said.

"What," he said, "are yore menfolks doin' while you're out huntin'?"

"They ain't but Pa," she told him, "an' he is laid up with a hurt leg."

Understanding immediately he nodded. "You've had no luck, though. You're in need of meat, are you?"

Hannah shook her head. "Not fer eatin', we ain't. Pa's leg could do with a piece of fat meat. I was hopin' to run up on a bear, mebbe."

From his height the man looked down at her and grinned. "What would you of done had you come up on a bear?" he asked.

Now she knew he was making fun. She forbore to look at him but she gave him a direct answer. "I would of kilt it . . . dressed out what I could pack . . . an' I would of bound Pa's leg with the fat."

She knew the man was looking at her and once more she felt a flush steal up her throat into her face. She quickened her step to pull a little way in front of him. In two or three paces he had closed the distance. There was no trace of laughter in his voice, now, when he spoke. "How did it happen yer pa hurt his leg?"

"His axe slipped."

He nodded. "Hit c'n happen. Bad, is it?"

"Bad enough," she admitted, and then, as if the remembrance of Samuel's red-streaked, sick-smelling wound drew the words from her she went on . . . "he was choppin' some firewood, not even fellin' a tree, mind, an' his hand slipped. The blade was sharp, jist whetted, not nicked nor nothin'. He warn't thinkin' but to chop up a little wood fer me to cook us a bait of vittles. Of a sudden his hand slipped. Next he knowed the blade was grindin' against the bone." She looked briefly at the man striding along beside her, then she confessed, "Hit's closin' up the poison inside."

Tice Fowler's face went sober. It could kill a man, that kind of thing. He'd seen it do so, with a bullet hole, a knife gash, or even with a long splinter of wood. When a wound closed over with the pus and poison shut inside, it could kill a man fast. There was never but one thing to do. "Yer ma," he said gently, "is knowin' of what to do, I reckon."

"They ain't but Pa an' me. My ma died when I was a youngun."

The man took that information in, then, still gently, he said, "Ma'am, I don't aim to be pryin' into yore affairs, but what are you a doin', jist the two of you camped way up here on the Kentucky, so fur from the settlements? This ain't in the path of no place, comin' or goin'. Have you done lost yerselves?"

It made Hannah angry that he should think they had lost themselves. Heatedly she said, "My pa is Samuel Moore, an' never in his entire life has he ever lost hisself, or me. Not fer a hour. We come down the Ohio on the flatboats with Major Clark. He told that he aimed to build a fort at the mouth of the Kentucky. They was several aimed to travel together up the river to Boone's fort. But he changed his plans an' went on to the Falls, an' them others was too fainthearted to foller their intentions. Not Pa, though," she went on proudly. "Pa held to his'n. Me an' him built us a raft, an' we have come this fur. We was doin' good, too, till Pa hurt hisself."

"You have done good," Tice agreed. "How long since you took up the river?"

Hannah counted silently on her fingers. "Seven days," she said, "an' we been in this place two."

"You done *real* good," Tice said, approvingly.

"Is it fur," she asked, "from here? Pa thought to make it in two weeks, give or take a little."

Tice nodded. "He would of done so, in my opinion, if he'd not hurt hisself. Hit ain't much further. If," he went on to say, "you'd not run into no Indians. The trouble is, ma'am, travelin' the rivers is the worst way they is of goin'. Old-timers in the country stay off the rivers, if they c'n do so. The Indians use 'em, mostly. It astonishes me some you've not done had a brush with 'em. This time of year, too. Come spring they take to prowlin' considerably. You've had good luck not to see e'er'n. Hit would of been best to strike inland, through the woods. I reckon where you come from you've not had to think much of keepin' clear of the redskins."

"Not in my lifetime," Hannah admitted. "Hit was mostly settled country. But Pa has fit 'em."

Tice kept to himself his thought that Pa must not have fought them lately, or he would not have forgotten that to make camp on the bank of a river was risky, and to go so far as to build a fire at night was purely asking for trouble. "You're from somewheres near Fort Pitt, are you?"

"Not real close, no. Hit was the border country. We allus thought it was in Virginny, but they been quarrelin' so with the Pennsylvany folks over where the boundary lays that Pa said we'd jist git out an' leave 'em have it whichever way they wanted. Said we'd head fer Kentucky. Boone's fort is where he picked. Is that where you're headin'?"

"No," Tice shook his head. "I'm from Logan's stand, a piece further down."

The hope that had showed in her face, unknown to her, died away. Quickly the man went on, "But I'd be pleasured to guide you to Boone's."

"No," Hannah said, "hit would misput you. Pa ain't able to travel yit, an' they's no knowin' when he will be. Hit would belate you wherever you're goin'."

"Ma'am," the man said earnestly, "we don't leave folks in trouble in this country. We're all used to bein' misput fer one another. Hit's the only way we've got along."

Hannah thought about what he had said, then acknowledged its truth. "I reckon it would be the only way, in a new country. You been here long, have you?"

"Longer than some, but not so long as others," he said. "I ain't been here from the first, like Dannel Boone an' Ben Logan an' Jim Harrod an' some others, but I been here a little over two years. I come from the Holston country, myself. I was at Boone's stand fer a time. Facts is, I come out with Dannel two year ago last September when he brung his woman an' younguns out from the Watauga. But I never took to the country up around his fort, nor to the people either, I reckon. I knowed Ben Logan an' David Cooper back on the Holston an' I kept wishin' to be where they was at, so one day I jist lit out from Boone's an' took me up a piece of land on the Hanging Fork. Hit ain't but half a day from Dave's place, nor much further from Ben's fort."

"I have heard Pa talk of Logan's fort," Hannah said, "but I don't know as I ever heared of David Cooper."

"It ain't likely you would. Folks off knows about the ones that heads up the forts, like Dannel an' Ben . . . but they's a heap more good men in the country never heared of."

"They would be, sart'n," Hannah agreed. "Hit takes a power of folks to settle a country. Is this Hanging Fork you named another river?"

"A creek . . . yes. Hit's but little settled yit."

"Hit's sightly, is it?"

"Well, it suits me. Hit ain't so level as some. They's hills about, but the land is rich an' good in the valleys, an' they's water aboundin', an' the cane grows good. If you've been brought up in sight of hills you feel more to home where they're at, though they's a plenty over all the Kentucky country. These is little hills that don't bear down on you none. They kind of back up to you, friendly like."

Hannah nodded. "I been used to hills, myself."

"I'd think it. I was once in yore country. Hit's sightly, but I don't know as I'd blame yer pa fer leavin' if his title warn't clear."

"That was the way of it."

"A man don't like the idee of workin' a piece of ground all his days an' never knowin' does he own the land or not."

"That was the way Pa held it."

"Then he done right, in my opinion, to leave it to 'em. He'll do good in Kentucky."

They had come, now, to the place where the hill plunged off into the valley. "You'd best let me go first," Tice said, "an' you tell me if I go too fast fer you."

"I'll keep up," Hannah told him, "I c'n manage."

"I believe it, but you tell me, now."

She promised and he led off. Going down was a whole lot faster than coming up had been, Hannah thought, remembering the long, laborious crawl up the steep slope. She kept hard on Tice's heels and watched approvingly as he picked the best places for his feet, hardly slowing as he made his choices, knowing, it appeared, almost instinctively, the stones that would roll, the branches that would give and crackle, the underbrush that would be stubborn about giving way, and avoiding them. He was mighty good in the woods, she had to admit—not, she thought loyally, as good as Pa, maybe, but as good as a man had need to be, and better, she remembered blushingly, than herself. Seeing as he'd offered to help out, and doubtless had the time, she decided that if she'd been unlucky about finding game this day, she'd had good luck anyhow, in running up on Tice Fowler. It was going to be a comfort to have somebody with them that knew the country, and she didn't mind owning it.

When they came to the bottom of the hill he stopped. "Where did you come out of this cane thicket at?"

"At the foot of the clift," she told him, "but hit's no matter. Jist take a sight on that highest sycamore yonder. Hit's not fur, then, to the camp."

Tice glanced at the sun and then hitched at the belt that held his knife and hatchet. "Well, we'd best be gittin' on, I reckon."

"Yes."

They waded into the cane. Tice looked around from time to time to see how she was getting along. He was careful not to let the bent canes snap back in her face, but otherwise he left her to follow her own way.

When they had got through they stopped a moment to rest. "A cane thicket," Tice said, blowing out his breath deeply, "is about the unpleasantest thing I know of to git through afoot. Hot, with all that growth up over yer head, an' no air to speak of down under."

Hannah nodded and brushed at her hair, laughing, "I tangled with most of it, head-on."

Tice moved on. "Which way?"

"Upstream."

They went more slowly, more silently, now. The woods were dim and still about them, and the ground underneath was spongy and damp. Hannah felt the dampness on her feet, and the sponginess, and the soles of her feet were suddenly cool after the heat of the cane thicket. It was a good feeling, for her feet were sore.

When they came by the hazel bushes she stopped at the small elm she had marked. "I had it in mind," she said, "to put a elm bark poultice on Pa's leg if I didn't run onto somethin' fer a piece of fat."

He drew his knife. "I've allus heared slippery elm poultices was good fer drawin' out the poison. I've not ever tried it myself, though. Where would you want that tree girdled?"

Hannah measured up about the reach of her arm. "There, I'd think." Below his hacked girdling mark she stripped off the bark. It came off loosely, in large pieces, a damp ooze forming instantly on the suddenly naked trunk of the tree. When Hannah thought she had enough, Tice gathered up the most of it and tied it around with a grapevine, tied it then to his belt, and Hannah knotted some long strips and slung them over her shoulder. "I've not ever," she confessed as they started on, "used elm bark on a gash before. But it's good fer drawin' a risin' to a head. Pa had a risin' once on the back of his neck. Hit riz up as big as a hen egg an' I poulticed it with slippery elm. Hit drawed it down in not more'n a couple of days. But fat meat is best fer a gash . . . leastways that's what I've allus heared. Hit jist warn't a lucky day fer runnin' onto e'er thing, though."

"Tomorrow I'll seek out somethin'," Tice promised. "I'll swing out over acrost the river an' likely come up on somethin'."

"I'd be obliged to you," Hannah told him.

They walked for a time in silence, then Hannah, in Samuel's way of worrying a subject, though she did not know it, went back to her day of hunting. "I got the track of one bear, up there on top the hill, but hit was a old track. I made it anyways a full day old, mebbe more. I follered it till I could tell they wasn't no use, an' I never seed e'er other trace."

She did not think, either, how she, in this short time, who had been so full of confusion at a strange man's appearance, could now talk so easily with him. There was no self-consciousness in her telling of coming up on the old bear track. The man walking beside her was a hunter, accustomed as Samuel was, as she herself was, to the woods. He would know the importance of what she was telling. He would put himself in her place and know how she had found the bear track, studied it, known it as an old one immediately, but he would have also known that you had to follow a track a piece to make sure. He would know exactly how her mind had worked, and how, when she was certain, she had made her decision to cease following the track. There was no need to explain to him. Any man used to the woods would know what had happened, would agree she had been wise to leave off.

Tice nodded his head. "They's times like that. Not e'er trace."

"I misdoubt," she went on, "hit was on account of game bein' skeerce. Hit was jist not a lucky day fer it."

"Not in these parts, it ain't," Tice told her. "Hit's skeerce around the settlements, now. But in these parts they's a plenty. Hit was jist a bad day fer it."

They came to a slough of brackish water backed up from the river. Across it lay a mat of fallen trees. Tice stepped onto them and they swayed under his weight. "Take keer," he warned her, "an' don't slip."

She watched him safely across, wonderingly. This morning she had crossed alone, sure-footed, bare toes gripping the limbs, the crossing taking none of her thought and little of her care. Here was a man warning her, her that had been taught when she was a little one and never needing warning since, her that could have given most men lessons in taking care. In all her life she had known well only one man, Samuel, although men had crossed their path many times, stayed in their home, hunted with them. She could not remember that any had ever said to her before, at least not since she had been a grown woman, "Take keer."

And he'd said, coming down the steep slant of the hill, "I'd best go first, an' you tell me if I go too fast."

Maybe he thought she was awkward on her feet. She wouldn't wish him to think that, but he could see for himself she wasn't. Maybe, seeing as he had caught her careless by the spring he was thinking she needed looking after. Likely that was it, she thought, and chagrin wormed around in her stomach. In no way could she undo that, now. She sprang onto the bed of massed limbs, swayed with them easily, then crossed as lightly as if she had been walking on grass, never wetting a foot. At the bank Tice reached out a hand to pull her up. She ignored it, but her heart sank. She knew for sure, now, that he thought her careless and needing help.

And then he further confused her. "Hit goes the quarest to me," he said, chuckling, "a woman huntin'. They is several of the womenfolks in the country kin shoot as good as a man. You take Esther Whitley or Jane Manifee. They are dead shots. I warn't in the country the time Logan's was under siege by the Indians, but I've heared 'em tell of it times without number. Dave Cooper has told me hisself, an' he tells it that Esther an' Jane both taken their places at the stockade as good as man could."

"Hit don't wonder me," Hannah said.

"Nor me, that part don't. But I don't know if they ever went in the woods an' hunted like a man. I have never heared of it if they have, an' likely I would. I reckon both have kilt birds an' rabbits an' squirrels, little game that comes around a house-place, but I never knowed of e'er woman was good at huntin' real game."

"Well, I ain't as good as Pa," Hannah said, quickly.

"Hit's to be expected you wouldn't be," Tice said, comfortingly, "but the wonder of it to me is you bein' any good at all. The way I make it, yore pa, they bein' jist the two of you, has raised you like you was a boy instead of a girl-child."

Hannah thought upon it. "Hit may be. I wouldn't say it warn't that way. But I've took keer of the house-place since I was a little youngun, too."

"That would go natural . . . but the other don't. Likely he never knowed e'er thing else to do, a girl-child left to him thataway, but keep her to his side in the woods. He never did take another woman?"

"No."

"Then that must be the way of it."

"Hit could be," Hannah said again. "I never thought nothin' of it before."

"No. Hit's what you been used to. I c'n see how you'd not think to ponder on it."

A surge of courage stirred up in Hannah, born of Tice's kindness and understanding. "I ain't," she said, struggling to find the right words, "I ain't commonly as keerless as you found me today. I don't recollect ever bein' caught out thataway before, an' you needn't to tell me that once keerless is once too many. I know it is. I was jist lucky it was you. But I was taught better, an' I misdoubt I'll ever be caught so easy again."

Tice laughed. "They's no call fer you to fault yerself. You never overlooked me. Couldn't nobody of seed me, fer I seen you comin', an' not knowin' if you was by yerself or not, an' bein' astonished, too, I hid. I was hid in that big crevice between the rocks. You couldn't of seed a thing had you looked. You wasn't in no way keerless. You had yer gun handy an' ready, an' you never ceased watchin'. That's all anybody c'n do, fer they's no way you c'n spy out ever' least thing in the woods. Nobody c'n do that, not even Dannel Boone hisself. That's how come he was took by the Shawnees."

Relief flowed through Hannah. "I am glad," she said. "I hated it, havin' you think I had been so keerless."

"I never thought it."

Hannah pondered what he had told her, seeing it in her own mind, how Tice had arrived at the spring, had perhaps been bending over it to clear it of leaves, had heard her footsteps, listened, then turned, seeing her, catching just a glimpse of her, maybe, and then hid. There'd been no chance for her to see him. A body, he'd said, couldn't see everything in the woods. That was why Dannel Boone had been took. "When was it," she asked, "Dannel Boone was took?"

"In February. In the cold of the winter."

"Jist this year?"

Tice nodded. "He's still captured."

"He was huntin', was he?"

"Well, he was huntin', but the way it was, him an' a bunch from all the settlements was up on the Blue Lick makin' salt. They was a big bunch of 'em . . . some from Logan's amongst 'em. Dannel was huntin' fer the party."

"Was they all took, or jist Dannel?"

"All of 'em . . . ever' last man-jack of 'em."

Hannah clicked her tongue sympathetically. "The pore things. An' you could ill-spare 'em in the country, doubtless."

"Hit was a main blow, all right."

Looking up Hannah saw that they had reached the camp. Pointing, she said, "There is the camp, now. Right there, under them trees."

3

SAMUEL had dragged himself out of the lean-to and was sitting propped against the bole of a tree, his leg stretched before him, eased by the folded blanket under it. He was dozing as they came up to the camp, his head drooped to one side, but his gun was laid across his good knee and one hand held it securely. Hannah thought how pitiful and poorly he looked, broken down, as if he'd been cast aside. A man's strength, she thought, was his proudest possession, and it goes swiftly, the pride with it, when he is struck down.

Samuel had always been a strong man and a proud one. She was used to seeing him so, his strength and cleverness a shield between himself and life. But here, in a moment he was struck down, and as helpless as a young one he had to sit, dozy, under a tree, his shoulders, which could square to the heft of a heavy log, drooped and sagged, his long legs which could track an elk all day without tiring, stretched, already puny with illness, useless before him.

She felt a pity at seeing him so, a great sorrow for him filling her, and a wish, which shamed her even as she wished it, that Tice Fowler could have seen him first in his great strength and pride, not broken like this. She wanted to straighten his shoulders, to lift his head, to waken him and have him stand whole and strong before Tice Fowler. He looked old sitting there, dozing. It took her by surprise. Pa looks old, she thought, he looks like a old, old man.

She had never really thought of his age before. She had not thought how time was passing for him. His strength had not allowed for age, had withstood it, so that she had been aware all her life of nothing but height and strength and cleverness. Years had had no meaning where Samuel was concerned. She could not remember when his hair had not been iron-gray, nor when his face had not been lined. He had remained, since her first memories of him, the same, tall and gaunted and tireless. But now she thought, He looks old, Pa does, and a brush of fear ran through her, nameless and barely identified it passed so quickly.

For Samuel awoke instantly at their coming and raised his head to peer at them, his hand moving instinctively on his gun. He blinked at them, stretching his neck to look up, and Hannah saw how corded were its muscles. "Well," he said, then, "who mought you be, stranger?"

"Tice Fowler, from Logan's fort." Tice grinned down at Samuel. "Kentucky has give you a hard welcome, I would say."

Samuel grunted. "I d'know as Kentucky had e'er thing to do with it. Bad luck with my axe, mostly."

"That's what yer girl was tellin' me." Tice leaned his gun against a fallen log and laid off the trappings of his belt, knife, hatchet, the bundle of elm bark. "You'll be wantin' a fire, I reckon, Hannah," he said, "to make up that poultice."

"Yes."

Tice looked around for the axe, found it in the lean-to, and hoisting it to his shoulder went off, whistling, to cut wood for the fire.

"How'd you come up on him?" Samuel asked, motioning with his head at Tice's retreating back.

Hannah told him . . . told him in detail as she knew he wanted to hear, as he himself would have told it—how she had reasoned to look first for deer along the river, then had decided to head for the hill across the cane thicket— how she had crossed, climbed the hill, found the bear track and followed it, leaving out nothing of her thinking or reasoning. Samuel nodded as he listened, following her, seeing her movements, reasoning with her mind, making her decisions with her. She worked with the elm bark as she talked, breaking it, cleaning it, piling it beside her. She told how she'd been drinking at the spring when Tice had come up on her, how she had feared she'd been careless, but where Tice had hidden and how he had excused her. "You warn't at fault," Samuel agreed. "You done good. He was right. You cain't seek out ever' livin' thing."

Now that Samuel too absolved her the last worry about it left her. She felt free of it, and she went on to tell how Tice had said he would guide them to Boone's fort. "Though," she said, "Boone ain't there no more. He was took by the Shawnees durin' the winter."

"I hadn't heared of it," Samuel said.

"I didn't figure you had. You'd not named it."

"The fort still stands, I reckon."

"I reckon. He never said different. They warn't at the fort when they was took. They was a party of 'em off, makin' salt."

Samuel shook his head. "Hit happens. I am sorry to hear of it. I taken a likin' to Dannel Boone. I had thought to have more of his company."

Hannah was mounding twigs and leaves for the fire, now. When she had finished she picked up the iron pot and went toward the river for water. She met Tice, his arms loaded with wood. "I got the fire ready," she told him.

"I'll git it goin' straight off," he promised.

He did not like the camp site . . . the openness of it, no cover anywhere about, that tongue of beach in the river, the easy access and ford, but he could see no help for it at present. Samuel's leg must be opened and poulticed. They could not leave with him tonight. He, Tice, could keep a careful watch . . . and hope. He said none of this, however. There was no use saying anything. Tomorrow, if Samuel could be moved, they would go inland and make camp until he could travel.

He had a fire blazing when Hannah came back with the water. She moved a flat rock into its heat and set the pot upon it. Tice laid fresh wood on the fire, stirred it until it caught. Hannah brought up the pile of elm bark. "We'll have to open that gash, I reckon you know," he told her.

She nodded, bending over the pot of water, watching it. Then she looked up at him. "I had done made up my mind when I looked at it this mornin'. You want to take a look at it now?"

"Mought as well."

They walked over to Samuel. "I'd best look at yer leg, now, Samuel," Tice said to him.

"I reckon so."

Hannah knelt and unbound it. The bandaging which she had wrapped about it that morning was tight on the leg now, so much had the swelling increased. The skin looked stretched and hard, and the red streaks went now almost to the thigh. The wound itself was puffed looking, its edges white and crusted. Tice looked at it, lifted it gently, handled it, smelled of it as Hannah had done. Samuel's eyes never left his face, watching intently for some change of expression. The fear of losing the leg lay there, naked in Samuel's eyes, the hope of saving it made him search Tice's face. But Tice was well schooled in hiding his thoughts. His face was grave, sober, as any man's face would be, looking at such a wound, but it did not reveal the shock he felt. He laid the leg back down on the blanket. "Hit's got to be opened, ain't it?" Samuel said, then, expelling a great breath.

"Yes," Tice told him. "Hit's full of poison . . . they ain't no use to lie to you."

"I figured it. I c'n smell it myself. Well, git it done an' over."

"Mebbe you'd ruther Hannah to do it."

Samuel looked at her. She was standing, her hands hanging loosely, waiting. Her face was blank of any expression save that of waiting. Whatever she had felt on seeing the leg again her face did not show. It was calm, expressionless. Loosely she stood, waiting. She was thinking one thing. What's got to be done, has got to be done. She was not afraid of it. She did not shrink from it. Life had taught her that there are some things you cannot escape. Hurt and pain are among them. What's got to be done, has got to be done. She accepted it, now that Tice had said it too. She would do now whatever they said. "She's good with animals . . . calves, cows, horses . . . I d'know," Samuel said.

"Whichever you'd ruther," Tice said, kindly.

"You ever done sich?"

"Once. Feller I was travelin' with got cut up in a fight."

"Hannah ain't never. You'd best, I reckon."

Tice bent over his belongings and drew out his knife, tested it. "You got any rum?"

"Git it," Samuel said to Hannah.

She went to the lean-to and came back with a jug. Tice took it and handed it to Samuel. "Drink all you c'n hold."

[26]

Samuel drank in long swallows, not lowering the jug until he had had enough. Then he dropped it. "That'll do, I reckon."

Hannah went to the fire, saw that the water was beginning to get hot and dropped into it a pile of the elm bark. She went back to the men, wiping her hands on her skirt.

Tice was cleaning his knife on a large sycamore leaf. "We'll give that rum a chance to take hold," he said to her. She nodded.

Samuel was leaning back against the tree, his eyes closed. They watched him and Tice took out a small whetstone and honed the knife blade. That was the only sound Hannah could hear, the slide and grate of the knife blade on the whetstone, like breathing in and out, regular and unhurried. Over and over and over Tice slid the knife across the whetstone, not watching his hands at all, keeping his eyes on Samuel. Finally Samuel's head lolled, he belched, his eyes opened, squinted, he grinned and belched again, then his eyes closed and his head sagged. "Reckon it's time," Tice said. "Hold his foot so's he won't jerk."

In spite of her strength on the foot, Samuel jerked when the knife went in. She watched Tice's hand poised over the wound, steady as if he'd been going to dress out a deer, saw it hover a moment then sharply descend and slice ruthlessly through the wound. Samuel's foot jerked suddenly, but there was no sound from him. Out of the corner of her eye, sidewise, she saw his hand grip the hump of a tree root beside him. She kept her eye on the knife in Tice's hand, but cornerwise she also saw Samuel's hand grip, saw the knuckles whiten, the fingernails claw, then the knife's work was done, the hand slowly loosened its grip and went limp. "He's swooned," Tice said.

She sighed. "Hit's the best."

"Yes."

Together they took pieces of the old bandaging and mopped up the re-opened wound, cleaning it as best they could. "I got a little piece of that linen left," Hannah said. "I'll git it."

Tice laid a square of the clean linen over the gash while Hannah made a poultice of the mash in the iron pot. Samuel stirred uneasily when she laid the poultice over the wound, but did not speak. "He'll sleep a while now," Tice said.

She nodded and bound the poultice in place, using the clean linen until it was gone, finishing then with what was left of the old. "Hit ort to help," she said, "gittin' all that stuff outen there. But I'd feel better if I had a piece of fat meat to put on it."

"I'll git you a piece tomorrow," Tice said. "Mebbe this elm bark will keep it drawed out till then."

They had finished with Samuel's leg. Tice laid him more comfortably on the ground and spread the blanket over him. "I'll go wash off my knife."

"Well, I'll fix us a bait to eat."

Tice grinned at her. "Hit'll be welcome. What we eat at midday has done wore out on me."

Dark came on soon after they had eaten and Hannah tidied up the camp

[27]

by the light of the fire. When she had finished she asked Tice, "Had we best leave Pa where he is at, or move him into the lean-to?"

"Jist leave him be," he told her. "I'll be handy."

"I'm goin' to lay down, then. You c'n have my blanket if you want. I'll not need it in the lean-to." She felt unaccountably weary of a sudden.

"I thank you," he said, "but I'm more used to doin' without than you."

She didn't argue. She rolled up in the blanket and lay down, gratefully, on the bed of leaves that had been Samuel's couch. She could see Tice making ready for the night. He scattered the fire first, and then picked a tree, beyond Samuel, laid his gun down and sat, propping himself against the tree. He's not aimin' to sleep, she thought, he's fixin' to keep watch.

She called to him. "If you'll wake me when it's time, I c'n watch out so's you c'n git a little sleep."

"I mought," he answered, but she didn't much think he would. She determined to wake herself. She could when there was need. She'd done it many a time when Samuel had wanted to get up earlier than common. All she had to do was think of it before dropping off, and, as if a bell had sounded, when the time came she was awake. She put her mind to it now, and then closed her eyes.

It was black dark when she awakened. She rolled over and edged to the front of the lean-to, looked at the sky. She judged it was near midnight. Certainly the dawn was several hours off yet. She shivered as she crawled out of the warm bed and reached back for the blanket to wrap about her shoulders, yawning. Tice heard her and called out softly in the darkness, "You needn't to git up."

She found her gun and made her way over to him. "I'd ruther to," she said. "If you're aimin' to hunt in the mornin', you'll need a mite of rest yerself."

He grunted and she could see a blur of movement by the trees. He was standing. "If they's e'er trouble," he told her, "hit'll come from acrost the river. I don't look fer it, understand. Hit's jist best to take keer. You got yer gun?"

"Yes."

"Well, then. . . . Yer pa ain't stirred. Reckon that rum purely knocked him out."

"Hit must of. The sleep'll do him good."

"Yes . . . well, come daylight, if I don't stir, call me. If *he* c'n stand bein' moved, we'd best make camp further away from the river."

"Ain't you aimin' on takin' the raft on up the river?"

"No, ma'am. That would be the last thing I'd aim on doin'. We'll move an' camp an' wait till yer pa c'n travel. Then we'll strike out through the woods. Well, I'll lay awhile now."

Hannah settled herself by the tree. She was fully awake now, felt fresh and rested. There was an open spot in the trees just over the camp and by leaning her head back and resting it against the trunk of the tree she could see the

[28]

stars, and a little, pale disk of moon off in the west. You could tell, she thought, the time of night by the stars and moon, when the night was clear. And you could tell, too, that the winter was over and summer coming on. They moved, the stars did, changing places in the sky with the hours, and changing places as the seasons passed them by. She thought about it, wondered about the stars and moon, wondered why they'd been put there to shine in the night . . . why they moved. It wasn't a thing she could study out, though. It was past e'er *human* body's knowing, she guessed. There were some things that couldn't be studied out.

She felt a breath of wind on her cheek. There, now . . . wind was one of them. What was it? Where did it come from? What moved it unseen around the world and across the land? It would stir through the night, ruffle the leaves and shake them, bend the limbs—but when the dawn was near, when the dark was just beginning to lift, not light yet but just ready to be, it would quieten as if it listened for the sun. As still as death it would be then, at that time just before the light streaked into the sky, so still that, if you were stirring then, you could hear your own breath coming and going in your throat, and hear your own heart beat. The way of wind . . . it went queer and odd to a human body.

And the way of rain, blowing up in the clouds, the clouds splitting and pouring it down. She named over to herself the things she could in no way study out . . . wind, the moon and stars, rain, sunlight, clouds, storm, the fall of rivers down the land, the rise and flow of water. There was a power of things, she told herself, no human body could ever know the straight of. You could, in time and with study, know the ways of birds and animals, and even folks. They had life inside them, they all bled and their hearts beat and they breathed in the air. One way or another they all moved, flew or walked, swam or ran. They all died, too. The sun, now, and the stars, the wind and the rain, the water in the rivers, those things went on forever. How could it be, she wondered, that a thing that lived should come to the end of its living, and those things that had no life in them should go on forever? "Hit ort," she told herself, "to be the other way round, looks like." Then she laughed, to think of the sun and stars and moon dying. "The folks would die fer sart'n, then," she said.

She never talked about such thoughts as these. Once when she was a child she had tried to tell Samuel about the sound the branch back of the house made, running over the rocks. It went, she had told him, like singing, real soft. "You c'n hear the words, I reckon," Samuel had said, grinning at her.

"I kin," she had told him stoutly. "Hit's a singin' 'Go to sleep, go to sleep, go to sleep.' "

Sam had not laughed then. Sternly he had bade her to keep such foolish talk to herself. "Hit ain't nothin' but water runnin' over the rocks," he'd said. "Don't go gittin' foolish fancies in yer mind, Hannah. They'll make you go quare in the head . . . folks'll think you're tetched, an' they'll mistrust you."

So she had never again named the things she thought to Samuel, or to anyone else. But she was always thinking them, just the same. It did no harm to *think,* as far as she could see.

Samuel moved in his sleep, stirred and muttered, threw one hand from under the blanket. She watched until he had settled, her thinking distracted, and when he was quiet again she thought about moving camp tomorrow . . . today, now. Wondered where Tice would pick. Wondered if Samuel could be moved. Thought of the problems and shook her head. Below, she could hear the liquid sound of the river, running shallow around the tongue of the beach. She smiled in the dark. In spite of Samuel, running water *did* make a singing sound.

4

IT WAS STILL half dark when she stirred, quietly because of Samuel who was still asleep, to waken Tice. With one hand she pushed herself up from the ground. The muscles back of her knees were cramped and stiff from her long sitting, and she stood a moment, flexing them slowly to loosen them.

The river, she noticed, showed lighter where there were no trees to cast shadows. It looked dull and gray, like tarnished pewter, and it was barely moving. East, across the river and back of the hills, the sky was beginning to come light, pale down next to the hills with a faint, pearly pink showing, but still dark overhead, with stars not yet dimmed. The air was very still, and there was no sound at all except the sound of the river, a wet, flowing sound. There was not yet any stir in the trees, of birds or of wind, no movement of any kind.

She stood and rubbed her legs, feeling the stillness, thinking how this hour was always the stillest of the night, as if every living thing was holding itself in waiting for the first red touch of the sun. Only she was awake and moving. She sniffed the air. There was the damp of the river in it, and the smell of the cold ashes, something left over yet of cooking smells, and the fresh green smell of the trees. You would know, she thought, without looking that you were camped in woods on the bank of a river. She studied the sky. No clouds blotted the stars. The sun was going to rise clear, and it was going to be a fair day. She turned and walked softly to the lean-to.

Tice came awake immediately when she called him, sitting up suddenly and hitting his head against the low roof of the shelter. Forgetting the woman he cursed briefly. She laughed and he remembered, spoke his apologies, and crawled outside. He took a quick look around. "Ever'thing all right, is it?"

"As fur as I know," she said, moving off and beginning to gather wood for the fire.

"I'll not wait," he told her, "fer somethin' hot. Jist give me some meat an' a piece of that cold pone. I'll eat on the move."

She handed him the meat and a chunk of bread. She knew he wanted to be several miles downstream by sun-up, knew he had to be if he expected to kill anything today. He saw to his gun and started off, chewing already on a hunk of the meat. He didn't look back at all, and she watched him out of sight silently. Then she busied herself with the fire.

He had been gone about an hour when Samuel awakened, and the first shafts of the sun were stabbing down across the trees beyond the river, dappling and darkening the water, giving it color. Samuel rolled over, winced and groaned. Hannah went to him, taking him a drink of rum and hot water. "You feelin' better this mornin', are you?"

He drank before answering, his eyes studying the morning, judging it and deciding upon the weather. "I d'know as I do. I feel all tuckered out, weaklike. I d'know as I could stand up even if both my legs was good, but I reckon the pain is some better. Hit's aimin' to be a fair day, ain't it?"

"Yes." She took it as a good sign that the pain in his leg was better.

The air was now full of sound, birds chattering and twittering, a squirrel barking now and then, and even as they talked a young fox squirrel ran, unafraid, across the clearing. Hannah looked at Samuel and laughed. "Now, ain't he the smart one?"

When she had fed Samuel and redd up the camp she got out her bag of odds and ends and took from it linen thread and a big bone needle and set herself to mending. Samuel's spare buckskin had a rent in it. Her own skirt was torn. The meal pouch was worn thin in two spots. Her big hands guided the needle and strongly pulled it through the materials of the skirt and skins. Samuel grew weary of sitting and hunched himself down into the blanket and dozed off. Once Hannah laid down her stitching and crossed to feel of his forehead. It was hot, but not, she decided, uncommonly so.

The morning passed, the sun warming the air even under the trees until the day was like summer. The warmth was good, and Hannah felt as if her skin stretched and loosened, and she had freer use of her body. Cold didn't bother her overly much, but given her choice she liked it best when you didn't have to hug a fire. She felt more alive, somehow.

When Tice came in around midday he had a great hunk of bear meat slung over his shoulder. "Had good luck," he told them, sliding it to the ground. Hannah took it over from him, smiling at the sight of the good streaks of fat, and Tice went to talk to Samuel. "You feelin' some better today?"

Samuel didn't know. "I jist feel tuckered. Jist ain't got no stren'th left, seems like."

"Yer leg painin' you any?"

"Some . . . but no more'n common. Seems like mainly I'm jist all gone inside of me."

Tice looked at him, critically. "I was hopin' we could move back away from the river this mornin'. Me an' Hannah could likely pack you between us."

"C'n try."

"We'll try, then, when we've eat."

"Where'd you run up on the bear?"

Tice squatted in the dirt. "Acrost the river." He picked up a twig and began to draw in the dirt. "I'd crossed over, up a piece . . . you recollect where the river makes a bend an' a little slough, like, backs up?" Samuel nodded. "Well, that's where I crossed, an' I'd went near five miles, I'd say, beyond.

[32]

I'd jist follered a little swale up a piece an' was climbin' out, an' they was a long patch of level ground lyin' there, woodsy but clean underfoot, an' I heared him snifflin'. I laid low, waitin', an' he hove into sight purty soon, lookin' big as a mountain. I waited till he got square in front of me, an' then I let him have it. You heared the shot, did you?"

Samuel confessed he had not. "I ain't been listenin' as good as I could."

"Well . . . I didn't know but you mought of. But hit was a right smart piece off. I brung the head. I got him right under the ear."

Samuel nodded. "Hit's the best place. Hit's the surest. You brung the head in with you, did you?"

"I thought mebbe you'd want to see how it was I shot him."

"I would like to."

Tice got the head from the pile of meat, brought it to Samuel, squatted beside him and turned the head to one side. "Right there is where the bullet went in. You c'n see."

Samuel took the head, turned it, studied it and nodded. "Purty a shot as I ever seed. You done good. Don't know as I ever done better myself."

"Hit was a fair shot," Tice admitted modestly. "I have done better, though. This one mought be a speck high, wouldn't you say?"

Samuel studied the head again. "I wouldn't say so," he said, finally, "no, I d'know as I'd say it's high. Mought be . . . jist a mite, but I d'know as I'd say it was at all. In my opinion you done real good. I d'know as I ever seed a purtier shot."

"Hit was fair." Tice tossed the head back onto the pile of meat and wiped his hands with a mat of grass.

"Wish I could of went with you," Samuel said, wistfully.

"I wish you could of, too. Hit won't be long till you c'n be on the track again."

"I d'know. The way I feel right now it's liable to be longer'n I'd of figured."

"That's on account of us havin' to cut that gash open again. Hit's weak-enin', that kind of thing is. You'll pearten up tomorrow or next day, likely." He folded his long legs under him and leaned back against the tree across from Samuel. "Some of that bear meat when Hannah gits it fixed is goin' to strengthen you, too. You been needin' fresh meat."

Samuel brightened. "Hit could be. They ain't nothin' like fresh meat to strengthen you, fer sart'n. I don't reckon you thought to bring along the liver?"

Hannah, hearing, called out, "He done so, an' it's in the pot right this minnit. You'll be eatin' the stew in no time at all."

"I love bear meat as good as e'er meat I ever put in my mouth, but I relish the liver best of all," Samuel confessed, laughing.

"An' me. Unless it mought be buffalo liver."

"Buffalo is hard to beat," Samuel agreed. "Any way you look at it, though, I reckon the liver of a animal is its best part. You take deer, now . . . I'd ruther to have the liver as all the rest of it put together."

Tice nodded. "To eat fresh, I would. But deer dries better'n buffalo. Don't dry out so hard."

Samuel agreed. They sat silent, then, each thinking over the qualities of game they had killed. It pleased them they had agreed upon liking the liver best. It made a bond between them, made them kindred souls. Hannah could tell they were pleased and it pleased her in turn that they should get along so well together. She didn't probe her pleasure, but she made the liver stew happily, glad to have it, glad to see the two men take to each other. Samuel didn't like every man he ran across. Some he purely had no use for, and she could tell within a few minutes how he felt. He liked Tice Fowler. Not that he wouldn't have been mannerly anyhow. He would have, but in a different way.

Samuel broke the silence. "Hannah was tellin' me that Dannel Boone was took by the Shawnees."

"He was . . . back in February."

"Said they was a party of 'em, makin' salt. Was it jist Dannel took, or all of 'em?"

"All of 'em. Thirty-eight in all."

"Hit puzzles me," Samuel said, "how a bunch that big could be took."

Tice hesitated before replying. "You know Dannel Boone, do you?" he said finally.

"Not to say know him . . . I don't. I talked with him one time, is all. I took to him, though, that one time I talked to him, an' when I got ready to come to Kentucky I said I'd make fer Boone's fort, fer I liked the man a heap."

"So do I. I like him as good as e'er man I ever knowed. But folks says they is somethin' quare about the way them salt makers was took an' one of 'em got away when they'd got as fur as the Shawnee towns, an' the way he told it when he come back was that Dannel had been took first. He'd been out huntin' by hisself whilst the others was boilin' down salt. He said of a sudden there come Dannel, amongst the almightiest pack of Indians he'd ever seed. Right in the midst of 'em Dannel was, a leadin' the way. The men all sprung fer their guns, but Dannel called out to 'em. Said it would be the best not to resist. Said they was too many of the Indians. Said they'd all git kilt, an' hit would be the best to go along peaceable. Now, they wouldn't of, without Dannel had said so. They'd of ruther died. But Dannel said he had the promise of the chief, Blackfish, that they'd come to no harm, wouldn't be mistreated nor nothin'. Said they would be treated like prisoners of war an' would be took to Detroit to the British where they could be ransomed. Said it would be best, fer they'd all be kilt if they tried to fight." Tice stopped talking then and Samuel waited. After a moment he went on. "The way this feller told it was that they was some thought the Indians wouldn't of found 'em had Dannel not led 'em to the camp."

Samuel stared at Tice. "That would be the same as sayin' that Dannel Boone had give 'em away."

"Hit's jist the same as, yes."

Samuel thought about it. "Well, from what I have heared of him," he said at last, "hit don't go to me like he'd be that kind."

"Hit goes against what ever'body knows of him. But this feller had a heap of bitterness about it, hisself. He told that they found out fer a fact, from listenin' to the talk, that Dannel had offered to take the Indians to the camp . . . *offered*, mind you, without waitin' to be asked. An' he said Dannel got along so good with the Indians you'd never know but what he'd lived amongst 'em all his life, way he set out an' put hisself forrard with 'em."

"This Blackfish, this chief feller . . . he kept his word about not mistreatin' 'em, did he?"

"He did on the journey. That was all this feller knowed about, fer when he got the chance to git away he taken it. Hit's purely a mystery. Don't nobody know what to think. Dannel's woman give him up as dead an' went back over the mountains where they come from, with her younguns. Had she stayed on a spell, she'd of knowed he was safe, though whe'er he's not layin' dead an' skulped by now, nobody knows."

Both men were silent, thinking. Then Samuel said, slowly, "What's yore opinion?"

Tice cleared his throat, importantly, now that he had been asked outright. "In my opinion, they's somethin' don't nobody know about yit. Hit'll take more'n what I've heared to make me believe Dannel Boone played the part of a traitor to his own folks."

Samuel nodded. "That's about the way I make it." He pondered again, then shook his head. "Thirty-eight took. An' ill-spared, I'd reckon."

"Couldn't be no worse, hardly. Hit weakens us terrible bad not havin' 'em amongst us."

"I'd think it."

Hannah came, then, with the pot of stew. She placed it on the ground between them and handed them each a pewter spoon. "Eat all you c'n hold," she told Samuel. "Hit'll strengthen you."

The liver had cooked until it broke apart and she had thickened the soup with meal so that the pieces of liver floated in a heavy broth. Samuel dipped into it, then took his knife and speared a piece of the meat. "Lordy, but that's good," he said. "Hit's what I been wantin', though I didn't know it."

When they had finished eating Hannah took the pot away and ate her own meal. Samuel and Tice wiped their knives, sheathed them, and Tice broke a green twig for each of them to chew on. "I don't aim to be pryin'," Samuel said, "but I have wondered some how you come to be in these parts afoot."

Tice lay back against the tree trunk. "Well, we been losin' several horses lately. Indians been plunderin' a right smart, so some of us said we'd make a raid acrost the Ohio ourselves an' try to git a few back. Me an' two others went."

"You never got yer horses back?"

Tice grinned. "We got 'em, an' the others taken 'em on. But I had a little mare they'd got which we never found, an' I had a wish to keep on lookin' a mite longer. Warn't no use the others hangin' round when we'd overtook seven, so I told 'em jist to take 'em on in an' I'd go on a little sashay of my own. That was the way of it."

Samuel chuckled and Tice pulled at his chin ruefully. "I found my mare all right, but I never to say got her. An' I lost the horse I was ridin'. But I felt real lucky to save my hair. The way of it was, they'd missed the horses we'd took an' they'd been follerin' us. I allowed they would so I back-tracked an' come up on 'em camped. I figured to wait till good dark, till they'd laid down, then sneak over an' take the mare. I'd saw her hoppled out. I would of, too, only the dogs give me away. I had to scamper out of there in a hurry, I c'n tell you. An' they cut me off from my horse. They never give up chasin' me till I'd crossed the river. Hit was nip an' tuck there fer awhile."

"I'd think it."

Tice sighed. "Hit was a good horse to lose to them varmints, too. I allus hate losin' a animal to 'em. They don't know how to take keer of 'em. Mistreat 'em almost as bad as they do a human. But I'll git 'em both back one of these days." He pulled his long length up and threw his chewed twig away. "Reckon Hannah'll be ready to be goin' by now."

"Likely."

Hannah had been sorting and tidying and now seeing Tice standing she left off and came to where they were. "How did you aim to work it . . . movin' Pa?"

"If we could make a kind of litter by stretchin' a blanket acrost two poles, hit'd be best. If you c'n carry one end, that is."

"I c'n carry it."

"I mought could lean on you," Samuel put in, "an' mebbe make out to limp along a piece."

Tice shook his head. "Hit would do harm to yer leg an' set us all back. Me an' Hannah c'n pack you, I figure."

He chose two hickory saplings and chopped them down, stripped them of limbs, brought them to Hannah. They laid the blanket over and under the poles and Hannah laced it in place with thongs, pulling and stretching to make sure it would not give. Then they laid it beside Samuel. "I'd best put a piece of the fat meat on that leg afore we git started, I reckon," Hannah said.

"Well," Tice agreed, "but don't waste no time. Hit's midevenin' now, an' we'd ort to git started."

"You got some place in mind?"

"Hit's a place I know, yes," he nodded.

"How fur?"

"Close to four mile, I'd say . . . an' it'll be rough goin' in places."

"I'll make haste," Hannah promised.

She unbound Samuel's leg, carefully laying aside the bandaging. "They ain't no more cloth," she said, "we got to keep on usin' this."

The elm bark poultice had dried out overnight and was stuck to the wound. Hannah fingered it and Samuel groaned. "I'll wet it," she told him.

Little by little she worked it loose, being as easy as she could, but by the time she had finished Samuel was white and sweating. All three looked at the exposed leg. It was no better. Not one of them could fool himself about that. It was no better at all. None of them said so, however. Each could see for himself and there was no use speaking of it. Hannah laid the moist, raw piece of bear fat against the wound and bound it in place. "I never did put much dependence in elm bark," she said.

"No," Samuel agreed, "but I don't reckon it did harm to try."

"No harm," Tice echoed.

The leg rebandaged, Hannah took Samuel's feet, Tice his shoulders and they started to lift him on the litter. But when the weight of his body pulled on the leg Samuel screamed out suddenly and then went limp. "He's swooned," Hannah said quickly, "make haste, now, an' git him on the litter afore he comes to."

When they had him on the litter Tice looked furtively at Hannah, wondering if she had thought at all Samuel might die of this leg hurt. If that leg was so touchy he couldn't bear to be lifted, it was in a bad way, and no doubts about it. She said so little of what she was thinking . . . and she showed so little, going on about doing the things that had to be done. He thought it was lucky for him she was turned that way, for if she'd been like some women he'd seen, grieving and taking on, it would have been harder on all of them. But it made him wonder if she'd even thought what could happen. She acted like she thought it wouldn't be but a few days till Samuel was on his feet again, ready to travel. But then, he thought, so did he. Likely she just wasn't giving any sign.

He looked at the tidy piles of belongings. She had sorted them well, he saw. In the lean-to were the things to be left . . . the spinning wheel, the bundle of clothing and seeds, the iron pot and pewter spoons, the extra bar of lead. But heaped to take with them were the powder, the meal, the guns, the axe, the pouch of necessaries, and a hunk of fresh meat. "I c'n make a trip tomorrow for the things in the lean-to," she said, seeing he had noticed.

She didn't need to explain that her sorting had taken into account the fact that if the things left were never recovered, they would have the essentials with them—axe, guns, powder and immediate food for Samuel.

They loaded themselves and laid Samuel's gun and the axe on the litter beside him. He moaned when they lifted him, but did not entirely regain consciousness. "Hit's jist as well," Tice said, "it's goin' to be rough on him any way you look at it."

He led the way, following the river upstream for about a quarter of a mile, then heading away from it. No cane grew there. Instead there was a flat, marshy swale through which they floundered, bogging down to their knees frequently, but keeping going for there was no place on which to lay the litter while they themselves rested. Both were winded and sagging when they came out of the marsh to firm ground.

They laid the litter on the ground and Tice swiped his forearm across his face. His face was red and wet with sweat. Hannah picked up the hem of her skirt and wiped her own face, across her forehead, around her nose and mouth and chin. Her hair had straggled loose and absent-mindedly she tucked it back in place, looking curiously about her.

They were in a meadow of rye grass and a few hundred yards away the woods began. Back of the woods, not too far away, a group of low-swelling hills lay. Tice saw her looking. "The place I got in mind," he said, "is at the foot of that least knoll to the left there. They's a spring handy an' a good rockhouse."

Hannah nodded. She stood with her feet braced apart, her hands resting on her hips. She was breathing easier now, as was Tice. She looked back across the marsh to the line of trees marking the river. Not any more would they follow its bending course. She didn't know but she was glad to put it behind her. She didn't care for water travel, and then you couldn't see, she thought, what the land was like from the river. Hardly ever did the trees open out so you could see what lay beyond. It was just sliding along on top of the water, the trees always moving past, not changing in their kind or color very much, the banks high in places, low in others, but always the trees closing them in. It was going to be good, she thought, to see the country . . . like this meadow, now, with grass already up to a body's knees, and the mounds of the hills beyond. She felt a small rise of excitement. There was such a lot of talk about this country. She wanted to see it. When Samuel could travel . . . She put the dart of anxiety from her . . . when Samuel could travel they'd be passing right through the midst of it. There'd be time to look about, and it would be spreading itself right before her.

"You got yer breath?" Tice asked, recalling her.

She nodded and stooped to her end of the litter. Not until then did she notice that Samuel's eyes were open. "You've come to yer senses then," she said.

Tice looked around. "We ain't jostlin' you too much, are we?"

Samuel shook his head. "Some. But not more'n you'd expect. Go on when you're ready."

In another hour they reached the place Tice had in mind. It was a good place, Hannah thought. The spring flowed from the rocks at the bottom of the hill Tice had pointed out. Ages of dripping water had cut away the rocks beside it until an overhanging roof was formed. Beneath the overhang was a flat space, a shelter from wind and rain. A rockhouse, Hannah thought, was just a wide, roomy, shallow cave. Before it, south, down the slope, the woods ran, opening into the wide, flat meadow. It was sightly, she thought, pure sightly, and a feeling of pleasure lifted inside her.

But Tice was working swiftly, piling leaves in a corner of the rockhouse for Samuel's bed. She went to help and he left her with it, going, himself, to cut boughs to give it more softness. When they went to move him, Samuel waved them aside. "Set me down there by the couch," he told them, "an' I'll git myself onto it. Hit'll go easier, in my opinion."

They watched him as he slowly inched himself off the litter onto the bed they had made. Very slowly he moved, first his hips, resting afterward, then his shoulders, with another rest. White and sweating he worked away at it, until finally he had humped all of himself over the pole onto the leaves. Then he sighed. "I ain't hopin' to do that no more fer a spell."

"No," Tice told him, "next time you c'n walk away from that bed." He turned to Hannah. "I'll go fer the rest of the things."

"I aimed to go tomorrow," she said. "They's no need you makin' e'er nother trip."

"They's no need you goin' tomorrow, either. You fix him somethin' hot to eat. I'll be back when I *git* back, but it'll be after dark."

"Well."

After she and Samuel had eaten she sat by the fire, drowsing, rousing now and then to put another stick of wood on it, comfortable in the warmth of the fire, aware of a snug feeling from having even a partial roof over her head again. It was going to be good, she thought, to have a cabin soon. She weighed her feeling, laughing at herself, looking at her big hands, thinking of her strong, big body. She could walk all day on the track of game, and loved to. She could swing an axe and fell a tree as quickly and as expertly as Samuel. She could wrestle a plow from sun-up to sun-down behind a team of oxen, and had. She could lift and work and endure, alone or beside a man. But, she reckoned, for all a woman could do what a man could do, she was different inside. She, Hannah, loved a house-place, too, and a fire on a hearth, and the clack of a loom and a slow-growing pattern in cloth. She closed her hands and looked at them and felt in their palms the shuttle and the taut stretch of the warp. She felt the flax tied on the beam and threaded through the heddles and the slay. She felt the treads under her feet and pushed with one bare foot against the earth as if the harness were there to respond. Oh, the ways of a woman were her own and not given to any man to know, the shadows and the lights in her kept still and strong inside. They were a secret to her and a strength. They were the sign of the Lord to her, that she was different from men.

She grieved for the loom left behind. But she would have a loom again, she told herself stoutly. She would have a better loom and a bigger one than the one left behind. In this land she would carve out her own loom. She knew how she would do it. She would search out a tree and fell it, and hew it square herself, and then she would carve out the beams and when they were done, she would peg them together. In time she would weave strong cloth upon it. She, Hannah Moore, knew her ways, and what she had to have.

She roused when Tice returned. "I brung it all," he said, "savin' yer spinnin' wheel. I aim to go fer the balance of the meat I hung up in a tree over there, an' I'll git the wheel fer you then."

She gave him food and he ate, and she could tell how weary he was by the way he ate, slumped and lifting the food to his mouth slowly. "You are aimin' to keep watch again tonight, are you?"

"We c'n risk it without in this place," he said.

When he had finished he pulled himself up and went to lie near Samuel. He was asleep almost instantly, his breathing heavy, mingled with Samuel's snores. Hannah covered him with her own blanket. Then she lay down near the fire, warmed from her long sitting beside it and sleepy, and in some way, eased and content.

5

WITH THE ROOF of the rock ledge covering her and her belongings, Hannah lost the feeling of temporariness, the unsettled and uprooted feeling which had lived with her during the long journey and the overnight camps. No matter how familiar things were, an iron pot, a blanket, even one's clothing, no matter how well known the routine of building a fire and making johnny-cakes, when you rose each morning knowing that the night would bring you to a new and different place to sleep, when you slept each night knowing that the morning would move you on, you had a feeling of something inside you, she thought, slipping out of place, uneasy and sliding and shifting. She had accepted it as necessary—she had even become adjusted to it, but she had never become accustomed to it. It was not a natural way of life to her. She was used to a fixed and steady base, from which she might go out each day in any direction, but which, inevitably, was waiting for her return. On this journey there had been no returning. There had only been going on, and on, and on.

Now she had something solid over her head again. Even knowing, as she did, that this was but another camp before going on again, it was different. It was fixed to the extent of at least a few days. It was a kind of a home. So the hours passed for her in a slow regularity, full of the familiar chores of the home-keeper, the cooking, the washing up, the tending of Samuel, and it was only when she totaled up the days that they seemed to have passed astonishingly fast. A week they had been at the rockhouse, she reckoned one evening, and, startled, she wondered that the time could have escaped her so swiftly.

Tice had gone after the spinning wheel and the rest of the bear meat on the second day. He brought the spinning wheel, but he did not bring the meat. "Somethin' had got to it," he said, "wolves, I reckon."

"Likely," Hannah agreed. "Hit would of spiled in another day or two, anyhow, seein' as it's turned off so warm."

Tice hunted almost every day, keeping fresh meat always at hand so that Hannah had meat for stews for Samuel and fat pieces to keep on his leg. In spite of the poultices, however, Samuel's leg did not heal, and in spite of the good, thick stews, he continued to waste away. Almost daily his face became gaunter and leaner, the skin gray under his cheekbones and loose over his jaws. His eyes had taken on a locked, clouded look, lusterless and dull. Hannah had the feeling sometimes when she waited on him that he did not see with them any more, that if she had passed her hand before them they would not have blinked.

He had sunk, also, into listlessness. He took no interest in anything that went on about him. Hannah came and went, brought him water from the spring, told him of a redbird she'd seen perched on the lowest limb of a tree nearby. If he heard he made no sign. When Tice came in from the woods, Samuel did not rouse to question him, and if, thinking to interest him, Tice told him about his hunt, he listened apathetically, seeming weary even of listening. He ate what Hannah brought him, but more and more often he had no appetite for it, picking at the meat and rarely drinking all of the broth.

While the rest of his body wasted away, his leg stayed swollen, and continued to swell until it was almost twice the size of his other one. It was so sore and tender to touch that he screamed when Hannah changed the poultices. This bothered Hannah greatly. "I've not ever knowed him," she told Tice, "to take on so over a hurt. It don't go like him."

"He has been bad hurt before?"

Hannah nodded. "Once he got his foot hung in a rock an' creened it somethin' terrible. Hit swole an' give him a right smart trouble, but he never let on. Not like this, leastways. All I ever heared him do before was to kind of groan a little."

Tice rubbed his hand over his chin. He was getting a pretty good growth of beard now, and it seemed to bother him. He rubbed at it often. "You know e'er other thing to do?" he asked.

"I never knowed of fat meat failin' before. I d'know as they *is* e'er thing else to do. Without they was some charm would help."

"I don't know of no charms." Tice was sorry now he hadn't paid more attention when he'd heard womenfolks talking about charms. He'd never put much dependence in them, but it was beginning to look as if only a charm could save Samuel, for he hadn't the strength now to raise himself alone from his pallet. One of them must always brace his shoulders and help him. He allowed them to do what they would with him, trying, when he was told, to eat or to drink. But neither of them could hide from themselves or from each other that he was failing rapidly. "If he could stand it," Hannah said finally, "hit mought do good to heat up some water real hot an' dip them rags in it an' lay on his leg. I have heared it would help."

"You'd best try it, then, I sh'd think."

But the first hot cloth laid to the leg was such an agony to Samuel that it brought him full upright on the pallet, screaming and clawing at Hannah, the sweat pouring down his face. "You'll have to hold him," Hannah told Tice.

So Tice held him and Hannah doggedly applied the hot cloths, each time Samuel screaming and writhing under Tice's hands, begging her to leave off. "Jist let me die. Jist let me die, but don't put no more of them hot rags on . . . *don't do it,* Hannah!"

She paid him no mind. She didn't even try to explain to him. Time after time she changed the cloths, keeping the pot on the fire, her hands looking

[41]

as if they had themselves been boiled from being dipped in the scalding water, until finally Tice could stand no more of it himself. "You'll kill him, Hannah. He cain't bear no more of it."

She left off, then, let the last cloth cool on the leg and walked to scatter the fire under the pot. She stood, drying her hands on the tail of her skirt, then brushing her hair back. Tice followed her. He took in a deep, slow breath. "I d'know as I could of done that."

"You cut open the gash," she reminded him.

"But that was quick an' over with. This . . . an' his takin' on so."

Hannah's face contorted. "I jist hope it helps. I'd hate fer him to be tormented so bad an' it not do no good."

They both saw the crows when they gathered in the tops of the trees down the slope that evening. They were sitting on the bank of the small run which flowed off from the spring. Hannah had washed the strips of cloth she used for bandaging on Samuel's leg and had laid them on the grass to dry in the sun. She had gone to gather them in. Tice had been to fill the iron pot with water. Hannah, tired, uneasy about Samuel, had dropped to the grass and Tice had stretched out beside her. The sun was almost down. Already they were in the shadow of the hill behind them, but beyond the light fell across the grove of trees and over the meadow with an effect of startling clarity. Each tree in the small woods stood out singly and purely against the sky back of it, turned green-gold by some mixture of cloud and sun. Beyond, the meadow lay bathed in golden light and the matted grass seemed plated with it, gilded, its green showing through only faintly. The air had a limpid languor and was still warm from the long day of sun. At the far edge of the meadow the tops of the hills were reddened, but their sides held the same peculiar golden light. "I have seed," Tice said, putting aside the stem of grass he had been chewing, "I have seed it look like this after a rain, but I d'know as I ever seen it on a clear day."

Hannah thought. "I d'know as I ever either. Hit's purty, ain't it?"

"Kind of puts a spell on a body."

Then the crows came, flocking in from the marsh, settling in the treetops and their noisy, croaking clatter began. Tice and Hannah looked at each other, but it was Hannah who had the courage to say, "Hit's a bad omen."

Tice shifted his eyes and muttered, "I d'know."

"I do. Hit's a bad omen fer crows to cluster an' croak thataway. Hit means a death. I've allus heared that."

Because he had always heard it, too, Tice said nothing for a time. They both sat, silently, and watched the black wings wheel and circle, rise, lift, settle again, and all the time the raucous cawing went on. Then, thinking to comfort, Tice said, "They's a heap of them old sayin's ain't true ever' time. I've allus heared it was a bad sign when a dog howls . . . you know, throws back his head an' howls that lonesome, mournful kind of way? But I had a hound, once, he'd howl that way ever' time I tied him up an' left him by hisself. They say it's a sign of a death, but in my opinion it's more a sign a dog's jist

[42]

lonesome feelin' of a sudden. Now, crows has got to cluster, an' gatherin' together they're bound to croak an' clatter some. I d'know as it means e'er thing."

"I d'know either, but I've allus heared so."

"I c'n skeer 'em off if you want."

"No. Hit wouldn't change the sign none."

"I reckon it wouldn't."

They watched a while longer, then Hannah pushed herself up off the bank. "Hit's gittin' late. I'd best build up a fire. He mebbe c'n eat some more of that stew if it's het up."

"I'll git up some wood."

Hannah stood a moment, looking down the slope over and beyond the crow-crested tree. To the left was the marsh and the green-banded river. Straight before her was the stretch of swelling, rolling meadowland. The light was fading but that peculiar golden quality lingered. The sky was clean of clouds except for a few broken curds in the south, they, too, touched by the gold. Beyond the meadowland the hills ran in a solid line, and, looking, Hannah had the feeling that the sky was pinned to the earth by the hills, pinned here behind her, stretched up and domed, and fastened once again behind those farthest hills. She searched it and the feeling increased, that she was tented here on a hillside, by the stretched gold cloth of the sky. She shook her head and smiled at Tice. He'd think she had lost her reason if she named such to him. She pointed. "That's the way to Logan's, is it? South?"

"That's the way. Straight acrost this meadow, an' through the hills."

"Hit's a purty way to foller." She stepped across the tiny stream with one long stride and went around the corner of the rockhouse. She gathered an armful of wood and began laying the fire.

Hannah reckoned it was about an hour before day when Samuel awakened her, calling, asking for water. She took it to him in the bowl Tice had whittled out of a piece of buckeye wood. He drank deeply. Then he began to talk, quietly and calmly. He spoke so quietly and calmly that it took her a moment to realize he did not know her, that somewhere in his mind time had eclipsed and her presence had become that of her mother's. "Hit is a good place to stop," he said, his hands moving restlessly. "They is water from the branch, an' a plenty of shade fer a house-place. You'll have water to hand, an' a cool place in the hot of summer. An' the ground is good an' rich. I'll lay the sill logs there, Ann, an' I'll make 'em stout an' strong. Hit'll be a pleasant home fer you I'll build. An' a chimbley . . . I'll build you a chimbley like the old one. I'll build you e'er kind you say. Whatever my hands c'n do, they'll do fer you, I give you my word. You'll not be yearnin' fer the old place long, I'll warrant. You'll not be missin' yer folks fer long. Soon, now, the little 'un will be here to take yer time an' mind. An' when yer time comes I'll walk acrost the mountain an' git that Granny Poe to do fer you. You'll not be forsook. Hit's a purty place to stop, Ann. A man c'n do better fer hisself in this new land. If you'd cease grievin' fer the old, Ann, hit would come easier to like . . . a man has got to do what comes best to him." His voice went on and on, pleading, anxious, hopeful, sad.

From his pallet Tice spoke softly. "His mind is wanderin', ain't it?"

Hannah laid the bowl down and sat beside Samuel. "Yes."

She picked up his hand and held it between her hands, rubbed it aimlessly, wishing, somehow, to comfort him, to ease this ancient grief, this long guilt he had suffered because his man's wandering ways had laid too big a burden on a woman. Hannah tried to find the words to say, but they would not come. She felt only the dumb wish to say them, not knowing what they could be, not able to find them. She sat, rubbing his hand, listening, remembering, as his voice droned on. "I never thought you'd take it so hard, Ann. I never thought you'd grieve so. Cain't you put it out of yer mind, an' learn to like here?"

She remembered her mother, a big woman like herself, a big, plain woman, but lacking the hard strength which Samuel had bestowed on Hannah. She remembered the black hair, so like her own, the dark sallow face, the ways she had about the house. She had been clean, neat, tidy, and until the day she took to her bed she had never let her work go. She had been a master hand at weaving, and she had taught Hannah well.

But she had been a sad woman, never talking much, rarely laughing. Occasionally she had sung to Hannah, one song, always the same song, and never all of it. Hannah could hear the high, quavering voice now. "O, sister, O sister, let's we walk out . . . To see the ships asailin' about . . . Bow down, bow down . . . I will be true, true to my love, an' he will be true to me. . . ."

"Go on, Ma," Hannah had pleaded, when the voice had broken off.

But Ann had always answered the same. "I have forgot the rest."

Hannah used to wonder, and did again now, did she, maybe, have a sister she yearned for? A dear sister left behind? Or was it the sea? Had the old home stood beside the sea? Or maybe a true love, before Samuel, lost in the sea? She never knew. But now that Samuel was revealing so much, Hannah remembered how her mother had stood so often in the doorway, looking southward . . . stood there and looked and looked, not speaking or even weeping, just looking. As young as she had been, Hannah had sensed that at such times her mother was not aware of her or even of the surroundings, and, as children will, she had often stirred restlessly to call attention to herself and to bring her mother back. If Samuel had appeared suddenly, Ann had been wont to leave off her looking brusquely, busying herself immediately with some task.

Sitting beside him now, listening, Hannah tried to recall if she had ever heard her mother complain, and she could not remember having ever done so. All her complaining had been done inside her, in her heart, which Samuel must have known . . . which must, when she finally died of an obscure ailment, have laid forever upon him an uneasy knowledge of his own part in her sadness and in her death. For what Samuel was revealing in his delirium was that what had been to Hannah a safe and beloved home had been to her mother a strange and terrible place, no home at all, a place to which she had never become reconciled, and from which she was always turning and fleeing southward to the place from whence she had come.

A great sadness settled upon Hannah that it should have been so, and a great wonder. Being part of them both, she could understand her mother's eternal longing, and at the same time she could feel amazement, as Samuel must have done, that she could not put aside her longing and let the new home take its hold upon her. A man's ways, Hannah thought, are his own, an' it's a woman's place to foller after, an' to do fer him. Thus she defended Samuel, and then, equally loyal, she recalled that her mother had done exactly that—she had followed after and she had done for him. It must be, Hannah thought wonderingly, that to some it is given to follow gladly, and to some the gift is withheld, and then the most willing following must be done with inner sickness.

Samuel jerked his hand away and began thrashing about upon the pallet. She reached out to quiet him, thinking he would hurt his leg with his turning and stirring. Her hand brushed his face. The heat of it startled her. She felt his forehead, and it was hot, with a dry papery feeling, as if it would crackle and split under her touch. Even as her hand lay on his forehead he jerked away, sat suddenly bolt upright and began to struggle and to curse wildly, yelling that the redskins had him, that he'd been took while he was asleep, come upon unawares, that he had to get away, get loose and free. Tice was beside Hannah in a moment. "Git in back of him," she said, "an' hold on to his shoulders."

In the strength of delirium and wild with fear Samuel threw himself against their hands, struggling, fighting, screaming out at them and cursing them, "Leave go, you redskin varmints! Leave go! You'll not take Samuel Moore alive! I'll not be took an' roasted on a spit. You c'n sink that hatchet in my skull if you're a mind to, but I'll not be took alive! Leave go, I tell you!"

It took all the strength of both Tice and Hannah to hold him as he threw himself about on the pallet, not aware at all of his hurt leg, reckless with it and feeling, apparently, no pain from it. Then abruptly his nightmare of Indians was over. He slumped in their arms and lay back down. He continued, however, to moan and to turn restlessly from side to side. "He's burnt up with fever," Hannah said, "his mind is wanderin' on account of it."

Tice knelt beside her. "Reckon I ort to tie him somehow?"

"I'd ruther not. If we c'n make out to hold on to him, I'd ruther not to tie him up."

"He's liable to hurt his leg, Hannah."

"I don't see how he c'n do any great hurt to it . . . not more'n he's done already."

Samuel began to talk again and to thrash about. He was poling the raft up the river, now, fretting. "We got to git acrost to yon side, Hannah. Hit's gittin' too shaller here. I got to pole over. You stiddy the things whilst I angle us over. Jist sit stiddy, Hannah, we c'n make it." He was blowing, panting with the effort. Then he cried out in sudden alarm, "Hannah! You're a tippin' the raft! I said set stiddy! Goddlemighty, girl, we're goin' to overturn!" And

[45]

then, thinking the raft had overturned, he was floundering in the water, struggling, clutching Tice, yelling at Hannah, "Git to the bank! Git to the bank fast afore yer skirts drag you down! Git on, I'll see to the things. I'll see to the raft. I got ahold of it, you git on to the bank." He was quiet again, moaning . . . "The water is too deep. Hit's draggin' me under, Hannah. Hit's closin' over me. Help me, Hannah . . . help me outen the water."

Hannah knelt at his feet, holding them as best she could, her head bent and her shoulders huddled. Tice heard her say, once, "I'm helpin' you, Pa, all I kin. I'm doin' all I kin do fer you." And after that she said no more. She looked up quickly when a sudden movement of Samuel's wrenched his shoulders free of Tice's hands, frowned, and then bent her head again.

Finally Samuel was still and quiet, moaning only a little and turning his head from time to time. Tice and Hannah relaxed their holds, eased their knees but continued to watch cautiously. "How long you reckon he's liable to be like this?" Hannah asked.

Daylight had come now and she could see Tice shake his head. "I d'know," he said. "I've seed 'em go on thisaway fer hours . . . sometimes fer a whole day, an' more."

But Samuel had spent his last strength. He was feeling pain in his leg again, but he did no more than whimper and twitch his big shoulders and roll his head from side to side. He died thus, hard, as he had lived, and without recovering consciousness. There was no peaceful drawing of a last breath as Hannah had watched her mother do. There was instead a buckling of the chest, a last feeble effort to rise again, to stand whole and strong on two legs once more, and a collapse, a twitch or two, and then stillness.

Hannah breathed in deeply, as if within her own lungs she would take enough air for Samuel too, held the breath without knowing she was doing it, then let it go in a long sigh. "He's gone," she said.

Tice said nothing. He turned around, picked up the blanket in which he had been rolled, laid it over Samuel, drawing it up over his face. Hannah watched him, and when it was done she braced one hand on the ground and pushed herself slowly up. She stood a moment, looking down at the blanket-covered figure, her hands hanging limply, then she lifted her head, pushed her hair back and slowly walked out from under the roof of the cave. The sun was rising and the whole eastern sky was alight. Down in the woods the birds were noisy with a kind of wild joy, twittering, calling, not yet singing but ecstatically and excitedly greeting the day. A clear, pearly light lay over the meadow, extending to the far line of the hills and thrusting them boldly into the glow of morning.

When Tice moved up beside her and laid his hand on her shoulder she winced, as if any touch, now, was unwelcome, but she gave no other sign and he did not remove his hand. "If they was e'er other thing, Hannah," he said gently, "you could of done fer him, I don't know of it. You done all a body could of done, an' more than most. Hit's a comfort to know that, I'd reckon."

She made no answer—continued simply to look across the meadow, south, toward the hills. "Hit's a pity," she sighed, finally.

[46]

"Hit is a pity," Tice said.

"Hit's a pity," she went on, as if he had not spoken, "he never got to Boone's fort."

They buried Samuel the same day. Together they dug the grave, Tice softening the earth with the axe, Hannah scooping it out with a makeshift shovel of bark and with the iron pot. Tice had not wanted her to help. He was uncomfortable about it, something within him rebelling. He had never known of a woman helping to dig a grave. "You needn't to help," he said.

"I'd ruther to," she'd said. "I'd ruther to do what I kin."

Tice forbore to argue with her. It was a man's work and it didn't appear seemly to him for a woman to be helping, but then she wasn't like any other woman, anyhow, this one—not like any he'd ever known. He reckoned that being raised by a man, alone with him all her days, she'd taken on more of a man's ways than a woman's. Let her help dig the grave, then. No one would ever know but himself. There'd never be one to shame her.

He looked at her from time to time as she worked beside him. She had not given way to tears at all, but that she was grieving was plain to see. Her jaw was set and her eyes looked sunken in her head. Her face was tired looking and white, and her mouth was tightly crimped. She would be the kind, he thought, who never gave way to weeping, not hardly knowing how. She would always hold her grief tight inside of her, not even wishing the comfort of tears, but hurting hard with a kind of knotted hurt that wouldn't come loose. He wished she *would* cry and be eased of it, but he didn't expect her to.

When the grave was dug she looked about as if searching for something. "What are you seekin' out?" Tice asked.

"Some green branches to line the grave with. He was used to layin' out, an' he'll lay easier, seems to me, if they's a bed of branches under him."

At the last, Samuel laid upon the green branches, she smoothed his hair as best she could, ordered his limbs and folded his hands. She did only one thing that betrayed her feeling. Lifting the hands to fold them over his chest, she held them a moment, rubbing the dry wrinkled skin between her palms, then she raised them to her face and laid her cheek against them for a second —no more than that, and a spasm of pain crossed her face. Then she put them in place and stepped back from the grave. She cut more of the green branches and laid them over him, and then, herself, picked up a handful of the loose dirt and scattered it over him. Tice raked with the axe head and Hannah shoveled with the bark scoop and soon the grave was filled. That done, Hannah knelt and smoothed it over. "I hate to say it," Tice told her, seeing what she was doing, "but we'll have to scatter rocks over it an' limbs . . . hide it so's the redskins won't find it an' haul him out, or the wolves or some wild animal."

Hannah looked up at him, and then, understanding, she nodded and gave over smoothing out the surface. She helped him find stones to heap over it until finally it was all done. The sun was just setting. She dusted her hands on her skirt and brushed back her hair. Tice watched her. He didn't think she ever knew she did it. Her hair wouldn't stay in place and a hundred times a day she brushed it back. Sometimes she stopped and repinned it, but mostly she didn't—just slicked at it with the back of her hand to get it out of her eyes.

"You'll be ready to eat, I reckon," she said to him.

"Not so's you could tell it. I ain't got much appetite."

She looked at him with a vague, absent look, and then recalling herself, lifted her shoulders as if they ached. "No. But a body's got to eat. I'll fix us a bait."

She built the fire, mixed the bread, set meat to roasting. She went about the work with the same quiet efficiency she always showed, not muddling things, not dropping and stumbling. She reached, mixed, fixed, with the slow steadiness Tice had already learned was characteristic of her. He watched her and wondered what she was thinking.

She was thinking nothing at all. She was finding, in the busyness of her hands, in their familiar motions at familiar tasks, a respite from both thinking and feeling. She was thinking, if it could be called thinking, of carrying water from the spring, of setting the iron pot on the fire, of putting a pinch of salt in the meal, or whittling sticks for the meat. With routine she was patching the cracks of her sundered world, piecing it out and laying the pieces back together, beginning in the quietest, most certain way in the world to give it a little meaning again. With routine she was snatching from death, for a little while, the victory. These things were real, the iron pot, the water, the meal and the meat. These things had to do with life. Samuel was gone. But life still went on. There were things to do.

When they had eaten their meal Tice spoke of plans. "You have thought of what you aim to do, have you?"

Hannah had finished ordering the clutter of making their supper and was sitting across the ashes of the fire, leaning against the solid rock that formed the back of the rockhouse. "Yes," she said.

He waited for her to continue. When she did not, he asked, "You aimin' to go on, or you want to turn back?"

"I aim to go on."

"I c'n take you to the Falls an' likely some of them folks that come down-river with you would welcome you till you could travel back up to Fort Pitt. Somebody'd be goin' afore the summer's over, I'd reckon."

"No."

"Is they folks back there where you come from would want you?"

She turned her face toward him and looked at him quietly. "I have got no folks," she said, "that I know of, nowhere. Pa was all of the folks I had."

Tice was silent, thinking it over. "Well," he said, then, "is it in yore mind to go where yer pa was headed? Boone's fort?"

"I've got no particular wish to go there. Pa had picked it, but I don't know as it makes any difference now. I'd be amongst strangers there same as e'er other place."

"Would you jist as soon go to Logan's then?"

She dipped her head and plucked at her skirt. "I believe I'd ruther to."

She did not say what she was thinking, that at least she would know him at that place. Coming and going there would be one she could lay eyes on she'd seen before, one she'd had speech with, and knew something of his ways. Oh, she thought, in the midst of strangers it would be a comforting thing to have one not strange! "If I c'n have my pick," she went on, her words not stressed by any emotion, "hit would be Logan's, I reckon. I wouldn't aim, though," she said, suddenly raising her head and with a motion of her hands emphasizing her words, "I wouldn't aim to be a burden to nobody."

Tice laughed at her. "A burden? Nobody that c'n do a day's work is a burden in a fort. Ben Logan's woman, Ann, will give you a welcome with open arms, she'll be so proud to have another hand to help. You don't have no idee how it is in a fort—folks comin' an' goin', all of 'em stakin' out claims an' tempery to git out onto 'em an' git started. They come in an' take shelter a few months, then they're gone till they's a skeer. The ones that stays there all the time has to carry the most of the load. Ones like Ben an' Ann Logan. Oh, don't ever think it, you'll be a burden. They'll be a plenty of things fer you to do."

"I'd hope fer it."

"You c'n do more than hope. You c'n put it down as sart'n."

She wondered that he did not mention his own woman to welcome her. Maybe she was the kind didn't take to strangers and knowing it he couldn't say, as she'd half expected him to, "You c'n stay with me an' mine."

He was talking again. "Hit would suit you, then, to start tomorrow?"

"Hit would suit."

He had thought it. She wasn't one to dawdle, and it would be in her mind, he knew, that nothing could be gained by lingering beside Samuel's new grave. "We'll stir soon, then, an' git a early start."

"Yes."

Hannah lay that night on Samuel's bed, and Tice rolled in a blanket near the fire.

6

WHEN IT CAME to dividing the load the next morning, Tice took the two guns, his own and Samuel's, and the axe, and he rolled the powder and lead into his blanket. Hannah carried her own gun and the iron pot and pewter spoons. Into her blanket she rolled the bag of necessaries and what was left of the meal and salt, not forgetting the clothing and bundle of seeds, which last she stuffed down into the iron pot. Tice looked uncertainly at the spinning wheel. "I reckon you set a heap of store by that there."

"Hit was my ma's. An' I'll be needin' it in time."

"I don't see e'er way we c'n take it, though, Hannah. We're loaded past easy packin' now."

"I done figured that out. I know we cain't pack it now. I aimed to hide it here an' come back fer it when I kin."

She set it back under the rock ledge in the farthest, darkest corner and heaped branches over it. Tice helped, approvingly. "I'll git it fer you the first time I'm up this way a horseback, an' it won't be long, neither. Two, three weeks at the most. I'll git it fer you, I give my word."

"You needn't to weary about it. I likely won't need it fer a right smart time. Jist anytime you got the room an' passin'. An' if it proves unhandy, I c'n come myself. I'd figure a way."

"You c'n put it outen yer mind. I'll git it fer you, like I said." Tice looked at her feet when they had finished screening the spinning wheel. "You got any footgear? The goin' gits rough in places."

Without argument Hannah opened her bundle, took out a pair of moccasins and tied them on. She knew herself her feet were yet too tender for traipsing. She was ashamed that she had needed reminding. I'd ort to thought, she told herself. He'll be thinkin' I'm plumb dozy.

Tice glanced around to see if they had forgotten anything. The rockhouse, save for the hidden spinning wheel, was as clean as when they had arrived. He nodded his satisfaction. "Now," he said to Hannah, "if I git to goin' too hard fer you, jist sing out. I'm used to makin' time."

"I c'n keep up."

"I don't think but what you kin, commonly, but that's a right smart load you're packin'. Hit mought wear you sooner'n you'd think. You mind, now, an' call out."

She promised and swung the blanket-wrapped load across her shoulders.

Tice stepped back of her to settle it evenly. Standing there, she could see the small, rough pile of rocks which marked Samuel's grave. If a body didn't know, she thought, they'd never guess it was a grave there. They'd just think it was a little small scattering of rocks had got riffled up together somehow. They'd not know at all there was Samuel Moore down in under the rocks and the dirt.

The remembrance of him, dead, who had been so much alive, came into her mind, and such a pain at this ending of a man's life shot through her, unexpectedly and suddenly, that she swayed on her feet. It was more than a mortal could reason out, she thought, achingly—the way of things. A body was born into the world, a little small, feeble thing, not asking to be birthed, nor knowing or remembering it. With nothing to do with it but to draw breath and eat and sleep, you come into the world and commence to live. And then you lived out your span—you grew up and you learned things, and you married and had young ones of your own, and you hunted or you kept the care of a house, and some things you laughed at and some things made you weep. You liked some folks and you misliked others. You journeyed and you stayed at home. You watched the sun rise and set, and the seasons in passing. You made out, this way or that, some folks better than others, but all in their own way making out to live. When your time came, like the last spark of fire put out, you died. And there was a little mound of dirt to show you'd ever drawn a breath. Why? Why did you ever? What was the use of it in the end? It was beyond a mortal's reasoning to know. All you could do, she thought, was keep on making out, this way or that.

Tice had shouldered his load now. He glanced at Hannah, saw she was looking at the grave, and waited. He reckoned that somewhere inside of her she was telling her goodbye to Samuel.

If I just didn't have to leave him here in this wilderness, she was thinking, in this new, strange country. He was gone and he would never know, but it wouldn't hurt so bad, she thought, if she could just leave him some place that was known to him in his lifetime. By her mother, maybe, close to home, or even in the woods he'd hunted and traipsed over, or by the branch back of the house. She felt as if she were forsaking him, leaving him here alone. He seemed to be lying so lonely and strange, and to be lonesome and strange, she thought, is the worst thing of all. Her lips moved, but no words came.

Seeing, Tice moved nearer. "Hannah," he said, "this is a easy place to find. Hit ain't as if you had to leave him in some woodsy place lookin' like ever' other woodsy place in the country. This here place is kind of marked. E'er time you're of a mind to come, it c'n be found as easy as the river."

She came back out of the fog of hurt and pain and looked at him. It was as if he had known how her thinking was going. He couldn't have found better words to say, and a wave of relief surged through her. "Why, hit's so, ain't it? This here rockhouse is like a cabin place. Hit would be easy to find. An' Pa is restin' close to the last house he lived in, ain't he? In a way he is, you could say. We have cooked an' eat an' slept here an' wore the strangeness off, an' he ain't restin' in a fur off unknown place at all."

[51]

"No."

He didn't hurry her, but she saw that he was loaded. It came over her that he had been waiting. She picked up her gun. "I never aimed to belate you. I am ready now."

"You sure, are you?"

"I'm sure." Tice had eased the leaving for her.

"Don't fergit to sing out if I git to goin' too fast fer you."

"I'll not."

He swung off ahead of her down the slope. Without looking back again she followed.

The sun was just coming up and the whole sky was flushed with a warm, rosy light. It lay over the meadow and beneath it the grass was silver with a heavy dew—frosted with it, iced with it, bent and sparkled with it. They walked down the slope from the rockhouse, through the woods and into the meadow.

Hannah was glad, now, to be journeying again. The country was spread wide before her eyes and she could see the lay of it, the curve and sweep and rise and swell of it. She could get the feel of it and the smell of it. She fixed the distance between herself and Tice, regulated her step to it and kept it there, comfortably near but not crowding. After that she could give her mind over to looking and seeing.

The meadow was wider than she had thought. It took them until the middle of the afternoon to reach the hills, a time of steady going. Hannah did not ask for rest. Samuel had taught her long ago that it was worse to rest frequently than to keep going. "When you feel yer legs givin' out on you," he'd told her when she yet reached no higher than his waist, "slow up a mite, mebbe, but keep goin'. Hit'll pass. You git yer second wind an' when you git yer second wind you c'n keep goin' all day." He'd pushed her to show her, tried her and tested her, and she had found it was true. Inevitably that first weariness and desire for rest came. If you gave in to it, a day's going was ruined. You'd have to rest every hour, likely. If you put it aside, kept going, in time you got stronger, the weariness passed, and you got into what was your real stride, tireless, easy and steady.

When they camped that night in the hills, she was tired, but she was not worn out. Tice said they would bait cold. "We had to risk a fire before," he told Hannah, "what with Samuel needin' his vittles hot, an' his leg tended, but that cave was kind of hid away. They's no call to now, an' I'd ruther not to take the chance."

"No," Hannah agreed.

They also kept watch, dividing the night as they had done on the bank of the river.

All the next day they were in hilly country. At first the hills were low and rounded, but as they penetrated ever farther south they became rougher, higher, knobbier. They were still not solidly about. There were long sweeps of meadow between, and beautiful valleys, but increasingly the hills gathered closely. "Is this the startin'," Hannah asked, "of the mountains?"

"My sakes," Tice told her, laughing, "they ain't no mountains in Kentucky savin' them in the east you got to cross comin' into the country, an' we ain't that fur over. No, these is jist hills, an' they ain't none much worse than these. An' they's allus meadowy places between 'em, an' valleys. Up north on the other side of the river hit's rollin' country, an' they ain't no hills to speak of. But mostly Kentucky is a country all broke over with hilly stretches."

Hannah felt a loyalty to the country already. "I'd ruther to have it that way."

"An' me."

"Hit's rougher, though, on the Hanging Fork where you got yore stand, is it?"

"Some," he admitted. "But like I said, they's meadowy places all over. My own place, now, it has got as purty a meadow as a body could ever hope to see. An' the game is plentier thereabouts. Not many has settled there yit, an' it's not been skeered an' kilt off."

Knowing how much simpler that made a man's job Hannah nodded soberly. "Hit is a thing to consider."

"You take, now," Tice went on, "if a man don't have to git out fur to kill his meat, he c'n put in a heap more time on his place. Not," he added, "that any of us has had the chance to put in too much time the way things is right now. But in time, when we git more settled an' the Indians is quietened, it'll be handy."

"You think they ever will be? The Indians?"

Tice looked at her quickly. "I think it . . . in time, that is. Ben Logan says that when we git enough men to make a march into the Indian country an' commence burnin' *their* towns fer a change, an' plunderin' *them* the way they've done us, they'll not be so ready to lay siege to us. In my opinion, that'll be the way of it."

Hannah thought about it. "When," she asked, then, "are they aimin' to make sich a march?"

"Oh, it's untellin'. But the way folks is comin', it won't be long. Mebbe next year, even. The next, fer sart'n. The settlements is thickenin' all the time. Why, three men from Logan's has went out an' built their own stockades, an' folks is already streamin' acrost the Gap an' summer barely started. Ben Logan says it wouldn't astonish him e'er bit if we couldn't muster five hundred men afore the year is over. Folks is commencin' to come from all sides, like you'uns down the river, an' as many as thirty, forty at a time, travelin' together, over Boone's Trail. Hit won't be long, I c'n tell you."

"I reckon Pa warn't the only one itchin' to git into the country, then."

"Not by a long sight, he warn't."

They traveled from first light until dark, Tice knowing each day the place he wished them to reach to lay over the night. Rarely did the land lie level. Even in the valleys and meadows there was a roll and swell to it that kept one pulling uphill and then bracing downhill. It was tiresome to the legs,

Hannah found. When he could, Tice kept to the valleys, skirting the hills, but occasionally a range of them lay across the trail so that there was nothing to do but make their way over.

One day they traveled for hours in a wide park of giant trees whose floor lay as level as a puncheon in a house. The tall, towering trees were widely spaced so that two or three riding horseback could have passed together. The trees were noisy with a brilliant, chattering bird—a bird that was green and gold and plumed sometimes with blue. Hannah asked about it. "That's a parakeet," Tice told her, "ain't they the noisiest ones you ever heared?"

"I d'know but they are," she admitted, "but they're awful purty, too."

The floor of the forest was thickly bedded with old leaves, but there was no undergrowth. Softly they paced through, scarcely a whisper of sound coming from their feet. Overhead the trees met, and the sun came through in small patches, scattered widely. Hannah took note of the trees. She made out ash and beech, walnut and gum, sugar trees and the broadest and girthiest of trees, the oak, and when they came out of the forest into the hills again she missed their tall stateliness. The hills were covered over with trees, true, but they were nowhere near as handsome or as tall.

Even in the hills, Hannah reckoned they covered about fifteen miles each day. She did not think she had slowed Tice much. He told her she had not. "You have done good," he told her, when they stopped at the end of the fourth day. "I don't know as a man could of done better."

"He likely could," she demurred modestly. "Pa could, I think."

"No, I don't think it," Tice insisted. "Him an' me, now, not packin' nothin', we mought of made better time, but with a load I don't know as we could."

Hannah did not tell him that without a load she had always paced Samuel, never asking or being given quarter. She wouldn't have worried about slowing Tice without a load. She would have known she could keep up. But she had been uncertain with the load. She let his statement stand, however. "I'd not want to slow you down none. You've done give up enough of yer time, the way it is."

"You've not slowed me none," he assured her again, "you've done good. Yer feet bothered you any?"

"Some," she admitted. "They ain't cut up none, though," she added quickly, "jist sore."

"Hit takes a while fer 'em to toughen," Tice agreed, reasonably. "Now the way of it is, Hannah, we c'n either head in fer Harrodstown tomorrow an' lay over there, or we c'n pass it by. If we head in fer Harrodstown, you could rest easy fer the night an' eat good afore we started on again. Somethin' hot mought taste purty good to you."

"Does Harrodstown lay right in the path?"

"Well, no. We're a mite west of Harrod's fort. Here," he said, "I'll show you the way of it."

He picked up a twig and squatted near her, rubbed a smooth place in the dirt and began to draw. "This here is about where we are at, now. Jist about level with Harrodstown. Mebbe four, five mile north yit. We c'n easy cut over there, though, an' take the night. Hit wouldn't be much outen the way."

"Where at is Logan's fort?"

"Down here." He made a mark. "We're on a due line with it."

"Is they e'er reason you'd wish to lay over at Harrod's?"

"Not in particular."

"If it was left up to you, you'd head straight on fer Logan's, would you?"

"*If*," Tice said, stressing the word, "I'd been by myself the whole time, I d'know but what I would. But it mought jist come in my mind to stop an' pass the time with the folks at Harrod's. A man don't rightly know what he'll take a notion to do. Till the time comes, that is. He mought, one time he's out, be of a notion to head straight as the crow flies fer where he's goin', without no stoppin' off an' visitin'. Again, he mought be struck with the notion of stoppin' an' visitin'. Jist depends, I'd say."

Hannah nodded. Samuel had been the same way. Often he had come home and said, "I jist taken a notion to go round the other side the mountain. Hit seemed like a good day fer runnin' on a bear." Or he would dress in the morning, stand in the doorway and eye the sun and turn quickly to say, "I've a notion to take a sashay over to the village this mornin'. If they's e'er tradin' you want done you c'n be thinkin' on it whilst I do up the work." She knew about a man's notions and how they were guided by his wants and humor.

"But," Tice went on, "seein' as I ain't been by myself, an' we are headin' fer Logan's, I d'know but I'd as soon keep straight on. If you would, that is, an' if you ain't too fashed out."

"Oh, I ain't," she said quickly, "why I could go on easy, an' I'd jist as soon."

"Then that's what we'll do," Tice said, throwing the twig away, "though it'll mean layin' out one more night."

"Hit'll not bother me none."

"No, I don't reckon it will."

Hannah was glad they were to pass Harrod's fort by. She dreaded coming to the end of this journey, now that it was in sight—dreaded coming, finally, to a settlement where there were people. If they passed Harrod's fort by there would be at least one more day before she need face up to it.

During the long days, following Tice, in the long silences of the hours, she had thought about what lay before her. She had thought of what Tice had said about Ann Logan needing help in her cabin inside the fort, and she had tried to picture herself there. She had called up to mind the tasks that would fall to her, the milking, maybe, and tending the milk, helping with the cooking, and redding up, helping, maybe, with the younguns. The work, she told herself, would come easy to her. She could do any kind of work that ever came her way, and not mind. She didn't recall that work had ever tired her or bothered or fretted her. But she shrank from the knowledge of living with, close to, near, people—being shut up in a town. I d'know as I c'n do it, she thought, and her feeling about it was a kind of anguished helplessness. But I d'know as they's e'er other thing *fer* me to do.

If Samuel had lived, now, he wouldn't have stayed in a fort any longer than it took to get some kind of a place started. He'd have taken them out of the town in no time at all. That was what he'd planned, and what he'd wanted, and it was what she wanted, too. She didn't know how she could make out to do differently. She thought about it, turned it over and over in her mind. She hadn't ever counted on coming out at this place, in this state. Then it occurred to her that maybe she could, alone, go ahead with the kind of plan Samuel had made. On the last day before they reached Logan's fort, she thought of it and she closed up the distance to Tice. "Is they e'er woman took out a claim for herself?"

"In her own name, you mean? An' worked it by herself without a man?" "Yes."

He shook his head. "I don't know of e'er one." He puzzled over it a minute or two. "No, I don't know of a one. I d'know as they *couldn't,* mind you. Not in law, that is. I d'know the law of it. But even if the law said you could, hit wouldn't hardly be a thing a woman *could* do. You got to raise a crop, an' you got to build some kind of a place on the land, an' you got to live on it a spell. I don't know as e'er woman *could* do all that without no man to help."

"I could," Hannah said, simply.

Tice looked at her. He saw the long frame of her body, the wide, strong shoulders carrying, now, a load almost as heavy as his own, and carrying it as easily as he. He saw the strong, big hands carrying the gun. From what he knew of her, and he had learned a lot, he judged that in most things commonly called a man's work she was as clever as any man. He watched her walking beside him, her stride as long and as effortless as his own, as used to the woods as his own, and he said, drily, "I d'know but you could," and then he laughed, "but my sakes, Hannah, they ain't no need you doin' that, even if the law'd allow it. No need at all. You'll have yore pick of men to marry afore you've been at the fort a month. If you're of a mind to git out onto a stand of yer own, what you'd best do, in my opinion, is jist make yer choice of the men that'll be beggin' you. Hit goes a heap easier that way. They's sich a rush as you never seen fer ever' single woman or widder that comes into the settlements. They ain't *no* woman has to make out by her lone self, without that's jist her own wish."

Hannah pondered his remarks. "Hit could be it would be the best," she said finally. But she didn't say what she thought about it, because she didn't know what she thought about it. Getting married was an idea entirely new to her. She would have to think about it some before she knew whether that was what she wanted or not. She'd have to see about it.

THEY MADE a very long march the last day. They had had good weather the whole journey—long, clear days with the air mild and sun-warmed. But they got up that morning to a drizzling mist which dribbled down out of a white-gray sky that had lidded over the tops of the hills. They were camped on top of a hill, near the rim where it broke into a rough hollow, and the hollow was filled with the misty drizzle, and the stretch of valley below disappeared in a gray, shifting fog. Beyond the valley there was nothing but the wall of gray. Tice shivered as they shouldered their packs. "Hit's like the time had got itself mixed up an' it was November, 'stid of May, ain't it?"

Hannah was untroubled by the weather. "Oh, they's days thisaway. Bound to be, 'fore spring c'n git itself settled in."

Tice grunted, settling the pack to his shoulders. "Now, we *can*," he said, "make it plumb in to the fort by night, or soon after, if we keep goin' today. Hit'd be the furtherest we've done, but it's possible. Hit's jist up to you, though," he added quickly.

Hannah could have laughed he was so poor at hiding his own wish. He'd been kind and patient, overly patient to help her out, but now that they were so near the fort he was like a horse headed for home. Likely he had a wish to get there as quick as he could—to the ones waiting for him . . . his woman and kids. "How fur do you make it?" she asked.

He appeared to be studying, though she guessed he knew within a quarter of a mile exactly how far it was. "Hit's too fur," he said finally. "Hit's a mite better'n twenty-five mile." Hopefully he looked at her.

She picked up her gun. "We c'n try."

He grinned at her. "I was hopin' you'd see it that way."

She grinned back at him. "I could tell you was."

"But, mind, now . . . we'll stop if you say so, an' I'd ruther you to say if you git too wore out."

"I'll say so," she promised, knowing he had said it to be polite, and she'd promised to match his courtesy. They'd go to the fort today, unless they came to disaster in some unforeseen way.

The going was no rougher than it had been, but the mist made the ground slippery in places so that footing was more uncertain and Hannah knew the miles were going to wear on them sooner. All morning they traveled in the hazy drizzle. "You cain't see," Tice told her, once, "but off there to the west is all hills now. Jist one after another like they'd been shook out of a box an' let lie where they fell."

He named off the biggest creeks as they came to them. "This is Knob Lick." And later, laughing, he told her, "This is Cooper's Branch. Dave Cooper fell into it one time with a full load of baled skins. Like to drownded hisself 'fore he could git loose from 'em. That's how come the branch to git its name." Still later, crossing a wider stream he said, "This here is the Hanging Fork."

Hannah looked at its clear, lazy-flowing water. "Is yore place close?"

"Not very. Hit's about ten mile upstream."

Hannah pondered on the name of the stream, thinking how Cooper's Branch had come to be called so. "How come this creek to be the Hanging Fork?" she said.

"I d'know as I know, exactly. Some says a coupla fellers was hung on it some place. They'd run afoul of the law, an' when they was caught up with they give the men had caught 'em sich a pesky time they jist got wore out with it an' hung 'em to git shut of 'em. I d'know as that's the way of it, though. Hit's been told, is all. Rightly, it's the Hanging Fork of Dick's River. Rises down close to where I got my stand, an' angles northeast-like an' runs into the Dick's River." He started chuckling. "Now, they's a story to the way *that* river got its name. Dave Cooper told me, an' he was along at the time, so I reckon he knows. He was in this country about ten year ago with a bunch of hunters an' they got friendly with a old Cherokee chief. Couldn't none of 'em say his real name so they jist called him Cap'n Dick, an' he was the proudest of that name. Liked it better'n his Indian name an' got in the way of callin' hisself by it. Well, one time they was trappin' an' huntin' down along the river an' he come up on 'em. He must of been in a bad humor or somethin', fer he didn't much like them huntin' there. He told 'em that was his river . . . hit was Dick's River, an' they ortent to be huntin' on it. He told 'em they could go ahead, though, since they'd got started but when they got through to go home an' not to come back, fer he didn't want none of 'em stayin' on there. That was the way it got started bein' called the Dick's River."

Hannah laughed appreciatively and said, "Well, I vow," and then she asked, "Did they go home?"

"Well . . . fer the time bein' they did. But they come back, as you c'n see. Him an' all the others come back, in time."

Hannah thought about the old Indian, and how he must have known even then what would happen to the country if the white men came into it and built their cabins and killed off the game and settled the land. She felt a little pity for him, but then, how else was a country to be settled? Ways had to change. There was plenty of room for the Indians in other places, if they'd only pick up and go. There wasn't anything making them stay on, after the white men came.

It didn't occur to her that the white men would always follow. There was only the present for her, the need, right now, to settle this particular country. Pity gave way to the impatience all the settlers felt with the Indians. Indians wouldn't live in this Kentucky country and make use of it, and they wouldn't go away and leave the white men in peace. It was a wide, big country, and the Indians had only to move over a little.

Along about the middle of the afternoon the drizzle let up and the sun shone out palely through the gray sky. It was a sallow light, but it slowly ate away the grayness and opened up the distances. For the first time that day Hannah could see farther than a quarter of a mile in any direction. It astonished her how this country could change in half a day's travel. You moved from meadows to hills, to valleys, to forested parks, back to hills. Only one thing about it was certain. You would never for very long be on a level place. The one distinctive thing about it was its billow and roll. High in the sky there was still a haze over the sun and its light was pale as if strained through gauze.

They slowly climbed a slope so long that it seemed not a hill at all but rather the slant of some gently tilted globe. When they finally reached the top, however, and began the descent on the other side Tice pointed ahead. "Hit ain't too fur now." He struck a faster pace, then, and Hannah grimly set herself to keep up. He was bound to get there, she thought, and she determined she would not hold him back.

It was not quite dark when they reached the fort. They had come up a long hill, wooded thickly, and had come across its top into the edge of the clearing. "There it is," Tice called out to Hannah, stopping and pointing.

The fort topped a rise in the middle of the clearing, looming darkly and overlooking a long, sweeping valley which lay between the hills. Hannah looked at it. She had thought she would dread this moment, but she was so tired that what she actually felt was relief they had finally reached it. Tice had set a hard pace, and she had been pushed to keep up. She was tireder than she remembered being for a long, long time. Her feet were sore, her legs ached, her back hurt, and as she stood she felt her knees trembly and weak, as if they were going to give way beneath her.

Tice explained to her, "Ben had us to clean all the woods away fer a piece, so's we could allus git a good sight around the fort. He didn't want no redskins creepin' right up to the gate unbeknownst to us. They come near doin' that once, last summer, an' he vowed then they wouldn't be a tree left fer 'em to hide behind within rifle shot of the stockade. Oh, it's a stout fort. The best of 'em, in my opinion. Why, you ort to see what passes fer a fort at Boone's an' Harrod's. They ain't half as stout as Ben's, but what Ben Logan sets his hand to is done the right way, an' you c'n put yer dependence in it."

The fort was oblong in shape, being a third again as long as it was wide, and the strong, sharpened poles of the stockade fence looked invincible to Hannah. Blockhouses overhung the fence at two corners. Fort Pitt, she remembered, was built that same way, only it was bigger. Some of her dread came back, then. She had hated Fort Pitt. She had felt strange there, oddly exposed and queerly different. She had hardly known herself among so many people. Everything about herself, so long familiar, had gone different, and she had felt as if she had put on a new skin and body, not so reliable as her old ones. She had hated the noise, the busyness, and she had hated the dirt which people herded together seemed somehow to accumulate. Her first feeling when the boats had finally slid away down the river had been one of ridding herself of something unclean. Some of that feeling of strangeness now crept back over her. But all she said was, "Hit looks to be stout enough."

"Oh, it is."

They crossed the meadow which lay at the foot of the knoll on which the fort was built and climbed slowly upward. Someone from the fort saw them and called out, "Who is it?"

"Tice Fowler," Tice shouted back.

The gate was open, waiting, when they reached it, and several men clustered about them as they came through. Hannah stood waiting as Tice helped close the gate behind them. She felt uncertain and awkward before the men, and she kept her eyes on the ground. They were gathered about, looking at her, frankly curious. One of them, standing near Tice, grinned and said something which she could not hear. Whatever it was Tice grinned too, looking at her. Her discomfort was so evident that he sobered quickly. "Men," he said, "this here is Samuel Moore's girl, Hannah. I run up on her an' her pa up on the Kentucky a piece. Her pa had got cut with his axe. We doctored an' tended him the best we could, but he died. I have brung her here."

The men were quick with their sympathy. "Hit's too bad, ma'am," they said, first one and then another, and then they told how it could happen to a man, did happen, times without number, they'd heard of it, known of it, seen it happen. They spoke quietly and softly, and Hannah took heart at their speech. She stood among them, her shoulders sagged under the pack, her hands folded on her gun, and waited, listening, accepting without reply their soft-spoken words. "I'd best take her over to Ben's," Tice said, then.

They walked away from the men and behind her Hannah heard their voices, murmuring together, still soft and quiet. She noticed now that the fort was divided into two streets inside the stockade, a row of cabins down the middle. The cabins on the outside rows were built in a solid line, each touching the next. But this row down the middle had space between the cabins—not much, but a little, and Tice headed for the cabin at the near end. "Ben lives handy to the gate," he explained.

There was a glow through the window of the cabin, a stronger glow than a fire would have made, Hannah thought, although smoke was curling from the chimney. They had candles, she thought. And suddenly the thought of seeing a candle burning again seemed very good to her. It had been such a long time since she had pinched out the one that had lit their last morning at home.

They came up to the cabin, whose door stood open, and Tice called inside, "Halloo, Ann . . . you here?"

"I'm here," a woman answered. "Who is it?" Hannah listened to the voice. It was pleasant, not scratchy or screechy like some women's.

"Hit's me . . . Tice Fowler."

"Well, come on in, Tice. I'm just givin' the children their supper. Ben's up at Harrod's. We'd nearly given you up, you've been gone such a time."

They stepped inside the door onto a floor—a clean puncheon floor, Hannah saw at once. In one more quick look she took in the rest of the room . . . the bed in one corner, covered with a woven spread, a chest against a wall, a dish cupboard against another, stools sitting about and pots hanging handy by the chimney, the ladder going up to the loft room in the chimney corner, a white-scrubbed table in the middle of the room, the candle flickering at one end of it. A woman sat at the table with a little boy standing at her knee and a smaller child on her lap. She was feeding the smaller one.

She was not actually a handsome woman, Hannah thought. Not really hand-some, but she was as pleasant looking as the sound of her voice had been. She was past her first youth, but still young looking, filled out as a woman was after children came, heavy-busted so that Hannah judged she still nursed the younger child. She wore a plain dress, dyed butternut, as was Hannah's own, on the dingy side with having been washed often, but her straight brown hair was crowned with a crisp, snow-white cap.

Hannah thought quickly and with a little shame of her own bare head. Her mother had worn a cap, always. She would almost as soon have been caught without her dress as without her cap, and it had been her pride to keep them snowy and freshly ironed. But Hannah had never worn one. Being in the woods so much it would have been in the way. She hadn't thought about it, though, to be honest. There had seemed no need to think about it, to decide one way or the other. She could have worn her mother's caps, she remembered. She had laid them away with the rest of her things. But it had not occurred to her to wear them. And the capped women at Fort Pitt had not made her wish to be like them. Only now, standing before this plain, pleasant woman, in the clean, fresh house, aware of her woods-bedraggled skirt, torn in places and unmended . . . aware of her creek-slimed moccasins on the clean plank floor—of her uncombed hair, tousled as it always was when she didn't take care, and uncapped, she felt shame for her appearance. She felt big and awkward and unkempt, graceless and ugly. She would have liked to turn around and walk out of the clean house and away from the woman. She moved restlessly.

The woman had risen when she saw that Tice was not alone, setting the child in her lap on the floor. Tice began his explanation of Hannah, and Ann Logan listened, her head to one side a little. Before he had finished talking, though, she motioned for him to hush, and walked with a small rush to Hannah. "You take off that pack from your shoulders this very minute," she said. "The ways of men are beyond me! To leave you standing with a burden on your shoulders while he talks! Drop it there on the floor and come here and sit. You're worn out, poor thing, and him without the eyes to see it! I'll bound he's walked you thirty miles today, just to get here!"

Tice sighed and grinned. "Not but twenty-five, Ann."

Ann Logan wheeled on him. "You ought to be strung up and whipped, Tice Fowler!"

He blinked at her, bewildered. "But she was fer comin' on in, herself, Ann. Hit was her said to."

"Of course she said to, knowing it was what you wanted. What else *could* she say!"

[61]

Tice looked at Hannah who was shedding her pack, disencumbering herself. She did look worn out, at that. But she'd not once complained. How was a man to know? "She's stout as a man in the woods," he murmured.

Ann sniffed. "For all she's strong and stout, and I can see she is with my own eyes, she's a woman, isn't she? A woman gets tired in ways a man don't know about, Tice Fowler. And just losin' her pa, too, grievin' inside of her. You could of thought of those things, seems to me."

Tice looked at her helplessly. "*How* could I? 'Thout she said so."

Ann spread her hands in a quick movement of impatience. "Oh, Lord love the breed—there isn't a bit of use tryin' to talk sense to you. Get on out of here and let me tend to her. Is what you've got there her stuff too?"

"Yes."

"Well, take it off. Drop it alongside her pack there on the floor, and then get on out."

Tice slid the pack onto the floor. "You got room fer her, have you?"

Ann put her hands on her hips and looked at him. "Of course I've got room for her. What did you think?"

"Well, you could of been full up with some others come since I left out."

"No, thank goodness I'm not. There's room and to spare. You go on down to the men's place, now, and get you something to eat. I'll take care of this one from here on."

Hannah had dropped onto a stool by the fire and was sitting, her hands folded, drooped a little between her knees, her eyes on the flames. It was a small fire, for there was no need of its heat. It had been built, she knew, to heat up the supper, and would be let die out soon. But she was glad of its cheer. She wasn't cold, but a fire was so pleasant a thing in a house. Even traveling, a fire was a comforting thing at night. She'd missed one these nights. She unfolded her hands and spread them to the brightness.

Tice spoke to her. "You'll be all right now, Hannah. Ann'll see to you."

A quick fear shot through her and she stood suddenly. Ann Logan was a nice woman, and good, likely, but she was a stranger. Tice stood in Samuel's stead, known to her, his ways and his talk. He was the only one she knew in this strange place, and he was going to leave her here. She had known he was going to have to leave her *some* place, she reminded herself. It was but what she'd expected. "Is where you are goin' to stay fur from here?" she asked. She thought if he just stayed some place inside the stockade it would be a comfort to her, knowing he was near at hand. But it could be he was going to his own place right away. She felt a fear of what he would say.

"Why, no," he said, wonderingly, "jist down to the blockhouse where the other men stays."

"You ain't aimin' to go out to yer own place right away?"

"I don't stay to my own place yit," he said.

"Oh."

He started backing out. "You let me know if they's e'er thing you need, now."

Ann motioned him away. "Get on out," and when he had disappeared she turned to Hannah. "Right now, first off, I'm goin' to fix you some good, hot supper, and I'm goin' to heat up some water so you can wash all over when you get through eatin'. And then you're goin' to lay down in a bed for a change and sleep the whole night through. My sakes, you been travelin' for months. I'll bound a bed'll feel good to you."

The two children had sat, the younger one with his thumb in his mouth, eyes round, quietly watching, but as their mother bustled about, dipping up a bowl of stew, breaking off a chunk of bread and crumbling it in, pouring up a noggin of milk, hunting out a spoon, the older child began noisily and rapidly to eat up his bowl of food. Then he started beating his spoon against the table. "Kin I have some more, Ma? Kin I?"

"You hush, now, Davey. You can have some more if you'll not make such a noise about it." She took the bowl of food she had prepared to Hannah, explaining, "That one is David. The least one is William."

Hannah took the food, looked first at Davey, then at the baby on the floor. She tried to smile at them. "They look to be in good health," she said finally. She had helped the Williams family on the flatboat with their children. She liked young ones, got along well with them, mostly by leaving them alone. She could find little to say to them, and thought probably there wasn't much anybody could say. Mostly it was doing, with young ones, she'd noticed.

"They're hardy," Ann agreed.

Hannah ate, at first with little relish for the food, and then suddenly with good appetite. From the taste of it, the meat was venison, and the broth was thickened with the crumbled corn pone. It was hot and rich and good. When she had finished Ann took the bowl and without question refilled it. Hannah tried to protest. It wasn't good manners to take seconds. But Ann hushed her. "You're not to stand on manners right now," she said. "You've been eatin' cold for several days. You fill yourself up real good. You need it."

While Hannah was eating the second bowl, Ann busied herself with the children, finished feeding the younger one, gave David another half bowl for himself. Then she quickly undressed them and hurried them through a back door into a second room. When she came back Hannah had finished, laid her bowl upon the table and was looking uncertainly about to see how Ann went about washing up. "Just let the things go for now," Ann told her. "That water is hot enough for you to rinse off with. Have you got anything of your own clean enough to change to . . . a clean shift or something, or have you been on the go and no chance to wash?"

Hannah hesitated. She did not have another shift at all. She had used it for Samuel's bandages. She hated to say so, but then she decided she'd better not start with Ann by taking pride when she had no call to. She explained. Ann clucked. "Well, there, now. You hadn't any choice as I can see it. Of course you had to use your shift on your pa's leg. I can find you something."

"I've got a spare dress," Hannah said, "an' it's clean. I ain't wore it since it was washed."

"You can put it on tomorrow, then," Ann said, "and we'll get this one washed out. For tonight, though, you'd best have a shift to sleep in."

She went to the chest, but before pulling out the drawer she turned and looked at Hannah. "You're some bigger than I am, and I misdoubt anything of mine'll fit you. I'll just run next door to Jane Manifee's and borrow one of hers." She moved so swiftly Hannah could hardly keep up with her, not in nervous jerks like some women she'd seen, but smoothly, as if she always knew exactly what she wanted and where it was. She made up her mind so easily. Now she said, "I'll just pour up the water for you and lay you out some soft soap and you can commence washing. You needn't to worry," she said, catching Hannah's look around, "there's no menfolks around. Ben's not to home, and nobody else will come in without warning. Just stay there by the fire."

Even as she spoke she was busy, pouring the hot water into a piggin, opening the lower shelf of the cupboard to dip out a bowl of soft soap and handing it out, moving from there to the chest again, drawing out a piece of soft old cloth. "You can dry off with this. I'll be back in a minute."

Hannah didn't know whether the errand was an excuse to give her the privacy to bathe or not, but she was glad of it. She hadn't ever been wholly undressed before another living soul, not clear naked, and she didn't know whether she could have made herself do it or not. With Ann gone she hurried to strip off her dress, and then sighed at the good feeling of the soap and water on her skin. An all-over washing, she thought, was the best thing in the world to take the tiredness out of a person's bones. Seemed like the heat and the soap and the water just washed the tiredness out, the same way it washed the dirt off. And, she thought, looking at the water with shame and disgust, there was a plenty of dirt, all right.

She had finished before Ann came back, and in her modesty had slipped her dress back on. But she hadn't liked to do it. It felt stiff with filth and she hated having to put it on next to her clean skin. She saw no remedy for it, though. And she didn't know what to do with the water . . . where Ann threw her slops. She looked for some container, couldn't find one, and decided Ann must empty it out. She would have liked to dash the water out without Ann seeing it, it was so dirty, but not knowing Ann's ways, whether or not she liked having water dashed on her doorstep, she decided to leave it.

She was sitting, taking down her hair, when Ann returned. "Haven't you washed yet?" she asked, surprised.

"Yes, ma'am, I'm done." She didn't explain why she had put the dress back on.

"Oh. Well, here's a shift for you. It took me longer than I expected. Jane had to ask a heap of questions, and wanted to come over herself and see if she could do anything. But I told her we could make out and you were tired and she'd best wait until tomorrow." She picked up the water. "I'll just empty this out back and you can slip into that shift. Jane's a big woman and likely it'll fit you real well. You can just crawl right there in the bed, then. There's pallets up in the loft room I generally put folks on, but seeing as Ben isn't here right now, you just sleep in the bed with me."

She went through the back room with the bucket of water and while she was gone Hannah slipped into the clean shift. Then she didn't know what to do with her dirty dress. She finally rolled it up and laid it on the blanket packs which Ann had lugged to one corner of the room out of the way. Carefully, then, she turned back the woven coverlid and crawled into the bed, sliding over onto the back side. Taking a big breath, she let it out slowly. The straw mattress crackled under her and she patted it gently. Lordy, but it felt good. She counted back. It had been four months, lacking a few days, since she had slept on a straw tick. She had almost forgotten how soft a bed it was, how a body could slump into it and let go, and any aches or soreness would just kind of ease away. She stretched her full length. It was a long bed. Ann's man, Ben, must have a good height to him, she thought, to be needing so long a bed.

Ann came back into the main room and began setting it in order. Hannah felt guilty and roused up on her elbow. "I'd ort to be helpin' you, 'stid of layin' here takin' my ease," she said. "I warn't thinkin' of nothin' but doin' as you told me."

"You keep right on thinkin' that way . . . for tonight at least," Ann said briskly. "You've had a rough time of it, and I'm used to reddin' up the things. It'll not take me but a minute. Go on to sleep if you can."

"I've been a heap of trouble to you."

"My sakes, Hannah, you'd do the same, wouldn't you? If a lone woman, worn out and troubled, came to your house, you'd do for her, wouldn't you?"

"Yes, ma'am."

But no lone woman had ever come to their house. Just men, Hannah thought, to take the night with Samuel, and none of them worn out and troubled that she knew of. But, yes, had there ever come a lone woman, she'd have done what she could. She lay back down and closed her eyes. The room was warm from the fire. Too warm, actually, for Ann went to the door from time to time and fanned it to stir up a breeze . . . but it felt fine to Hannah. She'd been wading cold creeks, sleeping out on chilly nights, feeling the ground cold beneath her. Now, with her flesh warmed by the bath and the bed, and the warm air of the room on her face, she didn't know that ever in her life had she felt any better.

The flame of the candle flickered now and then, and against her closed eyes she could see the flicker. That, too, was good. She'd gone to sleep many a time in the bed in the corner of their main room with Samuel and another man or two setting up, talking and talking and talking, their voices kept low so she could sleep, a candle flickering on the table. A house had always ought to have candles, she thought, for light at night. Not just a knot of wood, or a piece of rag in bear fat. A candle didn't smoke, and you could sit by its light in peace. And it gave a homey look, more suited to a house.

She was sleepy, and her thoughts went straggling off. She hoped Tice had a good bed, which he likely did, seeing he was home again. Something about the thought of Tice troubled her, and she opened her eyes again, puzzling at it. Finally she asked Ann. "Does his woman stay down there at the blockhouse, too?"

"Whose woman?"

"Tice's."

Ann laughed. "Tice isn't married. And there's no women stay down there. That's where the men who aren't married stay, or the ones that are here without their women for a while."

"I d'know why," Hannah said, wonderingly now, "but I allowed he was married, though he never said one way or the other."

Ann stacked the clean bowls in the cupboard. "He's old enough to be, and past. He never has been, though, that I know of, and I reckon never will be now."

"Don't he like women?"

Ann pondered a moment. "Well, he's not woman-shy, like some that never get married. He gets along with any and all of them well enough. He just never seems to need anything more than he's got."

Hannah nodded. "Pa was like that . . . after my ma died. He never aimed to git married again, though most men would of soon as they could. Pa seemed to like the way things was."

"There are men like that," Ann agreed, "and there are several of them in this country . . . men used to the woods, not wanting to be tied down. James Harrod was one . . . the man that built Harrod's fort."

"I've heared of him."

"He was past thirty before he married, and David Cooper waited a right smart while, and William Casey, down on the Green, has never got married, nor Silas Harlan, just to name a few that don't seem to want to. But, oh, there's plenty that do." She raised her hand and pointed a soapy finger at Hannah, started laughing, "You just wait till they hear there's a single woman in the fort! They'll come flockin' about like crows after corn. You wait and see!"

"That's what Tice said, only I thought mebbe he was pokin' fun at me."

"No, he wasn't pokin' fun at you. He was meanin' it. It happens all the time. There's no woman in this country has to do without a man, unless she's of a mind to. You can take your pick inside of a week or two."

Hannah laid her head back upon the pillow and rubbed her feet together under the coverlid in a kind of embarrassed wiggling. Again she didn't know what to say, or what to think. She hoped they wouldn't come flocking too soon. She hoped she'd have time to think upon it before they started clustering around. She didn't know as she wanted to get married. She'd been used to the ways of one man all her life, and she thought it might be pretty hard to get used to another's.

Ann said nothing more and slowly Hannah's eyes grew heavy again. Slowly her mind turned loose of people and places, of events and time. The last thing she was conscious of was the feeling of warmth, softness, cleanness, and then the velvet blackness of sleep overcame her.

8

THE SUN was high in the south and the sky was a bright, light blue. It had a polish like glazed china. Straight overhead some fat white clouds rolled and bunched together in lazy, overlapping billows. But the sun rode free of them and shone down strongly. The heat poured straight into the square of the fort.

Ben Logan had left but few trees inside the stockade, and they were small and grouped toward the middle. Standing under one of them, a little walnut, churning, Hannah wondered if the women, maybe, had argued for a little shade where the children could play. It was a nice thing for young ones to have a shady place during the hot time, and they'd used it, it was plain to see, for the ground was packed flat and hard all about. But with so many folks coming and going, it likely would have been anyhow, she thought, for more feet than children's stirred constantly up and down the two streets.

Hannah stood to churn, although there was a small bench handy that Ann Logan said she always sat on. She was kept on the go so much, she said, that she was always glad of a chance to get off her feet awhile, and churning was one thing you could do sitting down. But Hannah liked to stand . . . liked to grip the dasher with both hands and feel its thick plunging movement into the milk, up and down. Once her hands felt the exact thickness of the milk, for it varied with the heat and the length of time it had taken to turn, she set her stroke and kept to it steadily, seeming tireless until the butter had come. Ann had watched her the first time. "I don't believe it tires you at all."

"No," Hannah had said, "I d'know as it does. But I d'know as churnin' is a thing to wear on a body anyhow."

"It does me," Ann had said, laughing. "As long as I've been doing it, which is all my life, my arm still gets so tired it feels like it's going to drop off."

"You go at it too fast. You do ever'thing in sich a rush, like you had jist a minute to git it over with an' done. Hit is tiresome thataway."

Ann nodded. "That's what Ben tells me, but I can't help it. That's the way I am."

"Folks are different," Hannah agreed.

This morning Ann was down the row at the last cabin. Some travelers had come in during the night and one of the little ones was ailing. She was helping out. She was a good woman, Hannah thought. She had been good to her beyond all hope or expectation, though Tice had said she would be. And Ben had been good, too. Of course they were used to people coming and going in their house, staying the night, or maybe for weeks until there was a cabin for them to move into. They had acted as if she belonged with them, though. Right from the start, and it had been three weeks now, Ann had taken it for granted she'd help, and without appearing to be bossy in the least she had divided up the work so that Hannah was kept as busy as she herself. Hannah had turned her hand to whatever came up, minding the little boys, cooking, washing up, sweeping and cleaning, dressing out meat—all the things that the care of a family held, and more than once Ann had said, gratefully, "Hannah, you're such a big help."

And she knew she was. But she knew, too, that all she was doing, actually, was paying her way with the coin at hand. She wasn't doing her own work in her own way. She was marking time, still thinking, still pondering what, in the end, she must do.

Tice had gone for the spinning wheel the next week after they had reached the fort. The women had crowded about the wheel, their rough hands handling it and turning it, examining it with envious eyes. "Seems like," Jane Manifee had said wistfully, "I c'n feel the wool in my hands this very minnit, a threadin' through 'em an' fillin' up the bobbin. They ain't but one other in the country that I know of. Ann Poague, up at Harrod's, has got one. She brung it over the Gap when her an' William come on. She's got her a loom, now, too. I'm aimin' to have me one soon as we git settled out. If," she added fiercely, "we ever git shut of this bein' fortified, which it seems like we ain't never goin' to do!"

It was what all the women longed for, to get out of the fort, into their own homes, onto their own land. They put up with the fort, lived closely together quarrelsomely or harmoniously according to their natures, but they all looked longingly over the fence, yearned toward the time when they could walk out of the gate and take up their own lives again.

Hannah noticed that Ann Logan said nothing as the other women talked. She stood among them, listened, but there was nothing for her to say. The fort *was* her home. It was built on Ben Logan's land. Not ever, so long as there was need of the fort, could she get outside the fence. All the rest could go when the time came, but she was anchored, because her man was different, had in some way taken the lead and other men looked to him for help. Hannah felt pity for her and seeing Ann's hands on the wheel offered gently, "If they's e'er thing you got to use it fer, Ann, it's your'n to use."

Ann laughed and put her hands behind her. "By the time I have need of it, Ben'll see that I've got one, and a loom, too."

Hannah believed her. There would be nothing Ben Logan wouldn't see to, as time and opportunity came to him to see. "My ma had a good loom," she said, "but I couldn't noways bring it on. I c'n build me one, though, an' I aim to. Some day, I aim to."

The women had looked at her, nudged one another and laughed. Jane

Manifee had spoken for them. "Git you a man an' a place to put it first, Hannah, then build you a loom."

Hannah's neck and cheeks had grown warm. They weren't being unkind, she knew. They weren't poking fun. They were only teasing, saying what to them seemed inevitable. Get you a man first, and the other things would come. A woman belonged with a man.

They had all then broken into laughter and had begun teasing her about the men who had prinked themselves and come with one errand or another to Ann's cabin. "Are you aimin' to take Isaac, Hannah? Not for a year has he shaved off them whiskers, till you come. We'd done forgot the look of his naked face."

"Silas, now," Esther Whitley had said, "would be a good one for you, Hannah. He's a mite on the old side, but he's steady, an' he's been wed before. He knows the ways of a woman better'n some." Their eyes had winked and their elbows had flown about, nudging, and they had whispered behind their hands.

"John, I reckon," another had said, "is the handsomest, but he's flighty now. He cain't never make up his mind. He's staked off an' traded three claims of land already, allus lookin' for a better one. He mought be uncertain about his woman, though, would be the trouble. But he's handsome, an' no denyin' it."

Jane Manifee had sniffed. "Handsome is as handsome does. Now, in *my* opinion, you'd do best to marry William Whitfield. Of course he's been widdered, an' he's got them younguns, but you'd never want with William. He's a mite thrifty, mebbe, but not overly so. Not miserly at all. In my opinion you couldn't do no better than to take William."

Hannah listened, turning her face from one of the women to the other, thinking, as each spoke, of the man she named. There was Isaac Turner. He'd been among the first to come. "I brung you a little piece of meat, Ann, seein' as you got extry to feed." His face had been so recently shaved it had still looked scraped and raw. His hair had been slicked back with bear oil and clubbed with a thong of new elkskin. He was a little, thin, rabbity man with a nervous Adam's apple and he had sat perched on the stool by the doorway as if any sudden noise would send him skittering. He had spoken not more than half a dozen times, always to Ann, but his eyes had constantly sought Hannah across the room—not openly and curiously, but carefully and secretly, slewing sidewise when he thought she wouldn't be looking. It had made her feel like covering herself with something, hiding away where he couldn't see her. She hadn't in any way taken to Isaac, but he had been among the most persistent. Hardly a day went by that he didn't make an opportunity to come to the cabin. Ann had been patient with him, and Hannah had done her best, not wanting to hurt his feelings, but she wondered that he couldn't see she went out of her way to avoid him.

There was Silas Barnham. He'd come, too, the same day as Isaac. He was an older man, big and angled and bearded grayly. Forthrightly he had come, making no excuse with meat or any other offering. He'd come, spoken briefly with Ann, looked at Hannah boldly, watched her as she went on with her work. She had set out to scrub the hearthstone and she saw no reason to stop for him. She knelt, dipped the soft piece of deerskin in the soapy water and scoured and scrubbed until the gray stones shone with a clean glisten. Then she had emptied the water, hung the deerskin on a peg and returned to the room to help Ann shell the corn for hominy. She hadn't said one word to him, none coming easily to her to say, and hard searching not revealing any. He had sat and watched her, and then he had said, "Ma'am, I have need of a good woman, an' likely, from what I hear, you've got need of a man you c'n put yer dependence in. Ann c'n tell you what you'd want to know of me. An' I'd be obleeged if you'd have me."

She had felt an agony of confusion, not knowing what to say or even what to do. Her hands had suddenly felt too big and awkward and she had bent over the corn and shelled with a quiet fury, sending the separate kernels in a spattering shower into the big wooden bowl. She could feel Ann's look on her, and the man's, and she refused to lift her head, bending it instead even lower over the work in her lap. Silas had stood up. "You c'n give me yer word, or if you'd ruther, you c'n jist tell Ben," he'd said, and he had left with no further word.

When Hannah raised her head Ann was amazed to see that there were tears in her eyes. "Why, Hannah, you're cryin'. What did Silas say to hurt you?"

Hannah dashed the tears away. "Nothin'. He never said nothin' to hurt my feelin's . . . it's jist I don't know what to make of him, or the other'n. I ain't used to men takin' notice of me, an' it jist mixes me all up in my innards. Hit makes me feel foolish, an' I don't never know what to say to 'em."

Ann laughed gently. "What they're tryin' to get you to say is easy. They just want you to say you'll have one of them. They don't care what else you say."

"I wish they wouldn't. I wish they wouldn't none of 'em come about pesterin'. I wish Pa hadn't of died!"

But all the wishing in the world wouldn't bring Samuel back again, nor change the need for a decision. She knew that, but knowing it somehow did not make it any simpler.

John, the handsome one, had come, and in spite of her shyness he had made Hannah laugh with his frolicksome ways. William Whitfield had come, a sober, steady Scotsman, as forthright as Silas Barnham, telling her, accurately to the last pound of seed corn and the last of seven younguns, what he possessed, what he expected, what he had hopes of accomplishing, offering all of it to her to share.

All the unattached men in the fort had come, eventually, except Tice. In the three weeks since she had reached the fort she had seen him only three times. He was spending most of his time out on his place, now, clearing the land and planting. He had, of course, brought her spinning wheel to her, but he hadn't lingered long. He had come in for muster day and she had seen him drilling with the other men, but that day he hadn't even come up to Ben's cabin. And then one day the week before he had come in, needing a horse, and trading with Ben for one. He had eaten the noon meal with them that day, and he'd asked her if she was doing all right. Ben had told him, laughing, that she was doing just fine, but that if things kept on she'd have to make up her mind about one of the men flocking around pretty soon. Tice had laughed, too, and said, "Didn't I tell you, Hannah? You never had no need to weary about gittin' on yer own place."

Other men had come, too—from off, from Harrod's town, from Boone's fort and places just settled. They'd heard, roundabout, that there was a single woman at Logan's, an unattached woman, free to wed. Feeble excuses were made for coming. They were trailing horses that had strayed or been stolen. They were hunting in the neighborhood and stopped in to stay the night, to bring in a haunch of deer or bear. They had come to look over a piece of land. They all managed to end up in Ben's cabin for a meal or two, and to have a look at Hannah, to offer shyly, or boldly, according to their temperaments, a place in their lives.

Little by little Hannah came to feel so beleaguered that often when she saw Ben crossing the street with still another man she felt like ducking out the back, running to Jane Manifee's or Esther Whitley's, staying hidden out until they had gone. Only by great effort of will could she make herself keep on with her work, appear natural before the men. Instead of taking pleasure in being sought out, she grew to dread each day and the confusion within her deepened instead of resolving itself. There were even times when she wished, almost desperately, she had never come to the fort at all, that she had gone instead to the Falls and returned to the border country with some traveling groups. Or that she had even stayed on in the rockhouse alone. There were times when she looked wildly around the big room of the cabin as the men sat talking with Ben or Ann, or even to her, and wondered how she had ever come to this pass, how her life could so have changed in such a short time— times when she felt like a trapped animal, no way of her own choosing left to her.

She had talked to Ben about taking up a claim for herself. Gently he had advised her not to do it, even if it were legal. "You don't know anything about livin' in Indian country, Hannah, an' you'd be a burden to the settlement in the end. Somebody would always have to be lookin' out for you, worryin' about you."

It was so true that she did not argue. Her decision was thus reduced to the two alternatives. She could stay on in the fort, living with Ann and Ben, or she could take one of the men who had offered to marry her.

The dasher went up and down in the churn as she thought about it. She didn't want either one of them. She liked Ann and Ben well enough, but she hated the fort, walled in, dirty, full of talk and gossip, full of people. But she didn't know how a woman could just take up with a strange man and marry him and go off onto a place with him to live. It didn't even appear decent to her. Oh, what she wanted was what she had been used to—Samuel and the old cabin under the mountain, the branch trilling out back, the loom handy in the chimney corner, the bearskin rugs on the floor, the garden patch fenced with palings. What she wanted was to turn back the clock and have it all exactly as it had been before.

The sun, coming through the meager foliage of the small walnut tree, fell directly on her head. Her hair, as usual, was flying loose from the knot. She had no way of knowing that those loose, springy strands that were forever pulling free of the knot were the only softening thing about her face these days. As unconsciously as if she were brushing at a fly or mosquito she had the habit of giving it a lick with the back of her hand, until when finally enough of it had pulled loose that it became a conscious annoyance she would stop whatever she was doing and repin the knot. Then for perhaps half an hour she would be free of the flying curls. Sweat beaded her upper lip and she wiped her face with the apron Ann always made her wear, brushed at her hair again, bent to see if the butter had begun to gather around the lip of the churn lid.

When she straightened she saw Tice going into the south blockhouse. He was carrying a saddle and she guessed he had just come into the fort. He was hot, too. The linen shirt he was wearing had stuck to his back with perspiration, and his hair had pulled loose from its club and hung lank about his ears. It seemed odd to her, watching him, that she had spent days with him in the rockhouse, and more days on the trail coming to the fort. She tried to bring back into her mind the things he had said in her hearing, his ways of eating and rolling into his blanket at night, the look of his back ahead of her as they traveled. She could remember all those things, without effort, but she could not somehow connect them with that man down the slope by the block-house carrying in his saddle.

She had heard Ben say that Tice had a fine crop of corn planted. He'd had good seed, Ben said, and he'd planted when the sign was exactly right— in the arms—a mite late, maybe, for the whippoorwills had been calling two weeks or better before he got back from that trip into Ohio, and the oak leaves had been a speck bigger than squirrel ears, but he hadn't been overly late. With any luck he'd have a fine crop.

Hannah could see the corn, already up, tender and green and the leaves rustling as they unwound from the stalk, growing fast, almost overnight, and the stalks thickening and the leaves widening. She could almost feel it under her hand, and feel the turned soil under her feet. Tice had a plow, Ben had said. Ben had a plow, too. Once when he'd had to go back to the Holston country he'd brought in three iron plow points with him. The blacksmith had made them especially for him, and Tice had traded for one. "You take," Ben had said, "and carve you out a good plow, from whiteoak, say, stout and lasty, and then put one of those iron points on the share, and you got some-thing that'll turn the land good and deep—the way land ought to be turned. Tice was smart to trade for one of those plows. It'll pay him back several times over."

So Tice had plowed his land with a whiteoak plow, pointed with iron, and the land would be loamy and warm and crumbly when you walked over it with your bare feet. And the rows of corn would be like a long green line drawn over and over again across the field, hilled maybe one pace apart, with squash and pumpkins planted in the hills too. The squash would come up and wind itself up the cornstalk, fuzzy and prickly to touch, and the little yellow blooms would come out in July, looking like little bugles. She had seen the soldier's bugles at Fort Pitt, and she'd thought then that a squash blossom was like that, belled in just the same way. And the pumpkin vines would put out their broad, veined leaves and they would run over the ground between the corn so thick that before the summer was over it would look like a green braided rug. Hannah closed her eyes. It was almost more than she could stand, knowing that others were working the land now, and she was prisoned here, inside a stockade fence, with no home nor land nor family.

Ben had gone on to tell of the lay of Tice's land. "As sightly as any piece I've ever helped to lay out. There's a long rolling hill down to the Hanging Fork, and a grove of birches down by the creek. They're young yet, and small, but white and clean as bare bones. They bend a little towards the stream."

Hannah had opened her eyes. "Has he got a cabin built yet?"

"No. Don't anybody build a cabin right off, hardly. Without a family, that is. Not much need of hurryin'. He's got a fair shelter, though. That passes for an improvement and meets the law."

The ache she had felt then came back inside of her now—a deep, longing pain for a shelter of her own, and things about her once again that belonged to her, and work to do for herself. This churning, now—it was just passing the time. It wasn't her churn and it wasn't her milk and it wouldn't be her butter when it came.

Ben came out of the blockhouse. Another man followed him and they stood talking for a moment. He was a stranger to Hannah. Then the two of them started up the street toward the cabin. Suddenly Hannah could not bear to have yet another stranger coming, to make eyes at her, talk, look her over, make his offer of so many acres of land, so many head of cattle, so much land cleared and plowed. She wanted her own things, certainly—but she didn't want them tied with a string to a stranger.

She gave the churn dasher a vicious jerk, then turned it loose and fled, leaving it to settle slowly to the bottom of the churn. She ran around the corner of the cabin and hid, wiping her hands on the apron, ridding them of the grease of the gathering butter. She stood there, not noticing or caring if she was seen by people in the back row of cabins, wanting only not to be seen by Ben and the stranger.

They came steadily on, slowly, talking together. She could see that Ben was grinning as they came closer. When they had passed the front of the house and were well inside, she darted back around the corner. She stopped running, though, once she had cleared the house. She slowed to a walk, but went directly, nevertheless, to the blockhouse. She had never been inside. The men who were not married lived there, and women did not go in, except every month or so two or three, taking it turn about, would give warning that they were going to clean, and the men would pile their belongings out of the way and scatter.

[73]

She stood in the doorway and peered into the gloom. Tice was on the far side of the room, and a little knot of men was clustered about him. Ordinarily Hannah would have been too embarrassed to make herself known, but she had come to the end of her tether. She had decided what she had to do now. And she knew if she did not do it now and get it over with, her courage would ebb and she might never find it again. She called out to him. "Tice?"

His back was turned and she saw him swing around, slowly. The men stopped talking and stared at her. "Tice, I got to talk to you," she said.

"Why, sart'n, Hannah," he said, leaving the little bunch of men and coming toward her. "What did you wish to say?"

She waited until he was near enough that she could lower her voice. "I'd ruther not to say it here."

"Well, we c'n go up to Ben's then."

"No—they's somebody there."

Tice looked at her, puzzled, and rubbed the side of his jaw. She had been right about him. He didn't wear a beard when he was where he could shave, and he must have just finished now. There was still a faint smell of soap about him. "Well," he said, having thought it over, "I reckon we c'n walk down to yon end the fence. Would that do?"

She nodded, miserable.

She walked beside him the entire length of the street in silence, aware of every hidden eye in the cabins watching them pass, of every woman's tongue, stilled for the moment at seeing them, to be released volubly as soon as they had passed. Painfully she endured the long walk, keeping her head up, trying to forget where she was, thinking only of what she had to say.

Down the dusty road of the street the heat shimmered in a watery haze, and the glare of the white dust made her eyes squint. A fort, she thought, is the unsightliest thing on God's earth, and no two ways about it—and the poorest way man ever dreamt of making out. She *had* to get shut of it, and all its plaguey ways. She had to, or die.

When they came, finally, to the west fence, there still was no shade and she faced Tice in the white light of the sun, resting one hand against the peeled log of the fence, feeling its heat in her palm, and the sticky ooze of resin which had melted out. She took a good breath. Tice was not looking at her, which helped. He was looking back down the way they had come, frowning a little, thinking, maybe, of things he ought to be doing, but what she had to say wouldn't take long, and wouldn't keep him long. Only she had *had* to have a place out of the hearing of others.

She let out her breath and spoke. "Tice, I know you ain't wed, but it could be you've give yer word to somebody. I've not heared of it, but it could be you're promised. I'd like to know if you are."

He looked at her, and before he spoke she saw the small mark beside his mouth pucker and indent. It could be a scar, she thought, irrelevantly, but she thought more likely it was natural, just a little creasing of the flesh, a pocket, like, that formed when he went to talk or laugh. She kept her eyes on it, not daring to meet his. But she saw him shake his head, and the fear that had been gathering in her flowed downward a little. "No," he said, "I ain't promised."

She tried to go on, but she found her throat dry and lumpy. She saw Tice shift restlessly from one foot to the other and she thought, agonizingly, of turning and running away from him, as fast as she could. But if she did . . . she flung out her hands and blurted, "Then let's you an' me git married, Tice! I got to git shut of this fort, an' all these folks . . . an' all them men comin' an' goin'. I jist got to, Tice. I cain't stand no more of it. Hit's gittin' me sick inside of me, an' I cain't bear no more of it!"

She was astonished when Tice laughed. "Why, Hannah, I'd of thought you'd been pleased—so many wantin' to marry you."

"No!" She said it passionately.

"Most women would."

"I ain't most women. I don't know them men, Tice." She stopped and brushed at her hair. "You know I'm stout an' able, Tice. You've saw the way I c'n make out. I ain't aimin' to make any brags, but I'd not be a hinder to you . . . leastways I don't think it."

Tice stopped teasing and his face sobered. "No," he said, "you'd not be a hinder to no man."

She could look at him now, speaking of herself and things she knew of herself. "Hit's in my mind I could be of help to you. I c'n plow an' plant good, Tice, an' hunt." Her voice was eager now. "An' I c'n keep the keer of a house the best I was taught."

Roughly Tice spoke. "They's no need tellin' me . . . I *know* what you c'n do." He dropped his gaze then, to his feet, and with one toe made circles, round and round in the dust.

Hannah's eyes followed the circles. She waited for whatever he had in mind to say, certain now he wouldn't marry her, and miserably she wished she'd never thought of it. She ought to have known, she thought. She was too plain and gawky and too awkward, and Tice never had wanted to get married to anybody anyhow. She had shamed him and put him in the place of not knowing what to say. She had been too bold, and now he had to find a way to say so without hurting her feelings.

The toe kept repeating its slow circle and finally, thinking to make it easier for him, she reached out her hand and spoke. "Hit don't matter, Tice. Hit was jist a notion I had, but don't take it to heart. I'll make out one way or the other. Jist forget I ever named it."

He looked up at her. "Why would I want to forget it? I was jist studyin' on how it would be the best to manage. We c'n git married any time you say, but I don't know as you c'n go out to the stand with me yit awhile. Hit's awful risky, an' I ain't got but the shelter. I d'know as you could git shut of the fort that quick." He grinned at her. "But it would rid you of all them men comin' an' goin', that's sart'n sure."

She thought her heart was going to stop beating and never start again—just quit thumping and pumping in her chest. She'd thought he didn't want to, was ashamed of her asking, and all it was, he'd been studying how best to manage.

[75]

To her dismay she suddenly felt like crying and was terribly afraid she was going to. She struggled with her throat and blinked her eyes to keep them from wetness. "If you c'n make out with a lean-to," she said, "so kin I. An' I'd ruther to. Oh, I'd a heap ruther to!"

"Well, I d'know, Hannah. Hit's awful rough. A body c'n make out campin' when they're travelin', but you take it day to day, an' it c'n git awful wearisome."

"I don't keer," she said fiercely, "I jist don't keer how rough it is. Hit won't seem rough to me. I got my things we could take, an' they'd help some, an' I c'n make out."

But he still shook his head. "I'll speak to Ben first, about you goin' out to the stand." They turned and started walking back down the street. Tice said, then, a little shyly, "You would be willin', would you, to git married right now?"

"You mean the next day or two?"

"I mean right now. Ben c'n marry us soon as we git to the cabin, if that's what you want. He's a magistrate."

She didn't even have to think twice. "I would like it."

"All right. We'll git that done an' over, an' then we c'n decide whe'er you're to go out to the place."

"*I* ain't got no decidin' to do. When was you aimin' to go back?"

"This evenin'—but I c'n wait over till tomorrow."

"They ain't no need of waitin'. I c'n go as soon as you want."

Tice looked at her and began laughing. "My sakes, you do aim to git shut of the fort quick as you kin, don't you?"

"I shore do," she said firmly. But when she had said it, it came over her it didn't sound very nice. You didn't commonly pick a man just to get shut of something else. In her case it was the main reason and she couldn't deny it. But after all, she *had* picked. She had picked Tice when there had been a dozen others. Timidly she mentioned it. "I know you never come amongst the others, Tice, courtin', but I'd not wish you to think I've picked on you jist to git shut of the fort an' the men a comin'. Hit has a heap to do with it, an' I wouldn't lie to you, but . . . but. . . ."

"Well," Tice said, helping her out, "hit stands to reason you like me best, or you'd of took one of the others. That's the way I make it, anyhow."

"Oh, I do," she said gratefully, "I do like you the best. You are right to think so. Why, I don't even *know* them other men. An' Tice, as fur as I know how, I'll be a good wife to you. I ain't sayin' I'll be the best you could of got, for I know I'm plain an' gawky, but I'll allus do my part."

Tice cleared his throat. "I don't see as you're any plainer or gawkier than e'er other woman. You're built big, but you handle yerself good. I don't know of anybody walks any softer in the woods, an' a gawky person ain't up to that."

It was the kindest thing he could have said. She felt almost gay knowing he thought of her so. She laughed suddenly, not caring who heard, and not caring now who saw them walking together. "Ann an' Ben are goin' to be right surprised, I reckon."

The dent beside Tice's mouth twitched. "I reckon," he said.

The stranger had gone when they came to Ben's place. Ann had moved the churn inside and had taken up the butter. She was rinsing and working it with the wooden paddle. Ben had the bullet mold out and was melting lead in an iron ladle over the fire. He looked up when they came in, but went on stirring the lead. Hannah's hand flew to her mouth when she saw Ann finishing her chore. "I plumb fergot that butter."

"It had gathered," Ann said, "and all I had to do was take it up. I didn't know where you'd gone to, or when you'd be back."

Hannah looked at Tice who spoke up promptly. "Ben, you reckon you got time to marry me an' Hannah 'fore that lead's ready to pour?"

Hannah's eyes had dropped, but she saw that Ann's hands stopped working the butter and that Ben seemed frozen where he knelt. Neither of them said anything for a moment, then Ann laughed and said, "There! Didn't I tell you, Ben Logan?"

Ben pushed himself up from the floor. "You wantin' to get married right now? Right this minute?"

"Right now," Tice said. "We ain't of a notion to wait. Hannah wants to go back with me this evenin'."

Now that it was said, open and clear, Hannah could look up. Ann was smiling and Ben looked at her and shrugged. "It beats me how a woman always knows such things. She said all the time Hannah wouldn't take nobody but you. *I* said no woman would ever catch you . . ."

"Ben!" Ann's voice was sharp, and, reminded, Ben became confused and turned hastily away. "Let me get my book. I always forget how the words go without my book."

Ann came over and untied the apron from Hannah's waist. "Wouldn't you want to put on your other dress, Hannah? Comb your hair, maybe?"

Hannah looked down. Her dress wasn't dirty. It was her second best, but there was actually little to choose between them. The other one wasn't really any better, but she hadn't worn and washed it quite as often. Still, she thought, they'd be traveling, and there wasn't any use dirtying the fresh one. "No," she said, "I'll jist keep this'n on."

She did step over to the wash shelf and run Ann's shell comb through her hair and repin the knot. Then she was ready. Tice still stood where he had stopped, just inside the door. Ann motioned to the wash shelf. "Your hair could do with a combing, too, Tice. It's loose from your thong."

He made it fast and then ranged himself alongside Hannah.

Ben came back with the book and stood in front of them. He opened the book to a marked place, cleared his throat and peered at them. "You all ready?"

"We're ready," Tice said.

"Join hands."

Tice took Hannah's hand. It was the first time, she thought, he had ever touched her, saving the few times their hands had touched in passing when they'd dressed Samuel's leg. Not ever had they lingered and held before. Tice's hand was warm and hard, the palm deeply calloused. Her hand was large, but

Tice's was bigger and it closed over hers with a light, firm clasp. He was as steady as a rock, she thought. She'd heard of men being nervous when they were wed. If Tice was nervous it didn't show—not on his face or in his hand. She herself felt steadier than she ever remembered feeling. As if, now, she had come to a place toward which she had always been traveling, and having reached it, could stand quietly in its peace.

The words of the ceremony were a wonder to Hannah. Not ever had she seen anyone married, or heard those words before. They were read solemnly in Ben's deep voice, and she thought how a man and a woman stood and promised so much. It was what she meant to do, too, she thought. Maybe she didn't really love Tice right now. She didn't know what it meant to love a man in the way of a wife for a husband, but if you lived with one and had the care of him, it must surely be love you'd come to have for him. If love meant thinking about him, doing for him, seeing to him, helping him in every way she could, she knew that would be what she would feel for Tice. She didn't know about cherish—the word had no meaning for her except that it went with love, and obey . . . well, she was used to doing what a man said. She wouldn't have any trouble there. And as far as sickness and health went, life was like that and you made out the best you could. The same was true of better or of worse. There was always the good and the bad to be expected. She was aware suddenly that Ben's voice had stopped and they were all looking at her. "You're supposed to say 'I will,' Hannah," Ben told her.

"Oh, I will, I will!"

They all laughed and Ben went on, until finally he came to the end and said they were married. "All I got to do now is record it with the county clerk. But the knot is already tied good and hard."

Ann kissed Hannah and Ben shook hands with her and with Tice.

"What would you think of her goin' out to the place with me?" Tice asked him. "She's got her heart set on it."

Ben shook his head. "It'll be risky."

"That's what I told her."

"But I don't keer fer the risk," Hannah put in eagerly.

"There aren't any women outside the fort yet . . ."

"I don't keer fer that, either," Hannah interrupted, "I *got* to go! I jist got to go!"

"And she's going," Ann said, taking her part suddenly. "I know how she feels . . . and I'd rather take the risk, too, if I was her."

Ben looked at Ann queerly and then he gave in, arguing no more. "Well, it's just up to you all."

"All right, then, Hannah," Tice said. "Git yer things together. We got to git movin' if we aim to git there 'fore night. Ben, could I have the loan of another horse?"

"Sure."

"I'll bring it back in a day or two."

"No hurry. Any time you're comin' in."

"The folks," Ann said, "are sure goin' to be put out, not gettin' to chivaree you all tonight."

"That," Tice said grimly, "is jist exactly what I'm aimin' fer 'em to miss out on."

In a drawly sort of voice Hannah had never heard Ben use before he said, "It's a pity. You've dealt out so much misery to other bridegrooms, they'd ought to have a chance to get even."

Tice grunted. "I ain't riskin' it. Hannah, I ain't goin' to bring the horses inside the fence, come to think of it, so you jist take what you got to have. Jist make up one bundle an' put it inside that iron pot of your'n, an' in a little bit, jist long enough fer me to ketch up the horses, you walk down towards the gate like you was fetchin' somethin' fer Ann. I'll have the horses right outside the gate."

"Don't you want to eat your dinner first?" Ann asked.

"Ain't got the time," Tice said, heading for the door. "We'll git the rest of her things soon."

Hannah had never heard of a chivaree, but if Tice was so anxious to avoid it, she was too. She scurried to the loft and began to gather her clothing, then she stuffed the package of seeds inside the bundle, wadded the two pewter spoons down in the iron pot under the bundles, poked and prodded until they were nearly hidden. Then she was ready to go.

Ann made a parcel of meat and bread. "There's enough to keep you from havin' to cook tonight, too," she said. "If you're late gettin' there, it'll be a help."

"Hit's thoughty of you," Hannah told her, taking the parcel. She had to press it down in the iron pot on top of the other things. She went to stand in the door. "Tell me when to go," she said to Ben.

He came over and stood beside her. "Not yet."

She wished she could find a way to tell both of them how she felt about them—how good they had been to her, how thankful she was. If she could just say the words to tell them there was such a warm place inside of her now, and how they'd helped to put it there. They had ever been kind, and it wasn't their fault if she didn't like the fort and living with them. She tried. "Hit ain't," she said, "that I don't like you'ns. I reckon you know that. But a body has *got* to do fer theirselves."

Ann, who had come to stand on the other side of her, patted her shoulder. "Of course you do, Hannah. We understand that. We're glad for you. We didn't expect you to stay on. Tice is a good man, and he'll make you a mighty good husband, and we're just happy for you."

"Yes, ma'am."

"You mind one thing, though, Hannah," Ben said, then, "if Tice tells you to come into the fort don't argue with him about it. Do what he says, for it'll mean he needs to be free of having to worry about you. There are times when we need every man in the country, and the only way they can be free is to bring their womenfolks and young ones into the forts. If that time comes, and it likely will, don't be stubborn and risk it outside by yourself. It'll just make it harder on Tice."

"I'll not," Hannah promised.

There seemed nothing more to say and they stood silently in the doorway until Hannah, feeling uneasy, asked, "You reckon it's time yit?"

"Just a little longer," Ben said. "No . . . I see him, Hannah. He's ready. He's right outside the gate. He just signed to you."

Hannah saw him then and she picked up the iron pot. Awkwardly she turned to Ann and Ben. "Well," she said, "well . . . I'll be goin', I reckon . . ."

Ann gave her a sudden squeeze. "You take care of yourself, now, you hear?"

"Yes, ma'am."

She walked out the door and steadily, in her usual gait, walked toward the gate. It was just midday, the sun almost directly overhead. It was hard to believe that just one hour ago she had been standing under the little walnut tree doing the churning. Now here she was a married woman, going out to her own place. It was like a miracle, what could happen in one short hour. A body's whole life could be changed.

She met no one to ask questions, and she didn't care who saw from the cabins. They could speculate all they wanted. Soon they would all know. What she had to do now was walk straight to the gate and then Tice would close it behind her and she would be shut of this fort and its gabbling folks forever.

9

SHE WAKED slowly the next morning, drowsy and unwilling yet to move. Through half-closed eyes and with drugged senses she noticed the weather-stained shingle boards above her head. They were so near she could almost have stretched up her arm and reached them. She must, she thought, have somehow rolled her pallet nearer the eaves during the night, for usually the roof of Ann Logan's loft room was head-high over her. Half asleep as she was she took note of how well the shingle boards had been laid. Ben, she thought idly, was a master hand at lapping and laying a roof.

She sighed and turned on her side, warm and with a wholly peaceful feeling. As she turned she was vaguely conscious of a strange texture against her face. She rubbed her cheek against it, wonderingly, and then, as awareness took hold of her she came instantly and fully awake. She sat bolt upright, bumping her head against the low roof. She put up her hand. That was not the roof of Ann Logan's loft room over her head, and this was not the straw pallet on which she had slept lately. Those were the shingle boards of Tice's lean-to shelter and these were the buffalo robes he had thrown down to make their bed. But Tice was not there . . . Timidly she reached out to touch the rough pile of the buffalo skin. She drew her hand back immediately, embarrassed, feeling the heat flush her throat. It was as if she had touched Tice, himself, still there beside her. It was going to take some getting used to, his place there, and his right to be there. She had known, she thought, what to expect. She'd heard talk enough. There were some things, though, she guessed, you couldn't actually know about until they happened.

But even as she wondered that it was so, she remembered, too, how when the chill of the night had crept up from the creek into the lean-to he had pulled up an extra robe and tucked it about them, had whispered, "You warm enough, Hannah?" If he had been rough, demanding, he had also been thoughtful. It gave her a soft, sweet feeling inside—that special care for her. It flooded her with tenderness toward him, just remembering. Well, she was a wife now. She had stepped over into a new knowledge and had fully joined the sisterhood of all wives. Now she knew, and she felt a kind of pride in it, and oddly, a sense of self-respect.

Then she noticed it was broad daylight, almost sun-up, and horror overtook her. She had overslept herself . . . on her first morning, too. Mortified and ashamed she scrambled out of the shelter and looked about her. Tice was nowhere in sight, but he had built a fire, she saw, and brought up water from the creek. Her face heated and she mourned that she should have so failed on her very first morning. She hurried to wash her face and straighten her hair. She took comfort from the fact that the fire had not yet burned down very low. He couldn't have been up and stirring too long. He hadn't eaten, she saw, and in haste she set to work to make their breakfast. As she patted out the corn pones she heard his axe. She smiled. He was already at work in the clearing, then.

While the meat and bread cooked she looked about her. It had been after dark when they had arrived the night before and she had not yet seen the place. Tice had built his lean-to near a clump of young birch trees on the bank of the creek, and she remembered what Ben Logan had said of them. They were as he had told, young and strong and pretty. Except for being better built the lean-to was exactly like the one she had built as a shelter for Samuel, open to the front, steeply sloping to the back. The buffalo robes were heaped at one end for the bed, and Tice's belongings were piled at the other. This had been his camping ground for a long time, she saw, for the earth was well packed all around.

The creek was narrow here, not more than twenty good steps across. It was shallow and clear and bubbly over a rocky bed, and its gently sloped banks made it a natural crossing place. She smiled to see it. It made her think of the branch that ran across the back yard at home.

Back of the lean-to, to the north, the land was level for a stretch and it was covered with rye grass and clover, except where Tice had plowed and planted his corn. The corn patch lay to the west, down the meadow. She knew that was because he wanted grazing handy for his horse, and later for cows and sheep, maybe.

The meadow, at the far back, sloped very easily upward and then leveled off to make a wide shelf of land which was topped with a thin stand of trees. She could see beyond that the land continued to climb, more steeply and more thickly wooded. That was Tice's hill at his back.

To the east the meadow continued, but only for a little way because it then became a rank growth of cane over which she could not see except in the far distance. There, as if in the mouth of a canyon, loomed the massed hills.

As she looked the red rim of the sun pushed over their tops and the whole valley filled with light. Before her stretched a green world, the green of trees, green of cane, green of grass, a dozen different shades of green, a dozen different textures, all touching and blending, and now all overlaid and glossed with the glowing light of the sun.

She felt an enlargement of herself, an expansion, as if now she had become big enough to take in the whole land that stretched before her. She felt strong and able and full of a queer, bubbly exhilaration such as she had known sometimes as a child when some new adventure loomed. This was what she had been traveling toward, what she had been coming to, what her home was going to be, where Hannah Moore would live out the rest of her days. Remembering, she changed the old name for the new, repeating it to herself, testing it—

Hannah Fowler—Hannah Fowler. She liked the sound of it. This was Tice Fowler's stand. This was Hannah Fowler's home.

She heard Tice behind her and turned, her thoughts clearing, her hands ready to dish up his food. "You're up now, are you?" he asked. His linen shirt was wet through with sweat and his face was red and streaming.

"I'm up," she told him shamefacedly. "I don't know when ever I've over-slept myself like that before. I hope you ain't thinkin' it's common with me, fer it ain't. An' I'm too ashamed to speak of it, nearly."

Tice laughed comfortably. "Hit don't matter. I know yer ways, commonly. I could of woken you, but I reckoned you needed the sleep. A body don't git married ever' day. I only come back now to see to the fire. I warn't aimin' to git you up if you was still abed."

"I would of come to call you in a minnit," she confessed. "The things is ready to eat."

"An' I'm ready for 'em," he said heartily.

She handed him bread and meat and stood back, ready to serve him more. He motioned. "Git yores. They ain't no use standin' on manners out here."

She took her own portion without comment. Samuel had been like that, too. When there were guests he could depend upon her being mannerly enough to serve the men, but when they were alone he had liked her to eat with him.

As they ate Tice told her more about how the land lay. "Would you want," he asked her eagerly, "to take the day an' look at it?"

"I would like it," she told him, "but I don't want you to misput yerself."

"I'll not," he assured her. "I was girdlin' trees up there on the shelf but they ain't no hurry about it. Them trees," he said, laughing, "will stand there till I git to 'em."

"I reckon they will," she agreed, smiling.

"I've got it in mind," he went on, "to build me a mill on this creek . . . down a piece."

She looked carefully at the stream. "You'd need a good fall, I'd think, an' a right smart flow."

"That's jist what I got," he said, eagerly. "They is a fall jist about right, an' I ain't never seen the water low enough to dry the rocks yit. Of course it mought be in a awful dry season hit would git lower, but I misdoubt it would ever git so low as not to furnish a good flow. The way I make it, I could set the mill up . . ." He threw away the last of his meat, wiped his hands on his pants, grabbed up one of the pointed sticks Hannah had roasted meat on and began laying off his plan. "Here is the way the water flows, around a bend an' then straightenin' out . . . an' here, jist below where the fall is at is where I'd set the mill." He threw the stick away. "But you c'n see fer yourself. We'll go right by the place." He brushed his hands together. "You'll want to redd up first, I reckon."

Awkwardly she tried to decide. If she didn't clean up the camp he might think she was slack-handed. But if she did he would have to wait, and clearly he was anxious to start. She decided. "No, I'd ruther to see things first. Hit ain't much reddin' up to do an' I c'n easy do it when we git back."

"I was hopin' you would." He scattered the fire, making it safe to leave.

He led her an easy way down the creek, avoiding the cane thicket but calling her attention to the thickness of the growth, the height of the cane, its excellence for feed. He pointed out to her how the water changed, being here shallow, there a little deeper, here quiet and there swift. It was perhaps half a mile downstream that they came on the waterfall. "Now, this is the place," Tice said.

Hannah looked at it judiciously. There was evidently a sloped bed here which raced the water down very swiftly, for it boiled over the rocks and gushed down the drop in a white spume which spattered them where they stood. Tice went on talking, explaining exactly where he had thought to set the mill, stepping off the lay of it, showing the height and width he'd thought for the wheel, telling the kind of burrs he hoped to have. Finally he said, "Well, I don't think I've fergot e'er thing. That would be the way of it. But I don't think," he added, "to build the mill jist yet. I wouldn't want you to think I'd aimed to build it afore I git you a roof over yer head. I would of," he went on honestly, "if we hadn't got married, likely, fer a man don't have the need of a house a woman does. But now I aim to git the cabin built as soon as I kin."

"On my account you needn't," Hannah told him. "I c'n easy make out in the shelter. Hit's stout, an' even durin' the winter a body could stretch skins acrost the front an' be right snug."

"I ain't aimin' fer you to make out in a shelter, Hannah."

She saw it was a matter of pride with him, and she said no more, agreeing, "Hit would be best, mebbe."

For herself, she'd rather he wouldn't lay aside the work he'd planned for the season, but a man's pride was something she understood, too. A good man, a proud one, didn't want his woman living in the open. So it would be, and she felt a warm, glad pride of her own that he should feel so.

They went on, eastward, down the creek to the corner, which was an ancient sycamore tree, came into woods and began climbing. "They's might near any kind of wood a body would ever have need of in these trees," Tice told her.

"I c'n see they is."

There were some she didn't know, and he told her their names. "That'n there is a coffee tree. That'n is a sourwood. The next one there is ironwood. An' that'n that looks a heap like a horse chestnut, hit ain't. Hit's a buckeye. Hit's soft an' easy whittled. I'll make us some bowls an' things outen it when I git the time."

She knew the others, ash, beech, oak, hickory, elm, walnut, locust and sugar trees. She eyed the latter. "We'd ort to slash them sugar trees next winter an' ketch the sap fer sugarin' off."

He nodded. "We will."

Through the woods they now went due west, following the ridge. Tice hurried them on without stopping to talk or to point things out. He seemed eager to get on, and Hannah knew why when they came, finally, to a cleared spot. Like a small boy he pulled up and grinned at her. "I been wantin' you to see this." He pointed southward and to the east. "Jist look at that!"

Hannah had not realized the ridge was so high. There was a vast reach of country spread before her. She could see valleys and meadows and tree-rimmed watercourses, and tumbling ever higher and higher beyond, hills and more hills. In the far blue distance they nudged up against the sky, massive and blocked, so that she knew truly she could see from here to the beginning of the mountains. The whole space was bright in the sun, except for the dark shade of cloud-dappled spots. "Ain't it purty?" she said finally. "I never knowed they was e'er place you could see so fur."

"You c'n see the furtherest from right here," Tice said, "of any place I've yit been in the country, though I ain't sayin' they ain't others. I've jist not seed 'em, if they is. I come up on this by accident when I was huntin' one time an' I made up my mind right then I'd lay off this piece fer mine. I jist takened a likin' to it, an' I thought I'd never see a sightlier piece of land. Right down there," he went on, pointing, "is where I was clearin' this mornin', an' the camp is in that clump of trees straight in front. That shelf is level an' it will make a good field fer oats or fer some more corn."

Hannah studied the woods below them and Tice pulled at his chin. "Now you've seed the lay of the land," he said finally, "savin' the west stretch where the corn is at, an' I c'n tell you it ain't as sightly up thataway, you got e'er notion where you'd wish the house raised?"

"Ain't you done got a place picked?" Hannah asked, surprised.

"No . . . not to say picked, I ain't. I had in mind some place handy to the cane an' the mill site an' the creek, though they's springs all over an' that don't rightly matter. You say where you'd ruther to have it."

Hannah measured with her eyes the distances, down the ridge to the shelf, beyond it down the slope to the meadow and across to the creek. She measured up toward the corn and down toward the cane and the mill site. "Whyn't we raise it about where you was girdlin' this mornin', then? Hit would be handy fer ever'thing, near as I c'n tell. The ridge, here, in back would break the cold an' the wind in the winter, an' the trees would make a good shade in the summer. Hit's raised up fur enough from the meadow if they's a tide an' the creek overflows we'd be out of the water, an' they's room all about fer barns an' cribs an' a garden patch. The only thing is, you aimed it fer fields."

"That don't matter. They's a plenty of room fer fields other places." Tice looked at her admiringly. "You got the levelest head on you, Hannah. You've done got it all planned out an' I don't know as anybody could of planned it better. Right there is where we'll build it. Sart'n we will!"

Pleased, but embarrassed by his approval, Hannah fidgeted and could find nothing to say.

"Let's go down an' pick out the place," Tice said, and he led off down the steep side of the ridge.

When they came to the shelf of level land they wandered about, seeking its widest and most open space. They finally decided upon a place almost directly above the creek crossing and their present camp. There were great oak and walnut trees towering overhead, but it was open in the front and free of undergrowth and brush. Tice squinted at the sun. "I reckon it's gittin' too late to do much today, but we c'n mark off the house." He collected stones to mark the corners and then stopped to consider. "Say we make it eight axe handles long," he stepped it off, roughly, "that ort to be about right fer the length." He made a pile of stones and again stood, thinking. "An' say we make it five axe handles wide." He stepped off the width and laid more stones to mark the second corner. "That about right, would you think?"

Hannah pondered, trying to see the size of the house inside. "Hit'll be plenty," she decided. Then she said, "Are you aimin' to commence buildin' it right now?"

"Sart'n I am. I done got the corn planted an' fur as I c'n see this is the best time to git at it. Of course," he admitted, "I'll have to stop to work out the corn a time or two, but mainly I c'n hold to it the rest of the summer. Ort to git it done afore cold weather sets in."

"I c'n help," Hannah said. "I c'n help in the corn an' with the house, too."

"I don't doubt it," he told her, "an' I'll be glad fer you to do so."

Hannah looked about her, up the side of the ridge at their back, down across the valley and to its farthest ends. "How much land you got, Tice?"

"Four hundred acres. That's what the law allows, *if* you was settled on it before the first of this year, an' *if* you raised a crop of corn an' made a improvement."

"You done so?"

Tice nodded and pointed. "I built that there lean-to last year, which passes fer a improvement, an' I raised a little dab of corn last year. What I'd like, though, is to try fer the extry thousand the law allows when the land commission gits around to seein' to it."

Hannah looked puzzled and he explained. "They give you the four hundred if you meet the law, but they'll sell you another thousand alongside of it, at the state price."

"How much is it?"

"Hit runs around forty shillin's a hundred."

"That's a heap of money. I reckon they'd take skins."

"Sart'n they will, or *nobody* would be able to buy."

"When you got to have it?"

"Don't nobody know yit. Ben Logan says they'll not git around to sendin' the commissioners afore another year, mebbe two."

Hannah sighed. "We got time, then."

Tice grinned at her. "I reckon you're aimin' to help git them skins, too."

Hannah refused to smile about it. "The best I kin," she said.

Tice's face sobered. "An' I make no doubts but what it'll be a sight more help than a man commonly gits." He hitched at his britches. "I d'know about you, but I'm gittin' hungry."

"I'm as empty as a bear at the end of winter," Hannah confessed.

"Let's go eat, then."

They went down the easy, gentle slope, across the meadow through rye grass and clover to their knees, back to the camp.

10

It took Tice all the next morning to build a sled for hauling rocks for the foundation of the house. He cut stout hickory saplings for the runners, peeled them and laid them butt end to the front. Then he whittled the end upward so the runners wouldn't gouge too badly into the earth when moving. He laid smaller hickory poles across for the body of the sled, notching the runners to hold them, and then he bound the poles in the notches with rawhide thongs. He also notched the underside of the runner so the thongs wouldn't drag on the ground. "There," he said, when he'd finished, "I reckon she'll do. We'll git up the rocks fer the corners first."

For two days they hauled rocks and then Tice set to work building his corners. "I wish," he grumbled, "I had me a chalk an' line. I'll likely git these corners so unlevel the floor'll swag."

"Hit wouldn't matter," Hannah assured him.

"Hit would to me. I like to do e'er thing I set my hand to as good as I kin."

Dissatisfied as he was with trusting his eye, he came up with a device that helped him. He took two green sticks, measured the distance he wanted the sills to lie from the ground on them, notched them, stuck them at two corners and stretched a thong between them. "There, now," he said, "that's about as true as could be got 'thout a chalk an' line."

Another day was spent thus, building the corners, but then they were ready to begin getting up their logs. They talked about it that night. "You ain't got two axe heads, have you?" Hannah asked.

"No, I ain't. But I could git another head over at Ben's. You aimin' to chop down trees, too, are you?" He laughed, teasingly.

"No," she said, spiritedly, "you c'n do that, but I don't see no good reason why I couldn't hew 'em out once you git 'em down."

"Nor do I." He turned serious. "How would it be if I took the day tomorrow an' taken Ben's horse back to him, got the rest of yore things, an' brung back a spare axe head?"

"Hit mought be the best."

While he was gone, Hannah spent the time making a handle for the axe, patiently whittling it out of a piece of straight-grained hickory. When he came home, Tice admired it at length. He held it out, tried it after she fitted the head into it, felt the heft of it and the curve of it and said, "I d'know as I ever seen a purtier one. Hit's better'n mine."

"I d'know as it is," Hannah demurred, "but I've made a sight of 'em in my time."

"I c'n see you have."

They got an early start the next morning, making their way up the slope to the house site before the mist had lifted from the valley. Shreds of it curled about their legs and the sun had not yet touched the far rim of the hills. It was cool in the morning air.

When they reached the place Tice stood looking at it, thinking, considering. "Oak fer the sills, I figure. Hit'll last to eternity. An' we'll make the walls of walnut. You're used to winders, too, ain't you?"

"I c'n do without."

"No need of it, though I don't know how *many* we c'n put in. Depends. How would you want the door placed, now?"

Hannah squinted, seeing the cabin already raised. "The door," she said, then, "had ort to be in the middle, I reckon, about here." She stepped it off.

Tice thought about it. "I d'know," he said, "as we'd ort to weaken that front wall with a winder *an'* a door." He walked all about the four corners. "That back side had best be left solid, too. To be safe from Indians."

She nodded, understanding. "An' the chimbley will take up the east wall."

"Yes. Well, one, looks like, is all we c'n put in."

"One," she said, "is a plenty."

Tice was reluctant to settle for one. He would have liked to give her anyway two windows. He walked again about the corners, pondering, then he shook his head. "I wish I could put you one in that back wall, but it would be too risky. A redskin could sneak down the ridge an' lay a shot through too slick there. I wouldn't feel easy in my mind with a winder to the back."

"I ain't wishin' fer it," she assured him. "One will let in a heap of light. I'll scrape a piece of bearskin real thin to stretch over it."

"An' I'll make some shutters, so's we c'n close it up at night an' when it's cold weather."

All about them were the trees they needed for the logs, tall, virgin growth, great in girth, but they took a time to chop down. In spite of Tice's teasing, it worked out that Hannah spelled him with the chopping. It went faster that way.

They chose trees which would hew out a log half an axe handle deep and a quarter wide. They figured they needed six such logs to a side. They worked alternately, and side by side, at felling trees and hewing logs. Tice often watched Hannah work, when he was taking time to get his breath. She had a shorter stroke than a man, but she was more precise. Where she wanted her axe to go, it went, and there was rarely any chopping over of misplaced licks.

When they had a log ready they left it lie until the end of the day, then they levered one end of it onto the sled, hitched up the horse and dragged it to the house site.

Slowly the pile of logs rose, but so slowly that it was the end of August before they had enough. "We could," Tice said then, "git the men out an' raise the walls now, or we could go on an' rive out the shingle boards an' then when we raise the walls have the roof ready an' move right on in."

"Whyn't we do that?" Hannah asked.

So they set, then, to the slow, tedious work of splitting out three-foot slabs of whiteoak for the roof. It took many a one to roof a house.

They lost time occasionally. Three times they had to stop and work the corn, and once they lost two days because the horse broke loose from its hopples and strayed. They had to hunt through the hills and up all the hollows for her, until finally they came up on her placidly grazing on the edge of a cane thicket. Tice was so put out he said he felt like shooting her. "That wouldn't mend nothin'," Hannah said. "She don't know no better than to stray when she's loose. Besides, what would we do without her?"

Tice looked at her, amused by her literalness. "Well, Hannah," he said, "I wasn't actually *aimin'* to shoot her. I jist said I felt like it."

"Oh."

Her patience was something he yet could not always understand. It seemed to be limitless, with the horse, with him, with the weather, with the contrary way of the tools they used. When it rained he felt frustrated because he could not carry out the day's plans. Hannah sat in the lean-to and set herself to whatever task needed doing. She began riving out the shingle boards on such a rainy day. When an axe handle broke, he fumed for a good ten minutes over the loss of time. She went directly to cut down a hickory sapling and started whittling out another. When the horse strayed, as now, he went after it, but impatiently. She trudged along taking it as part of the day's work. Rain came, axe handles broke, horses strayed. She took each thing as it came. She never faulted him or herself, the horse or the weather. "I d'know," she said, when he spoke of it to her, "as they's e'er thing to *do* but what's got to be done. No need of frashin' yerself."

"I'd bust if I didn't," he admitted.

"Well, go on an' frash yerself, then. I ain't wishin' fer you to bust."

The one thing she showed impatience for was having to be forted up. That came in September.

They had eaten their noon meal that day and were already back at work on the shingle boards when they both heard someone holler. The sound came from the gap in the hills across the creek. "That's Dave Cooper," Tice said, standing. The shavings from the boards fell in a heap around his feet.

"Now, what could he be wantin'?" Hannah asked.

David Cooper and his wife, Bethia, lived on the headwaters of the Green River, but she had seen him around the fort.

He had not yet come into sight through the gap, but Tice walked toward the creek. "Trouble," he said over his shoulder, "I'll bound you."

He waited at the crossing. When the horseman came into view around the last shoulder of the hill he raised an arm in greeting. Tice waved in reply. "Hit's Dave, all right."

Hannah went on shaving the board braced between her knees, but she felt uneasy. This was the first person who had come their way since they had left the fort in June. Tice was probably right, she thought. David Cooper was bringing news of trouble.

He splashed through the water and flung himself off his horse beside Tice. Hannah could tell the horse had been hard ridden. He was lathery with sweat and foam. Tice led him into the shade and tied him, stripping some weeds of their leaves as he did, rubbing at the horse's hide with them. What the two men said to each other immediately she didn't hear, for they spoke in a low tone, but Tice then turned and said, "She jist as well to know, too," and they came on to where she sat. "Howdy, Hannah," Dave said.

"Howdy," she answered, "git you a stool there, an' set."

David Cooper was as tall a man as Tice or Ben Logan and as broadly built, although he was much younger than either of them. Sometimes Hannah thought there were no short men in Kentucky. They seemed all cut of one piece, to the same height and width. She had seen few less than six feet tall.

"Dave says the Indians has tore loose up at Boonesburg," Tice told her, "an' Ben is sendin' out the word fer all to come into the fort."

Hannah curled a fine shaving back over her hand. "I allowed as much. When did you want to go?"

Tice looked at David and it was he who answered. "Ben said not to waste no time, but," he laughed, "I got to rest my horse a spell. I'm goin' on home, then, an' git Bethia an' the youngun an' take them in afore the night's over."

David's place was some ten miles from Tice's stand, but angled to the southwest so that it was only an equal distance from the fort. Still, that was twenty miles of riding that lay ahead of him. Tice whistled. "You'll have to make tracks, then."

"I got a horse c'n do it."

To keep his hands busy while they talked Tice picked up the shingle he had been working on, settled it between his knees and drew his knife along its grain. "What brung it on this time?"

David shrugged. "What *ever* brings it on? There's some," he said darkly, "thinks Dannel Boone brung it on."

Tice looked at him and lifted his eyebrows. "Now, that goes plumb foolish to me."

"I don't reckon you know the whole of it. You've heared he got away from the Shawnees an' come on home, haven't you?"

Tice nodded. "An' brung the word the Indians was aimin' to march on Boonesburg straight off. But they never."

"Well, they have now. The word is they's more than three hundred of 'em, with old Blackfish himself leadin' 'em. Blackfish is the one adopted Dannel whilst he was among 'em. An' they're sayin', the Indians are, that Dannel give 'em his word he would surrender up the fort when the time come."

Tice's face sobered. "I don't believe that. I don't believe fer one minnit that Dannel Boone would give up his own folks. Hit don't make sense to me."

"They's British with Blackfish this time," David went on, "an' some says that Rebecca's folks, some of 'em leastways, has Tory leanin's."

"So," Tice said, "so his woman's folks has Tory leanin's—that don't make a

Tory out of Dannel. Likely," he laughed, "if Dannel *did* give them Indians his word to surrender up the fort he was jist promisin' 'em e'er thing they wanted to git good terms fer them that was took captive along with him. That would be like him."

David nodded. "Hit would jist his way . . . or to give his word to git on the inside an' learn what they was aimin' to do. But the main thing now, is, they're in the country, the Shawnees, an' Ben says fer ever'body to git into the fort quick."

Hannah took a deep breath and looked at Tice. "I d'know," she said, "I d'know as I c'n *make* myself stay there. I hate so bad to be behind them walls."

"Don't nobody like it, Hannah. Hit ain't to the likin' of none, bein' crowded up so. But they ain't no way around it, as I c'n see."

"Where will you be at?"

Tice looked at David and David looked uncomfortably at the ground. "Well, it's this way, Hannah. Ben wants some of us to go up to Boonesburg to help out. Me an' Tice an' some others has been picked."

Her lips tightened. "I thought as much." She stood suddenly. "I'm a goin' with you."

"Now, Hannah," Tice said, "you cain't do that. Hit's no place fer a woman."

"They's women inside the walls at Boonesburg, ain't they?" she said fiercely.

"They're done there. They won't be havin' to go sneakin' in, takin' the risks. They're inside the walls already. Now, you mind, Hannah, an' go on to the fort like Ben has said."

Her shoulders drooped. She turned slowly and looked across the meadow toward the shelf where they were going to raise their house. There would be a child in the spring, she knew now, though she hadn't named it to Tice yet. A woman didn't—it wouldn't be right to speak of such. He would know, though, when it began to tell on her. Maybe, she thought, he was right, maybe she ought to go on into the fort, though for different reasons than his. Maybe she oughtn't to take unnecessary risks with the child coming on. Sadly she looked up at the shelf of land where the stack of logs showed so proudly. In another week Tice would have gone after the men to raise the house. She sighed and put the thought of it aside. It had to wait, and that was all there was to it. "All right," she said, then, "I'll git the things ready."

What she felt while he was at Boonesburg, and all the rest of the country had given the fort up as lost, she never told him, but Tice figured he knew for he had to search her out when he got back. She'd been afraid to look on him, returning with the others, in front of other people and had run off and hidden in Ann Logan's loft room. He knew her well enough by now to know that had meant she didn't trust her own feelings. When she was strongly moved she had a tendency to hide away.

It would have made any woman fearful, though, getting the word that her own man had been taken captive. It had been the fault of William Patton, who lived at Boone's fort. He'd been out hunting when the Indians had attacked and was cut off. He'd climbed a tree and watched for a while and then he'd been certain the fort had surrendered, and he had made haste to Logan's with the news.

They never had thought of surrendering at Boone's. There were three hundred of the Indians, all right, and they were led by Blackfish as the talk had said . . . by Blackfish and a French-Canadian fellow by the name of De-Quindre. At first they'd dickered and parleyed but that was just to make time. They never meant to surrender. Then the Indians had attacked, and the siege had held on ten days, but they'd beat them off in the end.

Back home again Tice told Hannah how it had been. "The Indians sent word when they first got there they wanted to see Dannel—said he'd promised to hand over the fort when they come, an' now they'd come an' they was ready to take over. Hit made a body feel the quarest, I c'n tell you, an' they was a plenty ready to believe Dannel had meant it. Colonel Callaway come near foamin' at the mouth he was so mad. He sent back word to 'em, 'As long,' he said, 'as long as I'm the commander of this fort there'll be no talk of surrender, no matter what Daniel Boone has promised.'

"Then they asked fer a parley outside the gates. The colonel didn't want to parley with 'em, but Dannel talked him into it, an' *it* went off quare. At the end, when they'd got done talkin', the Indians said all the white men should shake hands with 'em. Well, they shook, then the Indians said they should shake *both* hands. Colonel Callaway figured that was jist a way to git their hands tied up to take 'em prisoner, so he jerked loose an' yelled at the others, an' they all commenced runnin' towards the gate. An' me an' the ones guardin' cut loose shootin' an' all hell broke loose. Then they laid siege to the fort an' tried to mine under the walls an' it was nip an' tuck there fer a right smart spell."

"What you reckon is the straight of Dannel a promisin' 'em to give up the fort?"

Tice shrugged. "Why, he done so. He don't deny it. Says he was jist playin' their own game with 'em. He'll tell it all at the court-martial, I reckon."

"The way folks feels," Hannah said, "he'd better tell it good."

Tice nodded. "I know it. Ben don't more'n halfway believe in him no longer. I never thought the day would come when Dannel Boone would have to answer to court-martial charges, but Colonel Callaway said he'd charge him, an' he has done so."

"When is the trial?"

"Next month . . . at Logan's."

"Will you have to go in to testify?"

"Well, I don't to say *have* to, but I'd not want to miss it. Dannel ort to know who his friends is."

"Yes." Hannah sighed. "I c'n see how you'd want to be there, an' ort to. Mebbe we c'n git the house raised first, though."

"I'd thought to," Tice told her.

It was a proud thing, the house-raising, though there was little ceremony to it. The men came, some twenty of them, from the fort and in one day they lifted all the logs into place. It was a wonder to see how they paired off, teamed up, and worked together so fast. Four men to a log they lifted, and two at each end making the chips fly as they notched. It looked easy the way they did it, but Hannah knew the weight of those logs and the nice touch it needed to notch just right so they would lie straight and level. They were master hands at it, she had to admit.

Tice had gone out several days in a row before the men were due to come and had brought in plenty of game for her to cook. There was deer meat, which was common, and buffalo hump and liver, which were not. The men ate heartily and praised Hannah's hand with meat. Tice glowed with pride in her. They drank heartily, too, of the rum Tice had provided. Men, Hannah thought, watching them, seemed to work better when a little wet.

Only one woman had come—Jane Manifee. Hannah wasn't surprised to see her. Jane was a stringy, gaunt woman who paid little attention to the conventions, going where she pleased with her husband, William, doing pretty much as she pleased. She had a raucous, hoarse voice which she never took the trouble to lower pleasantly. But Hannah liked her and felt at ease with her. "I warn't aimin' to miss it," she told Hannah. "The rest c'n stay shut up in that fort if they want to, like skeered chickens, but I git so all-fired tard of it myself I jist got to git out, times, redskins or no."

"When you think you'll git out fer good?" Hannah asked her.

"Not till spring, I reckon. If," she added wryly, "I live till then. William ain't the hand to stay with a piece of work the way yore man is. We could of been out now, like you'uns, if he'd stay with it. But he's allus got to go off in the woods, or traipse backards an' forrards any place but his own."

Hannah murmured sympathetically. Tice *was* a good hand to stay with a piece of work, but she couldn't admit it in the face of William's delinquency. "Hit'll be right snug in the fort come winter, I'd think."

"I wouldn't keer," Jane said bitterly, "if icicles froze on my toes, could I jist git shut of it."

Hannah laughed. "I know jist how you feel."

Jane helped with the dinner and helped vocally with advice on the raising, keeping the men laughing good-naturedly at her rough remarks. When the last log was in place and they were ready to leave, Jane called Hannah aside and for once lowered her voice carefully. "When," she said, "are you expectin'?"

Startled, Hannah looked at her.

"Oh, I got eyes in my head," Jane said, laughing, poking Hannah's stomach with one finger, "you're done already carryin' a youngun."

Hannah twisted her apron in embarrassment. "In April," she said finally.

Jane cackled. "You shore never wasted no time, did you?" She looked over at Tice where he stood among the men. "Well, I allus did say Tice Fowler was right smart of a man an' the woman that got him, if one ever did, would find it out." She patted Hannah's arm. "You jist send him in to git me when the time comes. I've helped birth many a youngun an' if I do say so myself, I'm as good a hand at it as ever was. You jist send fer me."

"I'd be proud to," Hannah managed to say.

"An' I'll be proud to come. Jist send fer me, night or day. But you'd best not wait too long. They c'n surprise you, times, 'specially with the first 'un, comin' early."

"How long ahead would you say to send?"

Jane considered. "Three or four days, I'd say . . . or a week, mebbe. Well," she tied her bonnet strings, "jist go with me."

"Cain't," Hannah said, "you jist stay on."

"Don't think I wouldn't if I was situated so's I could. You take keer, now. Along at the last you make Tice do any heavy liftin's got to be done."

"I will."

She watched Jane mount her horse. She's a good woman, she thought, a real good woman, and she thought how lucky she was that Jane would be with her.

When they were alone Hannah and Tice hated to leave the house to go back down to the camp. They walked around and about it, admiring it, loving it, laying their hands on it. "Now, hit's a stout one, ain't it?" Tice said, over and over again.

And over and over again Hannah agreed with him. "Hit's stout, all right. I misdoubt a tremor of wind'll ever shake it."

"No, nor nothin' else."

The men had only raised the walls. There remained the roof pole and rafters to set in place, the roof to put on, the chinks between the logs to fill, the floor to lay, and as a final, crowning achievement, the chimney to build. "They's a plenty to be done yit," Tice admitted. "We ain't moved in by a long sight."

But Hannah would not have it that way. "We're jist as good as," she insisted. "If it comes on cold, early, we c'n let the floor an' the chimbley go."

"We could, but if you'll put up with the first few cold spells we c'n git it all done afore snow flies."

"I c'n put up with 'em," she promised.

Day after day they kept steadily working at it, and by the middle of October it was roofed, with the strong, sturdy, whiteoak shingle boards tied down with locust saplings laid across them and bound at the ends, it was floored and chinked, and all they lacked was the chimney. "What you say we move in," Tice asked. "I'm gittin' tard of traipsin' backards an' forrards from the camp."

"Hit suits me," Hannah said.

"We got to quit fer a spell now, anyways," Tice reminded her, "an' git in the corn, an' I got to go to Dannel's trial."

They moved in, having very little to move. It was bare and clean and sweet-smelling in the big room, vaulted overhead, for they still had to floor off the loft room. Tice laid their buffalo robes in one corner. "I aim," he said, "to make us a bed first off. I ain't wishin' to sleep on the floor no longer'n we have to, an' I aim," he continued, looking around, "to git us a table made soon as I kin. I don't like shiftless ways of doin' in a house. In a camp, now, a body has got to make out. But when folks live in a house, they'd ort to act like it an' git things to *do* with."

Hannah set her spinning wheel in another corner, and Tice, seeing her hands linger over it lovingly made another promise. "I'll git you some sheep, too, soon. I c'n trade work fer a couple of yoes from Billy Whitley any time I c'n spare a few days. He's got a right smart flock."

"I'd like it," Hannah admitted. "They's nothin' I like better'n workin' with wool." She was wishing they could have got the sheep in time for her to have yarn to knit a coverlid for the baby, and some hosen, maybe. But no matter. There were some old linen shirts of Tice's she could use, and she could ravel out a pair or two of stockings that had been Samuel's. She had them stowed in the bundle, now, with her own things. They would do.

She set out her pewter spoons on the floor near where the hearth hole was, her iron pots and the buckeye bowls Tice had made. He laughed. "Kind of skeerce, ain't we, of housekeepin' things."

"We'll not be," she said stoutly. "We'll git what we need."

"In time, yes—we will."

"I ain't the least afeared but what we will. You've done good, Tice." That was as near as she could come to telling him what it meant to her, having her own house again, the promise of her own things about her. You done good— it was the highest praise she knew. It was always the sufficient phrase in their language. Tice took it so and smiled at her. "I done the best I could, an' you helped. We done it together."

11

HE TRIED to persuade her to go to the fort with him for Daniel Boone's trial. "Hit'll take several days," he told her, "an' I cain't hardly make it back home ever' night."

"You needn't to," she assured him. "I'll make out jist fine."

"I d'know." He was worried about her staying alone.

"Well, I ain't a goin'," she told him flatly, "not if the whole Shawnee tribe comes down on me."

"I ain't afeared of the whole Shawnee tribe a comin' down on you," he said tartly, "but one, sneakin' up, jist out a plunderin', would be enough."

"I c'n shoot," she reminded him.

"I know you kin. *If* you got the time to shoot. You ain't ever had any dealin's with Indians, Hannah. You got to watch *all* the time."

"I'll watch."

"An' e'er time you step out of the house fer whatever, big or little, take yore gun with you, an' see to it it's ready to fire."

"I'll do it."

Very nearly he didn't go, knowing her ignorance of Indian ways, but the pull of Dannel in trouble was too strong, and Hannah was, after all, a clever woman. He wouldn't put it past her to be able to bluff out one or two redskins. Besides, since the siege at Boonesburg, nobody had seen any Indian sign and it wasn't likely there were any lurking about, with winter so close at hand. And, finally, Hannah urged him to go. "Hit wouldn't be right," she told him, "fer you not to."

So in the end he saddled up and rode off. "I'll be back soon as I kin."

"Jist stay on till it's over."

He nodded. "But I'll come on quick as I kin."

She missed him. She wouldn't have thought how much you could miss a person you were used to having about. The bed, which was just a post nailed to the floor with poles going at right angles to niches in the logs and thongs stretched across to hold their bedding, seemed big and lonesome. She wondered that in the beginning, when they'd first got married, one of the worst things to get used to had been the feeling of him crowding her, lying beside her. Now she didn't know what to do with a whole bed to herself. Whichever way she turned there was too much room, and she got cold at night without him there against her back.

She found herself listening, too, for the sound of him working somewhere about the place—the ring of his axe, or the hammer of his maul, or his voice lifted to the horse. And at mealtimes she wasn't as hungry as common. A woman, eating alone, needed very little food, she learned. It took a man to cook for before food became very important.

She kept busy, though. The first day she made a corn-shuck mattress for their bed. She took several skins and turned the hair side in, stitched them together and stuffed them with the fresh, clean-smelling dried shucks. It pleased her when she had finished and made up the bed with it. A bed of skins did fine on the ground, did the best of all for that matter, but in a house, on a real bed, you needed a real mattress under you. When she changed the shucks there should be, she thought, enough straw for stuffing. Straw laid better than shucks, she'd always thought.

Then, they'd talked of a fence for what was going to be the barn lot, so when she'd finished the bed tick she worked at splitting out rails. At night, as long as she could see, she whittled on more buckeye dishes—platters, spoons, bowls, and she even attempted a tankard, though it turned out lopsided. She set it on the ground before her and laughed to see the way it tilted. "I reckon Tice will have to make the noggins," she said to it. "*You,*" giving it a push with her finger, which set it to rocking, "ain't fit fer nothin'."

Faithfully she kept the gun beside her all the time, but she had no need of it. She neither saw nor heard anything to alarm her.

On the fifth day Tice came home, walking beside the heavily laden horse, driving two ewes before him. He was weary to the point of illness and so disgusted with the sheep that he turned them over to her and said he hoped to never have to look at them again. "For downright dumb, foolish animals," he said, "I don't believe you could beat sheep, an' them two," pointing, "are the foolishest of all. You think they would *ever* stay on the trail, or move of their own notion? No! I thought to drive 'em home, but mostly I've drug 'em. I wish you well of 'em, Hannah. Fer my part I'd jist as leave never lay eyes on 'em again."

Hannah was overjoyed, but she had to laugh at the picture he drew. "They are contrary critters," she admitted. "You ort to waited till I was along to help."

"Well," he said acidly, "I done the best I could to git you to go."

She knew he was tired and put out with the sheep, but she was stung by the blame in his voice. "If you'd said," she told him, "you was aimin' on gittin' a pair of yoes, I'd of went—but you never. All I thought was, you was goin' to Dannel's trial."

"I know it," he said, repentant. "But it come handy to git the yoes now, an' I jist brung 'em along. Billy said if I'd come over an' help him with his chimbley next spring he'd take it as pay, an' I could bring the sheep on now. I hope you know more about handlin' 'em than I do, though."

"I do," she said. "We had sheep at home. I know all about 'em."

"Well, that's a satisfaction. An'," he grinned, "I brung you somethin' else."

He took a lumpy sack off the horse and there was an indignant squawk from inside. "Chickens?" Hannah asked, not quite daring to believe.

"Ann Logan sent 'em to you."

He opened the sack and the chickens flew out in every direction, squawking and flailing the air with their wings. Tice made desperate lunges at them, but he only frightened them more, and with their high-pitched, cackling voices splitting the air, they skittered away. In exasperation he watched them. "Now, look at them fool things!"

"They'll not go fur," Hannah told him, laughing. "They'll cluster after a time an' find a tree to roost in. I never seen how many there was, though."

"I c'n tell you. They was four hens an' a rooster." Tice threw the sack on the ground. "A free gift she made you of 'em. Said her little 'uns done good this summer an' she was gittin' too many." He turned to the horse wearily. "Man an' boy, I ain't ever had sich a time in my life, what with chickens squawkin' their heads off all the way, an' me not knowin' but what they was smotherin' out on me, an' them hard-headed sheep havin' to be drug by their necks, I've put in a day. Help me unload, will you?"

Hannah tethered the sheep and went to help him. He had brought a sack of meal, a bar of lead, powder, an auger, a small anvil, some wheat flour and salt. At the last he drew out another small bag. "Jane Manifee sent you a punkin," he told her, handing it to her. "Said she allowed you mought be wishin' fer somethin' tasted different from meat 'fore the winter was out."

Jane was thinking about her appetite getting finicky, she knew,—the way, in her fix, it was supposed to, but she felt awkward taking the pumpkin from Tice. She glanced quickly down the front of her dress. She knew there was a slight swelling there already, but Tice had apparently never noticed it. She didn't know for sure whether he had or hadn't. This was new ground she was treading and she didn't know its ways. But Jane had remembered, and while she didn't feel any particular yearning for pumpkin right now, likely Jane knew best, and she'd be wishing for something different before long.

Tice hoppled the horse and turned it loose and they carried the loads into the house. "I reckon them sheep will have to have a shed," he said, sliding the sack of meal off his shoulders.

"They ort to, to winter well."

He nodded. "I been aimin' to throw up a kind of shelter fer the horse. Mought as well git at it."

When they had eaten he sat on the doorstep and watched Hannah feed the scraps of bread to the chickens. She called them in a high, shrill voice. "Here, diddle-diddle-diddle-diddle—oooooo-eeeeee. Here, diddle-diddle-diddle!" And they came flocking about her feet, pecking jerkily at the crumbs on the ground. "Ain't they purty?" she said, stooping over them, "ain't they the purtiest things?"

"I never thought so today," Tice said, laughing, "but now I've eat an' rested somewhat, I c'n see they're healthy stock."

"Are they layin', did she say?"

"Ever' one. She said they was all layin' good."

Hannah looked down at them dreamily. "I ain't tasted a egg in I don't know when. Jist think. We c'n have a fresh egg whenever we want."

"Hit'll go good," Tice admitted.

He made room for her on the doorstep beside him and laid his arm about her shoulder. "You're pleased with the chickens an' the yoes, ain't you?"

Hannah looked at the chickens, still pecking at crumbs, and beyond them at the sheep nibbling grass. "Yes," she said, "I'm pleased. We got property, now, Tice. We got land *an'* a house *an'* property."

"I know it," Tice sighed, "an' comin' along today I wouldn't of give two penny pieces fer the lot of 'em, I was so sick of 'em. But I reckon mainly I'm jist as proud as you are to be gittin' a good start." He stretched and yawned. "Lordy, but I'm glad to git back home."

She wanted to tell him she was glad to have him back home, but she couldn't find the words. How could you tell a man of the great emptiness when he wasn't there, and of its sudden filling when he came in sight, when he sat beside you on the doorstep and laid his arm about your shoulder? Where were the words to tell how it felt? Empty? What was empty but a word, and how much did it say of how it felt? Lonely? Lost? What did they mean? You could say the words, but you still couldn't tell the feeling, the queer, strange, wandery feeling inside, as if even your stomach had come unanchored. "I'll bound you are," she said, letting it go, helplessly.

A comfortable silence lay between them, and then she remembered the trial. "What about Dannel?" she asked, "did he come off all right?"

"Well, I swear if I'd not plumb fergot about Dannel!" Tice squared around on the doorstep to tell her. "He come off, all right. He beat ever' single count they had him charged with. The way of it was," he went on, "they had four charges against him. The first one was they claimed he surrendered the men who was with him, makin' salt you recollect, when they warn't no real reason fer doin' so."

"How come him to?"

"He said when the Indians surprised him out huntin', they told him they was marchin' on Boonesburg, goin' to lay siege to it, an' Dannel said he done some quick thinkin'. Said he knowed the shape the fort was in, an' as many of the Indians as they was, they could take it an' ever'body in it, easy. Said he made up his mind them women an' younguns warn't goin' to be took if he could help it, so he told the Indians the fort was real strong an' they wouldn't git nowhere by makin' an attack on it, but they was a party of men close by they could take an' go home with prisoners jist the same. He got their word they'd treat the men like prisoners of war an' not misharm 'em in any way, an' they'd be took to Detroit to the British so's they could be ransomed in time."

"Did they?"

"Yes. Warn't a man amongst 'em laid a hand to, savin' Dannel. He had to run the gauntlet. The rest was treated good an' took on to Detroit, except fer the ones made their escape. So that was how he come off the first charge. He had a good reason to give up the men makin' salt."

"What was the next one?"

"The second charge was that he promised the British in Detroit, an' the Indians, he would surrender Boonesburg an' all the folks would go over on the British side."

"An' he *did* promise sich?"

"He did, an' he said he'd do it again, give the same situation. Said you had to match wits with wits an' he would of made 'em e'er kind of promise they wanted so's to learn more about their plans. He aimed all along to git away hisself in time to give the warnin', an' he done so when the time come. Said he never thought nothin' of makin' sich a promise, an' never thought it would be mistook."

"An' he come off that one, too?"

"He won out on it. The third charge was that he'd took a bunch of men away from the fort over acrost the Ohio after he'd come back, *sayin'* he was goin' to search out the Indians, but *aimin'* to have the men out of the way when the Indians come, so's the fort would be weakened. That one was so plumb foolish that even the judges never paid much attention to it. Hit stood to reason when the Indians never come when he'd heared 'em say they was goin' to, he would git wearied an' want to find out what they was doin'. Sart'n he taken out a scoutin' party. Any man would of done so. Well, he beat that one, too.

"The last one, the last charge against him, was the one I seen with my own eyes—but I never doubted but what Dannel had his own reasons. The charge was that when the Indians finally come, he advised the men in the fort to meet with 'em, an' that he was connivin' with the Indians to capture 'em. Well, I was there, an' he *did* advise the men to meet an' talk with the Indians."

"What reason did he give?"

"Well, when Dannel first made his escape an' ever'body was worked up over a big attack, word was sent to the Virginny council fer help an' they ordered out some troops. They hadn't yit got here when the Indians showed up, but Dannel said the reason he wanted to parley was to make time fer them troops to git here. He said he had no idee it would end up the way it did. He was skeered the fort would fall if the Indians attacked afore the soldiers got there—an' it come close to it, I c'n tell you that. I don't never want to see a settlement come no closer. Well, that was the way of it. Hit taken 'em two days on that last charge, but in the end he beat it, too. He was cleared, in full, of all four charges."

"I am glad," Hannah said.

"I'm glad, too. Hit was a poor repayance of all he's done fer the country to court-martial him, an' they's a heap of us glad he come off."

"You believe all he said, Tice?"

"I believe ever' word of it. I don't misdoubt e'er thing he said. I know jist how he figured it, an' put in his shoes I'd of done jist like he done. Dealin' with them redcoats an' Indians you got to be jist as shrewd an' clever as they are. But they's some," he said, "that never believed him, an' never will, an' till the end of their days they'll believe Dannel Boone was a traitor to his country. Colonel Callaway is one, an' I ain't too sart'n Ben ain't amongst 'em."

"You wouldn't hold it against Ben, would you?"

"No. I don't know as I would. A man has got to go accordin' to his lights. To my notion, Ben was wrong to side with Callaway. An' the reason he was wrong is because he is too all-fired strict an' religious minded. They ain't no gray to Ben. There is jist black an' white. Ben is a heap more liable to be just than he is to be merciful or understandin', an' he kin be awful harsh in his judgments. The trouble is, they *is* gray—a heap of times, an' you got to look at it real close up. Dannel hit a time like that. Ben, in his shoes, would of died 'fore he'd of give up the salt makers . . . an' likely Boonesburg would of fell. Dannel made a deal an' saved the fort. In my opinion, Dannel done right."

It was a long speech for Tice and he laughed when he had finished. "I'm gittin' as long-winded as a woman. You been all right, have you?"

"Yes." Hannah thought, then, to tell him of what she had been doing. "I made a shuck tick fer the bed."

"You got it done, did you? You been aimin' to a right smart time."

"The shucks had to dry out," she explained. "If they was the least bit green they'd sour."

"I'd think it."

She thought further about what she had accomplished. "I got fifty rails split out fer the fence."

"You never!"

"Yes. Chestnut, the way we said."

"Well, that was good, Hannah. In how many days, would you say?"

She considered. "Well, the first day you was gone I made the tick. Hit taken me longer than I'd thought on account of havin' to stitch the skins. I got at the splittin' early the second day, but I blunted the axe along about noon."

"Nicked it, did you?"

She nodded. "A purty good one, too. Taken me the afternoon to grind it out." She explained. "I was splittin' out a gnarly piece an' hit a knot a little on the slant. Seemed like the axe jist taken a kind of bounce, an' I knowed right straight I'd nicked it."

Tice thought about it. "I d'know as I ever had it to happen, in jist that way."

"I've not either, before. Hit may be I ortent to tried to split out sich a gnarly piece, but I've done so, many a time, an' no hurt done."

"No, I d'know as you ortent. If you give over *ever'* piece that's gnarly you'd come up short with rails. No, I'd say hit was jist overly tough-grained, an' mebbe the axe out of temper. I'll see to it. You got the nick out, though?"

"I got it out. I never had no more trouble. Say, three days an' a half I put in on the rails."

"You done good. Hit'd stretch me some to do better."

His praise pleased her, even though she knew he could have done much better. She had the strength to keep up with him splitting rails, but she worked more slowly. Still, fifty rails was a good start and she knew it. She relaxed beside him, content. Both of them had done well with the five days and neither of them could count the time lost.

Darkness was beginning to gather about them and in the clear, purpling sky the stars were starting to show. A slow chill seeped up from the valley and

Hannah rubbed her bare arms. Suddenly Tice took hold of her, roughly, and pulled her to her feet—stood grinning down at her. "I'd like to try that new shuck tick of your'n," he said, and he gave her a small shove through the door.

12

THE WINTER was a mild one. Some mornings there was frost, there were several snows, but they were not very deep and did not last long. Mostly, it rained a lot. Carrying her child Hannah felt a serenity in being house-bound which was unusual for her. It pleased her to sit by her hearth in the early darkness, hear the rain on the roof over her head, look out across the valley at the frost-crisped meadow, at the rain-swollen creek. She had a feeling of complacency rare with her.

They finished the chimney before Christmas, using the sled to haul up big, flat, slate-stone rocks from the creek bed for the hearth. They were water-smoothed, gray, satiny, and Tice dug out the ground to lay the foundation well. "If they ain't," he told Hannah, "laid below the frost line they'll split an' yaw in time."

Then they gathered smaller stones for the chimney piece itself. It took patience, they found, to build a chimney. The rocks needed to be of a certain thickness, and they were always having to find small ones to wedge under and in between to keep the chimney level. They plastered it with mud mixed with straw, for there was no clay on their land.

To them the chimney seemed to grow slowly, adding very little in height from day to day, but in all it only took them a month from the day they started until it was finished.

Tice hewed out a piece of walnut log for a mantel and drove pegs above it to hold their guns. On the mantel Hannah set out their wooden platters and noggins, proud that there was now a place to put them. When they built their first fire in it, Tice was mightily pleased that the fireplace drew so well. "There'll not," he told her, "be no smoke in yore house."

He hunted often that winter, eager to see the stack of skins accumulate in the loft room. "Hit'll take a heap," he said, "to git that extry thousand acres of land."

Hannah had planned to go with him. They could have acquired twice as many skins, and early in the winter she did go frequently. But after the turn of the year she noticed that she tired more easily, was short of breath, couldn't last on the trail with him. It was her legs and back that gave out on her, and she thought she would only hinder him, so she took to staying at home. She never said why, beyond giving the excuse of work of her own to do. He never questioned it, and she thought, then, he knew.

She wasn't certain, however, until he brought in a length of walnut log and began carving it out. He had first burned the heart out of it to make it easier to whittle. He made no explanation of what he was doing, and she didn't ask, and at first she had no idea what he had in mind. They had made a cupboard already, in the evenings, and she supposed he meant it to be another piece of furniture.

As he worked on it, however, steadily each night, and it took on shape, she saw it was a cradle. She was glad he knew, but still she would not speak of it before him. She did, however, openly ravel out some of Samuel's stockings, and with needles she whittled down very fine and then rubbed to smoothness, begin knitting the baby's hosen.

One night Tice looked up from his own work, caught the quick movement of her hands with the yarn, watched for a long time. She was aware of his look but kept on with the knitting. "I don't see," he said finally, "how it could be you manage four of them needles all at the same time. Looks to me you'd git 'em all tangled up."

"You don't use but two at a time," she explained, holding up the small stocking. "Them other two jist holds the yarn."

Tice looked at the stocking. "Ain't that awful little?"

"Well," she said, owning it for the first time, "a baby ain't very big on the start. Leastways, none I ever seen was."

"No," he said, turning back to his work, "I reckon not."

There, she thought. It's been said and owned. She wished, though, she knew if he was glad. You could, she told herself, take it he was, on account of him making the cradle. But then, you could take it he was just being forehanded, as was common with him.

He smoothed and shaved on the wood, the thin, fine strips curling back from his knife. "I ain't ever seed a little, small youngun, though. Not up close, nor I ain't ever helt one."

"You ain't?"

"Have you?"

"Once I did. Was a woman lived in the village close to home I used to visit when Pa would take me along with him to trade. She had a little youngun an' I was there jist after. Hit warn't but four days old. I helt it. But I've seed many a one . . . when they got up big enough to be took out."

"Well, I've seed them, too. Ain't no way you could keep from seein' them. But I d'know as ever in my time I've seed one jist birthed. Ain't you skeered a little, Hannah?"

She thought about it. "No. Not skeered, to say. I d'know as they's e'er thing to be skeered of. Younguns git birthed all the time, an' mostly it comes off all right. Jane Manifee," she told him, "said she'd come do fer me."

"Well," he said, letting out his breath, "I am proud to hear that! I didn't know but you was expectin' me to take keer of it an' I been studyin' whe'er I could or not. With a cow, now, or a mare, I'd make out all right, but I didn't put much confidence in doin' fer you."

She laughed. "Hit wouldn't be much different than you're used to in my opinion. You'd of done good. But Jane made the offer, an' I wouldn't want to hurt her feelin's."

"Nor me." He whittled in silence for a time. "I reckon that was at the house-raisin', was it?"

"That's when it was."

"She knows how to go about it, does she?"

"She said so, an' I'd think it. Jane ain't one to brag."

"No. She ain't give to braggin', you c'n say that for her. Likely she knows all right."

"That's what she said. Said she'd helped with many a one an' said she was real handy at it."

Tice nodded. "You c'n put yer dependence in her, then."

"I figure it."

He rested his hands on the cradle and obliquely went about learning when she expected the baby. "I d'know whe'er I'll git this done in time or not."

"You'll git it done," Hannah laughed. Then boldly she told him. "Hit won't be till April . . . the middle part, as I make it."

He grinned back at her, the bars of talk all down now. "I've knowed," he said, "fer a time an' a time, though you've thought to fool me."

She denied it instantly. "I warn't tryin' to fool you. I jist thought you had eyes an' could see fer yerself in time."

"You know when I first knew? Hit was when Jane sent you that punkin, back in October. That went the quarest to me, her sendin' you a punkin that way an' sayin' you was likely to want somethin' different to eat afore the winter was out. I got to studyin' on it an' I recollected I'd allus heared a woman carryin' a youngun had a finicky appetite, an' I made sart'n right then that was it."

"I didn't know but you did."

"You've not ever cooked it, though."

"No. I git tard of meat so steady, but I'd do that anyhow. A body does. But what I've wished for ain't been punkin. I've wished, some, fer dried beans an' some potatoes."

"Well," Tice said, "I don't know as they's a potato in the whole of Kentucky right now. I'd git some fer you if they was, but I don't know of any."

"Hit's no matter. I ain't sufferin' fer the want of 'em. They'd jist go good, is all."

"They would," he admitted. "I wouldn't keer a bit to have a mess right now." He whittled for a while in silence, then he said, "You'll not come to no harm, I reckon—not gittin' what you've a likin' to eat."

"I don't think it. I've not ever heared of sich, leastways."

"No. I've not either."

She thought she might now ask him if he was pleased, but not actually outright. She cleared her throat. "A youngun," she said, "will be a heap of company."

"Yes. Hit'll be that all right. But trouble, too."

"I'll not let it be no trouble to *you*," she said, hastily.

"I warn't thinkin' of myself. I'll be proud. But you'll have the tendin' of it."

She relaxed, a happy feeling surging up in her. He'd said he would be proud. "I'll not mind the tendin'," she assured him.

"Well, then, I d'know as they's e'er thing to weary about."

"No."

He rubbed the side of the cradle with his hand. "He'll sleep good in this, you think?"

"I'd think he would."

Tice took up his knife again, then laid it down to confess, "I ain't to say *used* to the idee yit, myself. Havin' a youngun of my own, I mean. I've thought on it a heap, how it'll be, but somehow I cain't git it straight in my head it's goin' to happen."

"Hit's goin' to happen, all right," Hannah said, smiling. "Ain't nothin' more sart'n in this world than a youngun bein' birthed, once it gits started."

"No. But you take a man . . . say, a man like me, never thought much on bein' married, to say nothin' of havin' younguns, an' it goes quare. Times," he went on to say, "hit's hard fer me to keep in mind I'm wedded. I ain't actually to say used to that, yet."

Hannah felt a pang of dismay. Her hands stilled and she looked at him. "You ain't sorry, are you?"

"No," he said, shaking his head emphatically, "no, I ain't sorry. I never meant that. Hit was the best thing ever happened to me. But . . . well, this is the way of it. I'm forty year old, or will be come June. I ain't to say had a place to call home since I was jist a tyke. Jist allus rambled around an' took to the woods, mostly. Never, to say, felt I wanted one. You c'n see, cain't you," he looked at her anxiously, "how it would take some gittin' used to, havin' a house-place of my own, an' a woman . . . an' now my own youngun. No, I ain't sorry, but it jist don't somehow seem real, times. I git the feelin' hit'll all drift away, the way a cloud does in the sky, an' I'll wake up out in the woods some place, jist dreamt it all."

Relieved, Hannah laughed. "You'll not. They ain't nothin' realer than me, nor this youngun when it gits here."

He laughed, too. "Well mostly I *know* you're real enough. An' I reckon in time the youngun will be, too. I was jist sayin' how it was when I git to studyin' on it hard. Hit's like it was too good to be true."

He went back to his whittling and Hannah took up her knitting again. The silence between them was deeply peaceful. It was as near as he'd ever come to saying he loved her.

13

THEY RARELY SPOKE of the child after that, but the knowledge of it, open and owned now, was between them, and as Hannah grew heavier and more awkward with her tasks, Tice seemed always near at hand to help her. He never hovered over her, but he saw to it that water was kept in the house, that wood was kept stacked near the hearth, and he never went so far into the woods hunting that he could not return before dark. Hannah was aware of his protective helpfulness, and, womanlike, she took deep pleasure in it. She did not take advantage of it, but she used it when there was need.

She grieved yet over the slowness with which the piles of skins in the loft room were accumulating. "I'm afeared," she told Tice, "the land commissioners'll come an' you'll not have enough." She felt as if she and the child had put an obstruction in his way.

He turned it off lightly. "Ben says they'll not git here fer another year, yit. No need to weary yerself."

"But supposin' they do come?"

"Then I'd jist not git the land, Hannah."

Commonly she took things as they came, but commonly she had only small things to worry about. It didn't matter too much if you lost a day of work because of rain. The work would get done anyhow. There was so much of it that you could shift and turn any of it to suit your need or the weather. It all had to be done anyhow. But this thousand acres was so big a thing, so important, that it hung over her constantly until a day came when Tice spoke sharply to her. "Leave off wearyin' about it, Hannah. If I don't *never* have but four hundred acres of land, it's enough. I'd like the extry thousand, sart'n I would, an' I aim to try fer it. But if I cain't git it, I cain't, an' I ain't aimin' to lose no sleep over it. An' I wish to goodness you'd jist put it outen yer head. Hit bothers me to see you botherin' over it."

She quit talking about it then. She knew by the way he spoke that it *was* bothering him, and that knowing she was fretting only made it worse. The only way, she decided, she could be any help to him until after the baby was born was to keep quiet about it.

Spring came on, slowly, almost imperceptibly, the days gradually lengthening, and on a day early in April when the sarvis berries and the dogwood were white on the sides of the ridge back of the house, the sun warm and the air silky, Hannah sheared the sheep.

Tice helped by herding them into the shed room for her and holding them while she clipped off the wool. It was thick, heavily matted, and it came off in great folds under her hand. "Jist look at that," she said, clucking happily, "ain't that a sight, now?"

"Hit's a good yield, is it?" Tice asked.

"Real good. I d'know as I ever seen better."

It made her back ache, stooping over the sheep, but she stayed with it, taking pleasure in doing a good job of it, shearing close and never even nicking the hide. "Looks to me," Tice told her, "you'd be bound to bring the blood, times."

Hannah sniffed. "I'd be mortified to death if I done so. A good hand don't never."

When she had finished she heated water and had Tice to fill the watering trough in the barn lot for her. Then she made a rich lather with her soft lye soap and put the wool to soak clean.

"Hit's awful trashy lookin'," Tice said, watching her stir it in the water. "All them burrs an' stickers."

"They'll pick out," she told him. "When it gits clean I'll dry it in the sun an' then git the trash out. No need botherin' with it till then."

She battled the wool with a flat paddle and kept it stirring and moving constantly until it was white and fluffy looking. Then she rinsed it and spread it to dry on the rail fence. "Now I don't know," she said, looking at it spread before her, "if I ever seen purtier wool in my life. Hit's goin' to be a pleasure to work it into yarn."

"Hit ort to be," Tice said, chuckling, "hit's enough trouble to git."

"No more trouble than e'er other thing that's worth gittin'," she retorted tartly.

"Well, fer myself," he replied, "I could make out with buckskin an' never miss wool things."

"You'll think different when we got enough I c'n make you pants an' stockin's an' things. You won't never wish to wear buckskin no more. Hit's a sight the warmest, wool is."

"Hit likely is," he agreed readily, "but I still say that fer myself I wouldn't go to the bother."

"No," Hannah said shortly, "most men wouldn't. Hit takes a woman to go to trouble."

Tice grinned. It was maybe the fix Hannah was in that made her more outspoken these days, or maybe that she was just getting used to being married, but there were times when she reminded him of Jane Manifee. He didn't care, though. He liked a woman with spirit, and if he got the back side of her tongue occasionally, he could put up with it. He'd rather she'd be like that than mealy-mouthed and puling. She didn't nag, that was certain, but she knew how to take up for herself. He didn't know, come to think of it, if a body that didn't take up for theirselves was worth anybody else doing it for them.

It took her two days to pick over the wool and then she laid it away in the cupboard. "There, now. Hit'll be ready fer cardin' an' spinnin' when I git to it."

It took him by surprise when she turned around from the cupboard and told him, "You'd best go fer Jane purty soon."

He felt a queer clutch in his chest. "Now? Soon?"

"No . . . when you c'n git to it, the next day or two. Hit ain't quite time yit, but Jane said send 'fore they was any hurry."

"I c'n go today if you say so."

"No. Go on with yer work. You c'n mebbe git done layin' the barn roof first. How much longer you figure it'll take?"

He had built a barn since Christmas and it was finished all but the roof. "Not more'n another day or two."

"Git it done up, then."

"You feel all right? You're sart'n?"

"I'm sart'n. I've kept a tally of the time. An' I feel fine. You c'n do as I say."

But he was uneasy and he made haste with the barn roof . . . didn't overlay the shingle boards as trimly as he would have, maybe, didn't take the pleasure in the task he would have. He felt as if something was behind him all the time, hurrying him and cautioning him. And finally, on the third morning he gave it over. "I'm goin' fer Jane this day," he said, coming back to the house to make ready.

"You git done?"

"All but a little." Sheepishly he admitted he hadn't the heart for the job. "I'll feel better if Jane's here," he said.

Hannah laughed at him. "Well, go on, then, an' git her. But you needn't of. She'll jist be settin' here, waitin'."

"Well, I'll not be in sich a sweat, whe'er she's settin' or workin'. I'm uneasy in my mind."

When he had caught up the horse, though, saddled it and was ready to go he was reluctant to leave. "Supposin'," he said, "that youngun was to take a notion to git birthed while I'm gone, an' you here by yerself?"

"Hit'd jist take a notion an' git birthed is all. But it won't." Impatiently she added, "They's ways to tell, Tice. I'd know. Go on if you're goin', or unsaddle the horse if you're stayin'."

"I'm goin'. I got plenty of water up fer you, an' wood."

"I know you have. I'll make out all right."

"I'll be back with Jane quick as I kin."

She nodded, and watched him ride off, noticed how he turned several times to look back. She didn't know why he was so twitchy about this youngun coming. She herself was very calm about it, confident. It was just one more thing she had to do. She'd heard her share of talk about birthings, knew, more or less, what to expect. She'd helped the cows and ewes at home in the border country, and while she didn't like pain any more than anyone else, she knew it could be borne, a great deal of it, and she thought she could bear it. She had everything as ready as she could make it, and felt that she was ready herself.

Tice and Jane were back just after sundown and Jane crawled down off her horse grumbling. "Sich a haste," she told Hannah. "I'm jolted to my teeth! Nothin' to do but come lickety-split!" She eyed Hannah expertly. "An' no hurry at all, as I knowed well enough." She snorted, followed Hannah to the house. "But I never seed a man didn't lose his mind with his first youngun comin'. You're doin' all right, are you?"

"All right," Hannah said, "fur as I know." She walked across the room to set the pot of stew over the fire. "I got you a straw pallet ready in the loft room."

Jane nodded and watched Hannah bend and straighten. "You got yer head set on this'n bein' a boy? Or a girl?"

Hannah looked at her, surprised. "Why, I ain't done much thinkin' on it one way or the other. Hit wouldn't matter much to me, though I reckon Tice'd ruther it'd be a boy. He allus calls it a 'he.' "

"He's goin' to be disappointed, then," Jane said, drily, "fer you got a girl there or I'll miss my guess, an' I don't, commonly."

"Kin you tell?"

"Well, I kin. A girl carries middle-ways an' deep. A boy, now, will carry high an' show a heap more. You're carryin' awful deep. Not knowin', a body'd think you warn't come to time yit. That's a girl you got, jist as sart'n as my name is Jane Manifee."

Hannah studied the matter and found she had unconsciously thought of the baby as a boy all along herself. But she didn't for one moment doubt Jane's knowledge. A boy would have been nice, for a man always needed boys about a place to help, but if it was a girl then they'd just have to get used to the idea. Maybe the next one would be a boy. She didn't doubt there would be a next one, plenty of them for that matter. Most families ran to ten or twelve children, and she didn't know of any reason why theirs shouldn't. She was young enough, and while Tice was getting on, she'd never seen that age made much difference in a man. About the only time off from bearing a woman had was during the nursing of a youngun, for as soon as her health came back on her she was caught again. That was why most women let a youngun nurse till it was a good three years old or longer. But Hannah thought of a large family placidly. That was the way of it, was all. Easily, then, she adjusted to the idea of a girl, pushing into the future the boys that would come. She didn't, however, tell Tice.

Within two days Jane had learned Hannah's ways with the house and had taken hold as if she had always been there. But Tice felt like a sore thumb, in the way, awkward and unneeded. The two women were so completely at home with each other, had so much to say, so much to do together, that he felt like a stranger in his own house. He didn't know what was expected of him, and no one told him. He didn't dare go very far from the house for fear he might be needed, but as several days passed and there was no sign of need, he didn't know when ever in his life he had felt so useless. If he hung about the house Jane looked at him as if he were in the way, and if he went off some place she was sure to come to the door and bawl for him to bring more wood or water. At such a time as this, he decided, a man might just as well go stick his head in a hole.

But he yet had his place by Hannah's side at night, though he knew he would inevitably be routed out of that. Only then, when Jane climbed the ladder to the loft room, with the invariable instruction to Hannah to call her and not wait till morning if she needed her, did he feel like himself again. With Hannah warm, heavy, sleepy, beside him, things settled rightfully into place and he was Tice Fowler again, in his own house, beside his own woman. And she was his own woman, in spite of Jane Manifee ordering them both about. He recognized the prickle of jealousy and put it aside. It would all be over soon and Jane would be gone and they'd be alone again. It couldn't come too soon to suit him.

But when Hannah awakened him in the night, the sixth one after Jane had come, he found it had come, after all, too soon for him. He had to be nudged several times, for he'd been plowing all day and had gone to bed wearier than usual. He came awake slowly, hearing his name. "Tice . . . Tice, you awake yit?"

Hannah's elbow hit him sharply in the side. "You needn't to poke my ribs in," he complained, still half asleep.

"Git Jane," she told him, keeping her voice low.

He came wide awake then, fear rising in him. He stumbled out of bed in the dark and scrambled for his outer clothing. "I'll git her," he said, "jist in a minnit. Wait'll I git my britches on."

But the pants were strangely jumbled and he couldn't find but one leg hole. He hopped around, feeling for the other in the dark, his heart thumping like he'd been running for a long time. "Jist as soon as I git my pants on," he said again.

It was reassuring to hear Hannah laugh. "They ain't that much hurry. Take yer time an' make sart'n you *git* 'em on."

There was no need to call Jane, however. She must have been sleeping with one ear tuned downstairs, Tice thought, for almost as soon as he'd got his pants straightened out and pulled up she was yelling down the ladder, "You got yer clothes on yit, Tice?"

"Come on down," he said gruffly, lighting a candle and setting it on the table near the bed. He'd heard about all he wanted from Jane Manifee.

She came backing down the ladder, rump first, her spindly legs, bare and brown, showing to the knees. "Now, you git," she told him, passing him with a swirl of skirts.

He looked around in bewilderment. "Where'll I git?"

"Any place," she told him, waving her hands at him, "the barn, the yard, any place you take a notion fer. Jist git till I c'n see what's goin' on. But don't go fur, so's if I need you I c'n call."

He went outside and sat on the doorstep, pulling the big slab door shut behind him. There was a moon, well over in the west, and very pale. Wouldn't be more than a couple of hours till daylight, he figured. He sat on the doorstep awhile then he decided to go on up to the barn and sharpen the plow point. It had turned a mite heavy, seemed like, yesterday.

At the barn he set it gently to the grindstone. Hannah was a good hand to turn a stone—never too fast or too slow. Just right, and you never had to tell her. He winced at the thought of her now. Women did die in childbirth . . . it was a common thing, and whether they did or not, it must hurt terrible bad. He poured water on the stone and turned it slowly, held the point against it. A man didn't think where his pleasure led for a woman . . . never gave a thought beyond turning to her of a night. He let the wheel slow and stop, laid the plow point down, carefully, so as not to crack it. He couldn't keep his mind to it. Might ruin the point. Then he heard Jane calling and on the run he started for the house.

"No need to rush so," she told him, laughing, when he reached the door. "I jist wanted to tell you it'll be up in the day, likely. She's jist commenced. I'll fix you a bait an' you c'n go on about yer work till noon, anyways."

He wondered what work she meant. What work had he planned for this day, which already seemed long enough to have ended, and it not daylight yet? "C'n I come in, now?"

"Sart'n. Come on. Ain't nothin' to keep you from it as I c'n see."

He looked to find Hannah in the bed but she was up, laying the table, and she smiled at him. She didn't look any different from any other time to him. Jane busied herself at the hearth. He sat down at the table. Hannah suddenly stopped what she was doing, walked restlessly about the room, turning finally to the bed post, hanging on to it. Jane watched her. "Hurtin' purty good, is it?"

Hannah nodded.

"Well," Jane said cheerfully, "hit's got to git worse afore it c'n git better."

Tice, watching Hannah, fiddled with the bowls and spoons, making a clatter with them. Jane turned on him. "Quit that. You're makin' me twitchy."

He got up and flung himself toward the door. "I ain't hungry," he said, over his shoulder.

Jane stared at the door. "Now, what got into *him?*" Then she looked at Hannah and laughed. "Reckon I ortent to spoke so short to him, but I cain't abide folks twitchin' things."

Hannah came back to the table, pushing her hair back, took up her task again. "He's thataway when he's uneasy. The pains ain't real bad yit, I reckon, Jane."

Jane sniffed. "Bad enough, an' well do I know it." She dished up the food. "You want I sh'd call him to come eat now?"

Hannah shook her head. "He wouldn't."

"Well, you know him better'n I do. He'd ort to eat, I'd say."

"He will. When he gits ready, he will."

When there was light enough to see, Tice hitched the horse to the plow and went out to the field where he'd been working the day before. All morning he plowed, back and forth across the field, at each turning looking toward the

[112]

house. Not once did he catch sight of Jane, and as the time slowly passed his uneasiness grew heavier. Hannah had been hurting bad, he could tell. He didn't know how a body could stand that kind of hurting all this time. But, he told himself, if e'er thing had gone wrong Jane would have called him. It was likely just taking a time. He made himself keep at his plowing until hunger caught him and gave him the weak trembles. When he got the weak trembles like that he had to put something in his stomach. He unhitched the horse and led it to the barn, leaving the plow standing at the end of the furrow.

He opened the door gently, easily, and peered around it. Hannah was hanging to the edge of the table, Jane beside her, but he could see her face. It looked awful. It was flat and doughy looking, the color all drained out of it except for great purple circles under her eyes. Her hair was drawn tightly back from her forehead, wet from her sweat, which stood in beads around her eyes, collected and streamed down her face. Her eyes were closed, her teeth in her lower lip and her breath came in short, puffing pants with a kind of low, moaning sound. As he watched, Jane wiped her face gently and spoke to her. "Keep a walkin', Hannah. Keep movin', an' don't hold back from the hurtin'."

Like some wounded animal Hannah swung her head from side to side, but obediently she turned loose of the table and moved away. Tice thought he had never seen anything so cruel in his life. What was Jane thinking of, to make her keep walking that way. He strode across the room and jerked Jane's shoulder around. "Cain't you see you're a killin' her? Git her into the bed, quick!"

Jane looked at him in amazement, but she quickly recovered. "I know what I'm a doin', Tice Fowler! A woman don't have a youngun in the bed, you ort to know that! I got things ready, an' this youngun'll git birthed the easiest way on Hannah an' it, too, when the time comes." She motioned toward the opposite corner of the room, and, bewildered he saw a kind of pallet made of white cloths laid on the floor. "Why ain't the bed better'n that?" he asked.

"Because," Jane snapped at him, "hit's easier on her to kneel there, you dolt. Now, git on out of here. She's doin' all right. She's doin' fine, matter of fact. Git out. Hit ain't decent fer you to be here. Hit'll soon be over."

Tice's anger swelled inside him until he thought he would burst of it. "Why ain't it decent?" he stormed at Jane. "Why? Hit was decent enough fer me to git her in this fix, warn't it? Hit would of been decent enough if you hadn't come, wouldn't it, fer me to tend her? Besides, I ain't keerin' if it's decent or not. What's to say a man ortent to stay by when the time comes? I ain't leavin' her no more, Jane Manifee. You ain't tellin' me to git out no more."

Jane stared at him, then suddenly capitulated. "Come to think of it, I don't know of e'er good reason you ortent to. Jist a notion folks has got, I reckon. All right, then, walk with her an' let her hang on to you. Hit'll be a relief to me. I'm wore out."

He went to Hannah, put his arm around her. She had paid no attention to them, keeping on with her walking, keeping on with the hurting. He doubted if she ever knew he was there. He spoke to her. "Hannah, hit's me . . . Tice. I'm right here an' I ain't leavin' you no more. You hear me, do you, Hannah?"

She looked at him, and tears came into his eyes as he saw the effort she had to make to focus her own on him. "I ain't leavin' you again, Hannah," he promised.

It was another hour before the baby came, and at the last it was so terrible that Tice wondered there were so many babies in the world. There would never be any more of his, he vowed. Hannah would never have to go through this again! He said so, when Hannah was finally, blessedly, in the bed and at ease. Jane laughed at him. "You'll have her in the family way again 'fore this'n is walkin', likely."

She was busy with the baby, which was crying lustily. Tice collapsed on the side of the bed, weak, wet to the skin with sweat. He marveled that Hannah could raise her head and look toward Jane and the child. He wouldn't have thought she could so much as lift her little finger, but there she was, trying to see. "Was you right, Jane?"

"I was right. Hit's a sweet little gal baby."

Hannah laid her head back down and sighed, looked at him slumped there beside her. "Do you keer that it's a girl?" she asked. It was a miracle to him that color was beginning to show again in her face. She looked tired, worn out, but the drawn look was gone.

He looked around at Jane. She had the baby on her knees, doing things to it, wrapping it. "Keer?" he said. Then he started laughing. Never in his life had he heard such a foolish question. He passed his hand over his eyes. "Lord, I don't keer if it's even human!"

Hannah was shocked. "Why, Tice Fowler!"

"Well, I don't," he insisted. "I'm jist glad it's here an' over with."

Jane came up, then, with the baby. "Here she is," she said proudly, "jist as purty a youngun as ever I seen in my life. Ain't you, lovey?" She ducked her head at the baby. "Ain't you?"

She held the bundle out for them to see. Hannah raised herself on her elbow and Tice bent forward, dutifully. She was as tiny as a doll, he thought, but a lot uglier. She was red and she was wrinkled and she looked exactly like a little, small monkey he had seen one time on the coast. He was aghast and looked hastily at Hannah, wishing he could spare her this disappointment. After all that pain and all that effort, to get this! But her look was tender and fond and loving, and she made small dovelike sounds in her throat. "Oh, ain't she the sweetest thing, Tice? Ain't she jist the purtiest thing you ever seen?"

He looked at the baby again. He'd seen calves and foals a lot more promising, he thought, but if Hannah said it was pretty he'd better agree. Cautiously he said she was, but he ventured to ask, then, "Ain't she awful red an' wrinkled, like?"

Jane chuckled. "All new babies is red an' wrinkled. Hit wears off. Don't take 'em no time to git white an' commence fillin' out the wrinkles. What you got to go by now is the way she's built. She's strong an' she's healthy. Didn't you hear her cryin'? Never heared a huskier cry on a newborn youngun in my time, an' I've heared a plenty."

[114]

She put the child on the bed beside Hannah and Hannah laid the folds of the cloth wrappings back a little. "Jane, look! Ain't her hair red? Ain't it?"

Jane peered. "Upon my word an' honor, I b'lieve it is! Hit was wet an' I never noticed, but now it's commencin' to dry, I do believe you're right."

Tice grinned. The feeling of fatherhood was slow coming to him, but it was coming. "Jist like her pa," he said. "I had red hair when I was a youngun."

"Well," Jane said drily, "I hope her'n don't go the way yore's has went. A thin-haired woman ain't the sightliest thing God ever made."

Tice stood up and stretched. Jane's barbs had no power to touch him, now that everything was over. A sudden cramp caught him in the stomach. "By golly," he said, "I'm as hungry as a bear. I ain't had a bite to eat all day."

"Well, stir up a fire, then," Jane told him, "an' I'll fix us all somethin'. I reckon me an' Hannah could do with somethin' to eat ourselves."

14

IN ADDITION TO a pair of willing hands and a neighborly heart, Jane Manifee had brought with her news of the settlers in the fort. "They're all scatterin'," she said, "gittin' out on their own. Me an' William moved out last month."

"You like where yore place is at, Jane?" Hannah asked.

Jane shrugged. William had taken up a piece of land about halfway between Tice's stand and the fort. "I like well enough. But I'd like," she said strongly, "e'er place in the whole country, jist so it warn't behind them fences."

Jane mentioned others Hannah had not known very well who had left the fort that spring, too. "Ben Pettit has took his folks out to his stand, now, an' I reckon you recollect William Casey," she said to Tice.

Tice knew him well. He was a young fellow who had never married, either, and many a time Tice had hunted and roistered around with him. "Has he took up a place, too?"

Jane nodded. "On the Green. Not fur from David Cooper's place."

Tice grinned. "He'll need him a woman, soon, then."

"Well, the way folks is comin' into the country he c'n have his pick afore long."

"The more," Tice said, "comes in, the better off we'll be. When we git *enough* men, we c'n do what Ben Logan's allus hankerin' after doin'—make a invasion acrost the Ohio an' give the Shawnees a dose of what they been handin' out fer so long."

"They's talk of that, too," Jane said, "an' sooner than you'd think. The *talk* is, hit'll be this spring."

"No!" Tice was astonished. "I'd not of thought it."

Jane nodded vigorously. "Ben says they c'n muster two hundred men now, an' ain't no use of waitin'. An' that colonel of the militia—what's his name? The one that's over the whole county . . ."

"John Bowman."

"Well, he's ready to go, he says. Says soon as the weather is right he'll send out the call."

"An' high time, too," Tice said emphatically. "Ben Logan is right. Them Indians'll not stop their plunderin' an' thievin' till we cross over an' do some plunderin' an' thievin' of our own."

Hannah looked at him bleakly. "I reckon that means me an' the baby will have to go in to the fort."

"Hit does fer sart'n, an' I ain't wishin' to hear no argument about it."

"You goin'?" Hannah asked Jane.

"No, I ain't. I have seed the last of the inside of that stockade. I'd ruther to be skulped as to go back inside. But then," she added, "I ain't got no youngun to be thinkin' of."

Hannah looked down at the baby. She'd rather be skulped, too, but she couldn't possibly take any risks with the baby. "Well," she said, hopefully, "hit ain't happened yit. Mebbe we c'n git the corn in an' I c'n plant the rest of my garden."

"Likely you kin," Jane offered in comfort.

It was the end of May when the militia was called out, ordered to rendezvous at the mouth of the Licking, where it ran into the Ohio. Forty-seven men went from Logan's, Tice among them, and without argument, Hannah took small Jane (for they had named the baby after Jane Manifee) into the fort.

It was a quick, punitive expedition, its sharp thrust being rapidly made in four days. The objective was the Shawnee town of Chillicothe, then located on the Little Miami. Wherever it was situated, the Shawnees always gave their principal town the name of Chillicothe, Eternal Fire.

On the twenty-seventh of May, two hundred and ninety-six men rendezvoused on the south bank of the Ohio. Tice traveled with the rest of the Green River men with Ben Logan at their head. They traveled swiftly and were at the rendezvous point in good time. They made their own camp and while they visited among the other camps and gradually got the feeling of being part of a considerable army, they cooked and slept to themselves. "We'll not cross over," Ben reported to them, "till morning. We're goin' to leave the horses here," he added, "and a guard to see to 'em."

They started crossing before daybreak, but it was well up in the morning before the crossing was effected. The men rafted over and the horses that were going on were swum. Once over, they strung out in marching order, and for two days they traversed the beautiful Ohio country, following up the valley of the Little Miami. The men marched well enough in the unaccustomed formations, and there was little straggling. They looked at the rich, green country about them with curious eyes. "Hit's purty, ain't it?" Tice said to William Manifee who was alongside of him.

"Purty an' rich," William agreed, "but I'd be willin' fer them to keep it if they'd jist stay with it an' leave us alone."

"Me too."

They were alert all day, but they saw no Indians, nor any sign of them. When they stopped that evening, Colonel Bowman called a council of the officers, and returning to the men, Ben reported, "We'll eat and rest here a spell. We ain't more'n ten miles from the town, now. We'll go on, then, an' get in position before mornin'. From here on there'll be no talkin' an' no more noise than you got to make. Don't clink them guns around an' don't trip an' stumble if you can help it."

"That's a purty tall order, Ben," Tice said, "in the dark."

"I know it is, but Bowman don't want the town woken up. The advantage will be in surprising them. Just do the best you can."

A sense of excitement rippled through the men. It was evident in their haste with the meal, in their care in seeing to their guns, in their fidgetiness to get on with the march. They stepped out, when the word came down the line, keyed up and nervous, but more eager than fearful.

There was, in truth, remarkably little noise for so many men in movement on so dark a night. There were occasional small clinks when a knife hit against a gun stock, there was a kind of rustling sound which accompanied them constantly, the shuffling sound of many feet moving cautiously on the ground. There was an occasional whispered expletive, a sigh let out unevenly, or a grunt when a man stumbled, but in the main it was a very silent army.

From the stars, Tice judged it was about midnight when they stopped. Ben collected his men in a circle about him. "Colonel Bowman has called another council. You all stay here, right here where I can find you, till I come back. You can stretch out and take a little rest. Don't talk above a whisper."

Most of them were glad for the chance to lie down, but Tice rambled about restlessly. "I'd say," he told William, coming back, "this here is a kind of prairie. Hit's level all about, fur as I've been."

William was sleepy. "Hit mought be," he agreed. "What's the difference? Whyn't you lay down an' ketch you a nap?"

"I aim to."

He stretched out and closed his eyes, but he couldn't go to sleep. He kept thinking of what lay ahead of them. There were some, he thought, and it could well be him, who wouldn't be coming back this way after tomorrow. There were some who'd be staying—for an awfully long time. Well, he shrugged it off, that's the way it went in a battle. You couldn't fight Indians without some getting killed.

His thoughts drifted to Hannah and to the baby, and he grinned in the dark. Hannah was mortally having herself a bad time right now, he guessed, being forted up and hating it so terrible. She'd given in pretty easy this time, though. On account of the baby, he figured.

He thought how it was at home, just the three of them. He thought how Jane Manifee had been right, and the redness and the wrinkles which had bothered him when the baby was so new had changed as she fattened and thrived. He owned he'd not seen many younguns that had done any better. Hannah had more than enough milk, had enough for two for that matter. When small Jane would nurse, the milk would pour from the other breast until Hannah would have to sop it up with a cloth.

He remembered Hannah, and a clear picture of her came into his mind. He could see her going about the house, doing up the work. He could see her face, broad, strong, with its angular bone structure, and the clean, dark skin stretched tightly across. He could see the dark eyes which moved so roomy and free in their sockets . . . and the heavy black hair which she was forever brushing back from her face. It made him smile, remembering the gesture. Not quite a year they had been married, and it was a thing to wonder at yet, how known she had become to him, all her ways and all her looks.

He thought how he had married her, feeling such a pity for her, how she'd had to do the asking because he was so blind. If he'd had the sense God gives a goose she wouldn't have had to come asking. *He* would have been the one that did it. But all it was with him then was he'd admired her strength and courage, he'd liked her straight-out ways, and he'd felt a pity for her. It was sure certain different, now. He didn't feel all here, being away from her.

He thought how it was you learned so much about somebody when you lived with them, things they never even knew themselves, likely, and how it made them so much closer, like a youngun of your own flesh and blood— sweet, somehow, and kin. Like the way Hannah had of being shy and awkward before folks, sometimes even with him, and the way she had of wondering about things, like a youngun—asking questions, wanting to know. She stumped him, times, asking. And for all her bigness and smartness, she liked it best when he was some place handy. She never would say so . . . but when you got to know her you could tell the difference in the look on her face when she was contented and when she wasn't. She didn't know how her face changed when he came in and told her he had to go off somewhere. Not that she would ever say one word against it. She would get busy and fix him a bait to take, roll his other shirt into a bundle, get him ready to go, not even knowing that the shine of her eyes had dulled and a little line between them had puckered. It made him wish he never had to go.

She was like a youngun, too, wanting to sleep near enough to touch him in the night. If it wasn't more than a toe, she kept some part of herself touching him, and she likely didn't know it, but if he rolled away from her, she always followed along. He wished he was where he could touch her now.

He dozed a little, and the next thing he knew Ben was back and routing them all up on their feet, gathering them around him. "Now, listen good. This is the way of it. We're aimin' to bunch the whole outfit in three divisions. The town is close now. We'll angle off to the left here and get between the town and the river, and sprangle out around till we join the next division in back. William Harrod is the head of that one. He'll take a position like ours, only to the right. Bowman will stay with the other division and they'll move up straight ahead and stay to the south, the way we are now. We'll have a tight circle around the town that way. When we get in position just lay quiet till we get the signal. It'll come from Bowman. Then we open fire and move up on the town. You all understand that, now?"

It was simple enough, and the men murmured their understanding.

"See to your things then and get lined up."

Ben went up and down the line, whispering now and then, straightening them out, and finally they moved off, single file, treading very softly.

It seemed a long time to Tice that they were on the move, although it was actually little more than an hour before he could tell from the damp feel of the air that they were near water. Shortly afterward he could hear the sound of the river flowing. It was, he knew, shallow here, with a rocky bed. Otherwise it would have made no noise.

Someone, he didn't know who, moved back along the line then, stopping the men, locating each one, warning him again to keep quiet, not to fire, no matter what happened, till the signal was given. "Hit'll come down the line to you," the man told them.

Tice's position was among boulders and he judged he was very near the bank of the river, which probably was broken here by rocky cliffs. It likely, he thought, sheered off in back of him. He wouldn't want to have to do much retreating if that were so, he thought.

The last hour, just before daylight, was the longest. Lying still, tense, uncertain, he guessed that William was next to him, but there was no way of knowing how far away he was, now that they were in position. He judged they had been spaced pretty widely, for there was nothing to indicate the presence of another man on either side of him, no breathing, no rustling, no sound of any kind save the liquid rushing of the river behind. Even the leaves on the trees hung without motion, and it was too early for any stirring of birds or wild things.

As time passed, various things occurred to annoy and distract him. His nose itched, uncontrollably, and all the scratching he did didn't relieve it more than a few seconds at a time. One foot went to sleep and he had to rub it back to life. His legs cramped and he wanted to move around. Then the itch moved from his nose to his eyelids, which were heavy from lack of sleep. He began to feel entirely miserable, and gradually the silence all about him became a living thing, oppressive, heavy, a great physical force which pushed against his chest, weighing him down. He found himself feeling choked by it and straining for some kind of human sound to relieve its intensity. Just anything, he thought, to make him know he wasn't lying in the dark and quiet by himself.

It came, a smothered oath from the left, and he sighed with relief. William had been there beside him all the time. He risked a whisper, calling softly, "That you, William?"

"Hit's me." William's answer was soft, also, but it was nonetheless strong. "I'm a spraddle of a goddamned root-wad an' hit's about to split me to the gullet."

"Whyn't you move a little?"

"They ain't no place *to* move!"

"Come on over here. I'm amongst rocks, an' they's room a plenty."

William made no answer, but there was the sound of movement, very slight, very faint, and in a moment he was beside Tice. "I don't reckon," he said, "hit'll upset Colonel Bowman's plans any if I don't stick to that root-wad. One thing is sart'n, I'd be no good to him if I done so. I d'know as I c'n walk the way it is."

Tice chuckled. "We'd best keep quiet, William."

William snorted.

The sky gradually paled, so gradually that you could hardly tell it at first. It was more a lifting of the dark, so that there weren't so many stars, and then a light gray band showed in the east. When Tice looked down, he was surprised that he could see his gun in his hands, and he could see William sprawled beside him. "Hit's comin' day," he said. But William had gone to sleep.

Then Tice noticed he could see the Indian town below. It was sprawled somewhat, but it was remarkably well laid out. There were log houses, very like the ones they built themselves, and at the center of the town there was a large house which he judged must be the council house. The whole village lay as still as death in the early dawn, nothing at all stirring. But even as he thought how quiet and lifeless it looked, a howling and yowling set up among the dogs of the village, a bedlam of yelping and barking. That's ripped it, he thought, somethin's set them dogs off.

William came instantly awake, clutched his gun, blinked. "Is it time?"

"The signal ain't come yit, but them dogs has seed or smelt somethin'," Tice told him.

William studied the scene below. "I'll bound they'll be no waitin' fer a signal, now. If them dogs don't bring ever' Indian in the town out to see what's goin' on, hit'll astonish me. There, there's one now!" He pointed.

An Indian had come out of a house near the lower end of the town, yawning, scratching himself and spitting. They could not hear him, because the dogs were making too much noise, but they could see him plainly. They saw him stoop, pick up a stick and throw it among the dogs, then stop, look around, listen. Then they saw him turn sharply and run back into the house, come back outside in seconds with his gun.

A shot rang out from across the village. The Indian howled, spun around and dropped, and then Indians began pouring out of the houses on all sides, running like stirred ants in every direction, howling, screeching, yelling. A consolidated fire opened on them from Harrod's men across the way and Tice raised his gun and sighted. "I d'know about you, William, but I ain't waitin' no longer."

He fired, and then William's gun went off. Both reloaded rapidly. "Git yore'n?" William asked.

Tice nodded. "Seed him drop."

"I missed."

"You won't next time."

All down the line, now, on their own side, the firing was taken up and Tice and William set themselves to aiming, firing, reloading, steadily. "They're millin' about down there so bad," William complained, "hit's hard to git a good shot."

"You couldn't hardly expect 'em to stand still an' let you take a good aim at 'em, could you?"

"No," William grinned, "but it'd help."

The confusion in the village was great. Fire was pouring in from all sides, now, and the Indians were yelling, firing wildly back in all directions, milling helplessly about, and the dogs were still howling. The noise was terrific, and slowly the smoke from their guns rose above the lines of the Kentuckians, drifted lazily and then settled back down, making it even more difficult to see what they were doing.

[121]

Then someone among the Indians, some chief or other, Tice guessed, took over and started herding them into the big house in the middle, and at about the same time the order came down the line to charge. Tice scrambled around a boulder and ran forward, seeing the line form on both sides of him. Out of the corner of his eye he saw that William hadn't budged. "Come on, William. The order has come to charge."

"Well, go on an' charge then. I ain't a goin' to. I'm stayin' right here behind this rock. Them Indians is goin' to commence givin' us a right smart fire when they git in that house an' I ain't keerin' to be in the line of it."

Tice wavered uncertainly. There wasn't much doubt the Indians could do a lot of damage when they got inside that house and were protected. It would be the reversal of their own sieges against the settlers' forts, and Tice knew from experience the deadliness of close fire from protected quarters. But Ben had told them to mind the orders, and he'd be mighty put out if they didn't. It could be, he reasoned, going hesitantly forward, that they had a plan they'd not told the men. It could be they intended to take the log house and take the Indians with it. He didn't know. But, Ben had put his dependence in them and they oughtn't to fail him. He made up his mind. William could stay behind if he liked, but he'd have to charge with the rest of them. He ran ahead, catching up the line.

When they came to the edge of the woods, however, the order came to halt. Tice ducked behind a tree. Some of Harrod's men were already in the town, setting fire to the cabins and plundering. A howl went up from Logan's men. "They're gittin' it all! Harrod's men is gittin' the best of the plunder!"

Ben was among them instantly. "Nobody will get the best of it. It's all to be pooled and auctioned. You'll get your share. Now—Tice, David, Billy," he named them off and a dozen others, "come with me. We got to work fast. Take logs and tie them together."

Tice looked at him in amazement, wondering if Ben had lost his mind completely, but Ben motioned to him. "Hurry up, Tice. We got no time to lose."

Ben pitched in and helped himself. "There's no need riskin' ourselves in the open. We'll make a breastwork and move it along with us. I'm aimin' to get right up to that council house, set it afire and smoke 'em out."

Rapidly they constructed the breastwork of young saplings, braced it and shoved it out in the open ahead of them. "Now!" Ben yelled, "bunch behind it, boys, and shove!"

Seeing what he meant, finally, they grouped and began shoving. The breastwork slid along, not easily, but with their strength behind it, not too difficultly, either. They moved into the town, past the burning cabins and onto the central street of the village. Slowly, but safely, they edged on. As they passed houses that had not yet been set afire they stopped to apply the torch. Gleefully Tice did his part. He felt exuberant, like a youngun let loose to do all the damage he could. Before long the entire village, with the exception of the council house, was in flames, and the smoke billowed around the men and set most of them to choking and gasping.

[122]

When William joined them, Tice didn't know, but suddenly he was there beside him. "You decided to risk yer skin, did you?" he said, laughing.

"I never knowed you was aimin' to charge in back of a pile of logs," William said. "Jist as good as rock, to my notion."

They never reached the council house, however. They had very nearly covered the distance when a messenger ran up to Ben Logan and told him, "Colonel Bowman says to retreat."

"Retreat!"

The men heard Ben's yell and stopped shoving, looking at him. His face showed his consternation. The messenger nodded. "He says the order is to retreat."

"But, why? We've just got in position to do some harm! Does he know that?"

"He c'n see what you're doin', if that's what you mean. But he said to retreat."

In disgust Ben Logan gave the order, and slowly the men fell back, inching their breastwork back with them.

Ben was so angered, so put out with the order, that he forgot and argued with the colonel in front of them all when they reached the woods. "I can't believe you mean that order!"

Colonel Bowman was a massive man, weighing, Tice judged, near three hundred pounds, and commonly when he talked he bellowed, but when he answered Ben Logan his voice was kept low. "Ben," he said, without heat, "that was worth tryin', but you couldn't see the whole situation. Without artillery it would have been hopeless tryin' to reduce the council house. There was no use riskin' the lives of any more men. We have done what we came for. We didn't intend to take prisoners. We've burned their crops and their town. My men have taken over two hundred horses and the plunder in furs and skins will be considerable. We've hurt 'em bad enough. There's no use killin' our men to no purpose."

Ben calmed down, but Tice could see that he didn't more than half believe the colonel. Still, it had been Ben himself who had reminded them this was an army, and orders had to be obeyed.

Harrod's men were called out, likewise, and the withdrawal commenced. It was orderly. A whisper ran through the lines that the real reason for the retreat was that word had come that Simon Girty, the renegade white man who lived and fought with the Indians, was bringing up the whole Mingo tribe, and Colonel Bowman wanted to get out of the country before he arrived. The talk went that a Negro woman had brought the word to the colonel, she having been a captive in the town for many years and understanding their language. It never was proved, one way or the other. No one had actually seen the old Negro woman, but all claimed they'd heard it on good report.

There was a sharp fight about fifteen miles away from the town, the Indians having had time to catch their breath and pursue. But the officers ordered the men into the woods, formed them into a square about the horses and plunder, and, each man to his individual tree as they were accustomed to fighting, they stood the Shawnees off. It took them nearly three hours to do it, though. The Indians hated to see those horses go.

After that they had no more trouble and the expedition was over save for getting back home. And save for the plunder auction. Once they got back across the Ohio they camped and spent two days holding the sale. Any horses that were recognized as belonging to some settler were excluded from the sale, but there were plenty put on the block, anyhow.

Tice was jubilant. He bid in two good ones, a stallion and another mare, and he was lucky enough to get a bale of skins also. He had some other odds and ends, too, he'd picked up in the village he thought Hannah would like.

In the main the men came prancing home. They hadn't suffered the loss in dead and wounded they'd thought likely, the total number not yet being known, but it was small. It was a proud thing for all Kentuckians, and they told each other the expedition would go down in history—the first invasion of Indian country by the settlers—the time, finally come, when they quit holing up like animals inside the walls of a fort and went out like men to seek and fight their enemies. And, they told each other, romping along home, pounding each other on the back, hurrying, eager to see wives and children again, they'd done good. Yes, sir, by grannies, they'd done good!

15

HANNAH was delighted that the stay in the fort this time had been so brief. She kept marveling at it as they rode out home again. "I never looked fer you," she told Tice, "under two weeks, to say the least."

"Oh, we never aimed to make a long thing of it. I knowed all the time hit would be soon an' over."

"You could of said so," she scolded.

"Well, a body cain't actually tell. Hit was jist what we was all thinkin'. I wouldn't of wanted," he went on earnestly, "to raise yer hopes an' have 'em dashed right down had somethin' went wrong."

"No," she agreed, "that would of been the worst—to be lookin' an' you not comin'."

"That was the way I figured it."

She admired the horses. The stallion was a beautiful young sorrel animal, and the mare was a pretty chestnut. "Ain't they purty, though? I swear, Tice, you was the luckiest to git 'em."

"I was, warn't I? They was two others biddin' on 'em, but Dave Cooper kept eggin' me on. Said he'd make the lend of his part of the plunder credit if they was need. So I jist kept on biddin' till I got 'em. Not," he added hastily, "that I paid more'n they're worth. I had my figure set in my mind, the highest I'd go, an' it never went there. Hit was good luck fer me, sart'n. I got the skins cheap, too, an' they're prime. Jist wait till you see 'em."

"That's what I'm aimin' to do," she told him, laughing.

He laughed, too, feeling joyous and full-blooded and triumphant. He couldn't have found the words to tell Hannah how good she looked to him and how glad he was to be back again. But, he had to own it, it had been exciting and he reckoned a man never felt so much a man as when he went to war. He'd been lonesome for her, but that morning they'd charged, once he'd got into it, there'd been a kind of wildness you couldn't explain. It had been a whooping, singing, shouting kind of wildness, and it belonged only where men were banded together, without women, danger like wine in their veins, ruthless, crazy and lusting with power. He doubted if he'd ever forget it, his first taste of organized battle.

He sobered, rode near to Hannah and touched her. She'd had the drab business of staying behind, being cooped up in the fort. He felt sorry for that. "You been all right, have you?"

Now that it was over Hannah felt no need to complain. "Jane taken a little sniffles, but they don't amount to nothin'."

"Changin' her bed, likely." He peered at the baby, chucking her under the chin. "Ain't she growin', though?"

"She's gittin' so heavy she's a solid weight to pack," Hannah said proudly.

When Hannah looked over the skins Tice had brought she had to admit that the women who had cured them had known what they were about. She hadn't ever seen skins any better dried or softened. They added them to their store in the loft room. "Hit ain't enough yit, though, is it?" she asked.

"Hit takes a heap of skins to make up what we'll need," Tice said, shaking his head. "But we'll make out, one way or another."

It was the old worry, whether they'd have enough by the time the land commissioners came. Never had Hannah seen a pile of skins grow so slowly.

Tice had brought back, too, an iron spider and two iron ladles and the bottom half of a little iron kettle with the three legs on it still good. "Jist picked 'em up," he told her. "They was layin' there, overturned, an' I figured you could use 'em."

"I kin," she assured him. But it surprised her to see such things from an Indian town. Somehow she hadn't thought they'd have kettles and things like white people. "I'd never of thought it," she said. "I'd of thought they had their own kinds of things an' their own ways of doin'. Hit makes me feel the quarest to handle this here spider an' know some Shawnee woman has het it up an' browned corn pones on it."

"They git 'em offen the traders," Tice told her. "They's been traders goin' in to them Indian towns fer a time an' a time. They go up into Pennsylvany or over into Virginny an' buy up a lot of stuff, beads an' lookin' glasses, an' cloth goods an' pots an' things, an' a heap of rum, an' then they take 'em into the Indian country an' trade 'em fer furs an' skins."

It was a good spider and Hannah liked to use it, and she soon forgot where it had come from.

The garden had taken little harm during the time they had been gone, though the wild things had done some damage—the rabbits, woodchucks, coons and things. "I got to make a fence," Hannah said angrily. "I ain't havin' my things eat up by wild things. An' hit'll have to be a palin' fence to do any good."

Tice helped, though not very willingly, on rainy days or in the evenings and they rived out the paling boards and tied them together with thongs, set them strongly in the ground. "There, now," Hannah said when they'd finished, "I reckon that'll keep 'em out." She touched one of the palings, then, and confessed, "I allus did like a palin' fence around a garden patch, anyhow."

"Well, you got one," Tice said, shortly, "an' about as pore a payin' piece of work as I ever set my hand to."

"You'll not think so next winter when they's things to eat besides meat," Hannah told him hotly.

"Humph," was all Tice could spare in reply.

The garden did do well. Hannah had planted all the seeds she brought out from the old home, the seeds that had been tied so carefully in the little patches of cloth. She planted turnips and beans, pumpkins and yellow squash, and a maize corn that was the best she'd ever seen for grinding into meal. She planted by the signs, of course, the things which rooted, like turnips, having to be planted in the dark of the moon or else they'd all go to vine, and the things which matured above the ground, such as beans and corn, in the light of the moon so they wouldn't go to root. It was especially important with corn and Tice was careful to plant when the moon was exactly between the half and full, so as to get the best light of it. They had a cow, now, and pigs, as well as three horses and the sheep to feed. He'd traded with Ben Logan for the cow and he'd got the pigs from David Cooper.

One thing Hannah planted which Tice laughed at her for was gourd seeds. "What," he said, "are you aimin' to do with them? Train the vines up over the doorstep to make a shade?"

"Jist wait an' see," she told him.

She did train the vines up over the doorstep and a pretty shade they made, but she knew the gourds would make new noggins and dippers and tankards, with maybe some left over from their own use to trade.

When Tice saw the gourds swelling and growing and she began to snap them off and lay them aside to dry and told him what she intended to do with them, he whistled. "You done good," he admitted. "You was smarter than me on them gourds."

"You jist never seen this kind before. I knowed all along what they'd be." She could afford to be charitable in her triumph.

She never did tell him, for she was shy about naming it, that she liked to grow gourds for another reason. She liked the little five-petaled white gourd blooms better than any other flower-pretties you could grow. She didn't know but she liked them better than roses, and she was certain she liked them better than lilocks and lilies. There was something about them that had always made her think of a star, and now that Jane had come, that made her think of Jane's small hand, the fingers spread, all soft and downy. She wanted, times, to lay her face against them, just for the feel of them. She'd never told anyone that was mostly the reason she liked to grow gourds. She guessed it would have gone foolish to others to hear.

The heavy garden yield kept Hannah busy well up into the fall. She was glad of it, but it bothered her a little that she wasn't getting her wool carded and ready to work with. "Hit's goin' to throw me awful late gittin' winter things fer Jane knitted up. But I ain't got the heart to waste e'er thing that's in the garden, an' I've got it in mind to gather up some of them walnuts an' crack 'em out afore the cold sets in, too."

"Well," Tice said comfortingly, "a body cain't do ever'thing. Jist do the best you kin, is the way I see it."

And there was always hanging over them the fear that the land commissioners would come before they were ready. It had been there so long, now, though, that they rarely spoke of it. Sometimes Hannah went up into the loft room and looked over the skins and thought how differently she had planned it. She'd thought to be such a help to Tice getting them in, but instead she had her hands full with chores about the place, and the baby to tend. And Tice had had to do different, too. A man *couldn't* hunt all the time when he had stock to see to and crops to mind. She hated in the worst way to think of somebody else, though, taking up the land all about them, and Tice losing his chance at it. She just had to put it from her mind when it got to bothering her too much. It was the way Tice said. They had to do the best they could.

Tice had to go to the fort once each month for muster day, and he came home early in October with a sober face. "The land commissioners is comin'," he said at once.

Hannah's heart sank. "When?"

"Next week. They're on the way, now. The word has jist come. They'll open up fer business at Logan's first an' make the rounds after that. There is four of 'em."

"They're Virginny men, I reckon."

"They're Virginny men. Ben told me their names, if I c'n remember. William Fleming was one, an' Edmund Lyme. There was a James somebody . . . James Barbour, that was it, an' a feller called Stephen Trigg."

Their names meant nothing to either of them. They were men sent from Williamsburg to enact the law. They wouldn't know about the country or its ways or its people. All they could go by was what the law said. Somehow, Hannah thought, she would have felt better about it if someone had been appointed from the country itself. But that wasn't the way the Virginia council worked. They always sent somebody of their own.

Silently, mutually joined in their concern, they climbed the ladder to the loft room and turned over their piles of furs. "How much you reckon we like?" Hannah asked.

Tice figured. "We got, I'd say, about three quarters enough."

They went back downstairs and pulled up stools to the fire, sat quietly looking into it, thinking. "Now is when I got to prove this claim, too," Tice said, almost absent-mindedly, pulling at his chin.

Hannah took alarm immediately. "What you mean, prove it?"

"Well, jist prove it, is all. Git witnesses to say you've met the law an' all."

"You've done so, ain't you?"

Tice moved restlessly. "I've done an' told you, Hannah . . . yes, I've met the law. Unless they want to come down real strict on the part about livin' on the claim that first year. I was comin' an' goin' all the time, an' tendin' it the best I could. What with the Indians plunderin' an' us havin' to chase them out all the time, I never, to say, actually stayed right with it till after I met up with you an' yer pa that time. You recollect I come right on out, then."

"Yes."

"But hasn't nobody stayed right with a place no better, that I know of. Couldn't. Not nobody, that first year. Ben'd come the closest to it. He says they'll not be too strict about it. Says if you stayed a night now an' then, an' tended yer crop, they'll take it."

[128]

"But they *could* be strict, could they?"

"I reckon they could, by law. But Ben says they won't. I ain't wearied none about that."

But Hannah was. This, now, was worse than not getting the extra acres. This involved the house-place itself and the fields and pastures and land. If the commissioners wanted to be strict about it, they could lose the very roof over their heads. And it was small comfort to Hannah that Ben Logan said they wouldn't be. The thought of losing her home threw Hannah into a frenzy of fear. "Ain't they nothin' we c'n *do* about it?"

"About what?" Tice pulled his thoughts back to her question.

"About provin' the claim."

"Jist what I aim to do. Ben'll stand witness fer me, an' Dave."

A chunk of log in the fireplace dropped and then blazed up. Its light flickered about the room and Hannah's eyes followed as each piece of furniture and each corner was lit up. She could never get enough of looking at it, handling and possessing her own things. It didn't make sense to her that they might lose all of it.

There was the bed in the corner. It was just a pole bed, but it was up off the floor, decently. Some day it would have a coverlid on it, a white one, like her mother's, and a patchwork quilt.

There was the table and the stools for sitting. She had her spinning wheel and next winter she intended to have her loom finished. She had the pieces for it hewed out already. She was letting them season a winter, was all. The baby had the cradle Tice had made, though you couldn't hardly call a cradle a piece of furniture. It was more like a cooking pot—when you got a youngun you had to have a cradle, just like when you cooked you had to have something to cook in.

Then there was the cupboard. It was the nicest thing they'd made. Out of black walnut, it was, and put together as stout as the walnut pegs could hold it. They'd hewed each piece exactly, and then they'd whittled and carved until they fitted perfectly. They'd rubbed it down with sand from the creek to make it smooth, and finally they'd rubbed bear oil into it and shined it with the palms of their hands. Tice had even made drawers in it and they kept their most valuable possessions in the drawers—their few pieces of silver money, a quill pen and some sheets of paper Ben Logan had given them. Hannah couldn't write, but Tice could sign his name, and a body never knew when a piece of paper and a quill would come in handy.

Of course, she reminded herself, they wouldn't lose the furniture and their belongings if Tice couldn't prove the claim. They could take them and the stock wherever they went. But she didn't know as they would ever seem the same in another place. She had a frantic feeling, as if they were already dispossessed and wandering, looking for some place to put their things, to raise another roof over their heads. She rubbed her arms and felt the cold-bumps her fear raised on them.

"Well," Tice said, standing and shoving his stool back, "no use wearyin' about it. Best git to bed an' git some rest."

She didn't feel as if she would ever rest again, or at least not until this nightmare of the land commissioners was over. She lay awake, Tice snoring heavily beside her, and the names of the men went over and over in her mind until they made a kind of sing-songy rhythm—Fleming, Barbour, Trigg and Lyme—Fleming, Barbour, Trigg and Lyme. But it was a nonsensical song, without end or meaning. She was just plain afraid of them and their law. They had so much power. They could turn Hannah Fowler and her youngun and man right out from under their own roof, and set them, travelers, on a strange trail.

Tice had put in to have his claim heard the first day the commission sat, having been at the fort when the news came and on hand to file, and Ben sent word it would be the twentieth. Dave Cooper brought the word. "Looks like ever'body in the country is the worst excited," he said. "I d'know as Indians would of worked 'em up as bad. They're already commencin' to pour into the fort. Ben said to tell you to bring Hannah, an' you all could stay with him an' Ann."

"We'll be there," Tice told him.

Hannah slept very little the night before, and she rose the next morning long before her usual time, unable to lie still any longer. Tice heard her stirring about and got up, too. "Jist as well," he said, "we c'n git a early start."

The chores had to be done and Hannah did her part mechanically. Then she dressed herself and the baby. Tice saddled two horses and brought them around. "You ready?"

"Yes." She pulled the door shut behind her, and then her heart failed her and her knees grew weak. She couldn't in any way sit the day out at Ann Logan's place, with folks all around her, having to talk and be pleasant, her hands idle and this fear eating away in her mind. She knew there was no way in which she could make herself do it. "I ain't goin', Tice," she said.

He was tightening the cinch on the mare. He turned and looked at her. "Now, *why* ain't you goin'?"

She hung her head, shifted the baby to her other arm. "I jist cain't, is all. I jist mortally cain't do it, Tice. Hit'd make me sick to go. I'd ruther to wait here an' keep busy." This last she said so low he had to bend his head to hear her. She looked up, grief and fear showing in her eyes. "Tice, I cain't bear the thoughts of mebbe losin' this place. I d'know as I could *live* through it."

"Hit's a sorrow to me," he said, slowly, "I ever named provin' the claim to you. Hit's jist to make it legal, that's all they is to it. I don't rightly know why you've got so worked up over it. I ain't in the least wearied."

He spoke the truth, she could tell. His thoughts were all on the extra thousand acres . . . but they had become unimportant to her. She was making too much of it, she knew, but until it was settled, until she knew this home was theirs, in the sight of the law, she wouldn't rest easy.

Tice ran his hand roughly over her hair and sighed. "All right, then. You needn't to go if you'd ruther not. I jist thought you'd take pleasure in visitin' with the womenfolks."

She shook her head and kept it down, hoping he wouldn't notice that her eyes had suddenly filled. Tice was the *best* man. Not many would give in to a woman's nervy ways like he did.

"Well, I'll unsaddle the mare if you're sart'n you ain't goin'."

"I'm sart'n." She felt better already.

He slid the mare's reins over his arm and started leading her back around the house. "Ann an' Bethia is goin' to ask after you, to say nothin' of Jane Manifee. An' I ain't aimin' to take the blame fer you not goin', Hannah."

"Don't. Jist say I had too much to do. An' it's true. I got sich a lot to do I ortent to thought of goin' noway."

When he had gone she changed her clothes and set herself to fill every moment of the day. She wasn't going to leave a minute for idleness and thinking. She decided to wash. That would take the most time. She'd intended to do it when they came back from the fort, so as to wash up the clothing they would have soiled there, but she'd do it today. She'd just gather up everything and take it down to the spring and get right at it. And then in the afternoon she'd start carding the wool. She should have done it long ago. She was terribly late with it, the way it was.

Almost happily she bustled about and when the thought of what was going to happen at the fort crept into her mind she put it resolutely away. She had this day left to her without knowing, and she was going to make a good use of it. And she wouldn't watch for Tice at all. He might get home tonight, but likely it would be tomorrow. She wouldn't wear herself out keeping an eye on the path.

But she did. When the warmth began to go out of the day and the sun's shadow on the east side of the house stretched out lengthily, her deep uneasiness, which had been allayed during the day, began to return and in spite of herself she found her eyes watching the trail. He would come through the gap in the ridge across the creek, to the south. That's where she would see him first if he was coming home today, and she knew, now, how much she wanted him to come. It would be an awfully long night if he didn't.

She kept busy, but as she worked she kept wandering to the door to look down across the meadow. Right there, he'd first come in sight. He'd be small at first, and too far way to hear even if she called out to him. But he might look up at the house and if she waved her apron at him, he'd see and wave back. Then he'd cross the creek, just where the clump of birches stood, and he'd let the horse water there. She knew just how he'd look, having watched him water his horse a hundred times or more. He'd loosen the lines, give the horse its head, let his own shoulders slump a little, lean forward and rub the horse's neck, then he'd wait, his hands crossed, his eyes fixed on the running water.

When the horse had finished he'd gather up the reins, cluck to the animal and they'd climb up the slope to the house-place. That was the way he would come home, the way he had come, time after time.

It was after dark when he got home, but not much. Hannah had barely finished doing up the night work, feeding, milking the cow, bringing in water from the spring, wood for the fire, when she heard the two mares in the pasture nicker. She knew by the sound of the nicker it was Tice returning. It was not a whinny of alarm, nor a snort of fear. It was the mares' welcome to Tice's stallion.

A knot tightened inside Hannah's chest and the muscles of her stomach suddenly cramped. All at once she wanted to run away, out of the house, any place where she need not see him and know, from him, the worst. She gripped her hands tightly and looked about at the room, thinking, trying to think, what to do. Then she got herself in hand and set the supper on to heat for him.

But she could not go out to meet him. She stayed by the fire and waited, hearing him take the horse around, then, after a time, hearing his steps approaching the house. She would not even look up when he came in, but the moment he walked through the door she knew it was all right. She knew it by the way he walked, by the springiness of his step. No man who had just lost his home could walk that way. He'd be lagging. The knot inside her chest eased and her stomach relaxed. She could wait, now, until he was ready to tell about it. She dished up a bowl of stew. "Well, you got back."

He hung his hat on a peg and sat down, taking the dish she handed him. "Yes, I got back. An' I'm so hungry my innards is cramped. I've not stopped to eat a bite. Jist as quick as the commission got done with me I crawled on my horse an' headed fer home. I've not had a morsel to eat since mornin'."

He spooned up the stew in big ladlefuls. Finding the ladle too small he threw it aside and lifted the bowl and drank directly from it. Wiping his mouth he handed it to her when it was empty. "Fill it again."

She watched him drink down the second bowl and then he turned, his eyes bright with pleasure. "I got the extry thousand!"

"You never!"

"I done so . . . an' you wouldn't guess in a hundred years how, either."

"Well, I'll not try, then. Tell me."

He squared around to face her. "Well, this was the way of it. I was standin' there, right in front of Ben's door under that little walnut tree . . . I was jist standin' there talkin' to William an' Jane, an' I was tellin' how I'd hoped to git that extry thousand but had come up short on skins, an' William jist up an' said, 'How many skins you figure to need?' Like that he said it, me not givin' it a thought. I told him, I said, 'Well, I reckon three bales of prime would be enough.' An' then he said, 'I reckon I got that many to spare. Take 'em an' welcome.' I swear I was so took aback I like to swallered my spit! Not thinkin' e'er thing about it, hit like to bowled me over!"

"Well, I never!" Hannah marveled. "William Manifee! I wouldn't never of thought it of him."

"Me, neither. The last man, the very *last* man I'd of thought would had skins to spare. First place, I wouldn't of thought he'd took that many skins."

"Oh, I wouldn't of been surprised at him takin' 'em. That's likely why he ain't put in fer an extry thousand of his own. He ain't aimin' to git hisself so tied down with land he ain't got the time to hunt when he takes the notion. But I'd of thought he'd traded as fast as he taken 'em fer more powder an' lead. What surprises me is him havin' 'em on hand fer the lend."

"An' they's no hurry about payin' 'em back. Said take my time. I tell you, a man like that'll do to tie to!"

"Oh, they ain't no better folks than Jane an' William. Hit's a lucky thing we got 'em fer door neighbors."

Tice was rummaging in his shirt front and he brought out a piece of paper. "There's the deed."

"Fer the extry thousand?"

"Fer all of it . . . fourteen hundred acres an' improvements."

Hannah's knees went suddenly weak. "You never had no trouble provin' the claim, then?"

"Why, no. They jist taken the witnesses, Ben an' Dave, like I said, an' it was over an' done with afore you could wink yer eye, hardly. You see how foolish yer fears was."

Yes, she saw, now. She laughed tremulously. It did seem foolish, now . . . but a man didn't know, there wasn't any way he could know, what four walls and a roof meant to a woman.

Tice laid the deed on the table and Hannah touched it wonderingly. It crackled. That little piece of paper was what said the place was theirs. It didn't hardly seem real it could. "Wait," she said, "wait'll I make a light. I want to see it good."

She lit a candle and set it on the table. Then she picked up the paper, turned it this way and that, examining it, trying to make it out. "C'n you read what's writ on it, Tice?"

He admitted he could not. "I c'n read printin' . . . some kinds, that is, but I couldn't never make out that fine script. Ain't it wrote up the fanciest, though?"

"I've not never seed nothin' like it before. Hit goes so little an' spidery all over the paper. Is they," she asked, puzzled, "is they folks c'n actually read writin' like that? Besides the ones that wrote it, I mean?"

"Why, sart'n they is. Ben c'n read it. Leastways he c'n read this here deed. He cain't to say read *ever'body's* writin', but he read this off real good. An' Ann now . . . Ben says she c'n read any writin' that was ever wrote, no matter who's. He says he never seed her stumped."

Hannah shook her head in wonderment. "I d'know how a body could make out to do it. I knowed Ann was smart, though. I allus knowed that, but to read things like this . . . hit's beyond my understandin'. Could you recollect what Ben said was on the paper?"

"I d'know as I c'n recollect *ever'* word jist the way he said it, but I recollect the way it goes."

"I would like to know the words it says."

"Why, sart'n." He spread the paper on the table and Hannah looked over his shoulder. "Hit says, to commence, October the twentieth, seventeen hundred an' seventy-nine . . ."

"That's today," Hannah put in.

"That's today. They got to put the day on the paper." He cleared his throat. " 'Whereas' . . . that there is the first word it says."

"Where? Where does it say it?"

"Right there . . . right there at the commencement . . ." Tice pointed, and then he went on to tell all the words in the deed as he remembered them, how he was entitled to fourteen hundred acres of land on the Hanging Fork of Dick's River, by pre-emption and by sale, and it gave the boundaries on all sides. The words said the land belonged to Matthias Fowler and his heirs and assigns forever.

"What is heirs and assigns?"

"Well, hit's you, should somethin' ever happen to me . . . you an' Jane an' whatever other younguns we mought ever have."

"Me . . ." she mused, touching the edge of the paper. The land commission, those men with the names she'd made a song of, those men with a quill pen and a sheet of paper had wrought a miracle. They had made Hannah Fowler rich. They had given her land to heir and to pass on to her young ones. They had given her possession of earth and water and trees and rocks and a house-place, to have and to hold forever. It said so. The paper said so!

"Put it some place it'll be safe," Tice said, handing it to her.

She wrapped it carefully in deerskin, so it wouldn't come to harm, and put it in the drawer of the walnut cupboard with their other valuables. She put it far back in the drawer and gave it a little pat as she released it, loving it, feeling almost as if it were another and cherished person in the house. Nothing, not ever anything at all could take her home away from her now. Now she had nothing to be afraid of.

16

THE FALL held on mild, warm, unbelievably beautiful, day after day. "Hit don't look like there is ever goin' to be any winter," Hannah said, when the middle of November had come with no great change in the weather. "I d'know as I ever knowed of a fall to last out so long."

"Hit ain't common," Tice agreed, "but I've saw a fall like this turn into a awful cold winter. Seems like when it does come on, hit jist tries to outdo itself."

Toward the last of the month there was a heavy rainstorm, after which the temperature dropped sharply to freezing and Tice, wrapping up to do the chores, laughed ruefully. "Well, here's the winter come, like I said."

Still, it was nothing more than the cold common to any winter for another ten days. Then, one day the snow began about noon, although it was difficult to tell what time of day it was. There wasn't even a sunrise that morning. There was just the gradual lifting of the dark to a kind of leaden gray, and like an opaque curtain the grayness continued to hang over everything the rest of the morning. The house would have been dark without the light from the fire. "What you reckon it's aimin' to do?" Hannah said, peering out.

"Make weather fer one thing," Tice said. "I aimed," he went on, "to split out fence rails today, but if that snow'd hold on it'd make awful good huntin'. Believe I'll make up some bullets, jist in case."

"Why don't you? I'm goin' fer some more wood."

Tice had dragged up some young trees the day before and he had chopped up a sizable pile of logs, but when Hannah went to pick them up, every stick was lying sheathed in a slick, glistening armor, glued fast to the one lying next to it. The rain, she thought, which had fallen in the night, had frozen them. It surprised her. She hadn't thought it was that cold.

She pulled and tugged, but couldn't budge them. She got the axe and chopped the wood free. It came loose with sharp, crackling sounds and the broken ice flew free in shivering white fragments. She kept at it until she had freed a dozen logs and tumbled them from the pile onto the ground where they would be easy to get at.

The snow was little more than a wind-driven spume as yet, just beginning to fly, barely visible. Hannah stopped in the lee of the house to wipe her eyes and face with the corner of her head shawl. She looked down the slope across the frozen meadow. It looked, she told herself, as if the sky had suddenly let go its hold and had dropped down on top of the earth. And the meadow, she thought, looked smoothed and leveled out. It looked shallow, like the little flat wooden bowl she had whittled for the baby.

As she watched, the snow thickened and the clump of birches and the trees along the creek became fogged in the white drift. Hannah shivered. "Hit's breedin' weather," she told herself, "an' mighty soon at that." She gathered up as much wood as she could carry and hurried into the house with it.

It was warm and cheerful inside. Tice had a good fire burning and he was hunkered down on the hearth in front of it. He'd laid out his bar of lead and the bullet mold and the old piece of broken iron pot he'd picked up in the Indian town. He used it to heat lead in. He looked up when he heard the door close behind Hannah. "What's it doin' out there?"

"Hit's fixin' to weather. An' it ain't wastin' no time doin' it. You're aimin' to git yer snow, in my opinion."

Tice went on shaving lead into the iron pot. "The hogs was all standin' with their heads to the north this mornin' when I fed 'em."

The baby was asleep and Hannah moved quietly, laying the wood on the floor. "I heared 'em," she said, "in the night, squealin'. They baited good last night, I reckon."

"Good as common," Tice said. "Or mebbe better. I het 'em up a mash of corn an' skim milk. But you recollect. You was grumblin' over me takin' up the fire with it."

Hannah rubbed her arms and stared sleepily at the fire. "They warn't hungry then. I've allus heared that hogs'll squeal jist before a uncommon cold spell, even if they've jist eat good."

"I've heared it, too, an' ever'body knows when they stand with their heads to the north, hit's goin' to weather fer sart'n."

"I reckon the signs all point the same way, then. An' that sky out there is a tellin' the same thing. Well, hit's the time of year fer a hard, cold spell."

"What day is it?"

Hannah crossed the room and took down from its peg a long, slender hickory stick. She counted the notches. "Hit's the fifth day of December, if I ain't out in my figurin'."

"You ain't out," Tice said, positively. He had never known her to be out. She kept the days and the months as straight as anybody he'd ever known. She *could* have kept them on a piece of paper, for she'd learned how to tally, and they had several pieces of paper in the drawer, but she said it would be a waste. She could keep the days just as good with a notched stick. He didn't know as he'd be as good at it as Hannah, for he sometimes forgot to notch a day and then he'd be off the rest of the month. But he didn't recollect that Hannah had ever been off as much as one day since she'd taken over the keeping of their days.

She laid the hickory stick back on its pegs and went to get her spinning wheel from its corner. In passing she bent and looked into the cradle. "She's sleepin' good today."

"She ort to," Tice snorted, "she was awake most of the night."

"Hit was them turnips I eat," Hannah said guiltily, "made her colicky. I was afeared when I eat 'em I orent to, but I was *that* hungry for 'em. I never even knowed they was any of 'em left up there in the garden till I went up to set a rabbit trap an' run onto that little bunch down in the corner. I would of eat 'em, I do believe, if I'd knowed they would give her an' me both the colic."

"They never bothered *you* none, did they?"

"No, but that was what was makin' her fidgety all night."

"I wouldn't of keered fer her fidgetin', hit was the yellin' bothered me."

"She never yelled sich a lot." Hannah started the wheel.

"No," Tice said, "she never yelled sich a lot . . . not more'n half the night."

Hannah stopped the wheel and peered at him over the top. "Now, she never yelled half the night, Tice Fowler! I seen to that. First place, I wouldn't let a youngun of mine yell half the night. I'd pacify it one way or the other, an' in the second place, she never done so. Best I recollect she had two little small colicky spells was all." Then she saw the pucker at the corner of Tice's mouth and saw his shoulders twitch. She gave the wheel a hard push. "You're a pokin' fun again, Tice," she said accusingly. "I c'n tell. You're jist tryin' to git me stirred up. You *know* she never yelled half the night."

"I know it," he said chuckling, "but you're worse'n a old hen with a flock of little diddles the way you ruffle up yer feathers an' git ready to commence floggin' if they's e'er word of blame put on that youngun. Hit's a temptation not to ruffle you a purpose."

Hannah sniffed. "You don't keer nothin' about her, I reckon. Have you done fergot that time she was croupy, an' had the catarrh in her throat? I like to couldn't do fer her, way you hung over an' nearly smothered me out!"

"That was different. She was sick then. I was wearied."

"So was I wearied, but I went on an' done what had to be done, 'stid of hangin' over the bed takin' on."

Tice said something under his breath.

"You needn't to mumble," Hannah said. "Jist say it out."

He started laughing. "I was jist sayin' they warn't ever no use commencin' nothin' with a woman."

"You," she said severely, "never told a truer word."

She set the great wheel to turning again, mounting it gradually to a steady rhythm. Its hum filled the room. Her free hand guided the wool, kept the tension right, the slack exact so that the spindle would fill evenly. The whir of the wheel made too much noise to talk above, but the rhythm of its turning, the flexing of her hand and foot, the smooth circling of the spindle, the roughness and prickle of the yarn in her hand and its even spread on the spool, were all so familiar to Hannah that her movements were automatic. She liked to spin. She liked watching the wool stretch and twist and wind itself into yarn. She liked settling the wheel into a regular rhythm. It took a fine foot to steady it just so . . . too fast and it buckled a little—too slow and it jerked . . . just right it had to be, and she knew exactly when it was right and how to keep it there. She never had a lopsided bobbin. Her mind could wander where it pleased but she'd know by the feel and the sound how the spindle was shaping up.

She watched Tice molding bullets. He was as particular about it as she was with her spinning. First he shaved up the lead in the iron pot. Then he set the pot in the coals, and when the lead had melted he ladled it out into the bullet mold. She watched the hot lead pour in a sliding, shining stream from the ladle into the molds. Always that thick, sliding stream fascinated her. It didn't look hot at all. It looked silvery and cool. "You'd find out mighty quick it's hot," Tice had told her once when she'd said so.

"Oh, I know," she'd said, "I know it's hot . . . powerful hot. I was jist sayin' it don't appear to be."

When the bullets had cooled he turned them out, took his knife and trimmed the roughness off, and as a final step he rubbed them with an old piece of deerskin that was worn and slick. She guessed he loved to make bullets the way she loved to work with wool, because he went about it so slowly and easily, so particular with each one.

The baby stirred in her sleep and murmured. Hannah reached out a hand and gave the cradle a push. The baby sighed and slept again. The wheel whirred and hummed in its unbroken rhythm. Tice looked up from the hearth. It could almost put a man to sleep, he thought, the whirring and humming. It had a homey sound he liked. A fire and a spinning wheel, he thought, and, he added, amused, a cradle . . . those were the things that made a home for a man. They all meant there was a woman in his heart.

They both heard the sound of the wind when it came, felt it, unbelievably, when the house strained under it. Tice stood up, startled, the bullets and the mold scattering across the floor. Hannah stopped the wheel. "Did you feel the house give then?" he asked.

"I did," she said, "fer sart'n. That's a terrible wind, Tice, to shake this house."

He clapped on his hat and reached for an overshirt. "I'd best git right out an' commence seein' to things."

Hannah moved the wheel into the corner. "Well, I'll heat up some supper. Hit ain't much too soon."

Tice pulled the latch on the door and before he could catch it the door was swung out of his hand and blown back upon itself, the wind driving the snow across the room. Hannah stared as Tice struggled to close the door again. When he had it latched he stood with his back against it and looked at her. "They ain't no use denyin' it, Hannah, hit's blowin' up a blizzard out there."

She got her shawl down and fastened it about her head. "Hit'll take us both to do up the work," she said.

They had to fight the wind and the snow to get the feeding and milking done, to bring in wood and water for the night, and it took them longer than usual to do it, but they settled down afterward, in warmth and comfort, with no real uneasiness of mind. It was a bad winter storm, was all. They'd both seen many a one. It would blow and snow for a day or two and then gradually it would blow itself out. Hannah even luxuriated a little in their snug security. "They ain't," she said, "nothin' like a storm to make a body feel warm an' safe inside."

When they went to bed Tice laid a good backlog of gum on the fire and banked it for the night, then he went outside for a moment. He came back in, shivering. "Still snowin' is it?" Hannah asked. She and the baby were already in bed, the baby asleep.

"Still comin' down thick, an' I'd guess it to be six inches deep already. An' cold . . . my sakes, but it's turnin' bitter." He pulled off his shoes and stood on the hearth warming himself.

Hannah hunched the covers higher around her shoulders. "Hit was bound to come," she said philosophically.

Tice made a dash for the bed. "Well, bound to or not, I'd jist as soon it never would git very cold. I c'n put up with the heat in summer as good as anybody, but when I git the shivers down my back, I purely don't like it."

Hannah laughed good-naturedly, gave him a pat on his thigh and settled herself in the curve of his body, her hand feeling the baby automatically. Jane was still dry, but before morning she'd be soaking wet, and her own shift tail would be as wet as the baby's. Tice grumbled sometimes. Said why didn't she let the baby sleep in the cradle the way she'd done in the summer. But she'd told him plain out no woman that even *tried* to be a good mother would let a youngun sleep by itself in the wintertime. "Why," she'd said, curt with astonishment, "she couldn't keep the covers on, Tice. She'd freeze to the bone!"

"I reckon she would," he had admitted. But after that she hadn't let Janie sleep in the middle any more. She'd put her on her own side, away from Tice. It wasn't very pleasant, she owned, to waken every morning wet to the skin, and a man likely was more displeasured with it than a woman.

The thongs creaked under her as she turned in the bed. Next winter, they reminded her, there'd be a feather tick on this bed. Tice thought that was getting pretty fancy, sleeping on feathers, but that was what she intended. That was why she'd traded Jane Manifee one of the lambs for a pair of geese. Jane had a feather tick, and so did Bethia Cooper. And of course Ann Logan had one. Ann had two, actually, though her mother had made one of them for her when she got married. They all said there wasn't anything that slept as warm in the wintertime. "You shake 'em ever' day," Jane Manifee had told her, "an' turn the tick over, an' when you crawl in at night they're as soft as a pillow, an' you sink down an' down till you think there ain't no bottom."

"My," she had said, deeply impressed. Jane had then let her lie down on her feather tick, and it had been just like she'd said, soft and sinky. It had been the ambition of her life ever since to have a feather tick of her own, and before another winter had come and gone, she intended to have it, Tice or not.

She slept soundly for a while and then, aware of discomfort, she stirred restlessly. Tice stretched beside her and snuggled closer. His movement awakened her. She was cold—that was why she had been stirring, and it was as cold as death in the room. She raised her head to look at the fire and tried to gauge the time. It wasn't more than the middle of the night, and the fire was smoldering, well banked to last till morning. But the cold had seeped in until it seemed as if there were no fire at all.

She edged out of the bed, slid the baby further down into the middle and pulled the covers up over it. Shivering she uncovered the fire and stirred it up, piled on fresh wood, poked and tended it until it blazed up in a fine warmth. She stood on the hearth, then, warming herself on all sides. She felt cold clear to the bones. Not since they had moved into the house had it been this cold, she thought. She wondered if it were still snowing, and she went to the door, opening it a crack and looked out. The wind had died down, but right in front of her face there was still a thick curtain of snow, coming down as if it never meant to stop, and she saw that it had deepened to at least a foot on the doorsill. She shivered and closed the door. There was something deadly and insistent about the snow coming straight down so silently and so thickly.

Tice heard the door close and turned over, his eyes suddenly flying open, startled at finding her up. "You all right?"

"Yes. I woken up cold, is all, an' got up to stir the fire. Hit's turnin' awful bitter."

He yawned. "I c'n tell it is, way the house feels. Still snowin' out there?"

"Hit's a foot deep an' comin' down harder than ever."

"Hit'll make good huntin' . . . if it don't git much deeper. Be hard goin' if it does." He yawned again and turned over.

Thoughtfully, Hannah went up to the loft room and brought down the few extra covers they had. There were only three skins left over from buying the extra land. They hadn't included them because they weren't prime.

The rest of the night they slept fitfully, each time the fire died down the room getting so cold that one of them had to get up to replenish it. Along toward morning Tice said, "Is this all the covers we got, Hannah?"

"Yes. I've looked out ever' extry pelt we got an' piled on. Hit's jist the cold bites through ever'thing."

"Well, it mortally is cold then. Ain't nothin' to do but keep the fire roarin', I reckon."

"I d'know as they is," she agreed.

17

As he did every morning, Tice went to feed while Hannah got breakfast. He was gone so long that she had to keep the food hot on the hearth for him. Usually he was through by the time she had it ready. She went to the door several times. The snow was still an impenetrable curtain right outside and it gave her a smothery feeling of being holed in to see it, so white, thick, deadly cold, falling so relentlessly and quietly and so steadily, just the thickness of that solid slab of walnut between her and it. It gave her a feeling that the heavy whiteness and the still cold were personal enemies, searching her out, ready to stab at her house and her child and her man, and at her, herself. Cold, she thought, was a terrible thing.

The wind was rising again, too, now that the night was over. She could hear it whining about the house corners, and it blew down the chimney, making the smoke whirl. Each time the fire died down she felt the chill bite into her shoulders and even with the fire burning high only a small circle near the hearth was really warm. The far end of the room was icy cold. The meat hanging there had frozen stiff during the night, and the water bucket hadn't thawed enough to tell yet. She'd broken the ice to get water for her bread.

When Tice came in, finally, he slammed the door behind him and stood leaning weakly against it, panting. Hannah looked at him, frightened. His face was blue with cold and his mouth worked stiffly. His eyebrows were quilled with frost and his eyes were squinted almost shut. She ran to him, took his arm, shook it. "Tice, what's the matter?"

"I'm froze," he said, shudderingly, "jist plumb froze. My eyes is even froze together."

"I c'n see they are. Git to the fire, quick."

He walked lurchingly toward the fire, rubbing his hands together, hunching his shoulders. "Hit's cold, Hannah—terrible, terrible cold. I d'know as I ever seed it this cold before."

"In this country, you mean?" She dipped him a mug of hot water and poured rum into it. "Here, drink this while I fix you somethin' to eat."

He warmed his hands on the sides of the noggin. "In any country," he said seriously. "I jist don't know if I ever in all my time seed it this cold, anywheres!"

It scared her, hearing him talk so. She watched him drink down the scalding liquid, handed him a platter of fried meat and bread. "What taken you so long?"

"I got lost. That's what taken me so long."

"You got lost! Ain't you even been to the barn yit?"

"I couldn't even *find* the barn, an' I like to not found the house again. Hit's a blizzard, Hannah, I'm a tellin' you . . . hit's a real blizzard. An' you cain't see nothin' or keep yer bearin's, or even hear nothin', it's so thick."

"What'll we do about the animals?"

"We got to git 'em all inside the barn, one way or another. They ain't got a chance, elsewise. The cow an' the calf, an' the two yoes, the lamb . . . they're done an' inside. On account of the snow I left 'em penned up last night, an' a good thing I done so, too. But the horses are out . . . an' the pigs, they ort to be brung in." An involuntary shudder rippled over him. "If they ain't done froze stiff, hit'll astonish me."

"You ort to waited an' got somethin' hot inside of you afore you went out in sich a cold," Hannah scolded.

"I never knowed how cold it was till I got out in it," he confessed.

When they had finished eating she took care of the baby and put her in the cradle, drew it nearer the hearth. The child whimpered and Hannah set the cradle to rocking. "Now, you'll jist have to yell if you're a mind to, Janie. They is too much to do fer me to set an' dandle you today."

Hearing Hannah's voice the child hushed, then, undecided since the voice did not continue, she whimpered experimentally again. Hannah smiled down at her. "No use you beggin' thataway. You jist be good, now. I got to go milk an' help yer pa. They's a bad storm a blowin' outside. Cain't you hear?"

She took two of the pelts off their bed and handed them to Tice. "Split them an' commence tyin' 'em around yer feet. I'm goin' to seek out the last of them wool hosen of Pa's fer us to tie around our hands an' faces. They's still several of 'em ain't been raveled up."

She found them in the cupboard. Tice put his fur cap on instead of his old buffalo-skin hat and she tied it down with one of the stockings. Then she wrapped his hands with another. "I d'know as I c'n feel," he said, "you got 'em wropped up so good."

"Hit'll be a heap better not to feel on account of 'em bein' too wropped up than not to feel on account of 'em bein' froze," she told him.

She then put one of Tice's hunting shirts over her dress and tied a pair of stockings over her own ears. Over the stockings she fastened her shawl. When she had wrapped her feet and hands she was ready. They looked at each other and laughed. "I misdoubt we'll freeze," Tice said, "though it may well be we'll skeer the animals to death."

Hannah took a wooden pail from its peg and rinsed it with hot water. "You ain't aimin' to *milk,* are you?" Tice asked, amazed.

"Why, sart'n," she replied, equally amazed at his question.

"You cain't bring a bucket of milk back through that storm, Hannah. Hit'll be all you c'n do to hang on to me an' git back yerself."

"If I c'n git back myself," she retorted, "I c'n bring a bucket of milk."

"You'll see."

"All right, then, I'll see. I'm ready. Let's go."

"I'm aimin' to make fer the fence this time an' foller it to the barn. They ain't no way we kin git lost that way, if we c'n make it to the fence in the first place."

Tice opened the door. A gust of wind blew the snow in a thick drift across the room. He struggled with the door and mumbled through the stocking tied across his mouth. She only heard the last part of what he said, " . . . hang on tight."

She took a firm grip on the back of his shirt and they stepped out into the storm. Tice managed to get the door pulled shut behind him. Through its thickness Hannah heard the baby let out a sudden yell. The cold air had fretted her, she reckoned. She'll yell, Hannah thought, till we get back, likely, and make herself ill-sorted for the whole day. But there was no help for it.

When they came to the corner of the house the full force of the storm hit them. Tice was staggered and stopped for a moment. Behind him Hannah gasped as the wind hit her like something solid. She stared unbelievingly at the thick, almost blinding wall of white that shut everything more than ten feet away into a wind-driven limbo. Tice turned sideways and crabbed along with the wind quartering behind him. Hannah held on, trying not to be a weight dragging him down, wanting only to keep in touch so as not to get lost from him. The snow underfoot was soft and mushy and they sank almost to their knees with each step. They stumbled along, managing to stay upright only by leaning into the wind and by bracing against each other.

Hannah knew how short a distance it was to the rail fence from the corner of the house, and she knew they couldn't miss it. They *had* to hit it some place, but it was taking them so long that she was beginning to wonder if they weren't traveling alongside of it instead of toward it. She knew, though, she had lost all track of time. In this white, blowing fury it was easy to become confused both as to time and place. It was even easy to become confused as to whether you were still alive or not. You got a feeling that somehow you had stepped clear out of the real, sane world, and that you'd wandered off into some kind of snowy nightmare. Her hand, clutching the back of Tice's shirt, had no feeling left in it at all. She thought it must simply have frozen into that tight hold.

Then suddenly she bumped into Tice's back. She heard his voice screeching down wind, but couldn't make out what he said. She guessed they had reached the fence, and knew it a moment later when they changed direction and headed directly into the wind. They had the help of the fence now, though. They could cling to it and pull themselves along by it. Hannah slid the milk bucket up her arm so she would have a free hand, and after a time she began to measure their progress by the length of her arm. She placed her stocking-mittened hand on the fence rail, pulled herself along until she had reached the end of her grasp, then she had to turn loose and reach forward to a new place. She figured each time she had to do this they had moved about two feet.

It seemed to her they had been battling the snow and the wind for hours, when Tice dropped to his knees all at once and her heart gave a jump. She felt for his shoulders and bent over him, putting her mouth near his ear. "You hurt?"

She felt his head shake. He pulled her down beside him. "There's the barn."

She rubbed the frost from around her eyes and looked. Dimly she saw its outline, looking big and dark in the whiteness all about it.

"Hang on," Tice yelled, "I'm aimin' to crawl the rest of the way. I c'n see better down close to the ground."

When they got inside the building they collapsed on their faces in the straw and lay there, the barn feeling warm to them after the bitterness of the wind and snow. Hannah thought how peaceful and warm it seemed in the barn. But she knew it was only because they had just come in from outside. Lie there long enough, she knew, and the chill would creep into your bones until you froze. She stirred, and Tice struggled to his feet, reaching down to help her.

The cow and the calf, the sheep, which had all sheltered in the barn, had fared well enough. Tice had forked them down plenty of hay the night before and they were all chewing. They needed water, mostly, for the watering trough was frozen over. He set about breaking the ice and feeding. He measured up a piggin of corn for Hannah to feed the cow as she milked.

Hannah thawed her hands inside her dress, shuddering as they touched her bare skin, but she couldn't milk with hands so cold she couldn't even hold on to the cow's teats. When a little feeling had returned she set the box of feed near the the cow's head and started. Doggedly she milked the bucket full, as she usually did, then she turned the calf in to take the rest. She set the bucket in a safe corner and wrapped her hands again.

Tice had been seeing to the two pigs whose pen was built adjoining the barn. He came driving them through the door. "I'm aimin' to bring 'em in here," he said. "I've done got a place fenced off in the corner there." He had laid rails across a corner and bedded it with clean straw. When the pigs, coated over with snow and ice, grunted their way into the straw, Tice heaved a sigh of relief. "Now I got to git the horses. You seen to yer chickens an' the geese?"

"Not yit. I ain't had the time. I will when we git the horses in. Where are they at?"

"Jist in the barn lot, thank goodness. I brung 'em up from the pasture last night. If they was still in the pasture, I'd jist have to leave 'em freeze, fer couldn't nobody find 'em there."

Hannah thought the wind had let up a little when they got out into it again. It didn't seem quite as fierce, but she wasn't sure. It may just have been, she thought, that she'd got used to it and knew what to expect. They headed down the fence on the opposite side of the barn this time.

The horses were not near the barn—not, at any rate, that they could see. Tice kept brushing the snow away from his eyes, trying to see, but Hannah knew if he couldn't see any better than she could, he might easily miss the horses.

They came to the first corner, turned with it and followed it down the north side of the fence. Now she was ready to believe she had been wrong about the wind. Her face felt as if the top layer of skin had been peeled off.

[144]

In the northeast corner of the barn lot, about a hundred feet from the barn itself, a grove of young locust trees grew. Tice had left them there to furnish shade for any animal using the lot. He was glad, now, he had, for they found the horses there, huddled in the meager shelter of the bunched, bleached trees.

They stood patiently, heads down, breathing heavily. Hannah thought they were frozen, nothing but breath left, but when Tice roped them and they started leading them back to the barn they could still move. They walked stiffly, like foals unsure of their legs, very wobbly and slowly, and a time or two one of the mares swayed and staggered as if she were going down. But she didn't. Each time she recovered and came on.

Tice led them into the hall of the barn and when they were inside where he could see their condition, he groaned. They were coated with snow and ice. Their bodies were sheathed with it and their manes and tails were sharded with frost. "I d'know," he said, "I d'know but they're gone."

He and Hannah set to work with handfuls of straw, rubbing them down, walking them slowly, talking to them, letting them have small, slow drinks of water. "Oh, I wish we had somethin' hot for 'em," Hannah mourned.

"Bein' inside out of the wind an' eatin' even a little bit will do a heap of good, *if*," Tice said, "they'll eat."

They both kept working with the horses, rubbing them, making them walk, until the snow and ice had melted off. Then Tice fixed them generous rations of oats and hay, and when they began to eat, he sighed. "I reckon they've come to no real harm. Hit was a awful close thing, though. Now we'd best see about yore things."

They went into the shedroom. The chickens, all of them, were huddled in the far corner, crowded together with their feathers hunched bleakly, their eyes glazed over, their heads drooped. At first Hannah could not find the two geese, but finally she saw them nearly buried in some loose straw. "Well," she said, "I've allus heard that a goose has got as little sense as God ever give to e'er thing he made, but them two has had more than the chickens. They knowed enough to burrow in that straw to keep warm, whilst the chickens has jist huddled an' waited to freeze to death."

She and Tice caught them. They still had life enough to squawk but they had no strength to struggle. "We'd best take 'em to the house," Hannah said.

"What about the geese?"

"Next time one of us gits out here we c'n bring them too. But they ain't hurtin' as bad as the chickens."

Tice stuck two chickens inside his shirt front and Hannah tied three in her apron. "You still aimin' to try to git the milk to the house?" Tice asked her.

Hannah looked at it. She had forgotten it. Then she laughed. "I reckon you was right. Till the worst of this is over you'd jist best turn the calf in with the cow."

When they got back inside the house Hannah had the feeling she had returned after a long absence. Everything in the room looked a little strange to her, new and different. She felt battered and tired. The house was very quiet and cold. Her first really conscious thought, thought that went beyond mere feeling and absorption of sensations, was that Janie had stopped crying. It made her move as quickly as her numbed legs would take her to the cradle. The baby was asleep, placidly making small sucking sounds on the thumb with which she had comforted herself. Hannah sighed. A squalling youngun would have been more than she could cope with just then.

She took the chickens out of her apron, took the two Tice handed her and set to rubbing them down with old rags while Tice built up the fire. Methodically she rubbed each chicken and when the kettle had heated she poured warm water down their throats. Then she went up in the loft room and dragged down her extra straw tick. She ripped it open and spread the straw in the chimney corner and set the chickens there, heaping the straw around them. "Now if you got sense enough," she told them, "to stay there, you'll thaw out in time."

She didn't know what time it was but she was suddenly very hungry, so she set the spider on to heat and mixed up a batch of bread. In the winter a pot of stew was always on the hearth, always warm, so that hot bread was all that was needed to make a meal.

Tice ate as he paced back and forth from the door to the hearth. "I got to git out to the woodpile," he told Hannah, restlessly. "We ain't got enough wood in the house to last the night."

"Eat first," she told him. "Eat a good bait an' then see if the wind has slackened up any. Mebbe it will."

"I misdoubt it. I disremember ever seein' the weather so fierce."

"Well, we got plenty to eat, Tice—for us an' the stock too. An' they's wood enough fer a month, I'd think. I don't see no cause to weary . . . not yit, I don't."

"No," he agreed, "not yit." He handed her his empty bowl and motioned that he didn't want any more. "I ain't hungry."

When she had redd up after the meal, Hannah set to spinning again. Come blizzard or not, the wool was still to be spun into yarn and time was fleeting. She couldn't afford, she told Tice, just to set.

Tice sat and dozed before the fire, whittled on a chair rung when he could keep awake long enough, went to the door and peered out, and always shut it again impatiently. "Hit ain't slackenin' e'er bit. If anything, it's still risin'."

"Mebbe," Hannah said, "we'd best not burn too much wood fer a spell."

But Tice would not have that. "No, we got to keep warm." He piled the logs high and kept the fire burning hot and strong. "I'll git out," he promised, "one way or another an' git in wood fer the night."

When finally the light began to fail and the storm was still blowing as fiercely as ever, he threw down his whittling knife and pushed his stool back. "I ain't aimin' to wait no longer."

Hannah helped him get ready to go out.

From time to time over the wind's whine she heard a thumping and bumping and she guessed Tice was laying wood up against the side of the house as he finished chopping it free. But when finally the door opened he stood in it empty-armed. He pulled the stocking down from his mouth. "I seen I couldn't git nowhere packin' wood backards an' forrards, so I jist drug one of them trees up to the door. I'll chop an' pile it in the door an' you c'n help haul it in."

That was the way they got the wood in for the night. And Tice did not try to get to the barn again. The animals were as comfortable as he could make them for the time being. They did not try to get to the spring for water. Tice filled the kettle with snow from time to time and they used the melted snow.

When night fell they were both tired, Tice almost exhausted. They sat in front of the fire drooping sleepily over their food and they went early to bed.

In bed, however, Hannah couldn't go to sleep immediately. Over in the corner one of the hens kept up a kind of low singing and humming. None of them had been laying since the onset of winter, but now one was singing just like a laying hen. It would be, Hannah thought, chuckling, just like the foolish thing to commence laying in such a time as this.

Finally the sound merged with the hum of the wind and she went on to sleep.

18

It snowed uninterruptedly for two more days and nights. On the second day the wind died away, but the snow continued to fall as thick as down shaken from a goosefeather tick. Hannah, cracking the door and peering out from time to time, wondered where it was all coming from. "You wouldn't believe," she told Tice, "it could be sich a heap of it. Hit looks as if all the sky had turned to snow an' was emptyin' itself out."

"I reckon that's what it's doin'," he answered her. "Fur as I've ever heared, that's what snow is. The clouds git mixed with ice an' it makes snow."

"Well, hit must of been a mortally big cloud."

"An' a awful lot of ice."

Once the wind had let up Tice cleared a path to the barn. He fashioned a wide scoop from a plank that was among a pile he had hewed and trimmed earlier in the fall and put to season in the barn loft. With the snow still falling so heavily the path kept filling and he had to keep shoveling, but using the path kept it packed underfoot and by scooping it out two or three times a day he could keep it fairly free. At least there was no danger now of getting lost going to the barn.

Feeding and watering the stock, keeping wood for the fire, keeping the path open, kept Tice busy every daylight hour. The first thing he did each morning was to shovel out the path. The second thing was to take to the barn the snow water he had melted the night before. It was a slow process, melting snow for every use. "If it ever lets up," he vowed, "the first thing I aim to do is git the path to the spring dug out."

Hannah brought the geese into the house. She had moved the chickens and their straw bed to the loft room and she put the geese with them. Tice grumbled at having chickens and geese overhead. Occasionally he would be caught standing under a crack in the loft room floor and would be splattered. Then he would threaten to wring a few necks. He didn't really mind, though, Hannah knew. But by grumbling at the fowls he could take out part of his impatience with the storm.

When the snow finally stopped the sun came out for one day, with little warmth in it, but bright and glary on the meadow. It seemed not to melt the snow at all, but there was some thawing, for the next morning there was a fine glaze of ice on top of the snow—thin, very slippery, blue-white. Then the sky turned overcast again, looking gray and soupy and forbidding. Tice looked at it uneasily. "*Now*, what you reckon it's aimin' to do? Commence all over again?"

However, the overcast sky did not produce more snow. About the middle of the morning the air suddenly warmed and a fine, misty rain which slowly turned to sleet started to fall. As it struck the already ice-covered snow it seeped through the top layer, then began to pile up. It fell all afternoon and gradually the trees, the fence railings, the roofs of the outbuildings, were layered over with a crust of sleety rain. Branches of the trees began to sag with it, and when Tice came back from feeding and tending the stock late that afternoon he said he had propped the shed roof because it was sagging so badly under its heavy load. He also reported it was turning bitter cold again.

Neither of them could guess how cold it actually got that night. They only knew that it was worse than anything they had ever experienced before, and they could no longer keep warm, even under all their covers, in the bed. When they had hunched futilely together for several hours, Tice threw the covers back and got up. "Hit's no use to stay in that there bed. The cold comes creepin' up underneath, an' my back has been shivery fer so long now I misdoubt it'll quit shakin' afore mornin'."

Hannah got up too and they moved the fur robes and blankets to the floor in front of the hearth. Tice built up a roaring fire and Hannah brought the baby and they rolled themselves in the covers and baked their backs in front of the flames. "Don't it feel good?" Hannah murmured when her back was so warm it burned to touch the blanket.

"We ort to done it sooner," Tice said.

"Hit's jist that this cold is so uncommon it takes a body by surprise an' you don't hardly know what *to* do."

"Won't nothin' about it surprise me no more," Tice opined.

But it did, for when daylight came they looked out on a world that was as rigidly iced and frozen as if it had suddenly been plated over with iron. The worst of it was that it had been encased in this frozen armor in such disarray as to make all the familiar landmarks look weird and strange. The woods all around them looked as if an angry giant had strode recklessly through, uprooting trees with a careless and fretful hand, sweeping them out of his way, breaking off limbs at will, strewing them and piling them and creating a massive, icy disorder. And over all the massed piles of uprooted trees and broken limbs, over the rolling, undulating bosom of the meadow, over the hills in the distance, there was this thick casing of ice, this rigid and inflexible frozen armor which made it look as if the world itself was frozen to the heart, would never melt and breathe again.

Hannah and Tice looked out upon it and then they looked at each other. "Never in my time have I seed sich," Hannah whispered, as if afraid even to speak of it.

"Nor me," Tice said, shaking his head.

When he came back from the spring there was a look of awe on his face. "Hannah, you'll not believe it. The spring is froze over solid!"

Hannah was rinsing the morning dishes. She stopped with her hands in the water and looked at the foam of lathery suds on top, trying to take this new thing in. How could the spring be frozen? It was a strong spring. It gushed out of the hillside at the back of the house in a never ending stream. How could a thing which never ceased moving freeze? Tice must have it wrong. "You're sart'n, are you?"

"I'm sart'n."

She knew, actually, he had not been mistaken. It was the way he'd said. You just couldn't believe it.

All that day the trees cracked with the cold. They made a sharp, explosive sound, as if a gun had been shot off into the still air. All around them, all day, the sharp, snapping, shot-like sounds kept going off. Tice winced each time. A lot of good wood was being ruined. But, he tried to think philosophically, a lot of firewood would be handy next winter.

Three days later they were still thinking a thaw would set in any day. They were still feeding the stock full rations of corn and hay, using up their firewood with no thought of being saving with it, and making heavy inroads on their meat and meal to keep a good stew inside of them during the cold.

Three weeks later Tice began dragging up firewood from the down trees and limbs in the woods. The snow had melted a little, then it had snowed some more, then it had melted and snowed, melted and snowed until Tice had lost count of the times, but it was still too deep to use the horses, so he dragged up only the smaller trees which he could handle alone. Then, seeing him so exhausted, Hannah helped, and he worked out a kind of harness he could hitch to the two of them and they could drag up larger trees. Even with the two of them it was terribly hard work. They floundered in the deep snow, slipped, fell and worked themselves into a sweat, which when they stopped to breathe and rest, froze their clothing solid almost instantly. Their cheeks and noses, their hands, were frostbitten time after time, became swollen and painful. But in three weeks they had burned the woodpile and all the smaller limbs they could find near the house. They gave thanks, now, for the down trees. It would have been too cruel having to fell trees in such cold.

Tice began to worry, too, about the corn lasting, and he started cutting down on the ration for the stock. He'd had a good crop of corn, better than most, for he'd had the help of Hannah and they'd filled the crib and some over when they'd gathered. But you couldn't feed all those animals twice a day with nothing else but a little hay and expect it to last out such a winter. Usually you could count on stock being able to pick a little in the pasture all winter. There was a hardy clump grass they liked and thrived on, which didn't freeze down much . . . and there were young cane shoots and willow sprouts, bark . . . lots of forage you could depend on helping with winter feed commonly. But he couldn't even turn the animals loose into the pastures. They would have frozen into carcasses in half a day with the cold so intense. Keeping them in the barn as he had to do meant feeding them every bite they ate.

He had to do something. He made a crude pair of snowshoes and began dragging the sled down the slope to the creek to cut cane and willow shoots.

He was awkward with the snowshoes, fell a lot, and they were imperfect enough that occasionally they tangled on him and tripped him through no fault of his own. He hated them and cussed every time he went to strap them on, but he was too worried about the corn not to keep working with them.

And the sled was heavy. It ran fairly easily going down the slope. In fact, it often overran him and knocked him down, bruising and skinning his back, making him stiff and sore later. Coming back up the slope it was a long, hard, heartbreaking pull.

Hannah couldn't bear it. She couldn't leave the baby to go as far as the creek, but she would watch and when she saw him nearing the foot of the slope she would go down to help him from there.

One day when she went to help him she saw a pair of turkeys lying on top the load of sprouts. "Oh," she said, "you got a shot at some turkeys. I'll relish somethin' different fer a change."

"I never had to shoot 'em," Tice said bluntly. "Take a good look at them turkeys, Hannah."

She picked them up and examined them. They were little more than feathers and bones. She looked at them in dismay. "What's the matter with 'em?"

"They was purely starvin' to death."

Hannah stood with the two gaunt turkeys in her hands and looked at Tice, her face slowly whitening. They had not yet begun to worry about food for themselves. It was true Hannah was not making the stews quite as rich, but there were still a few flitches of dried meat hanging from the rafters. Usually they ate fresh meat all winter, keeping the dried meat for when Tice went into the woods, or on a journey, or when they wanted it for a change. They never stored up fresh meat for the winter. There never was any need to. Tice could always go out and kill within five miles of the house-place. And they'd not thought but when it thawed he yet could.

There was still meal in the house, though the pouch wasn't more than a quarter full. Tice ground only one pouch at a time, for it got musty and the mice got in it. As long as the corn held out they didn't need to worry about meal, though, for Hannah could always soak it and make hominy. They had a little milk, yet, too. But as Tice had had to cut down on the cow's feed her milk had let up. The calf was already thinning from not having enough.

Still, they hadn't really worried. Any day the thaw would set in and Tice could go out and get meat and run a turn of meal off. But if the cold held on there wouldn't *be* any corn pretty soon . . . and if the woods things were starving . . . Hannah looked at the turkeys and her lips moved silently before she could bring the words out. "With the ice all over they cain't git nothin' to eat, kin they?"

Tice shook his head. "I ort to went sooner. I'm gittin' out into the woods tomorrow to see what I c'n find to kill afore things gits any worse."

He didn't have to get out in the woods the next day, though. At daylight when he went to the barn he found three gaunt, thin buffalo nosed up to the door, picking at the wisps of hay. He stopped short when he saw them, thinking he might frighten them away, but he saw immediately they were too hungry, too near starved and frozen to be frightened of anything. He didn't even bother to go to the house for his gun. He just picked up a fence rail and knocked them in the head, slit their throats and left them bleeding to death in the snow while he went on and fed.

That was the first time wild animals came to their barn lot searching for food, but it was not the last time. It got to be a common thing. Elk came, and deer, and more buffalo. The game Tice was accustomed to hunting came right to their door . . . and was hardly worth the shot it took to kill them, they were all so gaunt and so starved. There would be the liver, the heart, a little meat on the hams, and the buffalo humps still had some fat on them, but for the most part if he hadn't known he would fare no better in the woods, Tice wouldn't have wasted time dressing them out. Their skins hung loose about their ribs and their spines stuck up like the ridge pole of the barn. It was a hard winter all right—hard on the animals as well as on man.

It lasted, that deep, solid-frozen cold, for two months. In all that time Tice and Hannah never saw the ground. The snow never entirely melted and usually just as they had hopes that a thaw was on the way, the sky clouded over again and a new snow fell. It never was as deep as the first one, but the ground was always covered and every stream, every creek, was frozen solid and hard.

By sledding cane and willow shoots and young bark up to the barn, Tice managed to eke out his corn longer than he had expected. But the tenth day of February, according to Hannah's notch-stick, he came within sight of the end of it. He measured out a peck for Hannah to soak and cook for them, and there was less than a bushel left to feed. Something had to be done.

He went into the house and sat down before the fire, stretching his feet out automatically to the blaze. One thing, he thought, they'd never failed to have a good fire. If a body stayed warm—but a body had to eat, too. They had slowly used up everything Hannah had put by. He didn't know as he'd ever had such an appetite as he'd had this winter, just when they needed to be sparing of food. It seemed to him every time he sat down to eat he could have eaten all Hannah had in the pot by himself. And Hannah said she was hungry too. He guessed they were working their bodies so hard they just naturally needed more to eat.

There was one flitch of meat left. Hannah had said they wouldn't touch it if they could do without. They had no salt. The cow was giving but a trickle of milk and they were letting the calf have that. By rights, he knew, he ought to butcher that calf and eat it. He had supposed they would, but when he had mentioned it to Hannah she had looked so grieved he hadn't the heart. It was a heifer calf and she wanted to raise it into another cow. Then, as the cold had persisted, he had grown stubborn in his determination to bring them all, humans and animals, through without loss. "One way or another," he had told Hannah doggedly, "I'll git us through."

Now he sat in front of the fire and thought about it. If a thaw was ever going to come it didn't look like it. It was February. It could easily, now that the cold had lasted this long, be the end of March before they saw any let-up in it. And by the end of March every head of stock he had, to say nothing of his woman and youngun, would be either dead or in an awfully bad way.

He sat and pulled at his beard. He hadn't been shaving this winter. There hadn't been time to shave, even if he'd had the inclination, and he had a curly, sandy beard which grew spadelike around his chin. Hannah liked it so well he didn't know if he ever would shave it off now. He sat and brooded and pulled at it. Hannah was sitting across the hearth from him, sewing him a new pair of moccasins. He lifted his head. "How much money we got, Hannah?"

"Hard money or dollars?"

"Dollars. I know we ain't got enough hard money to be worth the namin'."

She laid down the moccasin and went to the cupboard and rummaged through the drawer. She brought the hoard of bills and handed them to him. "Hit's a little better'n five hundred dollars since you got yer militia pay fer that Ohio march."

Tice leafed through the bills, counting them for himself. He slapped them against his knee. "Wish it was five hundred of hard money."

"Don't you, though?" Hannah picked up her sewing again. "I d'know as I've ever got it through my head why them paper dollars ain't as good as hard money, seein' as it's mostly what we got to use, an' the Congress has put 'em out."

"Because they ain't got no hard money back of 'em. This paper money is American dollars, not British shillin's an' pounds. An' they ain't no American shillin's an' pounds to back up the dollars."

"Then whyn't we go back to usin' British shillin's an' pounds?"

"Because we're fightin' the British is why. When the war is over, if the colonies win out an' git theirselves set up right, these dollars'll be worth somethin'. An' we'll make out all right. You wouldn't want to be a Britisher all yer life, would you?"

"I d'know. I figure that's what I *been* all my life. Why's the use of changin' over now?"

Tice frowned at her. "You'd best not talk thataway in front of nobody else, Hannah. That's what gits folks in trouble . . . talkin' like a Tory. Now I know you ain't one. But they's plenty that might not. You jist don't understand what the fightin' is about."

"Do you?"

"Not the whole of it, I don't," he admitted honestly, "but I know hit's got somethin' to do with taxes an' sich an' wantin' to run our own show. An' I know enough to know I ain't on the British side. You'd jist better keep yer mouth shut tight around other folks, I'm a warnin' you."

"I d'know as you need to," she said spiritedly. "If you're aimin' on bein' an American, I am too."

Tice's eyes twinkled and he said to her, teasing, "If I was aimin' to be a Dutchman, would you aim to be a Dutchman too?"

Hannah pulled a fine thong through the moccasin. "If you was aimin' to be the devil hisself, Tice, with horns an' a tail, I'd git me a pitchfork too."

[153]

It shocked him, as she had know it would, and meant it to. It was very close to blasphemy and she felt daring as if she had teetered on the brink of something dangerous. But he was always teasing her, making her blush, making her hang her head. Sometimes something inside of her made her turn and hand it right back to him, and when she did, she usually ventured into an area which amazed Tice. She hadn't been raised by a man for nothing, after all.

There was the time when she had been carrying Jane, had been big and cumbersome and awkward and he had looked up at her coming across the field one day and had suddenly laughed, motioning with his hands to show how broad and big she was. She had laughed with him, but she had said, slyly, "Cain't nobody that sees me mistake how you been spendin' *yore* nights, kin they?" It had been so unexpected, so indelicate, that it had silenced him for the rest of the morning. Her tongue could be rough and her humor bawdy he had found out.

So, now, he looked at her, his mouth dropped open a little, not knowing what to say. She just plain flummoxed him, times. Hannah went on with her sewing. She let the silence hang until she turned the heel of the moccasin. "What did you want to know about the money fer?"

"I am aimin' to git some corn. I'm aimin' on tryin' to git through to the fort an' see if Ben's got any in the commissary he c'n sell me."

"You think he mought have?"

"I d'know. Hit's a chance. Only thing is, I mislike havin' to go off an' leave you an' Jane by yerselves. But you see how it is. Hit's either to go, or run the risk of losin' the animals an' goin' hungry soon ourselves."

"You needn't to mind. I c'n do fer us while you're gone."

"I know you kin. But it'll be hard on you. I wish it didn't have to be."

Hannah kept her eyes on her sewing. She punched the deerskin with her awl and then pulled the long strip of thong through the hole, overlaid and joining on the top and bottom and pulled the thong through the other side. Tice watched her. She made a good moccasin. She was never content just to shape a piece of wet skin to the foot, let it dry and then tie it. She always cut her skins and stitched them. She looked up at him. "When did you aim to go?"

"In the mornin'—soon as it's day."

He didn't say how long he'd be gone, and she didn't ask, but with the snow melted to where he could ride a horse Hannah could figure for herself that barring bad luck he should be back at the end of the fourth day. That would be allowing for slow travel, too.

At the end of the fourth day, however, she did not worry when he failed to come. She did up the work and set the house to rights for the night. She wished she had some more wool yarn to knit up. Knitting was the most comforting thing a body could do with their hands, she thought, and she could always sit and be easy in her mind if she had a piece of knitting in her hands.

There was the little pair of shoes for the baby, though, she hadn't finished. There was plenty of time, for she wouldn't be needing them until the next winter. Janie would likely start walking in April or May, soon after she was a year old, but it would be warm enough for her to run barefoot then, and it would be next winter before she'd have need of shoes. But she'd started them, so she got the pieces of soft deerskin out of the cupboard and began working on them.

The baby made a gurgling sound in its throat. Hannah gave the cradle a push with her toe. "You tryin' to say somethin'? Tryin' to talk?" She nodded at the baby and smiled at her. "Yore pa," she said, "has likely had to go some-wheres else fer his corn. Likely Ben Logan didn't have none to spare an' he's went up to Harrod's or mebbe even to Boonesburg. That's why he ain't come home yit in my opinion." She kept on sewing on the moccasin, kept the cradle rocking gently with one toe, and smiled and talked to the baby in the firelight. "He'll be back when he gits him some corn, yore pa will. He ain't one to give up easy, I reckon you know that, don't you? But I don't reckon you do, yit. You'll learn, though. You'll find out. You c'n all yer life hold up yer head an' know that yore pa is a man you c'n put yer dependence in, an' one that don't give up easy. But unless you fergit yer learnin' you'll never be the one to say so. You c'n jist take yer stand by the side of him, like I do, proud that ever'-body knows he's that kind of a man, an' not havin' to make no brags or boasts about him. Them that brags an' boasts generally have got nothin' to brag or boast about. Them that does, they c'n keep their mouths shut, fer ever'body else'll know it as good as they do. Hit would be a shame to him, an' to me, if you ever bragged or boasted on him. Savin' inside of yerself."

She bent nearer and looked into the baby's face. The child reached up a hand to touch Hannah's mouth, then she laughed aloud and went into a fit of frantic waving of her arms and legs. Hannah dropped her sewing and reached out to squeeze one small fat leg. "You look like yore pa, you know it? You look a heap like him. You got eyes like him an' even got that same little sunk-in place at the corner of yer mouth, to say nothin' of yer red hair. You want to know a secret, little Janie Fowler? I'll tell you a secret, then—one I ain't ever told a soul before, not even yore pa." She leaned down and rubbed her cheek against the soft skin of the child's leg. "Listen, close, an' I'll tell you. They's times when I look at yore pa, mebbe when he's jist settin' by the fire, or mebbe eatin' his stew, or mebbe feedin' the stock out at the barn, or mebbe even lyin' asleep—they's times when I look at him an' the heart in my bosom swells up till it feels like it's goin' to bust wide open . . . jist crack an' run down inside of me . . . jist on account of I'm so purely proud he's my man. I could jist sink down from the weakness inside of me, knowin' he's mine an' I'm his'n. That's the way I feel, sometimes, like my bones had turned to jelly, an' a shiver had run up my back an' made me have cold-bumps all over my arms. That's what love makes you feel like, Janie Fowler. That's what it makes you feel like. But, law . . ." she laughed and her voice trailed softly off and she sighed, "hit'll be a time an' a time afore you're old enough to know."

She slid from the stool onto the floor beside the cradle, and she sat with her face against the cradle, looking into the fire. Me an' him, she thought—we got us a house-place, and we got us this little youngun, and we got a cow and horses and pigs and sheep and chickens. Me and Tice—we got all this. And he's gone to get corn for the stock, and I'm left here to guard the house-place. But it's no matter, for soon he'll come riding back through the gap. She thought how the fire would burn warmer, and the bed would sleep softer and the stew would taste richer when Tice was at home again. She drowsed, staring into the fire, and then roused herself and went to bed.

The days passed with a little more snow, a three-day thaw, which was heartening, and then another freeze and hardening. Hannah stayed so busy during the daytime that she rarely had time to sit down except to nurse and tend the baby. There was less than a peck of corn for the animals, now. Each morning she went out into the woods and cut down sprouts and bushes and dragged them into the barn for the stock. Then she went back and stripped bark from the young trees which had been uprooted in the blizzard. At the house she boiled it with some of the hay and a handful of corn, into a kind of mash. Once a day was all she could manage to feed this mash for it took too long to gather the bark and boil the mash. It was all she could do for them, for she had to keep firewood chopped and dragged up, she had to cook a little now and then, she had to keep ice melted for water for the stock and for the house. By dark each night she was almost too tired to eat. When she drooped over her food, however, she made herself rouse. It was more important to eat than to sleep. She couldn't let her own milk start drying up, and Tice expected her to keep the stock going until he got back. So she doggedly swallowed down the thin stew, which was daily growing thinner.

It was on the night of the tenth day Tice had been gone that the wolves came. She awakened to the new sound of their howls very near at hand and was instantly out of the bed and into her clothes. She bundled Janie into the cradle and stirred up the fire. The baby did not awaken. Hannah reached down her gun, loaded quickly, snatched up her shawl and let herself out the door.

The moon was still up. It had been full three nights before, and caught at its zenith it would have brightened the yard and barn lot helpfully, but it was far in the south now and its light was frail and thinned out, almost milky, like the shifting gray light of false dawn. It blurred with the snow and appeared to come off the bosom of the snow as much as from the sky. Hannah followed the path, glad the snow was no deeper than it was. Snow only halfway to the knees didn't seem like much snow after what they'd got used to.

She couldn't tell how large the pack was. They were snarling and fighting among themselves in the barn so that it seemed to her there must be half a hundred. Something was down, some animal, and they were on it, worrying, slavering, gnawing at it. The rest of the stock was scared, squealing and milling about. She was too angry to be scared herself. She took cover at the end of the barn and fired into the wolves. They ran out the far end of the hallway, scattering easily as she had always heard they would. She knew they wouldn't go far, though, that they would be back, and she knew she had to hurry with whatever could be done.

She ran into the barn. It was one of the mares that was down. Hannah heard her breath bubbling with a dreadful, liquid sound and when she ran her hands over her, she found a great, gaping hole in her throat. They'd ruined her. She would have to be killed. The mare was struggling to get up, fighting to breathe. Hannah held the gun against her head, grieving, "Pore thing, pore thing," feeling almost as if she were killing a human being. It was the chestnut mare Tice had bought at the plunder auction. She made herself fire the gun and the horse buckled and lay still. Swiftly she turned away. She hadn't the time to spend on further grieving. Tice would hate losing the mare, but nothing could be done about her. She had to see to the rest of the stock.

The other mare was in the stall, panicky, wheeling about, throwing her head up wildly, whinnying and snorting. Hannah spoke to her, rubbed her head, calmed her as best she could, but the animal continued to snort and blow. At least, though, she had now felt a familiar hand, heard a familiar voice.

The cow and calf were backed into a far corner of their stall, the calf more than half hidden behind the cow, and the cow was standing with legs planted, her head down, rumbling threateningly. Hannah spoke to her, too, rubbed her head, her shoulders and flanks. "There, girl," she said, "hit's all right now. They's not a thing to be afeared of."

She felt relief that the cow and calf were safe and went on to the stall where Tice had penned the ewes and lamb. The ewes were huddled in a corner, heads almost hidden in each other's flanks, but the lamb was missing. She searched the straw to make certain it wasn't buried behind the ewes, but it was gone. Then she went to the far end of the hallway and saw the dark blots in the snow where it had been carried off. There was nothing left of it by now, she knew.

The mare and the lamb! What kind of an accounting was she going to have to give Tice of this night? She felt angry and besieged. She had to think what to do, what to do, or there'd be more loss. Wolves wouldn't leave for long with an animal down. They'd be back, and even now she could hear them snarling closer. Why hadn't they closed in the ends of the hallway when they built the barn! But nobody did. An open hall was the way everyone built. And now every animal in the barn was helpless, even more helpless, penned up as they were, than if they had been in the open. In the open they could at least have run. Here in the barn they were a standing prey.

Judging by the light, its thin quality, the oldness of the moon, Hannah knew it was between midnight and dawn, lacking two hours, maybe of daylight. For that long, then, the stock must be guarded. How to do it? She could settle down here in the hallway and fire off the gun every time the wolves came close, but it would be an awful use of powder. It would run her perilously close if Tice didn't come home soon. Then she remembered a thing Samuel had told once, of fighting off wolves with fire. That was it! She'd build a big fire at each end of the hallway and keep them going until morning.

She looked around, deciding quickly, her mind running on to the next problem . . . wood. There wasn't enough wood dragged up, to say nothing of being cut, to keep two fires blazing. Wood . . . wood . . . her mind ran over the possibilities. If she tried to get to the woods to drag some up—without even thinking further she dismissed that idea. Every animal in the barn would be killed before she got back.

Her eyes lit on the loft Tice had built across the far end of the barn, and the stack of planks he'd laid there to season. She'd burn the planks! But even as she started toward them she thought of a better use for them. She could close up the ends of the hall with the planks tomorrow. Best not to burn them. What? What could she burn? The shedroom . . . it came to her suddenly. It was well seasoned and would burn with a good blaze. She ran for an axe and then crawled up on the roof of the low shed, began prying the shingle boards loose. Twice while she was working on the roof she had to stop and fire into the wolves, but finally she had enough of the shingles loose to start her fires. Then she ran to the house for a shovelful of coals. She started a fire near each end of the barn. When they were blazing she began to pry the logs apart, working on the end of the shed where the logs were shorter. As each log came down she dragged it to a fire. When finally she had enough logs, she gave over tearing down the end of the shed.

She had been working without stopping and it was only then she realized how breathless and weary she was. She dragged up a log to the fire at the near end of the barn, dropped on it and pushed her hair back out of her eyes. She took a deep breath. The stock would be safe, now, though she'd hated to tear down the shedroom. They could build it back, however, easier than they could get a new start of stock, to say nothing of the poor things being eaten alive.

She kept watch the rest of the night, dozing a little now and then. As day was coming she heard a new sound and cocked her head to listen. She smiled. Janie was squalling, and from the sound of it she was mad enough to raise the whole roof off the house. She was wet and hungry, poor little tyke. Hannah lifted herself stiffly off the log, bent down to heave it into the fire, glanced at the other fire. They'd do till she got the work done up, then she'd come out here and board up the ends of the hallway. And that would be the end of the wolves.

Tice was gone two weeks to a day. He came back minus all his money and in debt for three hundred dollars more, but he came back with some corn and more of it in the commissary at the fort.

The evening was coming on when he got home. Hannah had been doing the chores at the barn and was coming to the house when she saw him coming through the gap across the creek. Her heart gave a great leap and one hand flew to her mouth. She stopped and watched him, trembly with her gladness that he was home again, feeling all at once like singing, or crying, gone all soft inside at the sight of him. He was leading two horses, both loaded. He had his corn, and he'd borrowed a horse from Ben to bring it home. And he was tired. She could tell by the way he bent into the slope and pulled his feet after him. He'd walked from the fort—maybe he'd walked from wherever he'd got his corn. She wanted to go flying down the slope to meet him, to reach him and touch him immediately . . . but something shy and awkwardly timid inside her would never allow her to show gladness openly. When she felt it, this sweet, compelling invasion, she could never even bear to look directly at Tice.

So she went in the house and busied herself, filling the kettle with fresh water, swinging the crane over the fire, brushing the hearth with the turkey wing. Not until she heard him speak to the horses outside the door did she go out to join him. He was unloading a pouch of corn. "Well, you got back, did you?"

He turned and his eyes searched her hungrily. "I got back. You've been all right, have you?"

A pulse beat back of Hannah's knees and they felt weak and trembly. She smiled and nodded. "All right . . . yes. I been all right." Then she made him let her take the horses to the barn. "You go on in the house. Set, an' I'll be right in to fix you a bait."

He looked lean and worn down, cold and tired. "I could do with it," he admitted, and without argument he turned the horses over to her.

He had brought one pouch of meal, and as he talked Hannah set the stew nearer the fire and stirred up a batch of bread. Her mouth watered at the thought of the crusty, brown, greasy cakes that would soon be ready to eat. She'd not had bread for a long, long time.

He'd been lucky, Tice told her, lying warm, now, on his stomach on the hearth, all his muscles thawing and stretching by the fire, his head pillowed on his folded hands. When he'd got to the fort, Ben didn't have any corn to sell. He barely had enough left to get his own animals and people through, but he had heard there was some at the Falls. "He said it was powerful costly . . . goin' fer sixty dollars a bushel, he'd heared, but that was all he knowed of in the country. He was sendin' a feller over to git a load, an' he allowed I could go along an' help, an' bring me back some with his'n."

"So you been to the Falls, have you?"

"I been to the Falls." Then he turned his head and grinned at her. "An' glad to git shut of 'em, too." He sat up. "That place, Hannah, is the tradin'est place ever you seen! All they think of there is tradin' . . . an' it's unbelievin' the prices they are askin' an' gettin'. Sixty dollars fer a bushel of corn . . . two hundred dollars fer a bushel of salt! An' you know what they pay fer a day's hire of labor? Twenty dollars, that's what they pay!"

Hannah ladled the bread onto the hot spider. "Humph," she said, setting it over the coals, "if it was me I'd consider that cheap. Who would want to work fer another man at any price?"

"Who, is right . . . not me. But some does, an' that's what they're payin'. Paper dollars, of course."

He lay back down, turned on his side so he could watch Hannah. She sat on a low stool, shielding her face with her forearm. Her hair fell forward and she brushed absently at it with the back of her hand. He laughed to see it. He wondered that she didn't do it in her sleep.

Every time he had to be gone nowadays he liked it less . . . for any spell of time, that was. He didn't mind being off for the day, in the woods, maybe, or even to make a trip to the fort and be gone one night. But when he had to be gone very many days it made him restless and uneasy. It was that woman sitting there on the stool, pulling and tugging at him . . . her black hair loose on her forehead, her face red from the fire, her shoulders rounded with stretching to tend the bread . . . it was that woman pulled at him. When a man took up living with a woman, he never was much good any more without her. Suddenly he felt a great need for her, now, immediately. He pulled her off the stool onto the floor beside him. She laughed softly and whispered, "The bread'll burn."

"Set it off. Hit c'n wait."

It wasn't until they had eaten that she told him about the wolves. "I had to tear down part of the shedroom to burn to keep the wolves off the stock one night."

"When was that?"

"Three nights ago."

"You made out, though?"

"I made out. Exceptin' I hated to tear down the shedroom. I had to use them planks you was seasonin' to board up the barn, too."

"Hit won't hurt 'em. I'm glad they was handy."

In detail, then, she told him what had happened. She hated to tell him about the mare and the lamb, but it had to be told. When she had finished he said, "You done good not to lose no more of the stock. Hit was my fault . . . not thinkin' to pen up the ends of the hall when I built."

Her heart lightened. She had done the best she could and he found no fault with it. "Well," she said, reasonably, "a body cain't think of ever'thing."

"No. Hit was bad luck to lose the mare an' the lamb, but it was good luck you never took hurt yerself."

"Yes. That's the way it was."

19

THERE WAS COLD WEATHER right on into May that spring, but the backbone of the winter was broken shortly after Tice got home. And the snows and the freezes and the thaws of the hard winter were good for the land. The soil cracked and mulched as fine as sand and was crumbly in the hands, blackened with frosted leaf mold. Never had there been such a crop year as that one. There was plenty of rain, but not too much. There was sun and heat when needed, but not to the point of drought. As the summer passed, the corn grew taller than any had ever seen it, weighted down with heavy, full ears, and until frost the leaves and stalks were lush for fodder. "I swear," Tice told Hannah, "I ain't ever in my time seed sich corn."

"Nor me," Hannah said, "an' the garden's beat all my hopes fer it. I ain't hardly got no place left to put the things I've dried an' laid away fer the winter. I ain't thinkin' we'll run skeerce *this* winter."

There was one bad Indian scare during the summer when two new stations on the Licking were attacked. A retaliatory expedition was called out and a thousand Kentuckians, Tice among them, led by George Rogers Clark, marched across the Ohio.

Hannah took Janie into the fort and spent a tedious month there. As endless as the time seemed, though, it passed somehow and they were all at home again by the first of August. "We done 'em enough damage this time," Tice said, "hit ort to keep 'em quiet fer a good, long spell."

"I wish so," Hannah said. "I git awful tard of this runnin' into the fort jist when the work is the heaviest here at home."

"Well," Tice said cheerfully, "we got plenty of time to git in the crops now."

As late as October, the air that fall was like a golden wine, light, sparkling, dry. And never had Hannah seen the hills so full of color as when the leaves began to turn. "Jist look," she told Tice one evening when they sat in the door, the work done, waiting for night. "Ain't it the purtiest sight?"

The hickory trees, the poplars, and most of the sugar trees were a hundred different shades of yellow, ranging from the palest, frailest, most delicate tints to the deepest, heaviest gold. Mixed among them were the sassafras and sumac, bright scarlet, and the deeper crimson of the ash. The gold of the beeches was touched with copper, and Hannah didn't know but she liked them the best of all. "A beech tree," she said, "is the proudest one of them all."

The oaks, stubborn and stolid, were still green. They would be the last to turn, the last to sever their leaves, the last to stand naked to the cold. "Ain't they strengthy, though?" Hannah said, laughing. "An' listen to that old katy-did. He's a sawin' slower an' slower these days. What comes of 'em in the winter, Tice?"

"They die off."

Hannah thought about it. "Jist one summer is all, ain't it, they got to live. Hit seems kind of sad."

"Well, hit's a lifetime to them. Ain't no sadder than what comes to folks."

"No. No sadder."

She thought about death and how it must come. It didn't seem, somehow, as if it could, to her. She knew it would, but it didn't *seem* like it would. There wasn't any way you could actually *believe* it would, though you knew. What was knowing, anyhow? She tried to think of what it was. It was handling a hoe in the garden. It was holding Janie and feeling the flow of her milk out of her breast. It was spinning wool into yarn. It was things you could touch and handle and take a good hard hold on. But, she thought, it was things you could only feel inside you, too. Like the gladness in her when Tice came home. And the fine joy when he turned to her at night. But you couldn't know somebody else's feelings, not actually. Not to say *know*, you couldn't—not the way you knew your own. You could guess at the way they felt, by your own feelings, but that wasn't to say knowing. A body was just kind of shut up inside them-selves, she thought, kind of walled in by their own feelings, and she didn't know of any way they could be otherwise. You couldn't, in any way, then, know death. Not till it happened, and then, she reckoned, there'd be nothing to know *with*. It was a wonder now, the way things went.

Tice shivered a little. "Hit's turnin' chill. 'Twouldn't surprise me none if they ain't a frost soon."

Hannah brought her thoughts back. "Hit wouldn't me, either. Bound to be. An' I got soap to make yit an' the wool to card, an' I'm aimin' to git my loom set up afore it turns off cold, too."

Tice stood. "You're aimin' to do that, are you?"

"Yes. I'm aimin' to make a coverlid fer the bed endurin' the winter."

In November the county of Kentucky was partitioned, and for a time the name, Kentucky, was lost to official records. The population was now too scattered, the distances too great, for one county seat to serve. But to the people it didn't matter whether they lived in Lincoln, Fayette or Jefferson County, one and all they lived in Kentucky. The largest county, and the one which took in their section of the country, was Lincoln. "How come 'em," Hannah asked, "to think of them names fer the new counties?"

"Well," Tice told her, "Jefferson is named fer the governor, an' the other two is named fer generals in the army. That's the way Ben told it . . . though I've not to say ever heared of them generals. The county seat fer our'n ain't yit been decided, though Ben has up his confidence it'll be at the fort. He aims, he said, to give 'em the land fer a courthouse if they'll situate there. He says he'd hate to see Harrod's git it."

[162]

Hannah thought about it. "Hit would be," she said, "kind of like a village startin' up if they put the county seat there, wouldn't it?"

"Them was his intentions—to git it commenced. He speaks of a tavern an' a smithy, an' they's done the mill, of course. Hit's a likely site fer a village, to my notion."

"An' mine. Would he aim, you think, to have the courthouse inside the fort?"

"I d'know as to that. Said he had fifty acres to spare, right near the springs. I reckon in the beginnin' it mought be inside the fence. He aims to build him an' Ann a house *outside*, though, but he ain't got all the planks he needs yit. Goin' to have real glass winders, too. Said he aimed to bring 'em on from Virginny."

"Well, what do you say! Real glass winders." She looked wistfully at their only window, covered over with bearskin. "They shore would lighten up a house, now, wouldn't they?" Then she stoutly insisted, "Well, they ain't nobody earned a fine house no more than Ann Logan, livin' inside them walls all this time, turnin' her house over to ever'body comin' an' goin'. I'm real pleased for her."

"Ben says he's aimin' fer Green River folks to have the first plank house in the country."

Hannah nodded. "He'll do it, too."

Late in November the first hard freeze came and Tice decided to butcher a pig. "I'll jist ride over," he told Hannah, "an' tell William hit'll be day after tomorrow, if the cold weather holds. Butcherin' a pig is somethin', I don't mind ownin', I like to have a little help with. I ain't to say the best hand in the world with tame meat. I don't allus," he admitted, "git a good scald on it."

"If Jane'd wish to come, bring her on, why don't you? I could use a hand with the lard an' sausage."

"Oh, she'll come. I ain't got no doubts of it. Bein' as they've got no pigs they'll likely enjoy the taste of pork fer a change. Butcherin' is a thing, seems like, a body'd ort to share. I'd feel awful miserly not to. Hit's kind of extry, not like game an' wild things, an' it'd be a pore out of a man didn't want to share with his neighbors, an' I don't know of nobody I'd ruther to share with than William an' Jane. Not," he added hastily, "that I'd begretch it to *anybody*, but I jist feel to share with them more'n some."

"An' me. Well, you ride on over an' give 'em the word. I'll git ready for 'em."

William and Jane came the next evening. "Thought we'd jist as well take a extry night with you," Jane said cheerfully, "so's the menfolks could git a early start in the mornin'."

"Well, now," Hannah told her, "I d'know as hit would of occurred to me. But it was downright thoughty of you. They c'n git to the butcherin' by good day, you bein' done here."

"That was the way I figured it. You been well, have you?"

Tice took William and the horses around to the barn and the two women went into the house. Hannah took Jane's head shawl and shoulder cape. "Well as common, I reckon. Now you set an' rest. I'll fix you a bait."

[163]

"I'll set, but we done eat. I told William I'd git us a bite early an' we'd jist come on."

"Well, I'm awful proud you done so."

Hannah liked Jane Manifee, better, she guessed, than any other woman she knew. She loved Ann Logan, loved her dearly, but she wasn't always comfortable with her. And she liked Bethia Cooper well enough, what she'd seen of her. But Jane, now—Jane was like a body's own folks. There was a kinship between them and they understood each other.

Jane looked around. "You got yerself set up awful nice now. I see you got yer loom done. I reckon that pleasures you a right smart."

"I d'know," Hannah confessed, "but what it pleasures me the most of e'er thing we got. I been used to a loom all my life. I never, to say, got used to doin' without, though I'd not of had no use fer one sooner. But a house jist don't look to be a house to me without a loom in the corner."

Jane examined it closely. "I'd say you done good on puttin' it together, Hannah. Hit appears to be stout-built. Them beams is oak, ain't they?"

"Whiteoak. Hit's as stout as I knowed how to make it."

"Tice give you a hand with it, did he?"

"No," Hannah laughed, "I wouldn't trust no man to put a loom together. No . . . I done it myself, an' I done it to *suit* myself."

Jane nodded. "With a piece you're aimin' to have the use of yerself, hit's best to *do* it yerself. Cain't nobody else git it to please. That's my way, too."

Hannah knew Jane would understand.

"Where's Janie?"

"She's asleep. Jist plumb tuckered out by early dark, she is, ever' day. Cain't stay awake till night, looks like. I never seen a youngun run about the way she does. Don't set still, nor *stay* still a minnit. Jist on the go the livelong day. Hit's no wonder she's give out come evenin'."

"They're all thataway," Jane laughed. "Them that's stout an' strong is. Never seed one that warn't. I allowed she'd be in the bed already, but I kind of hoped she wouldn't. I been wishin' to see her."

"I'll git her up."

"No, don't. Let her sleep. I'll git my fill of her tomorrow, likely."

"You'll do *that,* I c'n promise. She'll be underfoot ever'where you turn, in the way an' into ever'thing. She's the beatin'est youngun I ever seen. You all been well, have you?"

"We're here," Jane admitted grudgingly, "by bein' keerful. William had a spell of the misery in his back a while gone. Hurt him purty good there fer several days."

"What was the cause of it, did you know?"

"Sart'n I knowed. He stove hisself up layin' out overnight. Got on the trail of a elk. 'What,' I says to him, 'what is the good of a elk if you got to stave yerself up gittin' it? Hit'd be a heap better,' I told him, 'if you'd take keer, an' stay up to the work that's to be done.' But, law, you cain't tell a man nothin'. He'll *be* the way he was borned to be, to the day he dies, an' you jist as well to save yer breath. With William you had, leastways."

"With 'em all you had," Hannah agreed comfortably, speaking with wifely authority.

There was a small silence as the two women thought over what they wanted to say. Jane looked toward the ceiling, pondering. "Ain't them loft boards warped a mite?"

"Some, yes. They are. Tice said I got 'em on the thin side when I was splittin' 'em out."

"Hit's easy to do." Jane brought her eyes down to her hands folded in her lap. "Ain't you got nothin' we could be doin'? Seems awful wasteful of time jist to set."

"Well, I *have* got a batch of wool ain't been picked yit. I could set it out."

"Why don't you? I d'know of nothin' makes me fidgetier than jist holdin' my hands."

Hannah spread the wool on the table and they drew up their stools, began picking out the burrs and trash. "Hit's good wool, ain't it?" Jane said.

"You think so? Hit appeared a mite shoddy to me this year," Hannah said, modestly.

"No—I wouldn't say so. Hit looks real good to me."

"Well, I'm pleased to hear you say so. I couldn't come to no opinion, my-self."

They worked in silence for a time, then Jane said, "What you reckon William an' Tice is a doin'?"

Hannah laughed. "Why, Tice is a showin' William the new foal, an' how much corn an' hay he made this year, an' he's a braggin' on the size of the woodpile. He thinks he's been terrible put upon, me naggin' at him to git in the wood early this year. Hit's untellin' the times I've named it to him, till he finally done it. But I tell you I don't never want to see sich a time as we had last winter. Not ever again, an' they's no need of wearyin' about wood if a man'll jist git *at* it an' git up enough to do a spell."

"Ain't it so! Hit's the last thing they'll turn their hands to, if they c'n find e'er other piece of work to keep busy at. William don't never want to git up more'n one pole at a time. He thinks that's a great plenty an' it allus surprises him when it's went. Says I'm wasteful of it." She chuckled. "I'll wager William's a tellin' Tice about that there elk. I c'n jist hear him. I'll bound you, though," she added vigorously, "he ain't tellin' how he come in so stove up I had to lay him on the bed!"

"No, he wouldn't, I don't reckon."

Their hands moved swiftly over the wool, seeking, finding, pulling loose the burrs, stickers and trash. "Yer garden done good this year, did it?" Jane asked.

"The best I ever had a garden to do. Law, they was so much stuff I was hard put to make room fer it all. My potatoes done extry good."

"Mine, too."

"I allus did love to grow potatoes. They *reward* a body so. An' I'd ruther to dig 'em than any other kind of work I know of, savin', mebbe, workin' with wool. Ever' hill is different, an' you don't know till you git in it how many they'll be, or what size. Jist like goin' a different adventure ever' time."

"I know jist what you mean. Like you was a youngun, diggin' fer treasure."

Hannah smiled. Jane was the *best* hand at knowing just what a body meant —better, even, than Tice. Tice sometimes thought her notions foolish. Now, she guessed, was the time to tell her big news. She lowered her voice confidentially. "My health come back on me late in the summer."

Jane raised her eyebrows. "Hit's a mite soon, ain't it?"

"I allowed it was."

"Well . . . some does sooner than others. Hit's a pity, though." She laughed. "I jist as well to lay my plans to come in an' tend you again . . . along about next summer."

Unabashed Hannah laughed with her. "In May, I make it. One reason I was hopin' you'd come . . . I wanted to ask when you'd think I ort to wean Janie."

Jane pondered. "Well, I'd think you could nuss her on to the turn of the year—a mite longer if you wanted. Make sure, though," she warned, "to ketch the moon on the wane. You'll have a time if you don't. You jist cain't hardly *dry* up, 'thout it's a wanin' moon to draw it off."

"I've heared so."

"Well, I *know* so. You'll have a heap of trouble, an' she won't do no good. Ketch it jist right—about, I'd say, the last quarter, to make sart'n, an' it'll be as easy as ketchin' flies with molasses. No trouble at all."

"I'll keep it in mind."

The men came in. Their faces showed their satisfaction, their pleasure at having told and retold what they had been doing, what each had accomplished or failed to accomplish, what each thought of what the other had done, their communication and their agreement. Jane and Hannah looked at each other and nodded, wordlessly putting aside their own woman's talk and gossip, comfortably giving way to the men's presence.

The men seated themselves by the fire and the women went on with their work. Taking up apparently where he had left off, William commented, "Yes, sir, I'd say you was in about as safe a fix as a man *could* be fer the cold weather. I wouldn't say they was e'er man in the country in a better fix, or had put by more."

Tice stirred up the fire. "Well, hit has been a good season."

William agreed, but insisted, "You done awful good, anyways, Tice."

There was a time of quiet, each sorting over in his mind a topic of conversation to bring forth. It was William who came up with one first. "You heared about that feller's dog over at the fort, did you?"

"I cain't say as I have," Tice said.

Delighted, William laid his hands on his knees, took breath, and sailed into his story. "Well, sir, a new feller, I don't recollect his name right off, but one jist over the mountains, come in the other day an' amongst his belongin's was a awful handsome dog. He claimed, this feller did, that he'd trained the dog to bait bulls. Said hit'd circle the critter till he had his angle jist right, an' then

[166]

dash in an' seize him by the nose. Claimed he never missed an' warn't afeared of nothin'."

"Well, what do you say! Trained him to bait bulls, had he?"

"Yes, sir . . . that's what he claimed an' he could back it up, too."

"You seen it?"

"I seen it. I was there one day when the man put him to the test. One of Ben's critters it was. An' the dog done jist what the feller had claimed fer him. Circled round an' round, takin' his time, turnin' that brute like it was another dog, an' jist when he had him where he wanted him, he darted in quick as lightnin' an' latched onto that bull's nose with his teeth. Sich a bellerin' you never heared. Like to never got the dog to turn loose, either. But he shore proved what that feller claimed fer him, an' they was no misdoubtin' it."

"I'd like to of saw that," Tice said. "I d'know as I ever seen sich."

"No. Hit ain't common. An' it was somethin' to see, now. Jist dartin' in thataway, of a sudden, an' layin' his teeth into that old bull's nose an' hangin' on. Hit was really somethin' to see."

"I'd think it."

"Yes, sir . . . hit was somethin' to see." William paused, looked at the ceiling. "The feller claimed he aimed to have the dog hunt b'ars the same way."

Tice looked across the hearth at William, whose face remained innocent and placid. "Well," he said quietly, "I reckon it *could* be a dog that'd bait bulls could be learned to bait b'ars."

"That's what *he* said."

William studied his feet and the silence grew until Jane snapped at him, "Well, git on with it, William. That ain't all they is to it, is it?"

Pained, William looked at her. A woman never did understand the necessity for letting a story mull a little to get the best effect. She was forever ruining the telling by wanting to get on with it.

"No," he said, "that ain't all." He turned back to Tice. "This feller, he taken the dog out on the trail of a b'ar one day. Him an' several others. They got on the trail of the b'ar an' they knowed it was a big 'un. They come up to the b'ar finally, an' the feller sicked the dog onto him. The dog, he commenced circlin', jist as he was used to doin'. Circled an' circled, the b'ar turnin' with him, an' when he had him jist right, the dog lurched in to sink his teeth in the b'ar's nose, like he done with the bull."

There was another wait. They gave him silence, respectfully, although Jane sniffed audibly. "Well, sir," William went on, when he deemed the suspense had grown sufficiently, "that dog had done come up ag'n a different kind of animal, unbeknownst to him. That old b'ar, he jist swiped out with a paw an' knocked that dog side-windin', tumbled him head over heels, an' then he laid into him, cuffin' him which way an' 'tother till the dog was plumb addled. Clawed him a right smart, too. That was the worst amazed dog a body ever seen. He turned tail, quick as he could, an' he lit a shuck out of there, yelpin' like he'd been skun out of his hide." William paused, and then on a down note he added drily, "He ain't been seed or heared of since."

Tice and Hannah laughed appreciatively. "I figured hit'd come out that-away," Tice said.

It did not spoil William's pleasure in the story. He knew Tice would be smart enough to figure it out ahead of the telling. But that was part of the pleasure. Telling to one who could keep a mite ahead, but who had manners enough to bide and understand the mastery of the telling. "No, sir," he said, shaking his head dolefully, "that dog ain't been seed or heared of since. I reckon," he added, grinning, "that feller was some put out."

"I'd think it."

"To have his hopes pinned so high an' fall so low."

"Yes . . . I'd think it."

The talk turned then, as always when people came together, to happenings in the country. The men spoke of how Ben Logan had been elected the delegate to the Assembly in Virginia and what a proud thing it was, for his friends as well as for him. "Ben's a little shy on book learnin'," William said, "but they ain't a honester man in the country, nor one that knows its needs better."

They spoke of how the capital in Virginia had been moved from Williamsburg to Richmond, and how odd it went, and of the new governor, Benjamin Harrison. They wondered whether you could put your dependence in him, as they'd done in Thomas Jefferson. "Jefferson, now," Tice said, "was a man had the good of the country to heart."

William agreed.

They talked of the war with the British, and wondered if in their time it would be over. "Hit don't seem so," Tice said.

"They're a fightin' in Virginny now," William said. "Ben told .hat when he was in Richmond fer the 'Sembly meetin' they had to pack up an' git, the British had come so near. Feller name of Cornwallis is their main general there."

Tice shook his head. "Which way you think it'll go?"

"Well," William said, meditatively, "I d'know but the colonies'll win out in the end. They keep a hangin' on, an' you take an' hang on *long* enough, with *anything,* an' I don't know as they's e'er way you c'n be licked. Hit may, though, take a time an' a time of hangin' on."

They talked of how it was Ben Logan's intentions to grow a crop of tobacco the next season. "He says," William told Tice, "they ain't no reason why it wouldn't grow here same as back over the mountains. Says the land to his notion is jist as good, an' the weather a heap better."

"I been thinkin' on it some, myself," Tice admitted. "I d'know of e'er reason it wouldn't do good. Hit mought be I'll jist set me aside a little patch, too."

William thought on the matter, but he didn't announce any decision. The best he could do was say they might be right.

Jane rose, then, sweeping the wool on her side of the table into a pile. "Well," she said crisply, "if the menfolks has done expendin' their breath, I'd take it kindly to git on to bed. I'm feelin' kind of tuckered."

Hannah laid the wool away and stepped briskly to the ladder to the loft

[168]

room. "Tice," she said, "if you'll jist give me a hand with some extry covers, hit'd be a help."

Tice looked at her, astonished. She frowned at him and motioned with her head. Obediently he followed her. "I'll," William announced, "jist take a look at the weather."

In the loft room Hannah whispered to Tice. "I'm aimin' on givin' Jane yore place in the bed tonight. But I never wanted to spring it on you sudden fer fear you'd be amazed an' act it."

"Well, I would of been. Why you aimin' on fixin' it that way?"

"Jist because I aim to!"

Slowly it dawned on him. "Oh," he said, "hit's so's you c'n show off yer new feather tick, ain't it?"

"Hit ain't showin' it off. I jist want her to see how it lays."

"She could tell that 'thout layin' all night. You're jist wantin' her to see how you've come up, havin' a fancy tick an' all," he laughed.

"Well, suppose I am. You needn't to say it so's she c'n hear."

"I ain't."

"You are. Here, take this blanket an' git on down 'fore she ketches on, if she ain't already done so."

Back downstairs Hannah announced, a little grandly, that Jane was to sleep with her. Jane protested. "I ain't wishin' fer you to misput Tice."

"Oh," Hannah said, "hit ain't misputtin' him none." She glanced sideways at Tice. "He's a gittin' too big fer his britches anyways, an' hit won't do him no harm to take the night in the loft."

Tice snorted and went out to have a look at the weather himself.

The butchering was a success. The cold held and the morning was sharp and frosty. William said, when he'd gone out to get the feel of it, that in his opinion it was just about right. "Not froze too hard, but not liable to git too thawy, neither. Jist about right, I'd say."

"Hit's a relief to me," Jane said, "you think so."

They bickered constantly, these two, Hannah thought, and she'd noticed that she and Tice were leaning that way themselves more often. It didn't mean, though, she knew, that you didn't hold together awfully strong. It was just, she guessed, that when you'd been together long enough it came to be an odd, fond way of loving. She never loved Tice more than sometimes when she was scolding him the worst. She knew it was the same with Jane. Jane would have put her body between William and any danger that threatened him, unhesitatingly, just as she would with Tice. But there was a special privilege in being able to use that sharp, acid tone. It was the privilege you used only with someone very near and dear, and with someone about whom you were very certain. It stood, in its way, for the most complete understanding possible between two people . . . it was the compliment of entire confidence. It was, too, a way of expressing love which created no embarrassment, either in its giving or in its taking.

The women bustled about, heating water, sharpening knives, laying out all

[169]

the kettles and pots Hannah had. Shortly they heard a shot. "There," Hannah said, "they've kilt him."

They went out to lend a hand. The pig was lying on the ground and William was just rising from slitting its throat. Tice was putting aside the gun. "Hit was a good shot," William told them. "Right between the eyes."

The boiling water was poured in the trough in the barn lot and the pig soused in it, then scraped. Then he was hung on a pole between two trees and the butchering process began. As fast as the men handed them the cuts of meat, Hannah and Jane trimmed off the fat, collecting it in buckets and pails, laying aside the backbone and ribs for immediate eating, tidying up the hams and shoulders. William laughed jubilantly, seeing the good, fat meat. "I ain't had a bite of pork since I come into the country. I'm aimin' to eat my way clean down a side of them ribs."

"You c'n do so," Hannah promised him. "We'll boil 'em this day."

The hams and shoulders and sides were salted liberally and hung in the loft of the barn. "Give 'em a day or two to season," William advised, "an' then take an' smoke 'em a couple of days over a slow hickory fire, an' you'll have good eatin', man, I promise you."

Tice didn't say so, but he intended for William and Jane to take one of the hams home with them, and fully half of the fresh meat.

The women built a fire outdoors and Hannah started rendering out the lard from the fat. Jane kept busy with odds and ends of trimming, out of which the sausage would be made. "I wish," she grieved, "we had a mite of sage to put in it. Hit jist don't taste right without sage."

"I got some," Hannah told her. "I brung it on with me when me an' Pa come into the country. I been savin' it."

Jane's face cleared. "Now that'll make sausage fit to eat!"

William and Jane stayed another night, but they had to go on home then. Hannah and Tice loaded them with meat and watched them ride off down the slope. They watched them make the crossing, saw the water splash away from the horses' hooves, watched them climb the easy bank on the other side. Then they saw a parcel slide from Jane's horse and William dismount to retrieve it. Tice laughed. "I'll bound she made a way to lay that to William's fault."

Hannah smiled. "I've no doubts of it. An' likely it was . . . slack with the packin', more'n apt."

They watched the two grow smaller and smaller until they finally turned the shoulder of the hill and disappeared into the gap. Hannah sighed and turned back to the door. "I d'know," she said happily, "whenever I've enjoyed myself more."

"Hit was a good visit, warn't it? I do think a heap of William an' Jane."

"An' me. I d'know as they's any two folks that pleasures me more." She rubbed the cold-bumps on her arms and closed the door. "They're jist somehow," she summed up, "awful satisfyin'."

20

As if to atone for treating them so unkindly the year before the winter was unusually mild. February was an especially mild month, with long stretches of days so fine it was difficult to believe spring was not at hand. "I declare," Hannah said one morning, late in the month, "hit makes a body yearn to commence plantin', don't it? Though," she added, "it stands to reason it's way too soon."

They were at the spring where she had started her washing, and where Tice had come for a drink. Janie toddled up, fussy, crawled into Hannah's lap and groped for the opening of her dress. Hannah laughed at her fondly and cuddled her. "She jist won't give up that they ain't nothin' there fer her no more."

Tice watched, smiling too. "You reckon," he said, "hit was the best to wean her? You c'n use a cow's milk up to a month or six weeks of its time. Hit don't appear to me 'twould of done no harm to nuss her on a spell longer."

Tice had been more noticing this time and he had been aware almost as soon as Hannah that another child was on the way.

"I'd of been afeared to try it. Hit mought of made her sick or somethin'."

"Well, it's yore say, I reckon." He stretched, as if feeling the texture of the air. "Hit's like April. I d'know as it's too soon to git to plowin' an' plantin'. We used to git potatoes in by the last of February back home, an' I misdoubt they'd suffer hurt should it frost a little on 'em. Mought burn 'em a mite, but not to kill. Would you want me to turn up the garden fer you?"

"I'd of thought the Holston country was about like this fer weather," Hannah said. "An' you cain't put *no* dependence in it here till up in March."

"Hit warn't on the Holston I was speakin' of. I warn't borned there, Hannah."

"Well, I want to know! An' me allus thinkin' you was."

"No. I was borned in the Shenandoah valley. I never come to the Holston till I was up a big lad. When my folks passed on, I jist commenced driftin' like, first amongst the relations, an' then I taken up with a fambly was headin' fer the Holston. They needed a extry hand an' I hadn't nothin' else in mind, so I jist come along."

"Well, what do you say!"

She thought about it. She looked at Tice and it came over her that he'd lived almost forty years of his life before she had ever known him. Actually he had only begun living, for her, on the day he stumbled up on her at the spring and startled her so. He might as well have been just born that day, for all of her. She thought how two people, born and reared in separate parts of the country, could come together and live together until they knew each other so well it was as if they were one person, and yet how each had had a separate and individual life before. It went odd, she thought.

"Well, do you?" Tice asked again, impatiently.

She roused herself. "Hit wouldn't do no harm to turn up the garden, any-way. If it holds on fair I *mought* drop the potatoes, but if it don't, the dirt c'n be seasonin' out."

"I'll git to it, then."

As he went away she called after him, "Hit'd be good, Tice, if you'd spread the barn manure *afore* you plowed, fer a change."

He nodded, but did not reply.

Before he could get to the plowing, however, William came. He called, as all visitors did, from down the slope and Tice went to meet him. The two men then came on to the spring. "I reckon," Tice told Hannah, "I'll leave off turnin' up the garden today. William is aimin' on throwin' up another shed to his barn an' needs a hand with the logs."

Hannah wiped her wet hands on her apron. "Why, sart'n. The garden ain't hurtin' none. Hit c'n wait. You all been well, have you, William?" She snatched at Janie's dress-tail, tugging her back from the spring.

"Well as common, I reckon. Folks gits our age they cain't expect to have the health they once had. But we make out . . . we make out."

"I'll jist saddle up, then," Tice said, "an' be ready in a minnit."

William and Hannah talked on, mostly about the weather, how mild the winter had been, the hopes there were of early planting. Janie flitted between them, Hannah constantly having to interrupt the talk to dart after her. "She's the *wearisomest* youngun! Times, I cain't git nothin' done fer traipsin' after her."

William smiled down at the baby. "She's a flighty one, all right. Never still a minnit, is she?"

"No, an' it pure wears me down, I c'n tell you."

Tice came around with the horse and the baby ran to meet him, holding up her arms. She loved to ride on the horse and Tice, laughing, lifted her up to the saddle, holding her on, riding her in a small circle around the spring. "Now, that's all, Janie," he said finally, "I got to go. You'll have to git down now."

When he lifted her off, though, the baby set up a howling, sat herself down in the dirt and kicked and squalled, her small face turning red, her little heels beating out a tattoo on the ground. Hannah sighed. "She's got the strongest will. Jist look at that, now."

Tice picked up the child, tried to soothe her, but she squirmed and wriggled in his arms, trying to reach the horse again.

"Whyn't you jist take her with you, Tice?" William said. "Jane'd love the best in the world to see her."

"Oh," Hannah put in quickly, "she'd weary the sense out of Jane, havin' the keer of her all day."

"No, she wouldn't. Jane don't let younguns weary her. She jist gives 'em the run of the place. She'd be proud to have her. She thinks mought near as much of this youngun as if she was her'n."

Hannah knew that. Jane did love the baby, dearly. She looked at Tice. "Would you keer to take her?"

"Why, hit won't misput me none. You're the one to say."

Hannah pondered it. "Well, I don't reckon it'd do no harm." She laughed. "I don't mind owin' hit'd be a relief to me to git to do one day's work 'thout havin' her underfoot ever' minnit. I'll git her some didies."

She watched them ride off, Janie, happy now, sitting in front of Tice, her small hands holding the reins, clucking at the horse the way she had heard Tice do. Hannah smiled. It took such a little to make a youngun happy. It was a pity you ever had to cross them, for mostly they only wanted little, small things, like going riding on a horse, or digging in the dirt, or splashing in the water. But if you did up your work you couldn't *always* be letting them go their own way.

She turned back to her washing and, freed of Janie's hindering wants, finished quickly. She spread the clothes on the rail fence to dry, feeling a sense of well-being. Clean clothes looked the homiest, spread out in the sun to dry.

She thought what she would do with the rest of her day, sorted over the various things she could turn to. She believed, finally, she would work at the loom. She was making a coverlid for the little new youngun and she might get it finished if she stayed with it steady.

She worked the rest of the morning at it, but along about noon the light began to fail and she slid off the seat and went to the door. It must have come over cloudy, she thought. She swung the heavy slab door inward. Gray mist curled about her feet immediately, drawn in by the warmth of the house. "Why, hit's come on foggy," she thought wonderingly. The day had been so soft and fine, so drenched with sun and radiance that she could hardly believe the change.

She stood in the doorway and looked out on a sea of fog that swirled down the slope and over the creek. It drifted slowly up from the creek, curled into the meadow and rose quietly, like a tide edging ever nearer, until it lapped at the house, surrounded it, swallowing it in a smoky shroud. It ghosted the woods and dripped mournfully from the house and trees. The path which led from the house down the slope was wet and glazed over with it. Where it dipped into the meadow, the path disappeared into the bank of fog and was lost, as if it had wandered nowhere and had ended in nothing.

She worried a little about the baby. She hadn't sent any heavy wrap for her. But there, she told herself, Jane would see to her. Jane would wrap her up in one of her own shawls before letting Tice start home with her. No need to worry about Janie with Jane Manifee to see to her.

She looked down the path, one hand rubbing at the back of her neck.

[173]

There was a small cramp at the base of her head just where the great knot of hair rested. She ran her broad, square fingers under the knot and lifted it, set a pin in more firmly, rubbed at the cramped place again, then folded her arms across her bosom. It was turning off chilly, too, she noticed.

She stood leaning against the door for a moment, thinking if she should go on with the weaving, rubbing her arms absently, from wrist to elbow and back again, hearing and feeling the rasp of her calloused palms against the skin, but not noticing. It was almost too dim in the house to see. She'd been straining her eyes the past hour. But a better fire would make enough light to see by a little longer, she decided, and feel good, too, now that it was turning off cold. She lacked such a little bit having this piece finished she hated to quit before it was done.

She laid a fresh log on the fire, chunked it with her foot and watched it catch quickly. Then she went back to her loom.

The loom stood against the far wall in the chimney corner, and the light from the fire fell directly on it. Hannah slid onto the seat and picked up the shuttle, treadled the harness and took up her work. She worked methodically, with swift, sure ease. Her foot clacked the treadle rhythmically, one hand sent the shuttle flying, the other caught it, the released hand snapped the reed firmly against the completed strand. Over and over again the motions were repeated—raise the shed, throw the shuttle, snap the reed.

The monotony pleased her rather than troubled her. She liked a piece of work to have a routine. If it did not have one of its own, she gave it one. She liked her days ordered and fashioned according to the work to be done. She rose each morning and did the same things in the same way. She thought, as she bent over the frame of the loom, how Tice laughed at her for it. "If," he had told her once, "hit could ever be that I'd lay of a mornin', I'd know jist when to git up so's to be ready to eat. You do ever'thing the same way ever' mornin'."

She tried to think later what sound it was that made her turn her head. She could think of nothing. There had been nothing to warn her, nothing at all. There had been no sound that would have given their presence away, put her on guard. The dog had not barked, and he was a good one to give warning. William Manifee had given him to them. The geese and chickens had not been set to honking and cackling. She would have heard those things, even over the clack of the loom. But of course they would have slit the dog's throat, thrown a handful of grain to the fowls. And the noise of the loom *would* have kept her from hearing any softer sound they might have made . . . the turn of a loose gravel underfoot, the breaking of a dry branch, or even the soft sluffing of a moccasin on the doorstone.

But something, some feeling more than a noise, some intuitive knowledge that she was no longer alone, made her turn her head and they were there, two Indians, unbelievably and suddenly in her house, within the room, standing there, horrible, grinning, oily, greasy, and she helpless before them.

Her heart stopped beating for a moment and then lurched, began pounding madly. Instinctively she whirled around on the bench of the loom, wanting, without consciously thinking it, to face whatever was going to happen to her, to see what they had in mind to do with her. Through her mind ran frantic pictures of all the things she had heard of Indians, all blurred and run together —houses burning, women and children scalped, carried off, people tortured to a slow, anguished death. She did not know what to expect, and she was too paralyzed with fear to move, her throat too choked to scream. Her one conscious coherent thought was, Thank God Janie ain't here! Thank God I let Janie go with Tice! Janie was safe, anyhow.

She sat quietly, her eyes on the Indians, fearfully watching their next move. One of them was an old man, with silver ornaments in his ears and bracelets on his arms. He wandered about the room, pointing at things, jabbering, laughing. The other one stood in the doorway. He was, she judged, about Tice's age . . . in the prime of life. They both wore buckskin leggins and bright cloth shirts. The tall one, in the door, carried a gun. Neither of them was painted.

The old man prowled about the room, not disturbing anything, actually, just looking curiously, touching, talking to the other one. Then Hannah noticed that he was looking at her intently. He was standing near the doorway and he said something to the Indian who had not moved from there. He looked in her direction, too, and said something back to the old one. Hannah sucked in her breath. Maybe now they were getting ready to kill her. But the old man was grinning at her, and he had started walking toward her. Did they grin at you and then split your skull in two? She shrank a little, and then something made her straighten her spine, wait for him immovably, her eyes fixed on him. She did not identify it, did not label it as courage or pride. She merely straightened her spine. The movement said that she, Hannah Fowler, was not going to shrink from any redskin.

The old man reached her, grinning, speaking softly to her. He patted her head two, three times, like a mother patting the head of a good child. He felt of her arm, gently pinched it, and wildly Hannah wondered if they ever ate their prisoners . . . she would be fat enough, she thought ruefully, to satisfy the hungriest of them. Then the old man pointed to the bulge of the child, slapped his thigh, said something to the other, who also laughed, and they cackled together. Hannah felt her face turning hot and when the old man bent over and laid his hand on her swollen belly, still laughing, she felt suddenly outraged and she sprang up, casting his hand aside, yelling at him fiercely, "Keep yer dirty, heathen hands offen me!"

The old man, surprised, looked at her, frowned, and then began laughing again. He patted her shoulder, spoke to the other, motioned and moved away. The tall one had never moved from the doorway. He had silver ornaments in his ears, too, and he wore a red cloth shirt, even brighter than the old man's. He carried a shot pouch and powder horn slung around his neck, like a white man. He had on fancy, patterned moccasins, beaded and hung about with small silver brooches. Maybe he was a chief, Hannah thought. She didn't like his looks. He had a beaked face, close-lipped, cruel looking, like a hawk's. He had stood there like a statue in the door since they'd first come, just looking on, watching. He made her more afraid than the old one.

The old man padded about the house until finally he found the pot simmering on the fire. He took the lid off, smelled, then squatted on his heels and dipped into it. He ate noisily, filling his mouth and letting the drip run down his chin, wiping his hands free of grease on his thighs, cracking the small joints of the rabbits with his teeth, grunting now and then, grabbling for a piece of meat.

Hannah watched him in disgust. She had begun to remember something Tice had told her about the way Indians raided. "When they's a big enough bunch of 'em," he'd said, "when they got plenty of stren'th, they'll come whoopin' an' hollerin' down on a place, not carin' fer the noise or nothin'. They'll close in on a cabin, set it afire, burn the ones inside alive, or shoot 'em when they try to git out. But when they's jist a few, plunderin' mebbe, thievin', they'll hide out an' wait fer their chances. Wait till the man is off from the house, his gun with him, then they'll sneak up, steal the horses, kill the stock, plunder a house of its stuff, kill an' skulp the women an' younguns or carry 'em off, an' they'll not make no sound endurin' the whole time."

There were only two of these Indians—though of course the yard could be full of them, or the rest could be up at the barn. But she'd heard nothing outside. She thought likely this was all there was of them, just two wandering, thieving redskins. If there were only two of them, she thought, and she could get her gun . . . it was hanging on the deer horns over the mantel as usual, but though it was over the mantel, it was also loaded as usual.

She started sidling, an inch or two at a time, toward the fireplace. Maybe she could pretend to give the old man something more to eat, keep their attention centered on food. The old man had pulled the iron pot out to one end of the hearth and was squatted there. She had only to get to the other end of the hearth, reach up, get her hands on the gun's stock—it would be pointed directly at the old man. She could drive him, then, over toward the door. Hold them both off.

She moved slowly, slyly at first, inching along, then suddenly she moved boldly, with purpose, going to the cupboard, opening a door, taking out a bowl of milk. The tall, red-shirted Indian in the door moved as quickly as she, intercepted her, took the milk from her hands. He lifted it to his mouth, drank from it without taking his eyes from her, and then walked over and handed it to the old one. When the old man had taken the milk, the tall one quietly reached up over the mantel, lifted down the gun, handed it to the old man. The old one looked at it, grinned with pleasure, laid it by his side and went on eating.

Hannah looked on, her heart sinking. He had caught her looking at the gun, she guessed. She felt more hopeless now . . . more helpless.

The tall Indian began talking to the other one, then, frowning, gesturing. Laconically the old man answered him and the tall one spoke more fiercely, more hurriedly, more excitedly. He pointed at Hannah, at the house, his voice harsh and gruff. She guessed he was trying to hurry the old one, telling him to leave off his eating, kill her, burn the house, make off with what they had come for. But the old man would not be hurried. He kept on eating until there was nothing left in the pot, and then he lifted the pot and drained it of its last drop of liquid. He stood, belched and grunted, rubbed his belly and grinned.

They started talking again. They were talking about her, she could tell because they kept pointing. The old man would point and talk, frowning, insisting. The tall one would point and talk, more fiercely, more angrily, more insistently. They seemed to be arguing, almost quarreling. She watched them, feeling more helpless, more afraid than she had ever felt in her life, certain they were talking about her and what to do with her, but unable to know what they were saying, what alternatives they were discussing. She hoped if they were going to kill her they would do it quickly, mercifully. She didn't want to be taken captive and tortured, maybe. She didn't want to die a lingering, anguished death. She didn't want to die at all, of course. The child, this child which burdened her now, would never live if she died. Tice was certain this one would be a boy, and he made no bones about hoping it would be. He thought the world and all of Janie, but a man did want a son. And Jane Manifee said it would be. "You got a boy this time," she'd said, "you're carryin' it too high fer a girl, an' you're showin' a heap sooner." It was terrible to think it would die before it ever drew breath. She felt a spasm of pity for it.

The tall, red-shirted Indian was a big man, heavily built, and the color of copper. He didn't talk as much as the old man, but when he spoke his voice was harsher, quicker, more impatient. The old man had a very low voice, almost soft. He was small, withered, looking like a piece of dried apple, darker in color than the tall one. He clutched a badly worn robe about his lean old shoulders, and around his neck he wore a leather pouch which swung with the movement of his chest as he spoke.

Finally the tall Indian raised one arm, spoke with a kind of spitting hiss at the old man, lifted his gun, slapped its stock and then stalked out of the house. Hannah let her breath out on a sigh. She had not realized until then how frightened the tall Indian made her feel. In her relief she felt almost friendly toward the old man. She pointed to him and said, "Shawnee?"

Pleased, he grinned and began talking to her. There was a peculiar softness in his voice, a limpness and a blurred lack of emphasis. It all sounded alike to Hannah, only the occasional sound of a consonant coming clear and distinctly. The old man's lips seemed peculiarly immobile, the voice coming through them without altering their shape, almost as if he breathed the words out without effort. They had an oddly liquid sound. She shook her head. He nodded as if knowing she could not understand him. He pointed to his own chest. "Ne-nus-wa . . . Shawanoa," touching his chest again, swelling it out for emphasis. "Ne-nus-wa."

That, Hannah figured, was his name. He was a Shawnee and his name was Ne-nus-wa.

He bobbed his head laughingly, pointing at her. "I-kwä-wa."

She shook her head. "No, Hannah."

[177]

He laughed again, repeated her name, leaving off the aspirate. "Anna," he said, then he made a droll face and insisted, "I-kwä-wa."

Abruptly he turned from her, then. He began picking up the kettles, the sack of meal in the corner, grabbing at flitches of dried meat hanging from the rafters, and carrying them out. He stripped the bed of its blankets and robes, took some of them outside. He started piling the furniture in the middle of the room. Hannah had to move out of his way.

She looked on, feeling sick at heart. She judged they were going to take off what they could use, and would burn the rest with the house. She brushed her hair back and stood mutely watching. It was like watching something live being touched and mutilated and taken. The kettles and pots and ladles and spoons, they were as known to her as her own hands, her palms worn to their curves and fitted to them. She didn't know *how* she could get along without them. And the bed which the old man was hacking and pulling apart . . . Tice had hewed it out during the winter. He had carefully made the posts, quarter-turned, and had carved designs on the knobs at the top. He'd been so proud of their having a proper bed at last. The stools, the table, the loom . . . when the old man sank his hatchet in the loom she had to close her eyes. It took such a power of work to put a loom together just right.

The tall Indian came back. Hannah guessed that he had been out to set fire to the barn and kill the stock. He spoke to the old man, who nodded, and then he grabbed up a small iron spider in one hand, swooped a blanket off the floor and gave Hannah a rough shove to get past her. His touch set her off. Suddenly she was infuriated with them, plundering, destroying, mutilating her things. She grabbed the spider from the Indian's hand and began beating at him with it, belaboring him about the head and shoulders and berating him. "Dolty, plunderin', thievin' varmints! Don't know what to make of nice things . . . don't know no better'n to hack 'em up! Burn 'em up! Make off with 'em! Come in messin' up a body's clean house . . . shovin' 'em about."

Her fury enabled her to get in half a dozen good blows before the man recovered enough to seize the spider and twist it out of her hand. Afterward she wondered that he hadn't killed her, for there was murder in his look and his face was purple with anger. But all he did was hit her on the side of the head with the flat of the spider. It knocked her down and split her forehead so that the blood almost blinded her, but it did not knock her senseless.

As soon as he had disposed of her, the Indian went on with his plundering. The old man, who had been ransacking the cupboard, had not even looked up during Hannah's brush with the tall one. He appeared not even to know it had happened.

She wiped the blood out of her eyes with the tail of her skirt, caught hold of the stub of the bedpost and pulled herself up. She saw what the old man was doing. He was throwing aside the baby's clothing . . . things of Janie's she had laid aside for this little new one. There weren't many things, but there was a fine little white dress Ann Logan had given her, some bellybands, a stack of didie cloths, a little knitted shawl, some tiny shoes.

She picked the things up off the floor, smoothing them out. She plucked at the old man's arm, showed him the little dress, holding it up by the sleeves. He looked at it, grunted, "A-gwi," and shook his head. Supposing that meant he didn't want it, had no use for it, she folded it, laid it back in the drawer. He watched her curiously, suddenly grinned. He picked up the dress, turned around, picked up the other things and threw them into a heap on a blanket. He turned back to the cupboard and started taking out articles of Hannah's own clothing, piling them into the blanket also. He pointed, then, to the door.

That was how she learned she was to go with them. Numbly she looked at the clothing on the blanket. That was when she realized, too, that she had been hoping they would take what they wanted, burn the house if need be, drive off or kill all the stock, but somehow, by some miracle of kindness, leave her, unmurdered, whole, here where she belonged, where Tice would find her when he came home. Her heart clamped as she thought of having to leave him . . . and Janie. How would Janie get along without her mother? How would *she* get along without Janie and Tice? She hadn't consciously formulated the hope they would leave her alone, but now that she knew they meant to take her, she knew how strong a hope it had been.

She tied the clothing into a bundle and moved toward the door. Behind her the Indians tumbled the cupboard over, hacked it into pieces. She hardly heard the blows of their tomahawks. She was still too stunned by the fact that she was to be taken a captive. She was to go with them. That was to be her fate. They'd take her across the Ohio to one of their towns, likely, and she'd be made a slave—or they might put her to the stake . . . or maybe she'd be sold to some man for his woman. Her feet dragged. A scream rose in her throat as she thought of it, and she put up her hand to choke it back. She wished they had killed her. It would be better to be dead, she thought, than to have to live among them, under whatever circumstances.

But it wouldn't be just herself that died. There'd be this young one. There'd be two of them that died. If she died, this child would have to die, too—and he didn't have any say about it. He had to put his dependence in her. He could live just as long as she did. As long as she stayed alive, he was alive . . . he had a chance to be born and draw breath of his own. Then after he was born, he'd have a chance to go on living . . . if she was there to see to him. She was the only one who could give him the chance . . . to be born, and to go on living.

These thoughts of her baby straightened Hannah's back again. She was going to stay alive, she resolved—one way or another she was going to keep on living. As long as she was alive she had a chance of getting away from them. Tice would get all the men at the fort on her trail just as soon as he came home and found her gone. Ben Logan would help. They'd track down these Indians. They'd find her in two or three days. Before she ever walked out her doorway Hannah determined she would return to it. "An'," she told herself strongly, "I'll bring my youngun with me."

21

THE FIRST TWELVE HOURS of her captivity, however, made Hannah realize just how hard it was going to be to accomplish what she had set for herself. It made her know how shrewd, how quick and alert, how careful and how saving of herself she was going to have to be.

The fog had turned to a slow, drizzling rain by the time the Indians were ready to leave. When Hannah came outside she looked longingly down the slope. If Tice would only come . . . but he wouldn't, she knew. It would be hours, yet, before he started home.

The barn and crib were burning and inside the house Hannah knew the Indians were setting the fire to it. The last thing they had done before shoving her out the door had been to rip up the feather mattress and pile it on the ruined furniture in the middle of the floor. When the loosened feathers had floated free in the air the old man had been like a child, catching at them, blowing them, laughing, and sticking a few in his hair. It made her feel sick at her stomach to see it. She wished she could stand between her house and its mutilation, spread her arms and protect it. She made herself, however, turn to the things they had flung on the ground . . . the flitches of dried meat, the sack of meal, the powder and lead and bullets, the pots and kettles and blankets. She fussed with them, clucking to herself, paying no heed to what was happening in the house. "Ain't got no more sense than a bluejay," she scolded. "Flingin' things about . . . throwin' greasy meat right down on a body's good blankets 'thout wrappin' it up . . . don't keer fer nothin' . . . don't know the difference. Fling iron kittles about on the ground, don't keer if they git broke. Even a youngun'd know better'n to treat things so."

Muttering, scolding, fussing, she busied herself with things. She heard the flames taking hold of the wood in the house, heard them crackling, but she refused to listen. She broke open a small bale of dressed skins the Indians must have stolen some place else and took several of them, with which she wrapped the greasy, dried meat. She took three more skins and made pouches of them into which she divided the meal. She laid out the powder and lead differently. Cleverly and carefully she laid out a load for herself that contained meal and meat, powder and bullets, rolled them in a blanket and fastened it securely.

Having followed her out, the old man and the tall Indian watched her, puzzled at first, and the tall one had frowned and moved threateningly when she had broken open the bale of skins. She had looked up at him, frowning herself, but had gone deliberately ahead. When she took only a few and then retied the bale as expertly as it had been tied before, when they saw what she was doing with the loads and the blankets, the old man nodded approval and spoke to the other. The tall one grunted, took up the bale and heaved it to his shoulders. He spoke to the old one and the old man motioned to Hannah they were ready. She finished rolling her own pack, tied it . . . then without waiting to be told she picked it up, shouldered it, hung her favorite kettle on her arm and stood to one side waiting. The tall one shifted the bale of skins, turned and started off. The old man motioned for Hannah to go next, and he brought up the rear.

She did not look backward. In her ears as she walked off was the sound of her home burning, but she gave no sign she heard it. When she turned the corner of the house the body of the dog was lying there, its throat slit, its blood staining the path. She stepped over it without even seeming to see it. As they went through the barnyard she saw the dead geese, the dead cow, the dead calves and foal. She paid no attention. She acted as if there were no dead animals to be seen . . . as if the barn and crib were not burning hotly. There was no visible shrinking from what she saw, no moan from her, no weeping. She stepped out quickly and steadily, keeping on the heels of the Indian ahead of her, her shoulders braced to the load, the kettle swinging from her hand.

Inside she was torn apart. Inside she mourned each dead thing, and grieved for its death. Inside she could hardly breathe for the tears that choked and lumped her throat over her burning home. Inside she could have screamed and begged and pled not to be taken away. But when she had vowed to stay alive and to keep her baby alive, she had begun to remember things she had heard Tice and others say . . . that the Indians admired a show of courage more than anything else in the world . . . that whatever you said of their meanness and their cruelty and their treachery, you had to say one thing for them, they were brave. They never yelled for mercy, they never cried quits, and they never begged. You could draw and quarter them, strip the skin off of them by inches, scalp them living, and they'd never make a sound. And they admired it when they saw it in anybody else. You stood a better chance if you never showed fear, if you never took on, or weakened. Hannah remembered Tice telling what Dannel Boone had said. "Dannel said," he'd told her, "the best way to git along is to act as natural as you kin, like you wasn't botherin' none at all about bein' took. Jist go on like they was folks you was used to, do the best you kin, be cheerful-like, don't be stubborn or sulky. Dannel," he had laughed, telling it, "owned up he'd had a right good time with 'em. He said if they didn't kill you outright when they taken you, you could git along with 'em if you'd try. An' if you git along with 'em, he said, soon or late a chance'll come to git away."

She remembered she had sniffed and said, "Well, I ain't aimin' to try . . . if I c'n help it, that is."

But she was . . . unbelievably she was, and she didn't know anything else to do but give Dannel's way a try. So she shut her ears to the sound of her house burning, stepped unseeingly over the dead body of her dog, never even glanced at the dead stock. She made herself appear unconcerned and uninterested.

They climbed the ridge back of the house and headed northeast. The tall Indian set a pace which Hannah knew, immediately, was going to push her to her utmost limits, if he kept it up. It had been over two years since she'd been in the woods with Tice, so she was soft. Besides that, she was heavy and short-breathed with this young one, and awkward, too. Her usual, long, hip-swinging step was altered. A woman carrying the weight and bulk of a child cannot take long, hip-swinging steps. She cannot place her feet in the easy, tracking steps of unhindered movement. The length of her step is shortened and the width of her track is widened. But she had to keep up, she knew. Without understanding the words of the argument between the old man and the tall one in the house, she had known the tall one had been arguing to kill her—the old man, to take her along. If she failed to keep up, if she lagged, became in any way troublesome, the old man might be as willing as the tall one to kill her. Whatever it cost her in pain and weariness, she had to keep up.

They followed no trail. When they traveled along a ridge, they went through the underbrush and scrub growth. When they went down a ravine or hollow, they waded in the stream that inevitably flowed through it, and when they climbed out and up a hillside, they climbed where it was the roughest, steepest and most impossible for horses to follow. Hannah knew what the tall Indian was doing. He was making it as hard as possible for rescuers to follow. Stumbling along in the gloom she knew how he was thinking. He hadn't wanted a prisoner. He had wanted to travel swiftly and free of the burden of a captive. But the old man must be a bigger chief, she thought. The tall one had had to give in to him, and now they had a prisoner and would soon have white men on their trail. He had to make it as hard as he could for them. Hannah was afraid of the tall Indian. He, she felt, was her real enemy.

Once it was completely dark, Hannah lost all sense of direction. It was still raining and the stars were hidden so that she had nothing to check her bearings by, and it seemed to her, bewilderingly, as if they often doubled back on their tracks. She didn't know whether this was actually so, in order to throw pursuers off, or whether she was merely confused by so much turning, twisting and scrambling about. They went up so many hills, down so many hills, through so many briar patches and thickets, that in the dark she knew how easily she might have become turned around. She had a feeling they kept coming back to a northeasterly direction, but there was nothing to check by, and she knew a feeling could get you lost in the woods quicker than anything else. You went in circles when you started following your feelings.

They traveled all night, and not once did they stop for rest. Hannah lost all sense of time, too. She concentrated on one thing only . . . staying on her feet. After she had fallen innumerable times, the old man tied a thong about her neck. When she stumbled, then, the thong tightened cruelly and suddenly.

[182]

Her neck soon became raw, and frequently she was choked and left gasping for air.

The pace the tall Indian set never seemed to slacken, except where the going was naturally so rough it was impossible to make time, and even then there was the constant urge to hurry. There was urgency in the voices of both Indians when they spoke to each other—there was urgency in the pull of the thong about Hannah's neck, and there was urgency in the pace. In spite of her weariness as the night wore on, Hannah took a grim kind of satisfaction in this urgency. You didn't worry that much about an enemy you didn't respect, and you didn't run that hard from one that didn't scare you pretty bad. These Indians were afraid of the white men in this section, Green River white men who would most certainly soon be on their trail, and there was no doubt about it.

The rain never once let up. Hannah's skirts were draggled and wet to the thighs and hung coldly about her legs. The shawl she wore about her shoulders protected her somewhat, but she was damp and chilly, and the smaller shawl she wore over her head was wet enough to wring out. Her feet bothered her more than anything else, however. Her moccasins were soon cut to ribbons, and she bruised and cut her feet on the rough places, not being able to see where to step. They were cold and wet, too, and there was hardly any feeling left in them.

The darkness overhead had begun to pale and a faint flush of opal light had started creeping up the sky when finally they stopped at the end of a long, steep climb. It had seemed to Hannah as if they were climbing the sheer face of a cliff, and she had been afraid her hands, sore and torn from grabbing at trees, bushes, rocks, whatever she could find to help herself with all night long, would not have the strength to hold out. When she had pulled herself up over the last ledge, in the meager dawn light she saw that they had stopped in a rockhouse, and the Indians were laying off their loads.

The floor of the cave was thickly strewn with dead leaves, which, when she walked through them, crackled and blew lightly. A great longing swept over her simply to lie down in them . . . just lie down and lie there, snuggled under the leaves, covered with them, nested in them—be safe and warm and dry—and then sleep. She felt as if she could sleep forever. In that moment she felt the unreality of her situation more keenly than at any time since she had first spun around on the bench in front of her loom and looked upon the Indians. At this hour of the morning, in this thin, pearly light of new dawn, this could not be herself, Hannah Fowler, wet and cold and bedraggled, miles from her own home and faced with two heathen Indians. She could not be here. She must surely wake soon from what was a bad nightmare, reach out her hand and touch Tice's warm body, feel his arm even in his sleep respond to her touch, lift and encircle her. She would wake, surely, and feel the softness of the feather mattress beneath her, stretch and nest herself in it warmly, once more, before getting up to start the day. She looked about. This could not be real—this rockhouse, the Indians, the raw, cold, damp morning. She would waken soon.

But it was real and she didn't waken. She stood there, cold and wet and exhausted, trying to think what she must do. Her feet were in bad shape, she knew, and from the pains stabbing down her back she wasn't sure the child hadn't come to harm. She had fallen too often during the night, and while she had tried each time to guard the child, she wasn't certain she had been able to do it.

Neither Indian paid any attention to her. The tall one took his gun and went away. The old man was already sitting on the ground, chewing at a strip of dried meat. She didn't know whether they were to stay here during the day, rest, hide out, or whether they were only stopping for a brief rest and would then go on. She needed to tend her feet . . . dry them, warm them. And she wanted to get at the meat in her pack. She had been wrong to put it all in the pack. If she had had some in a little bundle she could have got at, she could have chewed on a piece off and on and she would have come through the night in better shape. She was going to have to think ahead better than that.

Suddenly she decided she was going to take care of herself. She was going to build a fire, dry herself out, tend to her feet, and eat some hot food. It would be a risk, she knew, but she might as well be killed quickly for trying, as to die by inches from neglect. She had the canny thought, too, that if she got by with it, maybe Tice and Ben and the others would come on the traces of the fire when they followed along.

She set to work scooping the leaves away from a place near the outer edge of the rockhouse. The old man watched her, but he went on eating with apparent unconcern. When she had the place scooped out to the damp ground beneath, she piled up dry leaves and laid on twigs and bark. Then, taking care not to go too far, to stay in sight, she gathered some larger wood.

The old man watched her open her pack and get out her flint. This was a moment she had been afraid of. Seeing the flint rock among the things flung on the ground she had packed it with her own things. She was afraid, now, that it might be taken away from her. She wanted it kept handy, for the time when she made her escape.

She felt a surge of relief when the old man neither said nor did anything. She struck the flint, caught the spark, and the fire blazed up. She laid open her pack and took dried meat from it and set a spit to roasting. Then she dipped up rainwater from the bowl of a sunken rock, mixed it with meal and set corn cakes to baking in the coals. Finally she stripped off what was left of her moccasins and held her feet to the fire. The old man got up and joined her, holding his hands out to the flames, laughing at her. He startled her by saying, "Good."

"You talk my tongue?" she asked him, eager to know. If she could talk to him, make him understand her, it would be a big help. He shook his head, continuing to smile so that Hannah knew it was not so much a negative as not understanding what she had said. He turned his hands, which, in spite of his age, were still strong looking, warming the backs of them, then turning and warming the palms. He repeated the word "Good," still smiling at her.

Tice had told her that most Indians knew a little English, she remembered. He said they learned it from the traders—just enough to make their trades with. He said they learned quickest what rum meant, and gun, powder, lead. They usually learned yes and no, and you and me. They didn't bother to learn much beyond that. Some of them did, he'd said, some of them learned to speak it right well, but most of them just learned what few words they needed to know, and let it go. Sometimes, he'd said, you'd run across one that wouldn't say a word of English, though you could tell from his eyes he understood when you talked to him. They'd taken a young chief once who'd been like that. Wouldn't let on he'd known a word of English for the longest time, and then all at once something had set him off and he could talk as well as anybody.

The old man, Hannah guessed, knew just a few words, maybe only the one. He pointed to the roasting meat and then to his own stomach, rubbing it. Hannah laughed. He wanted some hot meat. She tested the meat on the stick, then handed it to him, putting on more for herself. He squatted beside her to eat, talking between bites.

Indian talk exasperated her, she found. Even if she could have understood it, she couldn't halfway hear it. The old man would start talking but before he'd get even one word out it seemed like he ran out of breath. And it wasn't just the old man. The other did the same way, except when he was angry. Then he kept his sounds clear and distinct. Aside from that, however, the words just sort of died off in the air, and you couldn't tell whether they'd quit whatever they had to say, or whether they'd just run out of breath. She wanted to tell the old man now to speak up. But, she thought, you couldn't expect anything better of a heathen tongue like they talked. She had no idea what the old man was saying.

The meat on the spit was done and the corn cakes were brown. Hannah gave the old man a hot one, laughing when he tossed it from one hand to the other, grinning. She made her own meal and felt the strength from the good, hot food spread all through her. The rest, the warmth, the food, all made a great change in the way she felt. Even the pains in her back had eased some. She decided she had come to no great harm after all.

She had not heard anything, but all at once the old man cocked his head, listened intently, and then relaxed, smiling. "Ma-hwä-wa," he said, "pyä-wa . . . Ma-hwä-wa . . . Tsalagi." So that was the tall one's name—Ma-hwä-wa. As if she cared, Hannah thought. But another memory stirred in her mind. Ben Logan had said once that the Indian name for Cherokee was Tsalagi. The tall one, then, was not a Shawnee. He was a Cherokee. They wandered together some, Tice had told her, though the Shawnees lived north of the Ohio, and the Cherokees down in the mountain country, to the south. Well, Cherokee or Shawnee, she didn't like that one. A chill spread over her when she saw him coming. Just the sight of him made her skin crawl with uneasiness. There seemed no real harm in the old man, but that one—she wished he would go off and stay.

As he came closer the tall Indian sniffed, stiffened, then with an exclamation he bounded on up the slope and with long, loping strides was almost instantly beside Hannah. His movement was so unexpected that she had no time to do anything before he had hit her across the face with the flat of his hand, hissing something at her. He sprang past her to scatter the fire.

It was so hard a blow, and so unexpected that she was sent reeling backward, staggering to keep her balance until she was brought up sharply against the rock wall of the cave, and in spite of herself she cried out . . . but only once. Then she braced herself against the wall with her hands and slowly let them slide her to the ground. She felt sick and dizzy. The ceiling of the cave swung dangerously around and the figure of the Indian wavered in front of her eyes. She shook her head to clear it, because she did not want to faint—she did not want to take refuge in unconsciousness. She was too terrified. She didn't know what to expect next, but she fully believed it would be the Indian's hatchet, swiftly and fatally descending into her brain. She felt something warm in the corner of her mouth, licked it and tasted salt. The fact that her mouth was cut registered, but it did not seem important. Like a dog she licked the blood away, keeping her eyes on the Cherokee all the while.

After the one hard blow he ignored her. He stamped out the fire, muttering and growling, and then he went back to the other Indian. The old man had watched impassively, the calm expressionlessness of his face never changing. At that moment Hannah hated him as much as she hated the Cherokee. You couldn't count on him to lift a finger, she thought bitterly. And she had just fed him part of her hot food. She wondered if he would have interfered if the Cherokee had taken his tomahawk to her. She doubted it. At the moment she lumped all Indians into one basket and condemned them. There weren't any of them, in her opinion, fit to be classed as human beings.

Gingerly she pulled herself up from the floor, feeling of her jaw. It was numb but she could move it. If this youngun, she thought, ain't marked with a red Indian right on his jaw it'll surprise me. None was ever borned with a better chance fer bein' marked, that's sart'n.

A lump was swelling on the back of her head where it had hit the rock wall, her mouth was cut and swollen, and her knees still quivered, but she seemed all right otherwise. Anyhow, she thought triumphantly, I had me a good bait of hot vittles. He cain't undo that by kicking me around.

The old man went to help the Cherokee and Hannah watched them carefully erase all traces of the fire. They even doused the coals and carried the blackened wood down into the hollow, throwing it, scattering it. Then they covered the place where the fire had been with cold dirt, raked it and smoothed it, and finally laid leaves over it until you couldn't have told in a hundred years there had ever been a fire built in that place. Wryly she thought how she hoped Tice and Ben would come on the traces of the fire. That had been a mighty forlorn hope, she realized.

The Cherokee, she guessed, had been back to make certain no one was on their trail. Ruefully she thought how Tice wouldn't even know she'd been taken until he had come home yesterday. And the rain and the dark would have hindered them, tracking. They couldn't actually get started until this morning. The Indians, she thought, needn't have worried too much. She guessed they would be going on, now. She folded her pack and shouldered it, hung the kettle on her arm, and stood, waiting.

It was still raining, a slow, soaking rain, but they stepped out into it unheedingly. The same line of march was formed, the Cherokee leading, Hannah next, and the old man last. Hannah was not tied. She did not expect to be, for she figured the Indians knew as well as she that in her condition it would be folly to try to escape while marching. Some night, though—some night, she'd find a way, if Tice and Ben didn't come up with her. She trudged on and pinned her hopes on that. She'd make out as best she could . . . but some night she'd get away.

22

AT FIRST Hannah thought of trying to delay the march in every way she could. She had naturally to stop occasionally, and weariness and illness would have required little pretense to prolong the stops. But when she pondered it she didn't think she could actually delay them long enough for it to do any good. They had too much of a start, and there was too much risk of angering the Indians.

She knew they weren't keeping as swift a pace as they would have liked, anyhow, because of her. It was true they never stopped to rest, once started, but they couldn't go as fast as they would have, commonly. She could tell by the way the Cherokee got farther ahead sometimes, looked back uneasily and from time to time slowed for her to close up. Sometimes he yelled something at the old man, or at her, she didn't know which. The old man never answered, but he did once in a while prod her in the back.

At first she didn't know what to do when she had to go into the woods. Being pregnant she had frequently to stop. She waited as long as she could, and then her need made her desperate. She turned around and spoke to the old man, smiling to reassure him, motioning to the bushes. "I'll be right back," she told him. Then she simply shed her pack and walked off into hiding. She didn't look back, but there was no protest. Apparently he understood. She took care to return promptly. Too promptly, for once the old man was still making water himself. He grinned at her and motioned. "Good," he said.

Hannah's face flamed and a tart reply framed itself on her lips. Never in her life had she seen such a thing, and she wanted angrily to denounce the filthy, dirty varmint—tell him that no decent white man would expose himself so, much less speak of it! But she kept the words back. He wouldn't know what she was saying, anyhow. She bent over her pack instead, busied herself with it, slipped it on, and then without waiting for him, hurried to catch up the distance they had fallen behind.

As the day had begun she had tried also to think of ways in which she might leave a plainer trail. She had heard of many, such as breaking limbs of bushes, gouging your heel into the dirt, leaving strips of a petticoat. Her petticoat was stout and new and she couldn't have torn it without stopping and taking it off to get a good hold, and she didn't seem to have much of an opportunity for the other things, either. Not, at least, with the old man behind her —but, she figured, if there came a chance she'd leave any sign she could.

By noon of that first day of marching, Hannah had to face realistically the fact that it was going to be very difficult for Tice and Ben and the others to catch up with them. There seemed hundreds of little streams, and she knew they would lose a lot of time on all the crossings, some of the men having to track upstream, some down, until they came on the trail again. She did what she could to help. Once in a while she managed to stumble when they were wading up a stream, catch at a bush leaning over the water, strip off a leaf or two, maybe break a twig. Any little thing that would give them a clue as to which direction the Indians had taken would be a help, and would save time. She didn't know how much got by the eye of the old man, for she never looked around to see if he'd noticed. The only way she could hope to avoid detection was to stumble as naturally as possible, grab quickly and let go, and go on as if not concerned about anything but keeping her footing in the water.

Twice during the day she thought perhaps she had been able to leave a good heel print in soft mud. Both times they had left a stream in a place where the bank was gravelly instead of rocky, and mud oozed up in the gravel. She didn't dare pretend to slip. All she could do was shorten her step and bear down with her weight on one heel. She couldn't think of anything else to try.

From time to time during the day Hannah chewed on dried meat. This morning she had put some in the kettle she was carrying. And she didn't know, actually, what she would have done without it. By late afternoon she was so worn out she didn't think she could have gone on without the strength the food gave her.

It was her feet, mostly. They were now so cut and bruised and painful that she even forgot to worry about slowing up the Indians. She concentrated on trying to pick her way as carefully as possible. Nothing had ever hurt her more, she thought, not even when Janie was born. She knew she was holding them up. She heard them talking, and the old man prodded her constantly now. Finally the Cherokee came back and quarreled with the old one.

Hannah sat down while they argued. The Cherokee stood there, glowering and arguing, pointing backward the way they had come, pointing to Hannah. The argument was about her—that was plain to see, and she was scared, but she could not help it. She could do no better than she was doing. Not with her feet the way they were. No one could, she thought. It was more than any woman, in her shape, could do.

"Ki-nes-ä-pe-na," the Cherokee kept saying, pointing at Hannah. "Ki-nes-ä-pe-na."

Fearfully Hannah watched the old man to see what he would do.

What he did was very little. He listened to the Cherokee, looking where he pointed back down the trail, looking when he pointed at Hannah. Once or twice he said something in his softer, more gentle voice, looking at her as he talked so that she knew he was talking about her. The Cherokee grew more insistent, more vehement and angry, raising his voice, and then suddenly he leaned his face into the old man's, hissed a few words at him, and then pointed to Hannah, shaking his head violently. The old man pulled back from him, and then the Cherokee drew his hatchet, brandished it and made a swift, unmistakable, downward cleaving motion, spitting the word again, "Ki-nes-ä-pe-na! Ki-nes-ä-pe-na!"

The old one looked directly into the eyes of the Cherokee bent over him and straightened himself proudly. He folded his arms across his chest and shook his head. "A-gwi," he said, and his own voice was more harsh, and he shook his head again and pointed to his chest, "A-gwi."

Hannah went limp with relief. She knew by now that "A-gwi" meant no. There had been no mistaking the meaning of the word the Cherokee used. But for the moment, it was not important. The old man had once again said no.

The Cherokee stared at the old man, then walked away. The old one came over to her, shoved her back on her feet and prodded her on. She determined to try harder. The brief rest had helped her, but above all she wanted the old man to continue defending her and he had to see that she was doing her best.

It was no more than an hour later, however, before the old man himself called a halt. They were wading upstream in a small creek that wound along the bottom of a ravine. He called out to the Cherokee and pointed upward. There was another rockhouse, Hannah saw, almost directly above them. Without waiting for the Cherokee to answer him, the old one began climbing up toward it. Hannah scrambled after him. She wanted to stop this everlasting march just as soon as possible and if the old man wanted to stop here, she for one was going to stop with him. The Cherokee followed and there was a conference between the two Indians. They ignored Hannah, so she lay down in the leaves, so tired she didn't think she could ever move again.

She was tired in places that had never bothered her on a journey before, and she knew it was because of the imbalance caused by the child. Muscles that normally didn't come into use were called on, stretched and wearied. Her back ached as if it were coming unjointed. Her shoulders felt cramped and her thigh muscles were in knots that trembled and pained. But more than all else her feet hurt. "If they take a notion to go any further tonight," she told herself, "they c'n just take a hatchet to me . . . I ain't goin' one step more."

When they had finished talking, the Cherokee left as he had done before. Hannah sat up and took what was left of her moccasins off and looked at her feet. They were badly swollen and between the toes they had scalded and blistered. The blisters had broken and blood was oozing from them. The soles were badly cut in places, and they were bleeding, too. She was deeply worried about her feet. She *had* to keep going—her life depended on it, and she couldn't keep going with her feet in such a condition.

She was trying to rub them when the old man came up, saw what she was doing and began cackling at the sight of her trying to reach her feet over the bulge of the child. He made a grotesque motion to show how funny she looked. It made her think of Tice, teasing, and in spite of herself she warmed to the memory and laughed. That instinct for a little bawdiness in her humor overcame her and she sputtered at the old man, "All right, you old fool, you carry what I got in my belly around with you an' see how fur you'd be able to bend!"

Because she was laughing the old man knew she had said something funny and he doubled over, slapping his knees, his high cackling laughter screeching out. Hannah's humor soon passed. She wanted a fire, wanted to heat water and soak her feet. She got out her flint and by motions showed the old man she wanted fire, pointed to her feet to show she could not gather wood for it herself. He shook his head. "A-gwi . . . Logan, pyä-wa."

Hannah sighed. There would be no fire, then. Pyä-wa, she guessed, meant come. She wished Logan *would* pyä-wa, and make haste about it. She couldn't hold out much longer. She felt ill and weak. Fear for herself and pity rose inside her. She had to fight to keep the tears back. Oh, she did hope they'd find her. She was tired of this journeying—and sick of these redskins. She wanted this nightmare to end. She wanted to see Tice again. She wanted to see her baby, hold her. She rubbed her arms, remembering Janie's softness in them. It was a Lord's blessing, she thought, she had weaned Janie at the turn of the year. Jane could see to her, now, easy enough. Thank God, she thought, for folks! Thank God for Jane Manifee, and even thank God for the fort, bad as she hated it. It was there . . . you had to say that for it, and there were men, and there was Ben Logan, and they'd all be helping Tice now.

She hunted for a piece of meat and lay down, gnawing forlornly on it. When she finished, the old man came over and tied her. She looked at the thongs about her wrists and ankles. Well, she thought, she ought to have expected it. They were going to stay for a while, and the old man wanted to sleep. He had to tie her to make certain she wouldn't get away. But it depressed her. It made her feel her helplessness, having her hands and feet tied. It made her captivity very real.

23

It was still dark when she was awakened by a rough prod. When she sat up, Hannah saw that she had already been unbound and that the Indians were almost ready to leave. She struggled to her feet and hobbled to get her own pack. Hobbling, she saw with deep concern, was about all she was going to be able to do. Her feet felt stiff, and when she stood on them the pain was almost more than she could bear. They were swollen until the skin was tight and puffy. She looked at them with dismay. Would they last her out? Well, maybe, she thought, some of the soreness would work itself out as she used them.

The Indians had either already eaten or did not intend to take the time. Once under way Hannah chewed on the chunk of meat she had dropped when she fell asleep. It was, she judged, not more than the middle of the night. It had turned warmer and a storm was brewing. It would have been blackly dark except for the lightning which kept up a constant, pulsing play behind the clouds, turning the woods into an eerie, spectral place. The trees, mostly bare of leaves, looked like skeletons with hundreds of arms sprouted in every direction. They sprang up on all sides in the weird light of the lightning, taking on grotesque shapes and forms, looking alive and beckoning as the light flared and played over them, looking almost as if they bowed and twisted and turned and moved along with the little procession of people. Lightnin' in February, frost in May, Hannah thought, remembering the old saying.

Ordinarily she was not afraid of storms, and she was not actually afraid now. But this fitful, almost phosphorescent light awed her and she felt excited and uneasy. She watched it light up and line the clouds, the color glowing behind them so that they were silhouetted against it. The shape of the clouds was sometimes high and peaked, dark and formidable like mountains. Then in another place, the lightning would lift up billowing, low masses of clouds, looking like a tumbled feather bed. Or again there would be a solid bank of darkness, no break in it at all, its edges turned fiery red and gold. It was as if some unseen, powerful hand was shifting the light around all over the sky.

They had been traveling about an hour when the wind began to moan through the tops of the trees and the first drops of rain spattered down. Hannah barely had time to tie her head shawl tightly under her chin and secure her heavy one about her shoulders before the full weight of the storm crashed upon them. The noise was terrible. The wind in the trees, bending them, twisting them, sounded as if a thousand sobbing, crying, creaking wild things had got loose and were mourning together. The rain came in such torrents, with such force, that Hannah could have sworn something solid was pressing against the top of her head, weighting her down. She bowed into the storm, wondering if the Indians intended to keep on in it.

By the constant flash of the lightning she could see the Cherokee ahead of her, and she followed as best she could. The old Indian came up alongside of her, though, in a few moments and screamed something at her. She shook her head. She couldn't hear him, even if she had known what he was saying. He grabbed at her hand, then, and held on to her. Sometimes he helped, by getting behind her and shoving. The humor of it struck her, as miserable as she was . . . her, big as a cow, hobbling along, trying to scramble up a hill, and the old man in back, pushing, shoving, grunting and occasionally whacking her across the seat.

She struggled on, and just as she was beginning to think no human could keep going in a storm like this, it passed on. The rain, however, continued to fall, and it had turned astonishingly cold. Hannah was glad, now, to be moving. She would have frozen standing still, and her feet would have stiffened on her.

It was a dreary day's march, and a terrifying one for Hannah. About the middle of the morning they came to a river. She heard the word Chenoa, and she knew that was what the Shawnees called the Kentucky. It was running full tide from the rains and the storm, wide and heavy to the banks and full of drift and muddy foam, roaring swiftly along. It was cruel and treacherous looking. Well, Hannah thought, she'd probably get to rest a little here. They'd have to wait till the tide went down before they could cross. She threw her pack down on a large, flat rock, glad to be off her feet, sitting at last. She looked at her feet. They reminded her of the hams of the pig they had butchered in November.

The Indians stood looking at the water and talking together. Then the Cherokee stepped to one side and pointed downstream. All Hannah could see where he pointed was the mouth of a little creek which ran into the river just there. It was full, too, but it looked placid and calm beside the angry waters of the river. The Cherokee kept talking and finally the old man nodded. They both threw off their packs. They found a small log and dragged it up, quickly chopped it in two and bound the pieces together. Hannah, watching them curiously, knew they were making a raft of sorts and she began to feel uneasy. She couldn't believe, however, anybody with sense would try to cross that river right now. They must be getting the raft ready to use later, when the river went down.

They didn't finish what Hannah would have called a raft. When they had the two pieces of log tied together, they seized the bale of skins and tied it on, then tied on their packs. They came to where Hannah was sitting and took hers. She still wondered what they meant to do—wondered, now, if they intended to float their belongings downstream for some reason.

Then the Cherokee shoved the raft into the water and plunged in behind it, holding on, quickly swimming it into the swift current. Hannah watched fearfully, thinking it was the craziest thing she had ever seen anyone do. She looked for the man to be drowned right before her eyes. But as she watched she saw the current take the raft, swing it swiftly downstream and then in some eddy she had been unable to see but which had not escaped the Cherokee's eyes, float it into the quiet water of the creek. The Cherokee crawled out, rested a moment, then plunged back into the river and swam across again. Hannah could not help admiring his strength. Not even Tice, she thought, could have swum that river in such a current. He was a powerful man, no doubts about it.

When he had crawled out on the bank again, far downstream from where she and the old man were, he rested once more, then he walked back up the river to join them. The next thing Hannah knew the old man had seized her by one arm, the Cherokee by the other, and they had started walking her toward the river. She held back, fear rising. The old man gabbled something at her, pointing to the water and making swimming motions, and she understood that they intended for her to swim the river. "No," she screamed at them. "No—I cain't swim! I'll be drownded! No . . . no . . . no!"

She dug her heels in, struggling, then she started kicking, lashing out with her feet. She was frantic with fear. She had always been afraid of water, terrified of it. She couldn't swim, had never learned. Tice could never get her in water above her knees when they bathed in the creek in the summertime. She shrank back now from the frothing, swift current, so terrified she felt her mind reeling. She'd rather die than get in that water!

Someway, somehow, she jerked herself free of the Indians' hands and in unreasoning panic fled back up the riverbank. She didn't even think what she was doing. All of the practical common sense she had ever had left her. She became simply an instinct, fleeing from something so frightening she couldn't contemplate it. She went screaming up the bank, falling, slipping, sliding, catching at anything to help herself along, babbling to herself, "No, no, no, I cain't!"

It was the old man who caught up with her, and very quickly. He was sputtering angrily, provoked with her. He slapped her twice on each cheek, making her head ring, and then he dragged her, still fighting and clawing and struggling, back toward the river. He was amazingly wiry and strong for an old man. The Cherokee came to help him, looking at Hannah contemptuously. He took her arm and the old man turned loose of her. He was still scolding her as he walked around her, and in passing he hit her a good lick on the rear with the flat of his hatchet.

Hannah did not quit struggling. Every inch of the way into the water she fought them, and not until her feet left the bottom did she understand that they were going to swim with her, holding her up. Some semblance of sense came back to her then and she quit struggling, to make it easier for them. But she did not quit being terrified. It was the first time in her life she had ever been in deep water. It came up all around her head, ran into her ears, would have covered her head, she felt, if she hadn't held it high. And it was so muddy and so cold and so swift. She could feel how fast they were being carried with it. They'd be swept downstream and pulled under, she thought desperately, and that would be the last of them.

It seemed to her they were in the water for hours, and then again it seemed they had managed the crossing remarkably fast. They came out in the still water of the little creek, a quarter of a mile downstream. She had to give them credit. It was a pure miracle, what they had done, and it was no wonder they flopped on the bank of the creek and lay there, their breaths coming hard and fast, too tired to crawl up out of the mud. Hannah felt waterlogged herself and she was glad to lie still where they had dropped her. The earth felt very good to her, and solid. She touched it with her hand, patted it, pressed her back against it to make certain it was real. She closed her eyes and shuddered to think how awful the river had been. Water was so . . . so slithery. There wasn't anything to hold onto.

There was a sound beside her, and the squishing of footsteps in the mud. Her eyes flew open. The old man was standing up, still heaving for breath, the water streaming in rivulets from his greasy, almost naked body. He stood there squeezing small jets of water from the buckskin bag he always wore about his neck, and he looked so funny and bedraggled, with his topknot hanging forlornly to one side exactly the way the limp, flopped-over comb of a peckish hen did, that Hannah couldn't help laughing. She pointed to his topknot and made a motion of wringing it out. The old man laughed, too, and reaching up, grasped it and squeezed the water from it. Then he made a wry face at all the water dripping from his body, ran his hand down his sides and flung it off. Grinning, then, like a bad little boy, he slid the breechclout about his hips to one side and made an obscene motion of wringing water from a part of his body which Hannah had been taught to ignore.

The Cherokee laughed, and Hannah, embarrassed and ashamed, flung her arm across her eyes. It's all well and good, she thought indignantly, for Dannel Boone to say be pleasant and try to get along good with Indians. Being a man *he* could, but there are things, she told herself, no woman ought to be called on to see, and it did look as if every time she tried to be pleasant to this old man he took the advantage of her. She guessed they didn't think anything about it, being heathen, but she hoped the Lord would know that what her eyes had to be the witness of during this captivity she had little the choosing of.

After a little the Cherokee stood up, too, and motioned they must go on. Hannah thought longingly of just lying there. She didn't want ever to move again. She didn't think she could make herself get up. But the old man kicked her sharply in the side when they had recovered their belongings and handed her her pack. She rolled over, tried to push herself up. This child she was carrying was so much larger than Janie had been, even at the last, that she was so bulky and heavy it required her utmost effort to shift herself, tired and weak as she was also. She tried again, then patiently she rocked forward onto her hands and knees, heaved herself up, like a cow, rear end first. The old man laughed at her, patted his stomach and thrust it out in front of him in imitation of hers. She was so dizzy she could see three of him, but she grinned back at him. "All right, Grampa," she said, "jist go ahead an' laugh. Hit ain't no joke to me."

She watched while the Cherokee rubbed out every trace of their landing. Before he had finished she knew that no one, no one at all, no matter how good he was in the woods, could have told a living soul had ever set foot on this bank. This place, she told herself despairingly, is where Tice and Ben will lose the track for certain.

They went on, but the Indians, now, seemed in no particular hurry. They let Hannah take her time, without prodding, and they stopped, as usual, in a rockhouse, well before it was dark. She collapsed on a bed of leaves, not caring whether she ate, not caring about anything, only wanting to lie still, to rest, to stay off her feet.

She raised up on her elbows, however, to watch when the Indians cut bushes and stuck them in the ground in front of the rockhouse. They made a thick, solid screen of them all the way across the front, and she knew that from the outside it looked like a heavy thicket of undergrowth. They were shrewd ones, all right . . . you had to give them that. Then they built a fire.

Never had a fire felt so good to Hannah. She got up and spread her blanket, as the Indians were doing, to dry, and then she made her bed nearer the fire and lay looking at it, gnawing on meat the old man flung at her, soaking up the good warmth, absorbing it through every chilled and water-soaked pore of her skin. She felt as if she could never get dry and warm enough again.

Sometime during the night she dreamed she was being burned at the stake. She could feel the terrible heat through her clothing, the sweat ran down her face and the palms of her hands were clammy with it. She was filled with terror and began struggling against the bonds. Then she awakened. She was not even bound. The old man had not tied her, but the heat was very real. She was lying much too close to a huge fire the Indians had built up. No wonder, she thought, she'd dreamed she was being roasted alive—she very nearly was. She shoved herself back from the fire, coming wider awake as she moved.

The Indians were sitting by the fire roasting big chunks of fresh meat. They were greatly excited, laughing, chattering, very happy about something. The smell of the meat and the smoke and the heat of the fire filled the cave. The Cherokee was telling something, stopping to laugh at times, his eyes glistening in the light of the fire with his excitement and amusement. Once or twice he pointed . . . north.

As she took in the scene, Hannah's heart sank. It could mean only one thing. He had gone back along the trail far enough to learn that Tice and Ben had lost it. She judged, from his motions, that they had headed north, and remembering her feeling at the river she guessed it must have been there. That, of course, was why the Indians were so jubilant. Once again they had fooled the white men. She glanced at the meat piled in one corner, saw it was a nice fat young doe. The Cherokee must have killed it and brought it in.

She thought she had reminded herself often enough that it would be a miracle if Tice and the others could follow the trail, that she hadn't counted too much on being rescued. She had told herself over and over what a hard trail it would be to follow. She'd told herself they'd have too late a start, and the rain would have blotted out what few little traces had been made. She'd reminded herself of every disadvantage, she thought, had not allowed herself to count on it much. That's what she thought. But her heart told her differently, now.

Now that the hope was gone, she realized how much comfort she had taken from the knowledge that somewhere behind her Tice was following. Knowing he was coming had been a prop to her, even if he never caught up, and it must have been, she mourned, that deep inside her she had always thought he would be able to do the impossible. Having that hope dashed, now, made her feel abandoned and bereft—the most alone she had ever felt in her life. It was like, she thought, you'd waked up in the cold and the dark with a lost wind blowing all around you, and nobody else was there with you. It was like you'd come, and not another soul in the world to reach out your hand to, to the end of time and there was only a cloud of space ahead of you, to step off into, empty-handed. It was like, she thought, you were freezing inside of you, turning little by little to something too stone-cold even to weep. Tears wouldn't have flowed for turning to ice. She wondered, desolately, how she was to keep going.

Suddenly she was angry—at herself, at Tice, at the Indians, at the fate which had brought her here. One thing was certain, she thought, you couldn't keep going by sitting around grieving and brooding. You had to do something, and she was hungry, and she was going to eat. She kicked her blanket off and hobbled over to the old Indian. Without saying a word she jerked the spit stick in front of him out of the ground and walked back with it to her pile of leaves. They were so busy talking and laughing that they hadn't even noticed she was awake, and the old man looked at her now in amazement. Let him look, Hannah told herself, just let him look! He'd find out he still had *one* white person to deal with!

She slid the meat off the stick onto some leaves, and then she tossed the stick back. The old man dodged it, picked it up, then his astonishment passing he made some remark to the Cherokee. The Cherokee watched her, his eyes glisteny in the firelight. The old man put another chunk of meat on the stick and set it to roasting, but the Cherokee never took his eyes off Hannah.

Deliberately she bit into the piece of meat and the hot, red juice ran down her chin. She ate every bite of it, wiped her hands on her dress-tail, and then lay down. She pulled her blanket up, and closed her eyes. But she felt shivery. The Cherokee was still watching her.

24

THE NEXT MORNING he was gone when Hannah awakened. During the night she had known when the old man tied her, and he did not, with the morning, untie her. Instead he lay by the fire, taking his rest, alternately eating and sleeping. It did not greatly matter to her that she was bound. Her feet were now in such shape that she could not have walked on them anyhow. There was nothing she could have done but sit. If they had decided to go on this day, she thought, she could not possibly have done it. This day they would have simply had to kill her and be done with it. A body could stand just so much and no more, and she had stood it. Her feet wouldn't have held her up even to stand, much less to walk.

The day passed slowly, Hannah herself drowsing much of the time, waking with a start when the old man roused, eating when he threw her a chunk of meat, but mostly she just lay and slept, feeling the good warmth of the fire. She wondered if she were not lightheaded with fever, maybe.

Toward evening the Cherokee came back. He was riding a horse and leading two more. So *that,* Hannah thought, was where he had been—off plundering, stealing and driving off some poor settler's stock. They were fine horses and the two Indians were delighted with them. They walked around them, patted them, talked excitedly and laughed together. Horses were evidently riches to an Indian. Hannah herself felt great relief. Since the Cherokee had brought three, maybe they would let her ride. They must feel pretty safe, now, she thought, risking raiding a place. She guessed they would be going on, soon.

The old man untied her after the Cherokee came, and she rubbed her wrists and hands to bring the feeling back in them. They roasted more meat and ate, and as they ate they talked. Hannah, leaning against the wall of the rockhouse, found a small green limb which had probably blown in on a gusty wind. She fell to peeling its bark off, then it came to her she'd better start keeping a count of the days. She crawled over to the fire and took up a knife, motioning to the old man to show she meant to use it on the stick. He nodded.

She reckoned up the time since her capture and notched the days. It had been . . . only three days? That brought her to the first day of March. She rubbed her fingers across the notches and wondered how many she would make before the necessity for them had passed. If it took a hundred, she thought doggedly, she'd keep them. She'd know, when she got home, how long she'd been gone.

She had, too, a notion that these notches would explain her experiences to Tice when she told him everything that had happened to her. For she never doubted she would tell him. She would get away—in time, she would. She saw herself telling him, and she saw herself handling the notched sticks, showing him the notches, saying, "That day, that one right there, was the day we had to swim the river." And she could see Tice's hand, tracing the notch. "This day?"

And herself nodding, "That day." And she could hear herself telling him, in every detail, how terrible the river had been, spumed with muddy froth, swirled in fast-driven currents, full from bank to bank, and how she had been made to wade into that fearsome water, held by an Indian on either side, and had then swum with them to the other bank. He would think that was something wonderful, now.

"And this day," she would tell him, "was the day they stole three horses from some pore feller."

He would look at the notch and feel it.

To one not yet notched she would point and say, "The boy was birthed on that day."

Tice would smile over that notch, for he would be glad of his boy youngun.

And there would be that proud one, "This here one, now, this day was when I got away."

She had finished the notching and she sat, idle, holding the stick in her hands, thinking of Tice and home, seeing how it would be there when she returned, thinking of how it used to be before she was taken away. She was conscious of the warmth of the fire. It had been cold all day. There had been no sun, and a knife-sharp wind had blown out of the north. Now with the dark it had set in to rain again, a freezing rain mixed with sleet. There had been a skim of ice on the pools this morning. At home, now, the Hanging Fork would have been skimmed, too. She and Tice would have gone out to milk this morning, the breath from their mouths smoking up in front of their faces. In the barn the breath of the cows would have made steam as their fat sides heaved in and out, and there would have been the good barn smell, mixed of the hides of the cows, the straw underfoot, manure, hay, dust, and leather. No place smelled as homey as a barn, she thought. Remembering, she closed her eyes. She could smell it now, if she tried.

But the only smell which came to her was the rank, oily, stale smell of the Indians, whose bodies were dirty and smoky, greasy and rancid. Not even the rain and the river had washed their stinking smell away. She opened her eyes, affronted. Resentfully she looked at the old man and the Cherokee sitting on the other side of the fire. There they sat, she thought, talking, not even knowing or caring they smelled like a pair of old goats . . . just sitting there, with their legs crossed in a way no white man would think of crossing his, flat on the floor like a youngun. They were the filthiest lot, eating with their fingers instead of their knives, wiping their greasy hands on their stomachs and legs, and then always belching when they'd eaten all they could hold. They smelled and acted like animals, only animals were more decent and a lot cleaner. And they had burned her home. There wasn't any barn or house to go back to—no cows, or sheep or chickens. But that didn't matter, she told herself fiercely. There was the land left. Nothing had hurt the land, and they could build the house back, and the barn, and get another start of animals.

It came to her that the two Indians were doing a lot of talking. She didn't know that she'd ever seen them talk so much together. And they kept pointing, north and south. It must be, she thought, they were deciding something. Deciding, maybe, which way to go, or whether to split up. That might be it. She watched them curiously.

Suddenly the Cherokee pulled a buckskin pouch out from under his red shirt and started tossing it idly in his hand, up and down, his eyes on the fire as if not aware of what he was doing. It was larger than a shot pouch, but not too large to wear about his neck, stuffed inside his shirt. Hannah did not recall ever seeing it before, but she guessed it was where he kept his ornaments. It was greasy and dirty and badly worn, but it bulged full and it jingled a little as he tossed it.

Then, as if missing the catch, he let the bag fall onto the floor between himself and the old man. The Shawnee acted as if he had not seen or heard a thing. He continued to gaze steadily into the fire. The Cherokee suddenly pulled the thong which tied the pouch, upended it, and poured its contents onto the floor. Out flowed hundreds of small silver ornaments. They seemed to be endless as they poured out of the mouth of the bag. The Cherokee ran a caressing hand over them, mounded them, and they made a glittering pile. Hannah gasped to see them. Even to a white man they would have been very valuable.

They were flat and oval in shape, about the size of a one-penny piece, decorated with designs and carving. Each piece had been pierced at one end, and through these holes could be strung a fine thong for making a long strand of beads.

The Cherokee ran his hand into the pile and lifted it, sifting the bright silver pieces through his fingers. Over and over he did this, the ornaments ringing like little bells as they fell. He said nothing, however, and Hannah wondered at his purpose. Was he just showing off, bragging about his wealth in front of the old man? Was he, maybe, trying to make some trade? Maybe the bale of skins belonged to the old man and the Cherokee wanted them. Maybe it was the horses. She watched the scene, puzzled.

The old man moved, then, unfolding his arms, but not turning his head. He spoke to the Cherokee.

The Cherokee answered. "I-kwä-wa . . . the woman," and he slapped his hand down on the pile of ornaments for emphasis.

Hannah remembered that word—I-kwä-wa. It was what the Shawnee had called her in the cabin. The Cherokee was trying to buy *her!* She felt as if she had been plunged suddenly and nakedly into ice-cold water. Her skin curdled with cold down the whole length of her spine and she felt numbed with it.

Across the back of her neck small chills ran, so that the hairs were raised and hackled, and down her arms the hairs prickled in the same way. The Cherokee was offering the whole pile of silver brooches for her! Fear rose like bile in her throat and she knew that this was the thing which she had been most afraid of from the start . . . that somehow, in some way, she would end up the property of the Cherokee. Bitterly she thought how he had been ready to kill her at first, but now they were safe he wanted to buy her.

She had been so relaxed, so sleepy and warm. She had been only halfway curious about the Cherokee and his bag of ornaments. Danger crept up on very soft feet, she thought. She wanted to cry out to the old man, to beg and plead with him not to sell her. Her instinct told her to act, now, and it was so strong she made an impulsive movement to plunge around the fire . . . but she checked it. It would do no good. The old man would do as he pleased. If he decided to sell her, he would sell her. No amount of begging and pleading would sway him, and she would only shame herself and humiliate all white people in front of them, make them feel contempt for the whole race. There was nothing to do but wait and see what the old man did.

He did nothing for a while, as if pondering the matter. Each second seemed an hour long to Hannah. The Cherokee's eyes were bright in the firelight. It was if the red glow struck the luminous, moist eye and broke sharply, was refracted in splinters. He did not look at Hannah, but she knew that he was aware of her, and that he knew she had been watching. Quietly he sat there, contained, sifting the glittering ornaments through his hands.

The old man slyly eyed the Cherokee, then, and broke out into a delighted cackle. He pointed to the opening in the Cherokee's leggins, pointed to Hannah, bent over, laughing, gesturing obscenely with his hands. It was plain the old man was teasing the Cherokee about taking her for his wife. She felt her face go hot. They had no decency!

Angrily the Cherokee drew himself erect. The humor left the old man's face. He shrugged his shoulders and swept the baubles into the pouch, almost contemptuously, as if the Cherokee were a fool to pay so much for a woman. He tightened the thong and stood in one fluid motion. The Cherokee looked triumphantly at Hannah.

Frozen, with a kind of sick anguish, Hannah looked at the old man. She guessed, now, that he had protected her, kept her alive, for this moment, that he had known all along the time would come, when they were safe, that the Cherokee would buy her . . . and if not the Cherokee, some other Indian. Her only importance had been that bag of silver brooches.

The Cherokee turned to her, his brows beetling and his face stern, "Prepare meat," he said. "Make haste. Ma-hwä-wa goes to hunt the buffalo at the big mud lick."

Hannah heard him in amazement. He spoke English. He was one, then, like Tice had told about. Impatiently he gestured to her and she hurriedly rolled up some of the meat for him to take with him. When she handed it to him she found the courage to ask, "What do you aim to do with me?"

He grinned at her. "Ma-hwä-wa goes now to hunt the buffalo. The sun will rise three times before he returns. When he returns he will go to his own town on the Tanasee. The wife of Ma-hwä-wa will go with him."

"Is the old man goin' with you?"

The Cherokee shook his head. "The old one remains. He is an old man and cannot hunt well." He left, then, and Hannah watched him go out of the cave. She felt relief. At least he hadn't laid hands on her yet.

The old man came back after the Cherokee had gone and sat down across the fire from her. Bitterly Hannah watched him as he got out the bag of ornaments, spilled the pile of silver brooches out on the floor, picked them over, grinning, holding up first one and then another. He was pleased with his trade, she could tell. He was as vain as a woman, trying the ornaments against his ears, on his wrists, stringing some of them together on a thong and hanging them about his neck.

Wearily Hannah left off watching him and lay down, misery seeping all through her. This was the worst thing of all. She thought about herself and Tice, and she thought about how it would be to go home to Tice, if she had been this Indian's wife, had lived with him, maybe had his children. How could a woman go home after such? How could a man have her at home? How could Tice? Like a wall between them it would be. A man couldn't be expected ever to forget it. Every time he looked at her, every time he turned to her himself, he would remember it—remember that she had lain with an Indian. It made her feel unclean to think of it, made her shudder to think it lay ahead of her.

But how could she not go home? Never see Janie again . . . never see Tice again? Bring up this little new youngun to be a redskin. It wasn't to be thought of. How could she not take the first chance she had to get away?

Her flesh was sore with her desolation and even her bones seemed to ache with it. The slow, painful tears welled up in her eyes, filled them and spilled over, ran unheeded down her cheeks. She licked the salt on her lips and tried to swallow the lump in her throat. She turned on her side, turned her face to the fire.

Across it the old man had wearied of counting his baubles, had put them away and was sitting, his legs crossed, his back against the wall, his head beginning to nod down on his chest. The fire, Hannah guessed, and that bait of fresh meat, had made him sleepy. Idly she watched his head droop lower and lower. It would break her neck, she thought, to sleep with it bent so, but she had seen him the day before sit and drowse that way. Nothing ever seemed to bother an Indian.

The fire was dying down and its smoke drifted low above it. She watched it, thinking how near the floor it was settling. It went odd, she thought, how a fire died, little by little. She watched the small shred of smoke curling only a foot or two above the floor of the cave. The old man's gun lay there, to one side . . . her gun, she remembered, and the smoke curled around it as if it had just been fired.

Her head jerked up off the floor. If she could get to that gun, now—if the old man would just drowse long enough . . . Every muscle in her body tensed. The gun was loaded, she knew. She lay still, thinking, thinking hard. What a Lord's blessing it was they hadn't tied her. She guessed the Cherokee had left it to the old man, and the old man, since she no longer belonged to him, had for once grown careless. Or maybe the old man thought the Cherokee had tied her. Whatever, she wasn't bound.

Maybe, she thought, she'd better use the knife. It was handiest to her. It was right there by her side, where she'd been notching the stick. Her hand stole out and gripped it. But she'd have to creep right on top the old man to use the knife. She'd have to crawl clear around the fire. And if he waked she might have to strike too fast, might hit a rib and blunt the blow. The gun was between her and the old man. No . . . there were too many risks with the knife. It had better be the gun.

But she couldn't use the gun until she was sure the Cherokee was far enough away not to hear the shot. How far would that be? She tried to figure it out. In the cave a shot would sound awfully loud. He'd have to be pretty far away. How long had he been gone? He would have taken at least two of the horses, she was sure—one to ride, one to pack the meat back on. Not all three— surely not all three. But riding instead of walking, he could put a right smart distance between him and the cave pretty quick. Say she gave him an hour. He'd be several miles away. The old man could sleep like that, sitting up, for hours, she knew. Of course he wasn't as tired as he'd been yesterday, but he was full of meat, and the cave was warm. Likely he'd sleep a good hour.

She couldn't misfigure the time, now. It would go awful slow. She'd watch that log burning. It would burn, the way it was going, say one more knot— when it reached that next knot, then it would be time.

She fixed her gaze on the burning log, watched it hypnotically, taking her eyes from it only to glance at the old man. He slept on, snoring gently. Let him stay asleep, she prayed, please let him stay asleep. And then she thought how she was praying for a chance to take a human life. But she put the thought away from her. Human or not, he'd had no pity on her, and now it was her life or his, for she had to get away. But she didn't pray any more. She only watched. Tensely she lay without moving and watched.

Finally the fire reached the knot on the log and she eased up on her hands and knees. She started crawling, careful to make as little noise as possible. No more than a kitten creeping across a floor, she thought, listening, no more than the rustle of a leaf in the wind.

The old man never stirred. His breath was deep and regular and she knew he was now soundly asleep. She didn't allow that to make her hurry, however. Not more than a few inches at a time would she move, shifting a hand, shifting a knee, creeping so slowly that the gun seemed to come no closer at all. Each time she moved she looked at the old man. If he moved, *now,* she told herself, she would make a quick dash for the gun. She wouldn't give up this chance.

But he stayed soundly asleep and finally her hand touched the gunstock. Gently, gently she drew it toward her until she could pick it up. Feeling it, then, heavy in her hands, familiar and known to her touch, she sighed. Now she had only to shoot.

She raised up on one knee and sighted, but she was trembling too much to take a good aim. She lowered the gun and wiped her face where the sweat had broken out on it. She hadn't thought how it would be to coldbloodedly pull the trigger on a human being—him lying there helpless and asleep. She could keep the gun by, maybe, and creep around soft and easy—get away, and if he waked up she'd have the gun handy. And what, she asked herself, then, would you do if you don't kill him, and the Cherokee has maybe took all the horses, and there'd be this one left to track you down afoot—you, hobbling along on your crippled feet and him able and fast.

She raised the gun again—no, she'd have to kill him. She rested her elbow on her bent knee, held the gun as steady as she could. She was afraid to try for a clean shot between the eyes, so she aimed for the chest. Anywhere in the chest, this close, would blast him wide open.

The old man choked suddenly, coughed, and his head jerked up. His eyes flew open and he looked quickly around, found her. His reaction was immediate. His hand closed on his hatchet and his arm flung up with it. Hannah's finger squeezed as automatically on the trigger as it would have done had a deer in her sights leaped suddenly for the brush. The shot rang out and the old man, Ne-nus-wa, the Shawnee, slumped against the wall, the hatchet unthrown, still gripped in his hand.

She lowered the gun, watched him, slumped, now, herself. A sick, nauseating bile rose in her throat. She closed her eyes for a moment. Lord, she said, you know I had to do it. I *got* to git back to Tice an' Janie. You know that . . . I jist *got* to!

She made herself get up and hobble over to the old man's side. The blood was spreading from the great hole in his chest, dribbling down his side, beginning to make a pool on the floor. It looked, she thought numbly, like when they'd butchered the pig, the blood spreading just that way on the ground. He looked little, now, and withered away. He'd been a pretty old man. He oughtn't ever to have left his own town and gone plundering around with the Cherokee. He could have lived out his time if he'd stayed in his own village. In spite of herself she felt a deep pity for him. He'd been, times, just like a youngun to laugh and joke. She'd had almost a friendly feeling for him, then.

She laid him on his back and folded his hands across the hole in his chest. "You was part good," she told him, "an' part bad, an' I don't reckon you could help it no more than e'er other mortal bein'. Wherever yore soul has went now, if you got one, I hope it ain't too troubled." She knew it was foolish, killing the old man and then crossing his hands on his chest for him —but she somehow had a feeling to do that much.

She left him, then, and quickly thought what there was to do. First, she'd best see if there was a horse . . . then she'd know better what she could take with her. Holding to the rock wall she limped to the mouth of the cave. It was not quite dark yet and she peered out toward the meadowy place on the bank of the creek where the Indians had hobbled the horses. It was raining, and at first she could see nothing. Her hopes fell, and then she made out the dim shape of an animal picking at the clumpy grass on the far side of the meadow. She relaxed. She hadn't thought the Cherokee would take all three, but it was good luck he hadn't.

She turned back into the cave and decided rapidly what to take, hobbled about collecting the things. The knife . . . her bundle of clothing . . . the gun, powder, bullets. She laid out a blanket, tied them in it, picked up a chunk of the meat and wrapped it in her head shawl. Then she tied her heavy shawl about her shoulders and was ready to go. She looked about the rockhouse. She would never, she guessed, forget it, but she was going to put it behind her and see the last of it. By the time the Cherokee got back, she would be at home again.

She looked at the still figure of the old man. Well, she told him silently, you got your baubles, but you had little pleasure of them. And the Cherokee had nothing to show for his trade. Which, she told herself fiercely, was just the way it ought to be. He didn't deserve any better. The old man, now— she turned back and did one last thing for him. She covered him over with his old worn robe. She gave it a little pat. "I didn't," she told him, "git to do *much* more fer my own pa."

25

THE HORSE whinnied when Hannah came up to it but it did not move away. She reached it, spoke gently to it, patted its shoulder, and then she leaned against it, found herself sobbing. It was so good to be free, so good to have this horse here. It was still almost more than she could believe. She leaned against the horse's neck until the deep shudders began to die away, then she loosed the hobbles on its front feet. It was a mare the Cherokee had left, because, she guessed, she was the smallest of the three horses. She made a bridle, of sorts, from the hobbles.

She threw the blanket up, then slowly, patiently pulled herself up, bracing her sore feet on the horse's legs, hoisting and pulling. Then she looked around, looked up to take her bearings. There were no stars, but she remembered, generally, the way they had come yesterday. She headed the mare south. What a fine way that was to be going . . . south, not east, or north any more, but south—toward home and Tice and Janie. A body just don't know, she thought. They just don't know what their home and their folks mean to them until they think they're never going to see them again.

She set the mare at a good pace. It was dark, now, and still raining. She knew she was leaving a broad trail, but she didn't think she had to worry about that. What she had to do was make time, and get home. Even if the Cherokee didn't stay as long as he'd said, she had a good start of him. He wouldn't anyway come back before tomorrow sometime, and he'd likely figure she'd put too much distance behind her for him to overtake her. No, what she had to do was make time, and leave the tracks go.

The horse floundered in the mud sometimes and branches she couldn't see tore at Hannah's face. She was wet through and shivering with the cold, but she hardly took notice of it. She thought of the way she had to go. She dreaded the river, but as badly as she feared it, she prayed to hit it soon, for she knew that on the horse she should reach it within a couple of hours. When finally she heard its swift-flowing water she sighed with relief. She wasn't off in her directions, anyhow.

In the dark, knowing only that this deep, swift water lay there in front of her and somehow had to be crossed, she pulled up the horse. She couldn't even see the water, she could only hear it. But she remembered how it had looked. It made her shudder, just to remember. It was almost more than she could do to make herself kick the horse and urge her into the water. But

Tice had told her of swimming the Ohio many a time on a horse. He said they were good, strong swimmers and a man couldn't ask for a better way to get across a stream.

She leaned far forward, gripped her hands in the horse's mane, kicked her. The mare hesitated, took a few steps and stopped. She twitched her head nervously, snorted and blew. Hannah kicked her heels hard into the horse's flanks. "Come on, girl," she said, encouragingly. "I don't like it no more than you do, but we got to git acrost. Come on, now."

She wished she had thought to break off one of the branches that had been slapping her in the face. She needed a switch to make the mare take to the water. But finally, between Hannah's urging and kicking the horse waded into the stream, picking her way carefully, stepping delicately. Hannah felt the smoothness of her motion when she had to begin swimming. She closed her eyes and prayed. "Let her git to the other bank. Please . . . let her git to the other bank safe."

The water rose up around her legs, then farther to her waist and chest. The mare swam very deeply in the water. Hannah gasped. It must be, she thought, she was too heavy for the mare. She was surely sinking under, going clean down to the bottom with the two of them. They would never make it. She'd go down and down, and the water would strangle and drown them both. It was cold about her chest, and she grew panicky, hearing its swift rush all about her, feeling the current tearing at her. She thought about sinking under all that water, in the dark, her head and mouth covered by it, full of it, choked and drowned by it. Terror filled her and she threw her head back, screamed again and again—but she never turned loose her tight hold on the horse's mane.

And then it was over. The mare was walking again. The water fell back from Hannah's waist and legs and streamed off the horse like rain falling. There was a final heave and lunge as the horse staggered up the bank, and once they were up Hannah let her stand and blow. She felt her own breath come freer out of her chest. She patted the mare's neck. "Good girl. You done good!"

After a little spell of rest, though, she kicked her on.

Through the rest of the night she was often afraid she had missed her direction, but toward morning the clouds drifted away, the rain stopped and the stars came out. She took her bearings and saw with relief she was still headed generally in the right way. A little west, she thought, and she corrected by angling more toward the south.

At daylight she fumbled in the blanket for the piece of meat and chewed on it. She wished she could stop, for she felt stiff with the wet and cold, and her feet hurt her terribly. "Hit's them danglin'," she thought, " 'thout nothin' to rest on makes 'em hurt so bad. The blood is stopped off." She looked down at them. They were so swollen that she couldn't even tell by looking where her ankles were. She shook her head. They were in a bad shape, and and no doubts about it. Maybe she ought to stop . . . but she didn't really want to. She wanted to get on home. The Cherokee might decide to come back today, too. She couldn't afford to lose her good start. Her feet would just have to wait.

But she did ache all over so bad. She was worried about this little new youngun, some. She could have bad luck with it, easy, she thought. There was a nagging pain in the small of her back that threatened, and she put her hand there, trying to ease it. It was going to be a long way home, she thought —an awful long way, even on horseback.

Slowly the day passed. Along in the afternoon she felt so bad she thought she was going to have to stop and lay out the night. She didn't know whether she *could* go on. There wasn't a place on her whole body that didn't hurt, and she thought maybe she was getting light-headed. Or maybe she was feverish. But she didn't *feel* hot. She felt cold and shivery. She felt dizzy and trembly. She took some more of the meat and chewed on it. She couldn't let herself get so weak she'd fall off the horse.

She wondered that she didn't come up on a house. But there was nothing but valleys and hills and creeks. She was surely getting back pretty close to home, and it would be a big help, now, to run up on somebody's cabin. She could take the night and rest herself. There was nothing to do, though, but keep going.

By late afternoon the horse was plodding and Hannah was too worn, knew the horse was too worn, to urge her on. It was almost all she could do to stay on, the way it was. Her head kept bothering her, feeling light and empty, with a buzzing noise in her ears. She kept wanting to shake it, to free herself of the annoyance.

About sundown she came to another creek and she pulled up the mare to let her drink. She tried to think if she should get off and look for a log or something to bed down in. She was afraid to. She was afraid that if she got off this horse she never would be able to get back on. But if she let the mare have her head now, she ought to last out all right. She'd just have to stay on and keep going.

She wanted a drink, terribly. Her throat was dry and parched and ached badly. She looked longingly at the water as the mare drank. But she couldn't risk getting off. She clucked to the horse and obediently the animal moved slowly on.

She didn't, rightly, ever remember much of the rest of the journey. Telling about it later, she said, "Hit was jist like a dream. Seemed like ever'thing was heavin' an' movin' around. The ground, hit'd swell up of a sudden, like it was risin' towards me, an' the hills'd sway backards an' forrards, an' it fretted me that I couldn't make nothin' stay *put*."

"When did you come to yerself?" Tice asked her.

"Well, of a sudden I noticed hit was darkenin' again, an' it surprised me so I looked up an' all around, thinkin' I must of rode into a awful heavy shade, but I seen the sun was down an' it was night a comin' on. An' then I seen the mare was follerin' a track, an' when I taken good notice, I seen it was the trail to Jane's place from our'n. I knowed it by that old burnt place where William had burnt off fer a field but never plowed the field. An' I was headin' towards home. But it come over me they warn't nothin' there to head *to*, so I pulled the mare around an' made fer Jane's. I reckon," she said, "I never felt gladder of nothin' in my time. I knowed I had about come to the end of my journey."

But it had been good dark when she reached Jane's, and Jane's house had been dark. She tried to call, but her voice would make only a hoarse, croaking sound. The dog, however, was making a considerable fuss, so she sat and waited, knowing Jane would waken and stir to see what had roused him. Presently there was a light and then Jane opened the door a crack, peered out and spoke to the dog, "Be-gwine, Bryan! Who's there?"

Hannah tried again to call out, and she managed to croak loud enough for Jane to hear. "Hit's me . . . Hannah."

"The Lord have mercy on us, Hannah!" Jane came bustling out without bothering to put a dress on over her shift. "Is that really you, or is it yer ghost I'm seein'?"

"Hit's me."

"We'd done give you up! Tice has been in the worst franzy! They lost the trail an' Ben an' them come on back, but Tice ain't to say had good sense. Git off, Hannah. My sakes, but I'm proud to see you. Hit's like somebody risin' from the dead. Git down offen that horse an' come on in the house."

"Is Janie here?"

"She's here. She's sleepin' like a little angel right now. Right there in the house. She's been as good as gold, Lord love her. Git down, Hannah."

Hannah let her breath out tiredly. Well, she was here, and Janie was here, and soon Tice would be here. It was all over, now. "I d'know whe'er I *kin* git off or not," she said.

"Are you hurt somewheres?" Jane asked quickly.

"Not to say hurt, I ain't. I ain't come to no harm, that I know of. Hit's mostly my feet, Jane."

"Wait'll I git a light. I'll come back an' help you. You jist set there till I git a light."

Hannah waited, slumped on the horse. Not ever, not ever in her life had she felt like this before. She was sort of, she thought, out of her head a little. It didn't seem real she was here. Or maybe it didn't seem real she'd ever been captured, she couldn't decide which.

Jane came back, her dress on now, with a candle. She set it on the ground. "Now jist lean on me, Hannah. I'll kind of ease you off." She saw Hannah's feet in the light. "They look like two pieces of raw meat! Hit's no wonder you never knowed whe'er you could stand on 'em or not."

Hannah eased down off the horse, but she could not stand, even with Jane's arm around her. She slumped to the ground. "Leave me be, Jane. I cain't bear my weight on 'em. I c'n crawl to the house, an' I'd ruther."

"Oh, my sakes," Jane said, under her breath, but she went ahead, lighting the way, and Hannah crawled on her hands and knees to the house, crawled up the step, crawled through the door, then she fell forward on her face. "I ain't got the stren'th," she said, "to go no further."

"An' you needn't, love. I'll tend yer feet right there, an' then we'll git you to the bed. You jist lay there, an' Jane Manifee'll take keer of you."

Big, slow tears filled Hannah's eyes, welled over, flowed down her cheeks. She turned on her side and looked at Jane. "A body don't know, Jane, they jist don't *know* what their own kind of folks means to 'em till they think, mebbe, they ain't ever goin' to see 'em again. Hit was jist you, a talkin', made me come over tearful of a sudden. I don't know as I expected ever to hear you a talkin' no more."

Jane turned away. "Cry, if you want," she said brusquely. "I d'know as ever anybody had a better right. *I'd* be bawlin' my head off, had I been took by Indians."

Hannah swallowed painfully. "I'd like a drink of water, Jane. My throat feels like it's swole shut on me."

"Oh, my Lord. Sart'n you want a drink of water. I'll git it. Then I'll stir up a fire an' put you somethin' on to eat, an' I'll heat up some water to tend them feet of yore'n. I'm jist so took aback an' so astonished I've done lost my wits."

She brought Hannah a gourd full of water, helped her to sit up. "Don't drink too much, love. Jist sip a little . . . jist at first. Hit mought not stay down."

Hannah nodded, felt the first blessed coolness on her lips and held the drink in her mouth, savoring its wetness and coldness. "That tastes the *best*," she said gratefully.

"Whyn't you git you a drink along the way?"

"I was afeared to git off the horse," Hannah said, simply. "I knowed I couldn't git back on again."

Jane's eyes shone suddenly wet. She dashed at them with one hand. "I'll git you somethin' to eat."

Hannah stopped her. "Reckon you could jist lift Janie up—no need of wakin' her, but jist so's I c'n see her. Seems like I *got* to look at her."

"Well," Jane said, her arms akimbo in her disgust with herself, "if I was any more muddle-headed you could jist pen me up with the sheep! Sart'n you c'n see her. I'll git her."

"Don't wake her. She's ill-sorted when she's woken. Jist lift her up."

Jane laid back the covers and lifted the child gently. The baby stirred and curled herself more snugly in Jane's arms. Not heeding what Hannah had said she brought Janie and laid her in Hannah's arms. It was like, Hannah thought, taking her, it was like the first time Jane ever laid her there. Just like it, for wonder and for love and for the good feeling. She held her quietly, careful not to wake her, content for now with simply touching and looking. She marveled again at the silky, coppery hair and the white, tender skin, at the curled, limp softness of the baby hands. There never was, she thought, there just never was another youngun so fair and sightly. Then she looked up, handed the child back to Jane. "Put her back in the bed," she said, laughing, "put her back 'fore I fergit an' squeeze her till her little bones crack.

Hit's what I feel like doin'. They was times," she went on soberly, "when I didn't know whe'er I'd ever lay eyes on her again."

"I'd think it." Jane covered the child again. "Now, you got to eat somethin'." She brought a bowl of stew and sat on the floor beside Hannah, fed it to her laughing, "I'm afeared you'd take too big of bites."

"I mought. Hit's awful good."

Between spoons of the good, hot soup, she began to tell Jane about it, the capture, the Indians, the escape. "Whyn't you jist wait, love," Jane said. "Till you've rested an' then tell it."

Hannah looked at her, puzzled. "Why, I cain't," she said, "rest till I've told it." It seemed obvious to her that she *must* tell Jane what had happened, tell all of it, before she could rest or sleep.

Seeing she had to talk, Jane sat and listened as the whole story poured out, spewed out, almost, from Hannah's lips. She bobbed her head vigorously at the last. "I'm glad you kilt the varmint! I'd of loved to jist cut him up in little pieces, him a livin' to know it."

"I d'know, Jane. He warn't sich a bad old man. Hit was mostly he was jist Indian, I reckon. Never knowed no better. Hit goes quare to kill a human bein' . . . even a Indian."

"Hit wouldn't go quare to me!"

"Well, it give me a odd feelin', though I knowed I had to do it. I come over all sick inside."

"Don't think *no* more of it. He desarved jist what he got. Hadn't he jist sold you to the other'n? Now, you jist set there an' I'll git some hot water an' rags an' some grease an' tend yer feet."

Just the same, Hannah thought, she wished it had been the Cherokee instead of the old man. But then she'd had no choice. A body had to do what they had to, and put it behind them when it was done.

Jane brought water and bathed Hannah's feet, gently and tenderly, clucking all the time like a bothered hen. "Looks like yore moccasins give out on you, didn't they?"

Hannah laughed. "They never to say *commenced* with me. They was old ones I'd been wearin' about the place. My feet has been swellin' on me of late, anyways, an' I'd been favorin' 'em a right smart. But I wished mightily I'd had on a good, stout, new pair, I c'n tell you. I'm wearied, some, Jane," she said, sobering, "about havin' bad luck with this youngun."

Jane looked at her quickly. "E'er sign of it?"

"Nothin' but this pain in my back that won't leave off, an' I got a little small one in my side."

"An' hit's no wonder . . . all you been through. But if you ain't got no more signs than that, a few days flat on yer back in the bed will likely set you to rights. Hit mought be jist all that walkin' you done, an' then gittin' away an' havin' to ride sich a time a horseback. My sakes, I cain't ride no piece on a horse 'thout feelin' so shook up hit's like my liver had come unstuck. You'll have to stay in bed with them feet, anyway."

Jane smoothed on the bear grease and bound Hannah's feet in clean rags.

"There, now, they'll do, I reckon." She wiped her greasy hands on another rag.

Hannah leaned back on her arms. "Where is Tice at now?"

"I don't rightly know. Him an' William lit out some place this mornin'. Ben had give his word that he'd git out ten or twelve of the men an' they'd go seekin' you plumb to the Ohio towns . . . but Tice has been so twitchy he couldn't stay put. William has stayed by him."

"Now, ain't that jist like William, to stay by him thataway? Hit's the *best* of him."

Jane shrugged. "Tice'd do the same fer him. They'll be on. They's no need to weary about *them*. Now, you git in the bed an' git you some sleep. You're frazzled to the bone, I c'n tell."

Hannah looked ruefully at her bedraggled clothing. "I'm too filthy to git in yer clean bed, Jane."

"They ain't nothin' on that bed won't wash," Jane said crisply. "You're too wore out to clean up tonight. Now, git on in it."

Hannah crawled to the bed and Jane helped her in. She let out a long sigh. "I d'know as anything in my time ever felt so good to me." She patted the soft feather bed under her. "I b'lieve yore tick has got more feathers in it than mine. Hit lays softer." Then she remembered she had no feather tick any more. "Hit was burnt plumb to the ground, warn't it? The house."

Jane hesitated, then decided to tell the truth. "Yes . . . but it's no matter. You'll git you another house. You jist shet yer eyes, now, an' go to sleep."

Hannah reached out her arm and pulled Janie closer, obediently closing her eyes. No, it didn't matter. They would get another house. What mattered was, she was safe again, Janie lying here in the crook of her arm where she belonged, Jane Manifee's feather mattress under her, Jane Manifee's voice telling her to go to sleep. It was like a mother's voice, she thought, like an own mother's voice. Comforted, warm, cared-for, she drifted off to sleep.

26

TWO DAYS LATER Tice came back, riding, as Jane said, lickety-split. Hannah had slept, waked to eat, watch Janie and hold her, go back almost immediately to sleep again, for most of the two days. She had waked at noon of this day, feeling, for the first time, herself again, feeling slept out, rested and stronger. "My land," Jane said, "I was commencin' to think you warn't ever goin' to git done sleepin'. You feel better, now, do you?"

"I feel real good."

"Hit's a good thing you're built as able as you are. You'd of come to grief if you hadn't been. Me, now—I'd likely have jist passed clean on out."

Hannah laughed. "I've allus been stout."

They heard the horse, then, running. Jane went to the door, flung it open. "Hit's Tice," she said.

Tice flung himself off his horse, left it standing, blowing, and ran toward the house. "Is she here?"

"She's here," Jane told him.

He brushed roughly past her in the door. Quickly his eyes found Hannah in the bed. More slowly, then, he went to her, and when he reached the bed she saw that his eyes were full and swimming. He slumped on the side of the bed and looked at her, then he leaned forward, ran his hands over her hair and face and shoulders. "Hit's really you, ain't it? I ain't jist dreamin' it."

"Hit's me, all right," she said, laughing chokily, "or what's left of me."

He took a deep breath, dashed one hand across his eyes, but held tightly with the other to one of Hannah's. "I been near out of my mind."

"I know. How'd you know I was here?"

"Why, they had word at the fort. I come back there. They told me you was safe at Jane's."

Hannah looked at Jane. Jane spoke up quickly. "I rid over whilst you was sleepin' so good, an' give the word. I reckoned Tice'd head fer there when he come in."

"Ain't she the beatin'est?" Hannah said to Tice, looking fondly at Jane.

"Well," Jane said tartly, "they warn't no use the whole country to keep on s'archin' fer you. You was here, safe." She busied herself at the fire, then took a stool on the hearth.

"You're all right, are you?" Tice asked, then. "The word was you'd come to no harm."

Jane spoke up. "She's got two of the worst wore feet I ever seed in my life, an' she's been clouted over the head, an' she's all beat out—but outside of that she ain't took no harm."

Tice watched Hannah, and she nodded. "I'm all right. They never actually mistreated me none—an' the youngun is safe."

"I'm glad." He shuddered. "Lord, what a time it has been."

Then Hannah must tell, over again in every detail, what had happened. And Tice must tell, too, how he had come home, found the house burned, found her gone and the stock killed . . . tell how he had ridden like the wind to the fort and Ben had called out the men who were there and they had taken to the trail that very night. "By grannies," he said, "I never seed sich a trail to foller. We got misput on it a hundred times, I'd say, 'fore we finally lost it entirely. Them Indians was the best I ever seen fer hidin' their tracks."

Hannah nodded. "I thought it. I knowed you'd have a time. An' it rained the whole time. I knowed that'd wash out ever' track they overlooked. Where did you finally lose out on the trail?"

"At the river. We never seed a sign after that, though we went up an' down that river fer a good five mile both ways."

"I figured that, too." She told again how they'd swum across, rested on the mud flat, and how the Cherokee had blotted out every trace. "I knowed right then," she said, "you couldn't foller on."

Well, it was over. They sat, peaceful now, and looked at each other, touching only with their locked hands. Hannah's eyes, sunken, painfully shadowed, looked somehow bigger to Tice, but they shone warmly, fondly. As if absorbing him, they rested on him. She noticed, for the first time, how stooped he was beginning to be, his shoulders sloping, rounded, into his neck. She noticed his neck, too, beginning to look like Samuel's, the leaders sharp-drawn and corded. She looked lovingly at the weathered, creased face, at the sparse, sandy beard, always scraggly from his fingers pulling at it, at the eyes, a little faded, weather-squinted at the corners. Tice, she thought, with a rush of choking, fierce emotion, was the *best* man. Oh, she would have died had that Cherokee laid a hand to her!

Tice had said nothing when she had told how the old man had traded her to the Cherokee. His hand had tightened, was all. And she had hurried, then, with the telling so he would know the Cherokee had never touched her. She wondered why, but she guessed even Indians had some decency to want to be alone. And she guessed, too, that he had promised the old man meat for his journey on to the Ohio and wanted to get the hunting over with in a hurry so he could be on his way to his own town. Whatever had delayed him, though, she could give thanks for. It had made her able to come home without shame.

"The house," Tice said, then, "is burnt clean to the ground. I reckon Jane told you."

"Yes," she said. "But I figured it. I knowed from the way that fire taken hold it warn't goin' to quit till they warn't nothin' left to burn. The barn was goin' fast when we left out. Well, we'll jist have to git at buildin' it back."

Janie had toddled over while they were talking and climbed on Tice's knee.

He had been holding her, but now she struggled to get down and he set her on the floor, giving her a loving little spank on her round, fat little backside. Hannah smiled. That was the way he always set her down . . . never failed to give her that little spank. The baby ran to Jane Manifee and Jane took her up. Janie tugged at her dress and they all laughed. "You needn't to pull at me, youngun," Jane said, "I ain't got nothin' fer you."

"She ain't ever quit tuggin' at me thataway," Hannah said. She turned back to Tice. "They ain't e'er thing left, then."

"Nothin' but the land. Oh, the chimbley is still standin' . . . an' the doorstone warn't hurt none."

"Well, now, Tice," Hannah said, eagerly, "that'll be a big help. We won't have to build e'er 'nother chimbley, anyways. I d'know," she said to Jane, "but we worked the hardest of all on that chimbley."

"They're a sight of work, all right," Jane said, "to git jist right."

"An' it's the best-drawin' chimbley. Ain't ever a bit of smoke in the house. Hit's a relief to me to know it's still standin'. An' the doorstone warn't hurt none?"

"No—not even cracked by the fire."

"Well, we'll jist put the new door right where the old one was at. A body gits used to the way somethin' like a doorstone feels to their foot an' it goes awkward to change. I'm real proud about the chimbley an' the doorstone."

They were silent, then, almost talked out. Remembering her deep fear for their home and furnishings when the land commissioners had come, Hannah wondered at it. It had made her sick, that fear. Now the home was gone—and its furnishings, and all she felt was a peace that the three of them, Janie, Tice and herself, had not been harmed. She remembered how she had thought, when she put the deed away, that now she had nothing to be afraid of. She sighed. Sometimes it took something awfully big to make you know what mattered the most.

Jane put in, then. "You mought, Tice," she said, "tell me where William is at."

Tice laughed. "Oh, he's comin' on. He warn't in as big a hurry as me. He'll be on directly."

"Well, that's a relief. I didn't know but he'd took off after a bear or somethin'."

"No . . . he'll be on."

When he came, the story had to be told again, Hannah, Jane and Tice all telling it this time, William listening, shaking his head. "Well, all I got to say," he said finally, "is you done good, Hannah, you done awful good gittin' away like that. A man, now, he c'n ginerally make him a good chance . . . but I misgive you'd find many women that could." He started laughing. "That Cherokee, now—he shore paid out his pile of silver things fer nothin', didn't he? I'd of love to seen his face when he got back an' found the old 'un dead an' you gone. My opinion, he done some fancy cussin'."

Hannah laughed. "I'd think it."

William turned to Tice. "Well, when you aim to commence buildin' back?"

"Soon. The season's comin' on an' I got to git a house up so's I c'n git to the plowin'."

William scratched his head. "I got a little time to spare, I reckon. I c'n help."

"If you *hadn't* the time," Jane said shortly, "you'd make it. Not," she added hurriedly, "that I'd begretch it."

"I sh'd hope not," William said calmly.

"You c'n jist stay on here," Jane went on, "Hannah's got to take keer awhile longer. You an' William c'n ride over of a mornin' an' come home of a night. No need you layin' uncomfortable."

"We're beholden to you, Jane," Tice said. "We'll git on back quick as we kin."

"Fiddlesticks," Jane said. "I'm that fond of Hannah an' Janie. I'll love havin' 'em."

So it was arranged. Each day Tice and William rode over to the place. They cleaned out the rubble left by the fire, raked it, picked it over, hauled it away. "I'm jist leavin' the barn," Tice said, "I c'n clean up that mess when I git to it. Hit goes slow enough jist reddin' up that house fire."

At the end of the week the men came home and said they were ready to begin felling trees for the logs. "Dave Cooper rid over today," Tice said, "an' told that they'd rounded up all the men in the settlement to come over an' help. They're all jist comin' an' aimin' to stay on fer a few days, till we git the trees down an' the house raised."

"Now, ain't that good of 'em," Hannah said, "ain't that jist the *best* of 'em!"

Jane sniffed. "Hit'd be a mighty pore out of a settlement didn't all turn to an' help when folks has been burnt out."

Hannah looked at her and laughed. "That'll do fer you to say—hit ain't you that's been burnt out. Wait'll that day, which I hope don't never come, an' then you'll know how good it feels to know you ain't got to stand *all* on yer own. Hit's a heap of comfort to know they's folks about you c'n put yer dependence in. I wish I could help," she added wistfully.

"Well, you cain't," Jane said firmly.

Because she insisted on hobbling about on them, helping Jane with the work, Hannah had repeatedly broken the cuts on her feet open, and they were slow to heal. She had not yet been back to the house-place. She had such a wish to see it again. There were spring smells in the air these days. You couldn't, Hannah thought, rightly smell the sap rising in the trees and the buds swelling on the limbs, but you could smell *something* that told it was happening. There were smells and sights that belonged to each time of the year, but in spring they were sharper than at any other time.

For several nights now the little peeper frogs had been hollering down in the marshy place back of Jane's house. You could always hear them the earliest of anything, but it wasn't long after they started until the songbirds commenced. And yesterday when she'd stood in the back door and looked down toward the creek she'd noticed the willows turning . . . just a skift of green, just a little mist of it, like some kind of fine, thin veil drifted over them, but green just the same.

And across the hill she'd seen the pinky tinge of buds on the Judas trees. Soon the dogwood would bloom, and Hannah thought how the white flowers lay flat along the limbs, each flower marked like a small face turned upward toward the sun. And the wild plums would sprinkle out into blossoms about the same time. The ridge back of the house-place was thick with dogwood and wild plum trees. In the spring it was so white with blooms the green was almost hidden. Oh, she did have such a wish to be at home again by that time. She looked down at her still-bandaged feet. "I could jist whack 'em off, the plaguey things," she said.

"Now, that'd be smart," Jane said.

Hannah laughed. "I jist ain't used to bein' crippled up. But I reckon I'll make out."

"If you'd stay *off* of 'em, they'd cure up a heap faster."

Tice and William stayed at the place with the other men while they were working on the house, and Hannah held her impatience as well as she could. "Wouldn't you reckon," she said, one evening, "I could git around enough to go back with Tice when he comes next?"

Jane considered it. "You'd be awful awkward, campin', 'thout no roof or floor. Whyn't you jist bide here till he gits a roof on, anyways, then I'll not put nothin' in yer way."

That was the way of it, then.

The house walls went up, and there was no chimney to build. When the walls were raised there was only the ridgepole and rafters to set, the roof to lay on, the floor to build. "I c'n git you two winders this time, Hannah," Tice told her, "if you wouldn't keer to have the door set a mite off-center. Hit's William's jedgment, too, hit wouldn't weaken that front wall overly."

William nodded. "Move the door, say, a axe length towards the chimbley end of the house. Wouldn't do no harm at all."

Hannah considered it, thinking over the difference it would make in the arrangement of her things, when she had things again. It would throw her with a shorter wall, next to the chimney. But that would be a good place for the loom. She came to her decision. "Well, why don't you, then? I'd love a extry winder."

"I'd thought," Tice went on cautiously, "though, mind, I d'know as it'll work out yit, but I'd *thought* to git Ben to bring on some glass winders."

Wordlessly, Hannah looked at him, and even Jane was impressed. "Glass!" she said. "Well, what do you say! Glass, Hannah . . . real glass, like back home."

Hannah felt kind of trembly inside. "I never had glass winders back home. I d'know as I'll know how to *do* with 'em." Though Tice had been cautious, she knew they were as good as set in the window openings. He wouldn't have named it otherwise.

"Well," Jane said, "they ain't much *doin'* to 'em. You got to keep 'em washed, of course. Cookin' grease an' dust gits 'em dirty."

Hannah laughed shakily. "Oh, I'll keep 'em washed. I'll not let no speck of cookin' grease or dirt git on 'em. Tice, I couldn't be no prouder!"

"I thought you'd be pleased."

"Well, I am. Sart'nly I am."

There finally came an evening, a month exactly since the house had burned, when Tice came in and reported that the roof was on. "The floor ain't laid yit, nor the chinkin' done, an' of course the winders ain't come, but she's covered, now."

Hannah looked at Jane. All her life she would remember how good Jane was, all her life she would love her, but tomorrow . . . tomorrow she was going home. Jane nodded at her. And Jane knew how a woman felt about her own place. She took a deep breath. Tomorrow . . .

And there it was, just the way she had known it would be.

The ridge looked just like she had known it would look, white all over with the blooms of the sarvis berries and the dogwood trees and the wild plums, with the Judas trees making a little sprinkling of red in between. It was the prettiest hill, the highest and the friendliest of all the hills about.

The creek was shallow and clear and noisy in its chattering way over the rocks and stones. The meadow was green with rye grass and clover, and it stretched just as long down the valley, just as soft and plushy looking as it had always done. She felt as if she had been away a year. She felt as if she had only turned her back and then turned around again, it was so known to her, so dear and so loved.

The house . . . she exclaimed over the house, roomier, stouter even than the old one. She set Janie down and walked all around it, touched it wonderingly. The logs were so bright and clean and sweet-smelling. She put her foot on the old doorstone, felt its familiar smoothness through her moccasin. She felt like crying with her gladness. Oh, a house-place, a body's own house-place . . . it was the heart and the beat of a woman's life!

Tice came around the corner, his hands awkwardly held behind him. "Reckon what I got?"

She laughed at him. "I wouldn't have no idee."

Slowly he brought his hands around and Hannah's eyes widened. "Why, hit's the old red hen!" She reached out and took the hen, hugged her close to her. "I never in this world . . ." She smoothed the hen's feathers, felt the hot tears sting her eyes. "Oh, I'm the gladdest to see her! I allus had a fondness fer this 'un. She's the one commenced layin' endurin' the blizzard that time, recollect?"

He nodded. "I knowed you was fond of her. I was the proudest when I run up on her the other day. She's been roostin' up there on the hillside back of the barn all this time. An' she's been layin', too. They was a nest plumb full of eggs. Wonder they ain't done hatched out."

"She ain't broodin', I reckon, or they would of." Hannah bent over the chicken, clucked to her. "You never said you'd found her."

"No. I thought to surprise you."

[218]

"Well, you done so!" She couldn't say what it meant to her to find one live thing left to them. She could only stand and hold the hen, smooth her feathers, hug her close. "She'll make us the start of another flock. She was the best of that bunch Ann give me."

Janie was begging to hold the hen and Hannah let her have it. "All right, love, you c'n hold her. Take keer, though, an' don't let her peck you." She brushed her hair back. "Well, I don't know about you, Tice, but I'm gittin' hungry. If you'll unload them pots an' kittles Jane give me the lend of, I'll git a fire to goin' an' warm us up somethin' to eat."

"I'll do it," he said. "Hit'll go good."

Inside the house, Hannah hung up her shawl and set a fire to blazing. Then she looked about, waiting for Tice. They'd put the bed, she thought, in that corner, just like before . . . and the cupboard there, and the loom there in the chimney corner where she could get the light. Tice would have to make Janie a trundle bed when the little new youngun got here. But, law, there was a sight of other things to do before then.

Tice brought the loads in and she took the pots from him. "What's Janie doin'?"

Tice laughed. "She's made a nest out there in the corner of the fence an' her an' the hen is both a settin' on it."

"Ain't she the beatin'est?" Hannah swung a kettle on the blackened crane, pushed it over the fire. "You reckon," she said, "you'd have time to turn up the garden fer me tomorrow?"

Tice pulled at his beard, his eyes twinkling at her. "Why," he said, "I c'n make the time, I reckon, if you're in that big of a hurry."

She laughed. "Well, I jist thought I'd commence droppin' my seeds in the mornin'."

"I'll git to it," he said. "Hit's time."

She laid another stick on the fire, poked it and stirred it. "Yes," she said, "hit's time."